For my sister Mary, with love

AGENT PROVOCATEUR

Faith Bleasdale grew up in Devon, did History at Bristol University and then moved to London. After sampling a huge variety of rubbish jobs, she decided that she would put her passion for writing to good use. She currently lives in Singapore where the climate and the shopping definitely agrees with her. She writes full time. *Agent Provocateur* is her fifth novel.

To find out more about Faith and her other novels visit *www.faithbleasdale.com*

Also by Faith Bleasdale

Rubber Gloves or Jimmy Choos?

Pinstripes

Peep Show

Deranged Marriage

FAITH BLEASDALE

Agent Provocateur

FLAME
Hodder & Stoughton

First published in Great Britain in 2004 by Hodder and Stoughton
A division of Hodder Headline
First published in paperback in 2004 by Hodder and Stoughton

3 5 7 9 10 8 6 4 2

A CIP catalogue record for this title is available from the British Library.

ISBN 0 340 73492 2

Typeset in Plantin Light by Phoenix Typesetting
Auldgirth, Dumfriesshire

Printed and bound in Great Britain by
Mackays of Chatham plc, Chatham, Kent

Hodder and Stoughton
A division of Hodder Headline
338 Euston Road
London NW1 3BH

Acknowledgements

My thanks go to my family for unconditional love and support – I truly know that I'm lucky to have you all. Also to Thom, who looks after my website, it always turns out great and I think you're brilliant. To Jonathan, I always wonder what I did to deserve you, and know it must have been something really good. To all my friends, especially the ones who have to listen to each of my ideas: Holly, Jo, Sara, Deborah, Tyne – thanks for your patience! To Simon Trewin of PFD, a fantastic agent who encourages me and gives me confidence. To Mari Evans and all at Hodder, I appreciate, so much, all you've done for me.

Of course the final thanks must go to anyone who is about to read this book. I hope you enjoy it.

Chapter One

'Can I buy you a drink?'

Grace Regan raises her head slowly, instinctively knowing that it is him. She is pleased about the lack of originality in his approach; it makes what she is about to do so much easier.

She spotted him as soon as she walked into the bar an hour ago. The photo that she had been given was a good likeness – almost too good. Generally people bear some resemblance to their photographs, but most don't look identical. Mr X did. Not just his face, but also the details, right down to the spotted yellow tie, the slightly crooked smile, and the navy blazer. Standing at the bar was the real man, but she could have been looking at the photo. It was unnerving.

Grace sat down at a table in full view of the bar. She studied him, the man who looked like his photograph. He was talking to someone wearing a similar uniform to his, a colleague, perhaps. She waited for someone to take her drink order and she requested a glass of champagne. Champagne was part of playing the role. Then she scanned the bar before briefly letting her eyes rest on him. When she turned away, she knew that he was still staring, so she crossed her long legs. She imagined him turning to his companion and pointing her out. She could almost feel both pairs of eyes on her. It was just a matter of time.

And now here he is.

She looks at the almost full glass in front of her.

'I'll have a glass of champagne, thank you.' She looks directly into his eyes. They are grey and small. A little too close together. Small eyes sitting too close together are, Grace believes, an obvious sign of a philanderer. Although, in reality, philanderers don't have a specific look, Grace has met so many she really believes she has started finding common identifying marks.

'Why don't we make it a bottle and I'll join you?'

She smiles at him on the outside and on the inside wishes that she was with the photo. She chastises herself for behaving in an unprofessional manner but feels that she knows this man so well. Knows his type. From his slicked-back, lacquered dark hair (hair that could take itself out to dinner), to his shiny gold cufflinks and black loafers, she wishes that he were just an image on a piece of paper. She shakes herself out of the gloom. After all, she has a job to do.

He sits down and motions to the waiter; his friend has been discarded. While he orders she brings some amusement back into her evening by playing the game that she and her boss call 'Mr Potato Head'. She studies his features, picking out those she would keep and those she would change. She decides that the hair definitely needs revamping. She smiles at him as she imagines taking a pair of scissors to the heavily lacquered flick. The eyes need moving further apart, so he looks less suspicious, and the nose hair needs trimming. As he smiles at her, she decides that his teeth could do with some expensive cosmetic dentistry. The waiter pours two glasses of champagne, and Mr X picks his up in a toast. With a lot of work he might even be attractive, she decides.

Her earlier black mood forgotten, Grace picks up her glass and gives him her full attention as she prepares to do her job. As she sips at the champagne, he has a slightly suggestive smile plastered to his lips; the first real difference between reality and his photograph. She resists the urge to laugh. Why do they have to be so easy? she asks herself as she raises her glass in a second toast to the lying cheating bastard and the torturous, but well-paid evening ahead.

Two hours later she is in a taxi home. She calls Nicole, her boss from her mobile.

'He's a cheater,' she says. It's a triumph of sorts; a hollow victory.

'Full details in the morning?' It sounds like a question, but it is in fact a command.

'Absolutely. 'Night.'

'Night, honey.'

When Grace arrives home, the first thing she does is to take off her wire. She puts it carefully on the hall table, knowing she will replay the conversation in the morning. Then, remembering she is 'blonde', she removes her wig. Next she goes to check her fish. Her tropical fish tank sits in the centre of her living room on a custom-made shelf. Her cream sofa faces it. She has a small television but it is tucked into a corner. She rarely watches it. She prefers watching the fish to television; there is something that is both relaxing and mesmerising about them. She likes the feeling of company they give her, although that is not a fact she would openly admit. She is more attached to them than to anything else in her life. They mean more to her than anyone.

She goes to the kitchen to get the fish food from the freezer, but pauses as she reaches the door of her small study. It is closed; she always keeps it closed because although she works from home, she does not always want to be reminded of it. She opens the door and sees her answerphone light blinking at her. She sits at her desk, in her black leather chair and presses play. She doodles on her pad as she listens to her boss's voice barking at her. Nicole is perhaps the only female in Grace's life, or the only female that almost resembles a friend. Nicole announces that there are six jobs lined up for Grace, and they need to discuss them the following day. Grace is pleased, naturally, but she is also angry. Is there no end to women whose husbands or partners are cheating on them? What is it with men? She tries not to be angry; cheating men are her bread and butter, or her champagne and foie gras. That is her contradiction. She enjoys her job, but wishes that it weren't necessary. Occasionally she even likes the men she is paid to meet, although she knows she shouldn't. Although she is totally devoted to her work, at the same time she longs to meet the man who turns her down because he is in love with someone else. Of course, she could never share these views with Nicole, because she would be flayed. Fired. Or both.

There is one personal message on her machine, from one of her two lovers, boyfriends, or whatever they should be called, but she decides not to call him back. He can wait. The fish can not. She continues to the kitchen, gets the food and goes back to feed them.

She smiles as she lifts the hatch covering the tank and all the fish swim to the top. They know they are being fed. She puts the food in the net and places it in the water to defrost. She hates taunting them, and tells them so.

'Not long now, be patient.' She doesn't think that fish understand patience, but she believes they enjoy anticipation. She hopes they do. When she finally drops the food into the tank, they go for the food in a frenzied fashion, as if they haven't been fed for days. She loves watching them eat.

Grace holds her own beliefs about her fish. She believes that they are intelligent, that they remember, that they recognise her, and that they like it when she talks to them. She doesn't care if that makes her certifiable, because she is happy with those beliefs.

Forty minutes later she realises she hasn't moved from the sofa, so she bids her fish good night and goes to her bedroom.

She undresses and climbs under her duvet. She snuggles as far as she can into it for comfort. She knows that Nicole will see it as a job well done when she tells her about how easily Mr X fell for her charms, but, of course, Mrs X might feel differently. That is Nicole's job, however. She deals mainly with clients and only occasionally do they ask to meet Grace, or speak to her. Nicole delivers the news, something Grace is grateful for, although she still feels responsible. Even though she has no idea who Mrs X is, she feels immense sympathy for her that night.

She replays the evening in her head as she prepares for sleep. He was arrogant as soon as he started speaking to her. He seemed to think he was irresistible but, as if to make sure of her interest, he was so open about how much money he earned it was almost comical. For Grace it was *déjà vu*. So many men are made from the same mould. When she was a child, her mother used to make jellies in rabbit moulds. She would never make just one, but several because Grace came from a large family. The brightly coloured rabbits would wobble in a line on a shelf in the fridge. That is how she believes men like Mr X are made. Tragically.

He sported a wedding ring and she asked him about his wife. Ironically in her job, she always asks them about their relationships, mainly because the way they reply gives big clues to their characters. He, in answer, launched into the tired old story about how she didn't understand him, how she did nothing but spend all his money, how she made his life hell. Grace was, of course, sympathetic. He ordered a second bottle of champagne. Then Grace teased him – a tactic that some, or perhaps most, men found irresistible. The file that Nicole had given her on him said that he was intelligent, but Grace found little evidence of that. He was too convinced of his own superiority to be intelligent. He was ruled by his libido. But that was another thing she often discovered. The man described by his wife was rarely the man she met. They had drunk only half of the second bottle of champagne when he made a move. Grace hadn't even made it clear she was interested. She was about to give him a subtle sign that she was willing to take things further, but she didn't need to. He propositioned her with, 'I know a very nice hotel we can check in to.' Again, highly original. She smiled, made her excuses, gave him a fake number and left. The tape had captured all the evidence she needed.

He was such a horrible man that she finds it impossible to identify any positive attributes. Why his wife even cares if he is unfaithful is beyond her. Actually, why his wife married him in the first place is beyond her. But then, Grace knows that love doesn't work the way it should. No logic; that's what Nicole tells her. But as she is immune to love, she cannot understand.

That is the last thought on her mind as she snuggles further under her duvet and, like a child, puts her thumb into her mouth.

Grace Regan is thirty-two, technically single, and has an unusual job. She describes herself as a detective, specialising in the field of infidelity. Others call her 'the honey-trap woman', which she feels is a gross trivialisation. Her work is far more involved than people give her credit for. Although she is five foot nine, with long, slim legs, dark brown hair, huge hazel eyes and lips that always smile, she knows that her job involves more than her looks. Other people don't. No matter how many times she explains, some people refuse to understand.

Her friendships have depleted; her lifestyle has made sure of that. She doesn't have much normal social time because that is when she works. She found people either disapproved of her, or got bored of maintaining a friendship with someone they never saw. Grace regrets her lack of female friends, but can do nothing about it. She is resigned to her life the way it is, and the security it offers is a comfort to her.

Grace became a honey trapper when she met a private detective, Andrew Brooks, in a bar. At first, he was another bloke buying her white wine and trying to get into her knickers. Finally admitting defeat, he gave her his card, having learnt that she hated her job. She called him out of curiosity, and he introduced her to the art of infidelity testing. She was highly sceptical when he first suggested it.

'I've only just met you and you're offering me a job?' she asked. She was more than suspicious; it was as if this was his new ploy to get into bed.

'Yes, I am. Or at least a try at a job. What I do is far more specialised than anyone gives it credit for. I hire intelligent women, not bimbos; you need to use your head far more than your looks. Women who fear their relationships are being threatened call us and ask us to help.'

'Help how?'

'If they suspect their partners are being unfaithful they need proof. That's where you come in. Or you would. You go out and you test the man. It's quite simple.' He smiled.

She studied his face. He was in his late forties, she guessed, and not unattractive, but worn. She remembered thinking he was smart, he looked intelligent, well-groomed, but not sleazy. For some reason she had a strong urge to trust him.

'Why me?' she asked.

'I'm looking for intelligent, attractive girls to work for me.'

'I don't know . . . it sounds like prostitution.' She blushed as she said this.

'Not at all, Grace. I am not asking you to sleep with men for money, I'm asking you to become a detective. And for that you need a huge amount of skill.'

So, she wanted him to tell her more. Although he said men usually capitulate to a 'honey trapper's' charms, they wouldn't if the honey trapper didn't know how to play it. The woman has to use detective work to find him (with help, sometimes), her looks to appeal to him (sometimes using disguises), her personality to woo him (with inside information about his character), and psychology to reel him in. An infidelity tester will be socially engineering situations whilst making it seem that the man is in charge. She needs to possess intelligence, the ability to listen, to flirt and to gauge a situation. She has to be pragmatic; the mistress of contingency. From the job description, Grace was hooked, intrigued and she wanted to give it a go.

Instead of jumping in feet first, Andrew took her to watch one of his girls in action. As they posed as a couple in the corner, Grace paid Andrew no attention, focusing only on the woman working at her job.

'That was interesting,' she said afterwards.

'So, you're in?' Andrew asked.

Grace nodded her assent.

After working for the detective for a year, she was headhunted by Nicole. Nicole's agency is more specialist, and Grace was offered the opportunity to earn more money and be more in control. She is allowed more autonomy, has an office set up at home, and she is given more independence over the way she works. The biggest advantage to Grace is working for a woman. She trusts women.

Nicole is an ex-police woman, although she hates to talk about that. She left to set up her own detective agency specialising in infidelity because she had had enough of bureaucracy. The reality is that she earns a lot more money, and is her own boss, and the boss of others. Nicole, ironically (or so Grace thinks), has been happily married for twenty years. She is forty-one and looks slightly masculine – perhaps reflecting the tough side of the business. Grace once told her (after a couple of glasses of wine) that she would make a rotten honey trapper, and luckily for her Nicole agreed.

Ever since she started working in her line of business, Grace has never been able to work out Nicole's motives. She doesn't know if she is in it for the money, or if she genuinely wants to help women whose marriages/relationships are in trouble. She believes it is a combination, but she hopes it is because she wants to help women.

Because, of course, Grace works only for women. She doesn't just dart around trying to seduce men, then telling their partners on them. She is not a tart; she is a professional. She has her own rules and she does not sleep with any of the men she is testing, although she hears that some girls do. She won't, that is her rule and she sticks to it.

The business is based on the premise that the customer is always right. They have to be adaptable; cater for different needs, although the clients have one thing in common: all the women want to be told that their partners are not cheaters. Unfortunately, not many are ever told that.

After working in the business for a year, Grace developed her own formula for honey trapping, like a step-by-step guide. She has kept this as a mental guide and it has always helped her through a job.

Step one: Nicole gathers information from the client. This information includes a photograph, a list of the man's interests and his profession. Perhaps most importantly, they need to know if the man has a specific type of woman that he is partial to. When Nicole hired Grace, she told her it was partly because of her personality, partly because of her brains, but also because she would be most men's type.

Step two: they need to know where they will find the man. This is the difficult part, because the men aren't always where they say they'll be. If the client is unsure, then Nicole will send someone to follow the subject from his office (if they are testing after work) to the bar, to which Grace will then be summoned. The same applies if he is going out from home.

Step three: having identified the location, Grace will turn up, buy a drink and wait for the right time. If she has to talk to him when he is in a group (men are very rarely on their own), she will ease herself into the group before focusing all her attention on the man she has been employed to test.

Step four: catching the man. If the man is in a large group, this can be tricky. Often men don't mind being chatted up in front of their friends, but in order to take it further they want to be more discreet. (After all, if they are cheating, the fewer people who know, the better.) If this is the case, then sometimes Grace will give out a mobile number. She has pay-as-you-go mobiles, which the client is billed for because they are discarded after each case.

Step five: getting the evidence for the client. Sometimes it is enough for the client if the man calls Grace, but not always. A client will sometimes push for a date to be arranged, and then for a proposition before believing him a true cheat. Some women are so desperate to be wrong about their partners that they need to hear them asking for sex before they will admit they are rats.

Nicole explains the seduction techniques to the client before they proceed. The women will wear clothes that are attractive but not overtly sexy, they will make eye contact with the man in question, they will laugh at his jokes and tease and tell jokes. They are not employing any new techniques: they go with the tried-and-tested. They go with what works.

The client will get a verbal report or a recorded one, depending on what she wants. Some women want just to hear the conversation; others go so far as to want to see their men in action. Grace has small cameras and tape recorders that she can easily hide. Whichever, she always reports to Nicole, who reports to her client with total honesty. This, Nicole admits, is the hardest part of the job, and Grace agrees – breaking hearts, because that's how they see it. But Grace tells herself that she is working for the greater good, because no woman wants to be with a man who is so willing to cheat on her. She is breaking hearts but in the process she is saving hearts. And she really does believe that.

People might assume that a woman working at such a job hates men, but Grace doesn't, she is really quite keen on them. And she cites Nicole as another example: she has been happily married for so long, she adores her husband, she certainly can't be seen as a man hater. However, Grace has always believed in fidelity. She has never believed that men should be allowed to use weakness as an excuse for cheating, nor listened when told that men can't help themselves. She has no respect for men who cheat, but she has even less respect for women who excuse them. Every man can resist and every man should. She would love to tell a woman that a man has resisted her. However, she has never been in that position.

She thinks that perhaps her job has taken on new proportions. She now takes it personally; she needs to find him. She needs to find the man who will be faithful, the man who, when approached by the beautiful and sexy Grace, will say, no, no, because he has someone he loves already.

She had many discussions with Nicole about it. She needed to put things into perspective and her boss helped her.

'Why do you do this?' Grace asked.

'I'm a detective, and one thing you learn pretty quickly in my business is that most disputes are about relationships. I didn't set out to specialise but, God, the number of people that wanted their partners followed, or tested, was huge. Now, it's pretty much all I do.'

'But how does it make you feel?'

'Grace, I'll be honest with you. Sometimes it makes me feel shitty, and it's not just about infidelity in men. I am also hired by a number of men who think their partners are cheating – not as many as women, but it's growing. I see what other people do to each other and it makes me sick. No one deserves to be lied to, to be cheated on; no one deserves the inevitable broken heart. You can let it get to you, totally consume your being, or you can just get on with it and think that every time you save someone from a bad relationship you're almost doing them a favour. They may not see it straight away but one day they will.'

'Do you think all men are cheats?' Grace still held some hope of romance in the days when she started working for Nicole. She wanted to think that men weren't all bad.

'I wouldn't be married if I thought that, Grace. No, not all men are cheats, but most of them are. I sometimes wonder if Paul is faithful because he knows that I'd be able to catch him. I wonder if he thinks I have tested him or will test him so he's terrified of talking to another woman, but at the end of the day I think he loves me enough. Also he sees what I do and the hurt that can occur, and he's just a decent man. And if there is one decent man, then there will be more. It's just a case of finding them.'

At that moment, Nicole took a maternal interest in Grace, which she still has now.

When she wakes the following morning, Grace goes straight to her fish. She smiles and chats to them while they wait for breakfast, and once they're fed she goes to make coffee. She stares blankly at her percolator and only when she is satisfied that it is filling properly does she go to the shower. By the time she has pulled on a tracksuit (her working-from-home uniform), her coffee pot is full and ready. She pours a cup of black coffee into her large round breakfast cup, and takes it to the study. She isn't wearing any make-up.

She sits at her desk and looks at her notepad with messages from her machine last night. She switches on her computer, and while she waits for it to whirr away through the bits she doesn't understand, she makes her first call of the day. It's nine o'clock.

'Oliver Williams, please,' she asks the receptionist, and she types her password into her computer as she waits to be put through.

'Oliver.' He sounds so self-assured, but she knows he is not.

'It's me.' She stares at her screen as she waits for him to say something. He always pauses whenever she calls him, as if he needs time to think about what he is going to say next. He never has that problem when he calls her. She finds it endearing and annoying at the same time.

Grace met Oliver just over a year ago, while she was actually working. When the man she was testing went to the loo, Oliver came over and gave Grace his card. He didn't say anything and Grace decided that she liked his style. She liked his cheek. And he was really quite sexy. She has been seeing him, casually, ever since.

Oliver – or 'Occasional Oliver', as she calls him – has a busy lifestyle that should prevent him from making too many demands, although he still does. But because he isn't the busy-businessman-with-a-neglected-wife-and-an-indulged-mistress cliché, Grace sees him whenever they both have time. It isn't as often as he'd like. Oliver bizarrely wants to turn Grace into the neglected-wife cliché, but she refuses. She likes Oliver; she likes that he likes her enough to want to neglect her on a permanent basis, although, of course, she will never agree to it.

He works in the music business, but Grace couldn't describe his job. They are lovers but only in the way that Grace will allow. When they first met, she told him all about her job, and he tried to make her quit, which is when she told him that if they were going to continue they would do it on her terms, not on his. Which is why she continues to see Eddie, her other lover. She does not have to answer a charge of infidelity because she is totally honest. They both know about their non-exclusive status and even if they don't like it, they accept it. They are her men who cannot cheat.

Eddie, like Oliver, accepts the situation because he believes he is in love with Grace, and is convinced that one day she will wake up next to him and realise that he is the love of her life. Then she will quit her job. Neither of them is married, but Grace believes they see other women. She needs to believe this. There is nothing underhand about the arrangement: it suits her and, according to the men, it suits them as well. No one can cheat on her because she won't put herself in that position. It's as simple as that.

Eddie is the man who has been in Grace's life the longest. Eddie is a fashion buyer. She used to be his assistant, but they didn't sleep together until she had long given up her job and started in her current role. He is single, in his early fifties, and is too much of a confirmed bachelor to settle down. He never pressures Grace because he enjoys his life and their arrangement too much. He thinks he might be in love with her, but he is in love with his freedom more. They don't see each other very often. With Grace having little social time anyway, and with two men to entertain, she neglects Eddie for long periods.

Grace sometimes thinks of the time when she was working for Eddie, in a nine-to-five type of role, but it seems like another life. She didn't enjoy the industry, the rigid hours, the confinement to an office full of people who were equally as fed up as she. However, sometimes she misses the normality and sometimes she can barely remember it.

Eddie and Occasional Oliver are not just her lovers, but they are also her friends. They are the ones she calls if she is having a bad day, or a bad night; they are the people she trusts. If someone analysed her relationships, they would probably say that she has to have more than one man because her rota of lovers is her protection, the armour she wears on her heart. They would also say that they stop her from being alone. Because without them, that is exactly what she is. A mad woman, alone with her fish.

Grace doesn't believe there is anything wrong in the way she has chosen to live her personal life. She is no longer sure that she is capable of falling in love, so she is doing what she needs to do to keep her happiness. She isn't trying to hurt anyone, and she always says that if that were going to happen, she would walk away from him. Nevertheless, she is a young, single woman with an unusual career and lifestyle.

Oliver finally decides what he wants to say. 'You didn't call me back last night.'

'Sorry, but I was working and I got in late.'

'So you nailed another bastard?'

'I did. I need to call Nicole, who will have to tell his wife.' Nicole has a golden rule: she doesn't start work until ten every morning. She says she needs to exercise before work, and that is the earliest she can make it.

'Poor cow.'

'I know, and the thing is he was such a prat. He was this arrogant prick who came on to me with hardly any encouragement. It makes me really sad that he has this lovely wife at home but he'd rather be in a bar chasing skirt.'

'You even sound like a man.'

'I've been around too many cheats.'

'Anyway, tonight? My trip was cancelled at the last minute.' He knows how Grace needs to keep things at arm's length and acts accordingly.

'Yeah, OK.'

'Don't sound too keen.'

'Sorry, Olly, I'm just a bit tired.' Grace thinks she slept well, but she is finding it hard to shake off the sleepy feeling she woke with.

'If you didn't spend half the night trying to trap men, you might not be tired.' She detects disapproval in his voice, which always riles her.

'I was not out half the night.'

'Maybe, but you do have an amazingly tacky job.' She should have known that he was dying to say that to her; he always needs to make one comment at least.

'Olly! You know how I feel about what I do. Don't start.'

'Sorry. I'll come round after work?'

'Not before eight.' Because he has annoyed her, she decides to annoy him.

'But I was going to finish early.'

'Shame. Bye.' She puts the phone down with a smile.

After another coffee, she types up a report of the previous evening to email to Nicole, and she listens to the tape. She shudders at his voice, dripping with – what is it? Desperation, lust, greediness. Then she removes the tape, puts it in a padded envelope and addresses it to Nicole, who will send a courier for it. At five minutes past ten she dials Nicole's number.

'It's me,' Grace says.

'Morning, honey. So, the spider went for the trap.' Nicole likes to use what she thinks is 'spy speak'. It always makes Grace want to laugh.

'Yes, he did. Have you spoken to his wife?'

'She called me last night; couldn't wait until today. I told her that he went for it and I'd call her today to see if she wanted a copy of the tape and the report. Poor woman was beside herself. Kept me talking for hours. I didn't get to sleep until gone two.'

'Poor thing. I've emailed you a full report and the tape is sitting here waiting for you to send a bike.'

'Well, she does want the report, obviously, but I think she's made up her mind to throw him out. Apparently she doesn't want her daughter growing up thinking all men are cheats. Anyway, you're pure gold, Gracie. So, how are you?'

'I'm OK. Tired, for some reason.'

'Darling, chasing cheating men is a tiring business, and don't let anyone tell you otherwise,' Nicole laughs.

'Don't I know it. You know, I would just like one to tell me to bugger off.'

'Well, one of my other girls did get turned down, if that's any consolation.'

'No, really?'

'Yeah, but I think she went a bit wrong with the tactic. Anyway, I'm going to take you to lunch soon, because you sound thin.'

'How can I sound thin?' Grace tries not to be too attached to Nicole, because of the work connection, but she is.

'You just do. And when we have lunch we'll natter about your quest for a faithful man. Also I've got something else I want to talk to you about.'

'OK, Nicole, I'll look forward to it.'

When Grace puts the phone down she feels sad, because she doesn't want Mrs X's daughter thinking all men are cheats, but she also doesn't want to think that herself. But they are, aren't they? Or is there still hope?

A couple of hours later, after organising her files and her upcoming jobs, she breaks for lunch. She makes herself a salad and she eats it in the sitting room, where she sits on her sofa, facing her fish tank.

'You guys might be a bit aggressive with each other but at least you aren't lying cheating men.' She smiles at them.

Chapter Two

'Johnny, stop it. I'll be late,' Betty Parkin begs unconvincingly, through her giggles.

'OK, fine. Go to work.' Johnny sits up in bed, and folds his arms, dropping Betty like a stone on to the mattress.

'Well, maybe I can be a bit late . . .'

Johnny turns to face her. 'Really?'

'Oh, well, the buses were a nightmare and the tube was stuck in a tunnel for hours.'

'Choo, choo, here comes the train. Get the tunnel ready and switch on the green light.'

Giggling hopelessly, Betty obliges.

An hour and a half later she runs, breathless, into her office.

'Sorry, Hannah,' she says to her assistant. 'It was the train.' And at her private joke she bursts out laughing. Hannah looks at her oddly. Although she is used to her boss's early morning euphoria, she still doesn't understand it. Nor, she suspects, does she want to.

'Betty, when you've composed yourself, Fiona wants to see you.'

'Thanks, Hannah. Anything else?'

'There's some messages on your desk, but nothing much.' Hannah turns back to her computer screen and Betty takes her coat off, flings her bag on her chair and goes to her boss's office.

Betty has been working at *Modern Woman* magazine for six

years, and now she is a senior features writer. She climbed up from work experience girl, and now is enjoying her job almost as much as she enjoys her marriage. She also has a lot to be grateful for. After all, it was her job that gave her Johnny.

She and Johnny have been together for four and a half years, and married for just under two. They are still honeymooners, which Betty thinks is unusual after so long. She fell in love with Johnny almost instantly when she went to interview him for a feature in the magazine about personal finance. She still laughs now when she thinks back.

One of the topics chosen for features was the financial independence of young women. It was considered the short (and somewhat boring) straw. Then she met Johnny, an independent financial advisor with a lot more than just ISAs going for him. She managed to string the feature out long enough to get him to ask her out and she has never looked back. Neither has he.

From the word go, they were seen as the perfect couple. Friends envied the way they went so well together. Even now, that envy lives on. Betty and Johnny enjoy each other, and although they acknowledge they are sometimes a bit sickening, sometimes a bit smug and definitely far too happy, there isn't a damn thing they can do about it. Nor anything they want to do about it.

Everything has gone their way ever since their first meeting. Their relationship, although not without rows, has been relatively flawless. The proposal was perfect: he went down on one knee whilst they were on a weekend away in Barcelona. They bought a small but lovely house together and got a cat, Cyril, from the cats' home. They had the wedding of the year: one hundred people, a church and a sumptuous sit-down meal – and it didn't rain, even though it was September.

Betty, however, is not without her demons. She sometimes feels like two people: Betty at work, Mrs Parkin at home. *Modern Woman* is a magazine aimed at independent career women, and although there is room for husbands and boyfriends within that definition, Betty sometimes wonders if she still fits that mould. She loves her job and would mourn it if it went, but she is not as independent as she used to be. She doesn't leave her husband at home and go for wild nights out with the girls, she hasn't been to a club in years, and she is more interested in buying things for the house than clothes shopping. She dresses well, she looks the part, but she just doesn't always feel it. She worries sometimes that she will be seen as a fraud: 'You are too devoted to your man to fit the modern woman profile, off you go.' But at other times she thinks she is a modern woman – just one who has landed on her feet and seems to have it all.

She is good at her job; she is a good writer. Before Johnny she used to be the whole *Modern Woman* package. She tried out men, she discarded men, she speed dated, she two-timed, and she had longish relationships where she called the shots. She was an independent modern woman. Her career was more important to her than anything; she would cancel dates for work without a second thought. But then Johnny happened and everything changed. Betty admits that to herself. She cannot explain what happened, or why it happened. She fell in love and her life turned itself on its head. This she tries to keep from work. It is her secret, her terrible secret. When she is at work she will ogle male models, she will talk about sex, she will be the way she was. But she knows, deep down in her heart, that she isn't that way any more. Work Betty is a very different animal to home Betty.

Her social life outside work revolves around being married. It wasn't a conscious decision to drop her single friends, but it just seemed that activities involving either just herself and Johnny or other couples – dinner, theatre, movies, parties – seemed to consume all their time. She sometimes worries that it was a decision, albeit a subconscious one, to slide her single friends out of her life, but she pushes the thought away, and likes to think that maybe they slid her out.

She not only feels contradictions between her home life and her work life, but she feels guilty for being so happy sometimes, although she is not sure why.

'Morning, Fiona.' She smiles as she plonks herself down in the large leather chair, which swamps her small frame. 'How are you?' She sometimes wonders if she will ever be editor. Fiona works frighteningly hard, horribly long hours, but she does have a really cool office. It's quite large, with a massive glass desk, two large leather chairs, a sofa in the corner (for naps), and framed *Modern Woman* covers all over the walls. There is also a television, which is the thing that Betty covets the most. Catching *Neighbours* at lunchtime, or the news, or even the Channel 5 afternoon movie would be fab. She is sure that Fiona does exactly that. The only problem is that Fiona is feared universally throughout the magazine. She and Betty put on a friendly façade, but Betty is aware that Fiona could eat her for breakfast and throw her up by mid-morning.

'Hi, Betts. How are things?'

'As good as they were yesterday.' Her boss is older than she is (Betty is thirty-one), but decidedly single, or actually divorced, something that slightly scares Betty. She thinks that if she even hears the word she might be contaminated with it.

'How's the cat?'

By the same token that divorce scares Betty, the mention of marriage scares Fiona. So she never says Johnny's name to Betty. In fact, Betty thinks she seems to deny his existence. Fiona is anti-marriage. When Betty told her that she was marrying Johnny, Fiona really lost it. 'What the hell do you want to do that for?' she screamed, and she didn't speak to Betty until after she got back from her honeymoon. Betty tried to be understanding. Fiona had a terrible experience with her ex-husband, who was sleeping with her best friend and a number of other women before she discovered his multiple infidelities. A nasty divorce followed and Fiona nearly fell apart under the strain. However, now she copes with it by hating men and hating marriage. Betty doesn't think it is exactly healthy but she feels more loyalty to Fiona than is necessary and she always humours her rants.

'Cyril is fine.'

'Right, then, down to business. I have a fantastic assignment for you.'

'Oh, good.' Betty is dying to get her hands on a good story, after spending the last month making up embarrassing sex stories. She wants to write a proper feature, one which demands research.

'You're going to spend some time with a woman.'

'What woman?'

'A honey trapper.' Fiona sits back in her chair and folds her arms.

'What on earth is that?'

'Her job is a little unorthodox but not as rare as you might think. She tests men's fidelity. Women hire her to go to a bar, for example, and be the sort of temptation to see if their men fall for her or remain faithful to them. They call it honey trapping. Putting temptation under a man's nose and seeing how he reacts. Most of the time she is hired by women who have good reason to suspect their men are cheats, but other times she is hired by paranoid women.'

'But she must be really twisted to make her living that way.' Immediately Betty dislikes this woman, and is shocked by that fact. Normally being a professional, she doesn't judge and she certainly doesn't hold opinions on her subjects. She ignores the dislike and concentrates on Fiona.

'Perhaps I jumped in a bit quickly.' Fiona has a habit of doing that, leaving her staff flummoxed about what she is saying half the time. 'I met this woman at a dinner party who, wonderfully, is a detective. Her firm specialises in the area of infidelity and one of the strongest parts of the business is the honey-trapping side, which I just explained to you.'

'Right . . .' Betty is slightly lost for words.

'It's fantastic. I love it. A woman who goes out and traps all those cheating bastards. Nailed. Banged to rights. Of course, they should all be castrated but this is the best legal thing.'

'So, you want me to write a feature on her?'

'No, one of her girls. I ran the idea by her and she said she was interested, in theory. It'll be like free advertising for her firm. But she said she would have to ask one of the women who actually do the job and take it from there.'

'So I would be following this woman around, whoever she is, documenting everything she gets up to.'

'From the moment she wakes in the morning until the moment she goes to bed.'

'But it isn't confirmed?'

'Not exactly, but Nicole, the woman from dinner, said she would call me with someone I can put you in touch with this week. It's going to make a great story.'

'It should be interesting at least.' Betty knows better than to argue with Fiona.

'I hope so. For the story's sake.' The meeting is over.

Betty spends the rest of the day researching, and discovers that honey trapping isn't uncommon. She shudders at the women who test their husbands, but then she also shudders at the thought that men cheat. She knows that Johnny would never cheat on her and she knows that she would never test him. Her marriage is her certainty. Her rock-solid belief. Her religion. It's not insecurity that makes her angry, it's the fact that the honey trappers feed off insecurity. She doesn't like deceit, and to these women deceit is an industry.

She is already forming the profile in her mind: a devious witch of a woman who wants to wreck marriages. Betty knows if a honey trapper came anywhere near hers she would kill her.

She keeps a photo of Johnny on her desk, her one concession to bringing her married status into work. As she looks at him, with his white-blond hair, his pale blue eyes, his sexy smile, she knows that she is going to struggle being impartial with the new assignment. She curses her boss, who would herself be perfect to do the actual feature. After all, hating men would give her and the honey trapper something in common.

When she arrives home, she fusses over ginger Cyril and feeds him, which is all he really wants from her. Then she goes to the bedroom and changes out of her work clothes. Everyone at the magazine dresses as fashionably as possible (they all feel obliged, as at least half the magazine's pages consist of fashion), but as soon as Betty gets home she opts for comfort. She wrote an article a few months ago about women getting complacent when they have bagged their man, and she sees herself falling into some of the traps that she pointed out. Wearing baggy trousers and big sweatshirts was one, but Johnny never complains. And Betty does make an effort for him; she hasn't turned into a total slob. She hasn't put on weight (another thing on her list), or started burping in front of him, and she always keeps her bikini line, her underarms and her legs waxed. And she never, ever, greets him at their front door with spot cream plastered all over her face.

Cyril is cleaning himself when she re-enters the kitchen. She goes to the fridge and pulls out a bottle of white wine. Pouring herself a glass, she hears a key in the door so she pours another glass and goes to greet him with it.

'Wow, you really know how to make a man happy.'

'Oh, yes, I do,' Betty replies, handing him the wine and planting a huge smacker of a kiss on his lips.

Betty likes making Johnny happy. She is hardly a domestic goddess but she tries to take care of him. They have a fairly equal marriage, she would say, because they take care of each other.

They eat dinner together at the small dining table and she tells him about her latest assignment.

'Apparently, women pay to test their husbands' fidelity. Don't you think that's bizarre?'

'What, that women test men, or that men cheat?'

'Both. I mean, could you imagine how you'd feel if I set you up like that? You'd be mad. But then I guess if you were cheating on me . . .' She shudders again at the thought.

'I would never do that. But you need to hear what they have to say before judging them.'

'Yes, but you know I just can't help thinking that the job is marriage wrecking.'

'But you said they work for other people; they only do what they're paid to do.'

'Imagine being paid to do that.'

'I know.'

'Rest assured, my darling, that I would never pay anyone to test you.' Betty smiles at him. It often astounds her, takes her by surprise, just how much she loves him.

'And I promise never to cheat on you.' They kiss, then they go to do the washing-up. Together.

Later, as she lies in bed awaiting sleep, Betty wonders again how she can be so lucky. How she is allowed to be so lucky. Her thoughts drift to the honey-trap woman she is going to have to meet, interview and write about, and fear rips through her. Whoever she is stands for everything Betty doesn't. They are at odds; they have to be. Betty knows that whatever happens, it is going to be a tough assignment.

She looks at Johnny, feeling the physical jolt of love. How

could a wife do that to her husband? How could she test him? She shudders again, as she knows that she never, ever will.

The next day, when she arrives at the office, she finds that there is a stack of papers, articles and pamphlets about honey trapping. She knows that Hannah has probably been there half the night collecting research. Betty remembers when that was her. Sleep wasn't something she had much of in those days. She sits at her desk with a cup of black coffee and reads. She wonders when she will actually be introduced to the honey trapper, or the fidelity tester or whatever she calls herself. She wonders if Fiona's friend has got it wrong and these women will all refuse to be interviewed. That is just a dream.

She decides to spend the day researching so when she is given someone to interview she will be prepared. She wants time to try to understand, or maybe she just wants to delay the inevitable. For some reason she believes that this feature could challenge her work façade, especially if she doesn't get over her phobia of it. She emails Johnny to tell him she loves him. Just that action makes her feel better. Then she emails her friend Alison to ask if she and her husband, Matt, would like to go for a drink that evening.

Alison and Matt replicate Betty and Johnny to a spooky degree. Although maybe that is not such a surprise as Alison was Betty's best friend at college, and Matt was Johnny's university friend, so they were introduced two months after Betty and Johnny got together. They married just under a year later, and live nearby. The two couples' social lives cross over to a large degree. When Alison mails Betty back saying that a drink would be great, she tells Johnny and feels her equilibrium return. So she will spend the day reading about women who wreck marriages and about men who cheat, but that evening, she will be married Betty with her oldest friend, and the man she loves by her side. Her sanity and certainty are unquestionable when she is in that situation.

Fiona sends her an email asking her how she is getting on. She mails back saying fabulous, and asking if she has her case study yet. Fiona says not yet. Then Betty goes back to reading the research and she just about manages to stop herself from shuddering at every sentence.

Chapter Three

Grace sits in her office until seven. Her organiser is full; business is booming. Nicole had given her two new cases that day: one, a woman who suspects her husband of cheating, and the other a woman who thinks her boyfriend is too flirtatious and wants to know if that flirtatiousness is really as harmless as he claims. The wife is desperate, but also resigned to the fact that her marriage is over. She had asked for someone to test her husband (blatantly tempt him), in order to have more ammunition for the divorce settlement. The woman with the flirt for a boyfriend is in love with him, but needs to know she isn't being taken for a fool. Both women are the type Grace likes to work for. They aren't victims; they are taking control. She has spent the day reading files and preparing for the jobs.

Finally, she leaves the office and takes a bath. As she lies in her bath, soaking in expensive aromatherapy bubbles, she thinks about the day behind her and the evening ahead. She is glad that it is Oliver she is seeing, because he is, perhaps, her most relaxing lover. She believes that if she had met him before the honey trapping, she would have married him by now. They would be a normal couple, with a normal life. Of course, at some point in that normal life he would cheat on her. That is the thought that stops her from loving. That knowledge is the thing that ensures she can't fall in love.

She dries herself and covers her body with Aveda moisturiser, liberally spreading it to ensure that her skin is invitingly soft. Then she pulls on her lacy black underwear and a pair of stockings. She wears a short, black dress and high heels. As she stares at her reflection, she knows she looks stunning; as if she were going out for an expensive dinner, which she is not. She is staying in, because that is what she does when she isn't working. But that doesn't mean that she shouldn't make an effort, and it doesn't mean that Oliver won't be grateful for that effort.

It is complicated. Grace always meets her lovers at her flat. As her job is spent in bars, restaurants and sometimes clubs, she can only separate what she does at work from what she does in her spare time by confining her social life to home. She has turned normality on its head.

At first she wanted to keep her flat private, so she visited them. But she found their homes depressingly masculine, which made her uncomfortable. She visited Eddie's flat only once, but that upset her because it was all big televisions and sounds systems. Oliver has a large house in Holland Park, which is unlived in. Grace couldn't help thinking that a family of six would be comfortable there; it seems unfair for one man, who is barely ever there, to have all that.

When she thinks back to life before fidelity testing, she assumes that men's flats were the same then. But she didn't recognise it, or it didn't affect her. It is only now that she has a problem with such maleness.

The intercom buzzes at her on the dot of eight. This annoys her. She imagines him standing on the doorstep looking at his watch, counting the minutes until he is no longer early. The thought of him doing this scares her, so she stands in her doorway, looking at her own watch until she has kept him waiting. Teaching him a lesson. Grace is looking forward to seeing him – has been all day – but she gets easily annoyed and punctuality is one thing guaranteed to annoy her. If he was early and buzzed straight away, then she would have been fine. Ditto if he was late. But being exactly on time (and Grace's watch is set with a precision that could not be questioned) was calculated, and therefore a little bit spooky. Of course, if Grace decided to be generous she could tell herself that his watch was not as exact as hers and therefore to him he could have been either early or late, but she doesn't wish to be generous. She wishes to be in control.

The buzzer continues insistently, like a child having a tantrum, refusing to be silenced. Despite this, Grace stands with her hands on her hips, watching, listening and feeling in control. After five minutes she succumbs to him and answers the intercom.

'Where were you?' he snaps angrily.

'In the bathroom.' She buzzes him in, with a faint smile on her lips.

She stands holding the door open while she waits for him to climb the stairs. Her flat is on the second floor of a mansion block. It takes him a matter of seconds before he appears. Grace feels excitement fluttering like a butterfly in her stomach. She chooses to ignore it.

'Wow, you look gorgeous.' He lunges forward clumsily, and kisses her cheek. His lack of sophistication turns her on. After the well-groomed, expensively dressed charmers she encounters in her work, his clumsiness is not only appreciated, it is necessary. She gives him a light hug and stands aside for him to enter. She takes in his attire and again feels relief wash over her. He is wearing faded jeans and a check shirt. On his feet are a pair of expensive trainers. His light brown hair is slightly too long for his thin face; normally he wears it shorter and it makes his thin nose and his blue eyes stand out more. His slightly scruffy appearance isn't deliberate; Grace learnt early on that he has no idea that he is scruffy. She likes that about him.

He walks straight into the sitting room and says hello to the fish. Grace stands back slightly, observing him as she would a painting. Her arms are folded, her head slightly tilted; she is trying to see into him, trying to understand.

'So, what are we doing?' His question brings her back to reality.

'Takeaway, I thought,' she replies.

He smiles at her. 'You look really sexy tonight.'

'Don't I normally?' She raises one eyebrow and the reticence she felt at his presence has now dissipated.

She knows that she takes a while to warm up. Like a comedian, she starts off trying too hard, not with him, but with herself. She is trying to melt the ice before it is ready to melt. But she wishes that it wasn't there. Whenever she sees one of her lovers she acts at first as if she doesn't know him very well. She acts as if she should beware; she acts as if she is addressing a stranger. That is another side effect of her job; one she understands but does not like.

Oliver sits down on the sofa and studies her.

'You look tired.' He is concerned. He wants to protect her, but she won't let him. Grace is the most infuriating woman he has ever come across but he is in love with her, so there is no question that he can walk away. He worries about her, not about her job. He believes that her job is destroying her but also that that is because she is Grace rather than because of the honey trapping. The job doesn't worry him, but the results of it do. He believes that she is cynical, detached, and terrified because of it. He believes it affects her more than she should let it. After all, it is only a job. However, there is no way of telling her. She is a relatively passive person until you criticise her job. Oliver thinks that Grace is riddled with contradictions, like an old table riddled with woodworm. She cannot get rid of them, but they only serve to make her more attractive – not something most people would say of woodworm.

Grace goes to the sofa, and sits next to Oliver. She leans over and kisses him gently on his lips. Then she pulls back and looks at him. He leans in and kisses her. It is a tender kiss. He reaches his arm behind her head and rests his head gently on the back of it. He takes her other hand and touches her fingers lightly while kissing her. His eyes are shut.

She falls into the kiss, feels herself changing, physically. Her body is warm, her head is fuzzy. She touches his fingers lightly. They feel hot.

Eventually she pulls away. Reluctantly perhaps, but necessarily. Grace's evenings don't start in bed, they end there, and so she needs to regain control.

'Wine?'

'Sure. I'll come with you and get the takeaway menu.'

Grace opens a bottle of red wine and pours two glasses. Oliver decides that they will have Chinese takeaway and he orders for both of them. Grace lets him do this. They sit back on the sofa with their wine.

'You didn't tell me what happened with that man's wife,' he says, sipping his wine without taking his eyes off Grace. He doesn't approve of her job, but it is important to her, therefore he always tries to talk about it.

'Nicole said it was horrible. Apparently she was so nice, but so sad. You know, most women don't hire us unless they're pretty sure, and I guess that's why I prove so many of them right, but it's heartbreaking for them to have confirmation. I guess when it's just a suspicion they can tell themselves they are being paranoid and you can bet that that's exactly what the men tell them. Bastards. I wish sometimes they would turn me down. Maybe then I'd feel better.'

'No sane man would turn you down.' He smiles, but then sees the scowl appear on Grace's face, and immediately starts back-pedalling. 'What I mean is, you just said that they don't hire you unless they're pretty sure, so the men you get to meet are all cheaters. You just don't meet the faithful ones because their wives or girlfriends don't need to test them.'

'Do you really believe that?'

Grace would like to think that is the truth, but in her heart she doesn't. The truth is that most men cheat, and that is based on some sound statistics. If it were true that the faithful men never needed to be put to the test, then that would perhaps make the world better, but that is a truth that eludes her. If her clients were convinced, they wouldn't come to her; they come to her because they are unsure. And all she does is prove that they're right to be unsure. That is her truth.

'I do.' He takes her hand and kisses it. 'If a supermodel tried to tempt me I wouldn't be interested.'

'How's work?' She abruptly changes the subject because he sounds too much like a boyfriend.

'Fine. As usual too busy, but we're making money and we're hiring some new people . . .' He tries to sound cheerful but he is hurt by her rebuttal.

'So it's a nightmare?'

'A bit.' The conversation is stilted. There is a cheerful pitch to her voice that sounds fake, and he is trying to cover his feelings, but is unable to string a sentence together. The evening is in danger of disintegrating. This is a typical meeting for Grace and Oliver.

The buzzer saves them, announcing the arrival of dinner. He goes to the door to collect the food and pay while Grace goes to the kitchen to gather plates. Her shoulders are hunched as she reaches into the cupboard; she feels tense. Oliver joins her, carrying two bags, and they begin to serve food up.

'You've got an extra spare rib,' she says to him, determined to lighten the mood.

'I'm bigger than you,' he replies. Grace winks at him and removes the rib from his plate and puts it on to hers. He takes it back.

'I'm having an extra prawn ball then.' By the time they take their full plates to the table in the sitting room, they are friends again.

After dinner they clear up and they feed the fish together. Then, scared of any tension reappearing, they go to bed. They make love for a long time, gently and silently. Afterwards he holds her, gripping her tightly as if he is scared she will slip away. They lie like that for a while, until he falls asleep. Then, as per his fear, Grace gets out of bed. She lights a cigarette (she hardly ever smokes) and she sits, tasting the combination of cigarette and salty tears, that for an unknown reason are rolling down her face.

Chapter Four

At six thirty, Betty manages to leave the office. She still has a little bit of work to do, but she takes her laptop with her so she can do it at home. She prefers to work late at night, once Johnny is asleep, rather than stay in the office, and as long as she gets the work done then there can be no complaints about when and where she actually does it.

She says her goodbyes and leaves. Most of the editorial staff are still working, but Betty is no longer a junior so she doesn't need to worry about impressing anyone. Thankfully, those cruel days are behind her.

She gets the tube home and thinks about all the research she has read. She wonders if she'll get her case study tomorrow. She wonders what she'll be like, how open she'll be and how willing to do the feature. She wonders what sort of person the woman will be. Betty already thinks of honey trappers as brash, confident and bossy. That is the image she has, and although she is dreading the case study part of the feature, she wants to get it underway. The sooner she starts, the sooner she will have it finished. It is confusing her.

She arrives home, her musing having distracted her enough to carry her all the way there. As she puts her key into the front door, her mobile rings. It is Johnny.

'Hi, hon.' She cradles the phone under her ear, juggling the laptop and the house key.

'Hey. I'm going to be a bit late. Shall I meet you at the pub?'

'Sure. We're going to Barnie's. About half seven.'

'I've just got a couple of problems to deal with. I shouldn't be much past then.'

'No problem. See you later.'

'Bye.' He hangs up and Betty renegotiates the opening of the door.

She picks the mail up off the mat and puts it on the hall sideboard. She isn't a huge fan of opening the post straight away, because normally it is junk mail or bills. She hangs up her coat, leaves her laptop in the hall and goes to the kitchen to pour herself a glass of wine. She then goes up to the bedroom to change into her jeans.

Barnie's is a bar down the road from her house, only a five-minute walk. It is a regular haunt due to convenience. As she has plenty of time, Betty takes it easy getting ready. She sips her wine as she changes, reapplies her make-up and brushes her long, unruly hair. She clips it back, then decides she looks like a schoolgirl so she unclips it. It doesn't help that the clips are silver glitter – a sample stolen from the magazine office. She brushes her hair again and, satisfied, she is ready.

Dropping the empty wine glass into the dishwasher, she grabs her handbag and her keys and leaves the house.

It is just getting dark, and it is also warm as she walks slowly to the bar. When she pushes open the door she sees that Alison and Matt are already there.

'Hi.' She kisses Alison on the cheek and then kisses Matt.

'Shit, what is that smell?' he asks, with a smile. He is always overpowered by Betty's perfume.

'Gucci Rush – don't you like it?' Betty pretends to be hurt.

'I think it's sexy,' Alison says, shooting her husband a look. Alison is overprotective towards her.

'It is quite, actually.' Matt grins, and goes to the bar to get Betty a glass.

Betty gives Alison's hand a squeeze. She adores her best

friend and secretly sees it as one of her biggest triumphs that she got her together with Johnny's best friend. It is a ready-made social life; everyone likes each other equally. This is important to Betty. If she is living in an acute world of coupledom she doesn't mind. She likes it.

'It's quite a nice Chardonnay,' Matt says, when he returns to the table and pours a glass for Betty.

'Flash?' Betty asks.

'No, quite cheap actually,' Alison explains. 'Well, not cheap but not expensive.'

'Where's Johnny? I need some football talk.' Matt stares at the door.

'He'll be here soon; he got caught up at work.'

'Yeah, right.' He makes a face.

'Stop being a moron,' Alison snaps, slapping his arm. She glances at Betty, but Betty knows better than to be bothered by Matt's suggestions.

'Thanks, Ali. I was only joking.' He rubs his arm.

'Not all your jokes are funny.'

'Can you two stop bickering? I feel like a mother.' Betty is used to Matt's teasing and their constant arguing. Although the arguments are rarely serious, they sometimes seem continuous. Betty wills Johnny to hurry up.

'We don't bicker, we discuss,' he retorts, and kisses his wife.

'No, we don't, we bicker,' Alison replies.

Betty puts her head in her hands and then takes a large swig of her wine. It immediately warms her up.

'You're right, this is a nice Chardonnay. Matt, go get another bottle, there's a love.'

Johnny walks in while Matt is at the bar. He kisses Betty, gives Alison a peck on the cheek, then goes to give Matt a hand.

'You are so soft, the way you go all cute when you see him.'

'Piss off, Ali. Anyway, I can't help it.'

'You've been married for two years – doesn't the sight of him annoy you yet?'

'No. Does Matt?' Sometimes, Betty panics when she thinks her friends are not as in love as she is, but she has no idea why.

'Only sometimes,' Ali laughs, just as the men return with another bottle of wine.

'Did you sort your problem out?' Betty asks as Johnny refills her glass.

'Almost.'

'What problem is this?' Matt asks, and Johnny explains. Alison makes a face.

'Guess what, Ali,' Betty says when the men are safely talking about work.

'What?'

'I have this new assignment.' Alison is envious of Betty's job at the magazine. She herself works in retail; she is the area manager for a number of stores.

'Which is?'

'I have to interview a honey trapper.'

'What on earth is a honey trapper?'

'A woman you pay to test your partner's fidelity.'

'No way. Tell me more.'

'Well, say you suspect your husband is unfaithful or capable of being unfaithful, then you pay this woman to tempt him, and if he capitulates you know.'

'Women really do this?'

'I'm glad you said that because I'm having a few problems getting my head round it, but yes, women really do it.'

'Are these women really attractive?' Alison looks worried.

'Apparently. I don't know who I'm going to be interviewing but Fiona says they are all good-looking, as does all the research I've read. That's what I find hard to understand. You've got this man and this gorgeous woman who is being paid to tempt him. I think that's just wrong.'

'Yeah, but if you thought that your husband was cheating, wouldn't you want to know for sure?'

'Johnny wouldn't cheat.'

'I know he wouldn't. I'm being hypothetical.'

'No. I'd just ask him. What is the point in being in a relationship with someone you don't trust?'

'Yeah, but not all men are trustworthy.'

'I just think it's sick. I mean, there are other ways of finding out if he's cheating. I think hiring this woman who is blatantly no better than a common whore to tempt him is wrong.'

'Shit, you do feel strongly about this.'

'I know, and I have to follow some woman around for a week or something to do a feature.'

'When?'

'As soon as. I'm waiting to hear.'

'Not talking about the honey-trap woman again, are you?' Johnny asks, joining in the conversation.

'What?' Matt asks, and Betty explains again. He pales.

'I am not sure I like the idea of you women doing that. It shows a lack of trust and respect.'

'I agree. I'd never do it,' Betty says.

'Well, I bloody well would. If you gave me cause, obviously,' Alison adds with a wink.

'And obviously I wouldn't, but I'd rather you confronted me if you had any doubts.'

'My point exactly,' Betty agrees, taking another drink.

'Christ, you're drinking quickly today. Is something wrong?' Johnny asks.

'Not at all. I'm just thirsty. But maybe we ought to eat before I get really pissed.'

'Good idea.' Betty and Johnny have one repetitive argument: her ability to get drunk quicker than anyone else and her insistence on forgetting that fact. Johnny doesn't mind her getting drunk – he's not a caveman – but sometimes when they're out and she is tipsy so quickly he finds it embarrassing. He just wishes she would slow down. Betty drinks because she thinks it increases her confidence, not something anyone else thinks she lacks but she sometimes does.

Johnny asks at the bar for some menus, and he also buys another bottle of wine while he is there. He is tired, and although he happily buys the wine he hopes he won't regret it when he has to carry Betty home. He is a little bothered himself. He received an email today from an old school friend, Simon, saying that they never seem to have time to see each other and for some reason it made him think about all the people that he hasn't seen in ages. It isn't that he even wants to see Simon – they had nothing in common at school and it doesn't look as if that has changed – it just made him look at his life. It bothers him because he seems to spend his entire life with Matt and Alison and, although he adores them both, he thinks that perhaps they are too cosseted. The problem is Betty. He knows that she likes that about them and he is unsure how to broach the subject. But for now he has a wife to feed, so he tries to push those thoughts away. He will think of something.

'Anyone want to share some nachos to start?' he asks, plonking the wine on the table and distributing menus.

'I will.' Betty leans over and kisses his cheek.

'Let's get two lots then,' Alison suggests.

Matt nods and pours more wine into everyone's glasses. 'So, what are you guys up to at the weekend?' he asks.

'Nothing. Nothing planned, anyway. But our spare room needs painting,' Betty replies.

'Exciting,' Matt responds.

'Yeah, well, you can help us then,' she bites back.

'Betty, thanks for the invitation but I think we might have better things to do.'

'Everyone has better things to do; even I have better things to do.' Johnny looks at her, and strokes her hand.

'Um, but when we've got a lovely guest room your mother can come to stay more often.' Betty laughs and strokes his hair.

'God, can you two stop mauling each other long enough for us to order?' Matt asks, and they do.

'I feel drunk,' Betty says, as they get up to leave. Despite the food, she is more than tipsy.

'You are drunk,' Matt replies.

Johnny takes her hand and guides her to the door. They say good night and they make their way home.

'You're going to have a hangover tomorrow,' Johnny says, desperately trying not to mind.

'It'll be easier to work on the marriage-wrecking whore story then,' Betty says without thinking.

'How can you be so bothered? Betts, you've never been this upset about anything you've worked on.'

'Not upset, couldn't care less.'

'Fine. Come on, let's get you home to bed.'

'Are you propositioning me?'

'Certainly not, you lush. I'm going to make you drink water and then I'm going to tuck you in.'

'Johnny, I feel horny.'

'No you don't. You're drunk.'

Betty giggles. 'Drunk and horny. Horny, horny.'

'Betty. . . I'm warning you.'

'Oh, you're so sexy when you're being strict.' She giggles some more.

Chapter Five

The alarm beeps at six o'clock. Grace rolls over and snuggles into Oliver, who has reluctantly opened his eyes.

'Hey,' he says, kissing the top of her head.

'Morning,' she murmurs, kissing his armpit.

'I wish I could stay in bed with you, but I'd better go.' He kisses her properly on her lips before moving the duvet and getting up.

'See you later,' she mumbles before falling back asleep.

He watches her from the door, knowing that she can't see him and knowing that if she could she would probably get angry. But that is his indulgence. Instead of a few extra minutes in bed with her, he prefers to watch her sleep. She looks so peaceful, so beautiful, and he knows that he loves her. He knows that the image of her sleeping will stay with him all day as he works, and he showers, dresses and leaves feeling good about that.

Grace waits for half an hour before she opens her eyes again. She knows he has left, having heard the door open and close. She knows that he was staring at her, which is why she pretended to be asleep, because she doesn't know how to deal with it. She gets up and goes to make coffee, feeling uncharacteristically tired. She barely slept, although she knows that she probably slept for longer than she believes, because that always tends to be the case.

She takes her coffee into the living room where she watches the fish for a while and feeds them their breakfast. She loves the way that they swim, open-mouthed towards the food, often missing it. Misguided. Like her. She decides that it is time to lighten her mood and she wonders why she has felt so unbalanced lately. She hopes it isn't to do with Oliver; she would miss him if he had to go.

She showers and dresses (usual work uniform of a tracksuit), and she goes to her office and switches on her computer. She checks her calendar; she has a job that evening, so she pulls out the file on her client. She always gives each case its own file, which she sends to Nicole when the job is complete. Each woman provides her with a photograph of her partner, a list of his likes and dislikes, as well as details of his job and his usual haunts. Then Grace will research his main hobby or his job so she has something she can talk to him about.

That evening's case is a boyfriend, rather than a husband – a boyfriend who after four years still refuses to commit to his girlfriend.

Men, Grace thinks, looking at yet another contradiction in her life. The ones she works with (or her victims) will not commit and want more than one woman. Oliver is the opposite. She tells herself to stop thinking about him. She doesn't have the time to think about him. She wishes it didn't have to be this way, but it does.

She is absorbed in her work when the phone rings.

'Grace Regan,' she answers.

'It's me,' Nicole says, in her brash, slightly hard voice. Grace often thinks that she still sounds like a policewoman arresting someone.

'Hi.'

'Lunch today. Zigli's.'

'That sounds like an order from my boss.'

'It is. I've got a great opportunity for you.'

'Really? Tell me more.'

'I will. At lunch. Be there at one sharp. Bye.' She has put the phone down before Grace can question her further.

She finishes her preparation for that evening before she changes out of her work uniform, into a pair of jeans and a stripy long-sleeved top. Zigli's isn't too formal and neither is Nicole. She leaves the flat and, without realising why, she is smiling. She is smiling because today will not be another solitary day. She will have a welcome distraction in her boss.

Nicole is sitting there when Grace arrives. She goes to join her, ignoring the waiter, who tries to accost her on the way. They hug; their affection for each other is genuine. Then they make small talk while they order drinks and study the menu.

'Ready for tonight?' Nicole asks. Business first.

'I've read the file, I've got the photo in my brain. The only thing is, as you know, I've got a list of four bars to try. What if he's not in any of them?'

'Call me, and I'll call her and we'll take it from there. I think he probably will be in one of them, though. She says they're the only places he goes to. Luckily they're close to each other so you won't have to chase him across London.'

'Fine. Then hopefully I'll get him at some point. So what's all this about? I'm sure you didn't invite me here just to feed me.'

'Well, I'm not sure that you'll like this because I know how private you are, but I want you to hear me out before you say no. I met an editor of a well-known women's magazine at a dinner party. Quite a good dinner, not the usual bunch of boring people. Anyway, we got talking and I told her what I did, and all about fidelity testing, and she was really interested. So, then she asked me if perhaps I would be interested in doing some sort of feature for her, to which I said of course because it's free advertising for the firm, but then she came back with a better idea, which was to spend five days shadowing one of my workers, i.e., you.' Nicole smiles and sits back.

'I have to have this editor follow me round?'

'Not her, a features writer – she didn't say which one. But you'd be perfect. You're the best woman I have working for me, you're beautiful, intelligent, sassy, independent. You'd be more than perfect. Now, of course there will be no photos, and no mention of your name. It'll be changed. But the events will be real.'

'And if I don't agree?'

'Well, it is your choice, but I think it makes sense. Shall we eat?'

They order lunch, and then Nicole turns to Grace again. She prepares herself to be persuaded but Nicole knows better.

'Do you remember Maggie, the woman you helped train a month ago?'

Grace nods, feeling suspicious because her mind is still with the previous conversation.

'Well, we sent her on her first mock job last night.'

'How did it go?' Grace remembers how scary the first test job was for her.

'Not good. She was supposed to be chatting up Mike.' Mike is a detective whom Nicole employs on a freelance basis. He has worked with Grace, trailing men that were hard to pin down.

'And?'

'She got to the bar, and Mike was standing there prominently. She'd seen a photo of him but not met him. Anyway, she made a beeline for some random man who she thought was Mike. Mike said he didn't even look like him. This man thought his luck was in, so at the end of the evening she asked him if she'd passed, he was completely confused and Mike finally stepped in when he'd stopped laughing. I told him it was a bit cruel of him, but he said that she deserved it. Not sure what I'm going to do with her now.' They both laugh.

'Are you sure I'm the best choice?' Grace asks, reverting to the feature idea.

'Grace, this is about the business, your job. You know that you're good at your job, which is why I asked you. If you take this personally then don't do it.'

'What do you mean?'

'It's your job, Grace, that's what I mean, and I don't think it should be anything more than that to you. Of course it's our livelihoods – both ours and the other people I employ – but it isn't your life.'

'I think I know what you're saying.'

'If it's too much, too personal, then we'll forget it.' Grace is her best worker, mainly because she is so dedicated. Sometimes Nicole worries that she's too dedicated, but because she is such an asset she tries to ignore those feelings. She wishes Grace didn't take everything so personally. Nicole recognises her fragility and it worries her. She wouldn't want to ruin her life. She fears that that is exactly what she is doing.

'Would I be able to meet the writer first, before we committed to anything?'

'Sure. Great idea. I'll get her to call you.'

Grace leaves after lunch feeling as if she has been steam-rollered. She goes home and waits for the phone to ring.

'Hi, Grace, my name is Betty Parkin, from *Modern Woman.*' Betty braces herself (rubbing her throbbing head slightly) to be charming. Charming, she decides, is much easier with a hang-over.

'Ah yes.' Grace is expecting the call, but not so quickly. Nicole probably had arranged it prior to lunch. She doesn't mind, though.

'Regarding the proposed feature, I just wondered if you would be prepared to meet for a chat.'

'Sure.' Grace thinks she sounds nice, if not a little busi-nesslike.

'Perhaps I could take you to lunch and we could outline our

proposal and see what you think.' Betty is being friendly, the hangover is making that easier, although she is already regretting suggesting lunch.

'Fine.' Grace is unsure why she is being quite so uncommunicative, but she is finding it hard to think of things to say.

'When would you like to go?' They arrange to meet the following day at a restaurant in town. At least Grace is being well fed over this. Then they say their goodbyes.

Grace stares at the phone. She knows the magazine, but she never imagined she would be in it. Nicole likes the idea, she loves the idea of publicity, but Grace needs to ensure that it is the right thing for her, personally, to do. She feels vulnerable, even behind a false name. She would be open to criticism, although no one would know it was her. Perhaps she is being oversensitive about it. After all, free publicity could do wonders for the business, and although it is Nicole's business, the more she works the more she earns. She replays the conversation again in her mind, unable to deduce much about Betty the journalist from their short chat. She thinks that perhaps she should do it, but she decides to ask someone for advice who doesn't have a vested interest. She almost calls Oliver, but knows that he will probably be flying off somewhere or holding one of his millions of important meetings. Oliver adores her, she knows, but he cannot always be there for her. Instead, she calls Eddie.

He answers the phone immediately. 'Eddie, it's Grace.'

'Hello. Are you calling me to arrange a well-overdue date?'

'Not exactly. I need some advice.'

'OK, but in exchange for advice I think I should get to see you.'

'I'm working tonight, and I need to talk to you before tomorrow.' For some reason she sounds slightly hysterical. As she hears this in her voice, she calms herself down, unsure what is wrong.

'OK, OK, what's up?'

'Nicole's asked me to do a profile with a women's magazine. I don't have to do it, but although it means a lot to her, I'm scared they might, you know, be horrible about me.' Her objection sounds lame when she says it aloud, that much she acknowledges.

'What magazine?'

'*Modern Woman*. It's a glossy monthly, quite popular, I think.'

'Photos?'

'No, no photos – of course I couldn't agree to that – but Nicole seems to think they'll be sympathetic and that it might get us business.'

'It probably will, or at least get you a load of enquiries. Can't Nicole get one of the others to do it?'

'I'm sure she could, but she wants me.'

'Of course, because you're the best. If you said no, would she be angry?'

'I get the impression that it wouldn't carry too much favour. You know how maternal she is, and I love her, so I wouldn't want to upset her. I think this is a good opportunity for her business, which in turn benefits me, of course.'

'It sounds like you've made up your mind.'

'I'm having lunch with the magazine woman tomorrow, so I don't have to decide until after that.'

'See how you feel. But it could be a very good move. For you and Nicole.'

'Do you want to spend Saturday with me?'

'Day?'

'Day and night?'

'My God, what did I do to deserve this?'

'Nothing,' Grace laughs.

'Shall I come round in the morning?'

Grace shakes her head: too keen, Eddie, far too keen.

'Come round at lunchtime. I might even make you some lunch.'

They hang up and Grace types her new appointments into her diary. She wonders what Betty will be like. She begins to feel excited about the story.

Then she studies her diary again. Eddie will be a welcome sight at the weekend, a stabling force. Eddie is a friend. If Grace had enough people in her life to categorise them, that is what she would say about him. There is a physical attraction, but that really developed from an attraction to his personality and his manner. He calms her down and he makes her feel safe, whilst at the same time he doesn't place too many demands on her. Their relationship is almost platonic. Almost, but not quite. Not quite, because that reminds her of who she is; of who she has to be.

Betty scribbles the time and the address of the restaurant in her Filofax. She has already booked it, or Hannah has, anyway. She replays the conversation with Grace over in her head. Grace's responses were so brief that Betty was unable to gauge her character at all. Was it indifference or fear? She cannot imagine that someone doing that job would be scared. But Grace did not sound the way Betty expected. She guesses that it is all an act. She probably flaunts a nice, friendly front, when she's really a bitch. Whatever it is, she will not find out until tomorrow.

Betty has a feeling that Grace will do the piece and she doesn't know if she is happy about that or not. Part of her would like her to say no, but part of her knows that this could be a good piece, and a good by-line. A lot meatier than the sex tips, diet tips and work-related issues that seem to have dominated her time lately. Instead of features where she invented research, this time she has a real story. One that, despite her personal feelings, the readers would find interesting. So why, deep down, is she feeling so scared?

Betty isn't a big baby; she can take of herself. She has always done so, although now more successfully than before. The timid creature that lived in her body for most of her childhood is gone. Betty is the sort of woman who knows what she wants and gets it. Her job and her husband are perfect examples of this. So her behaviour over the honey trapper, so wet, so pathetic, isn't something she welcomes, nor something she truly understands.

Her hangover is still gripping her, so she decides to call someone for reassurance. She calls Johnny.

'Hi, how's the head?'

'Pounding. Why did you let me drink so much?'

'I can just imagine how you would have reacted if I'd tried to stop you.' He laughs; his anger has dissipated as it always does.

'I called her.'

'Her, being the honey-trap woman?'

'Yeah, she sounded OK, but I think it's a front. I'm meeting her for lunch tomorrow.'

'Betty, you have to be nice to her if you want her to do this.'

'I know and I was very nice.' Betty is going to do a good job with this assignment and she is going to be nice to Grace.

'I bet you were. Shall we go out tonight?'

'No way. I need a long bath and an early night.'

'Now that I can do.'

She hangs up and looks at the clock. She is willing the time to pass because she could really do with a hug from Johnny. Some reassurance from her faithful, trustworthy husband.

Chapter Six

Betty gets to the restaurant early, ten minutes early. She sits at the table and imagines what sort of person will walk through the door. She is expecting her to be stunning, that much she knows, but she also imagines well groomed, expensive-looking. In Betty's mind she looks like the mistress of a rich man. In Betty's mind that is exactly what she is. No better than a mistress.

Betty has made an effort. She is wearing a cream trouser suit, high-heeled boots and her hair is swept up on to her head. She raided the beauty department for some make-up and also persuaded the beauty assistant to apply it for her. There was no way she will let Grace upstage her. She is unsure why it bothers her so much, but it does.

She orders a mineral water and sips it while watching the door. Every time a woman walks in she wonders if it is her. Suddenly she stops as she sees the door open again and in walks a woman who is so beautiful that Betty is immediately terrified it is her. She is not sure she can cope if it is her.

She is tall, almost six foot at a guess. Her hair is long and sleek (not like Betty's bird's nest), framing her face, which is a masterpiece. She is wearing a dark grey suit: knee-length skirt and long jacket, which is buttoned up, with nothing underneath. As she gets closer Betty notices her huge hazelnut eyes and her lips; she has never seen lips like them. As she follows a waiter to Betty's table, Betty realises instantly that she hates her.

She could have any man at all, with her looks, yet she insists on trying to seduce other people's. She may say that it is her job but Betty knows this is a guise. She can spot a bitch at one hundred paces and Grace is a bitch.

Grace doesn't know what to expect. She doesn't know what journalists look like, but she is convinced that she will be either smart or trendy. She isn't sure if she herself is trendy. Her work wardrobe is more classic, her casual clothes are quite simple. She thinks she passes as fashionable, but that is as far as she goes.

The maître d' leads her to Betty's table. As soon as she sees her she pauses for a moment to collect her thoughts. Betty is attractive, her wavy hair is off her face, her make-up looks as if it was done by an expert and she is, as Grace thought, trendy, or very modern-looking. Grace feels relieved she is wearing her grey suit. She is relieved she is wearing a jacket that blatantly has nothing underneath and shows a hint of cleavage. She is pleased she applied lipstick.

Betty stands up as Grace approaches the table. She puts her hand out a little sooner than she should so it is there, sticking out like a branch of a tree. Grace moves herself toward Betty's outstretched hand and shakes it lightly. She is not someone who is used to formal handshakes.

'Hello, how are you?' Betty asks.

'Fine, thank you,' Grace replies, sitting down.

'Can I get you a drink?'

'A tomato juice would be lovely.' Grace smiles and, like a mirror image, Betty smiles back. Grace, unused to much female company, feels intimidated by the confident, soldier-like Betty.

Betty thinks that Grace is far too self-assured, and refuses to let her intimidate her.

After Betty orders the drinks, she picks up the menu and gestures for Grace to do the same. She looks at the food, and tells Grace what she thinks is the best the menu has to offer. She wants Grace to think she dines here a lot. Grace is only half listening as she looks around the restaurant, taking in the lunchtime trade. She sees a number of business people, some chattering women, some lovers. She looks at Betty over the top of the menu and wonders what the other people make of them.

They order the food when the drinks are delivered. Betty tries to talk Grace into a starter, but Grace insists on only a main course. Betty thinks she is one of those women who don't eat, which would explain her thinness. Truthfully, Grace doesn't like eating too much at lunchtime. Betty orders a glass of white wine with her meal, while Grace declines. Betty thinks that Grace is a control freak; Grace wishes she could have a drink, but knows that lunchtime wine goes to her head and she doesn't want to risk saying anything silly. As they make small talk, they seem to be sizing each other up. Betty is looking at Grace the way a predator looks at its victim; Grace is looking at Betty the way a victim looks at its predator.

It is not until the food is in front of them that Betty broaches the subject of the magazine feature.

'We want a profile, a sort of week in the life of a honey trapper.'

'I hate that term.'

'Sorry. What would you prefer?'

'Detective, specialising in infidelity.'

'But it is known as honey trapping.' Betty looks at her sharply. 'Detective specialising in infidelity' hardly sounds catchy, she thinks, rolling her eyes.

'It is.' Grace sighs. She realises she will have to capitulate.

'Well, anyway, what we want is to follow you round. I would observe you at work – you know, before a job – and then when you are on a job. Of course I'd keep out of the way – I just want to watch – and then we'll profile you as well as talk about the industry as a whole.' Betty sounds more confident than she feels; Grace feels far less confident than she sounds.

'I'm not sure I'm comfortable being followed.' She wishes she could articulate better.

'I promise you'll get used to it. I guess photographs would be a problem.' Betty wishes that she hadn't said this, as she already knows the answer.

'No way.' Grace feels her face redden. Then she feels stupid; she is getting upset over nothing.

Betty looks at Grace sharply; she feels that the tone of voice she used was a little unnecessary. 'We can do without photographs,' she says kindly.

'You'll have to.' Grace knows that she is being needlessly harsh, but she cannot seem to help herself.

'So, tell me, in theory, how do you feel?' If you have feelings at all, Betty thinks. Despite her resolve not to be riled by Grace's job, she is already riled by the woman herself.

'The publicity would be good for business and, of course, I believe that the industry is interesting to women, and necessary, absolutely necessary. I'd like to see a proper proposal, of course, and I'd like to be given some sort of say on the final draft. I also want to run it all by my boss. She set this up with your boss, I believe.' Grace hopes she sounds like she knows what she is talking about; in reality she is clueless.

'I'm not sure about final say, but I will ensure that you agree the proposal before you start, and I give you my word that we will stick to the proposal.' Uptight and whore don't generally go together, but then control freak and whore maybe do, Betty thinks. She is growing to dislike Grace more by the minute, but she is glad that her instinct was right.

'OK, well, I'll wait for your proposal and we'll take it from there.' Grace can't explain what it is about Betty that makes her dislike her so strongly. She certainly didn't turn up for lunch expecting to feel such animosity towards her. She wonders if it is just intimidation, but she can't shake the feeling it is something more. However, she will do the piece, she has already decided that. She'll do it for Nicole.

After a painful and forced conversation over coffee, Betty signs the bill with a flourish, another action that Grace finds irritating. They get up to leave.

'It was lovely to meet you,' Betty lies, air-kissing Grace's cheek.

'It was lovely to meet you too,' Grace lies, wondering if Betty's blusher will be attached to her face when she moves away.

When she gets home, the first thing Grace does is call Nicole.

'Hi,' Nicole says.

'How come you're always at your desk when I call?'

'I feel like I've been grounded! Really, there is so much admin to this damn job that I don't get to do as much detective work as I used to.'

'Doesn't that bother you?'

'No, actually. I'm getting lazy in my old age and I like to sit on my arse all day.' They both laugh. 'So, how was lunch?'

'You know, this is going to sound really weird, but I get the impression she disapproves of me.'

'Tosh. She doesn't know you. Grace, you can be a bit paranoid sometimes and sensitive, especially when it comes to people you don't know.'

'My job is based on my confidence,' Grace protests.

'Yeah, but your personal life is based on something else. Gracie, I love you, everyone loves you, and don't you let anyone persuade you otherwise.'

'I asked for a proposal before we agree it.'

'Good. Let's make them think we're in the driving seat.'

'But we are going to do this?'

'I told you, it's your decision. But I would be pleased.'

'Then we're doing it.' Grace basks in the pleasure of doing something to please Nicole.

'That's my girl.'

Betty is sitting in Fiona's office.

'So what was she like?'

'Stunning with a capital S. My God, she's straight out of our fashion pages. She seemed a bit quiet, not terribly chatty. I'm not sure if that's because she's really arrogant or because she's only used to chatting up men.' Betty is trying to display her diplomatic side.

'If she's so gorgeous, it's a shame we can't photograph her.'

'No way will she agree to that, or your friend her boss. They'll lose all their business.'

'I think that's a bit dramatic, but never mind. You can describe her as stunning; we'll have to content ourselves with that. So, is it all agreed?'

'She wants a proposal to run by her boss, but apart from that, I think so, yeah.'

'So we can get going soon?'

'I don't see why not.'

'Betty, you're brilliant. This is going to be a great story.'

Betty smiles weakly at her boss and hopes that she is right. 'OK, I'll go and write the proposal.'

'Will you email it to me before you send it to her? I'm sure it'll be fine but I'd like to check. You know, I think this honey-trapping thing will really appeal to our readers.'

'You do?' Fiona seems a little too enthusiastic.

'Yes, and I wish I'd used one years ago to nail my bastard ex.'

'But you divorced him anyway.' Betty knows that Fiona is going to take this feature personally, which makes it worse for her.

'But I couldn't get him for infidelity, which was so unfair because he shagged half of London. I think honey trapping is a great industry.'

Betty sees the glint in Fiona's eyes and knows that she has no choice but to write a brilliant feature.

Chapter Seven

Saturday.

'Let's go to bed.' Eddie says this with a knowledge that the answer will be no. That does not stop him trying.

'No, Eddie. I'm all dressed up to go shopping.' Grace is wearing her one pair of trainers, flared black trousers and a jumper. Eddie is wearing a shirt and some chinos, his normal uniform. Eddie is the older of her lovers, and he has lost most of his hair. He is also a couple of inches shorter than she but she thinks he is adorable. Reliable and adorable.

'I can't believe you invite me over on a Saturday and you want to drag me round the shops.' He looks exasperated but is wearing a hint of a smile.

'I need new clothes.'

'You have a million clothes.' Eddie rolls his eyes. He will never figure Grace out, which he knows is probably why he is still with her. The minute she starts to make sense (which he is sure will never happen) is the minute he falls out of love with her, or infatuation – he is unsure which.

'I need more.' Ever since she met Betty, Grace has felt that something new is needed in her life. New clothes, new shoes, and maybe a new handbag. A female solution rather than a Grace solution. She thinks it is actually a Betty solution.

'Well, can't you go on your own and I'll wait here?' He is teasing her. He knows he will go with her. He knows that he is grateful for any time she gives him. It does not annoy him, it is merely fact.

'Eddie, I might have to get cross.'

'OK, you win. Where are we going?'

'Selfridges, of course. Where else?'

Grace kisses him hard, to thank him, which he appreciates. He puts on the coat he discarded half an hour ago, and they leave. They get into his car; a TVR Tuscan, his pride and joy. Grace teases him about the car, saying it is a 'chick magnet', and Eddie responds by saying if that were the case he'd have had her knickers off in there long before now. Grace kisses him when he says this. There is no way there is room in a TVR Tuscan for her long legs.

They park, having crawled through the Saturday traffic, and go to Grace's favourite store.

Two hours later they go and get a coffee in the bar.

'Christ, Grace, I'm knackered.'

'Just how I like my men, completely tired out.' She smiles as she looks at the bright yellow shopping bags lying loyally at her feet. She has bought herself some trendy outfits; perfect to wear when Betty starts following her around. Or at least perfect for her to almost compete with the amazing outfits that she is sure Betty will be wearing.

'Well, you got me. What do you want to do now?'

'Do you know what I'd really like?'

'No, but I bet it doesn't involve bed.'

'No, it doesn't. I would really like to go and see a film. I haven't been to the cinema for ages.'

'OK, but as I came shopping with you, I get to choose.'

'Deal, but if you choose you have to buy the popcorn.'

They seal their bargain with a kiss.

A thought keeps popping into Grace's head and she tries to use the mechanics of her brain to squeeze it out again. The thought is the way that she feels like part of a normal couple.

Shopping and a film: a totally normal activity for people in a relationship on a Saturday. Utterly normal. Grace squeezes as hard as she can to expunge the idea. She is not normal; they are not a couple. And that is the way it is. Eddie notices her mood darken, as it so often does when they are together. He also knows to ignore it. It will pass. They sit in front of an action film, Eddie's choice, lightly touching each other's hands and sharing a monster bucket of popcorn. By the time they leave, Grace has regained her earlier mood. She is not part of a couple, but that does not mean she cannot enjoy her day out. It does not mean that she cannot enjoy Eddie. She vows to relax more.

They return to her flat, where she insists on unpacking her shopping and hanging it up. She even changes into her expensive new jeans and a tight, sexy top. Eddie watches her as he always does.

'Drink?' she asks, once she's finished. She is not the best of hostesses.

'Whisky, thanks.'

She pours him a whisky and pours herself a glass of red wine. She likes the distinction between the drinks of her two men. Oliver drinks brandy or wine, Eddie, whisky.

They sit on the sofa, with their drinks. Grace feels tired, shopping type of tired, and she rests her head on Eddie's shoulder.

'You didn't tell me what happened with the magazine woman.'

'Oh, well, she was quite scary. You know, ultra trendy, really confident. I know I'm confident and outgoing in my work, but for some reason she made me feel really nervous. Actually I turned into a moron, barely able to string a sentence together.'

'I doubt that. Anyway, she probably felt just as nervous.'

'God, no, she wasn't intimidated at all. She was actually a bit bossy. Anyway, I agreed in principle but asked for a proposal. I said what you said and asked if I could give editorial approval but she said that wouldn't happen. Gosh, I hope this isn't going to be a big mistake. Nicole is so excited that I said I'll do it, I now feel that I'd be letting her down if I back out, but I'm still apprehensive.'

'Why?'

'I don't know, but this Betty woman is going to be shadowing me and I'm not sure I like that. She'll probably put me off and cause me to falter on the job.'

'Don't be so stupid. You're a pro, Grace.'

'Could you imagine, though? I see her watching me and I fall flat on my face or something equally embarrassing. She might make me say something stupid like: "Do you come here often?"' Grace laughs, but she is a tiny bit worried.

'Well, if you do fall over, and then give them a crap chat-up line, and they fall for it at least you'll know they're proper cheats.'

'Could be a new way of doing business.'

'Grace, now, I think you should do this, but first I think you should tell yourself that this woman is only a woman, and maybe you could even be friends.'

Grace shudders. 'I'm not good at that.'

Eddie sips his whisky and puts his arm round her. No, he will never understand Grace, which totally ensures her place in his affections.

Saturday.

'I love your job, Betts.'

'Me too.' Betty and Alison lie side by side on massage tables in London's latest day spa. Betty won the review tickets in a raffle, and while their husbands are playing golf the two women are enjoying a pampering. There is not a paintbrush in sight.

'I might have a steam next.'

'Then a swim. I wish we could come here every week. I would be so relaxed and happy.'

'You're happy anyway.'

'Yeah, but I get stressed at work, don't I? And to come here and do this every week would mean I got rid of all my stress.' She closes her eyes and imagines it for a minute.

'I suppose you could book yourself in for a massage once a week.'

'Yeah, but not here. Have you seen the prices? It's criminal.' Betty shudders at the thought of how quickly she could bankrupt herself.

'Talking of criminal, how did your lunch go with that woman?'

'The honey-trap woman? Just as I thought, really. She was uptight, absolutely stunning, too confident and sure of herself.'

'And you managed to be civil?' Alison knows how cutting Betty can be. Although she is not scared of her best friend, she knows many who are.

'I didn't give her the "I think you're a whore" speech, if that's what you mean. I was actually very civil. But I still don't think what she does is right.'

'Me neither, but then maybe we shouldn't blame her. After all, it's the women who hire her who want to test their men and it's the men who are untrustworthy.'

'But as you said, why not confront them? Seriously, Ali, Grace was incredible-looking; having her chat a man up isn't just slightly tempting, it's unrealistically tempting, which is bloody unfair. I know Johnny wouldn't go for it, or Matt, but most men would be so flattered to be chatted up by someone like her that they'd capitulate. Now, if you want to do this sort of thing, give them an averagely attractive woman, nothing special, and then see – not that I agree with that, but you know what I mean. Sending Grace to test your husband is like sending Kate Moss. They don't stand a fucking chance. Ow.' The masseuse pounds harder when Betty gets excited. She mentally curses and tells herself to calm down.

'So now you object on the basis that the woman is too

good-looking? First you were opposed to the whole premise.' Alison's voice is soft.

'I still am. I'm just saying that there's this woman who is stunning and knows it, and I know that the only reason she does the job she does is because she likes seducing other women's partners. It gives her massive ego even more of a boost and that is the only reason she does it.'

'It's going to be a fair interview then?' Alison laughs at Betty's intensity.

'I just say it how I see it.' Betty giggles too. Massage really is good for relieving stress.

After the spa, they make their way back to Alison's house where they are meeting their husbands. Betty flings her arms round Johnny.

'Good game?' she asks, planting a kiss on his slightly flushed cheek.

'No, I lost.'

'I won,' Matt pipes up, as if there is any doubt.

'Talk about mass humiliation, losing against him,' Johnny adds, wrapping his arms round Betty. 'Um, you smell gorgeous.'

'Massage oil.' A rush of love fills her. She knows that she is the luckiest woman in the world, but still she cannot understand why Grace and her honey trapping bothers her so much. Johnny is the one man she is certain of, the one man who wouldn't capitulate to the charms of Kate Moss or anyone. She is so sure in their love, she really is. So why are her thoughts behaving so irrationally?

'Do I smell gorgeous?' Alison asks, sidling up to Matt.

'Can't smell anything but my own success,' he replies, but gives her an affectionate squeeze anyway.

'We've decided that we need to have a massage once a week,' Alison says.

They are sitting at Alison and Matt's small round dining table, and eating tuna steaks cooked by Alison with a warm rocket salad. Alison is a far better cook than Betty, although most people are better cooks than Betty. She can manage pasta and baked potatoes but would rather not try anything more adventurous than that. Johnny isn't much better. Their local takeaways benefit from this fact.

'Which means we're free to play golf,' Matt says.

'We're turning into boring marrieds,' Johnny bemoans. 'The men play golf, the women go to the beauty parlour. Shit, we're middle-aged.' Although he doesn't sound too serious, his outburst visibly upsets Betty.

'We're not, we're only in our early thirties,' she protests. She will defend their lifestyle at all costs. She loves it so much that anyone criticising it makes her nervous; especially if that anyone is her husband.

'I know, in order for us not to feel so old, let's have a party.' Johnny suddenly sounds excited, although it is not as spontaneous as he is making out.

'For what occasion?' Matt asks.

'That's the point, there is no occasion. It's just because we're still young and we still have the ability to do spur-of-the-moment things.' Johnny looks animated as he warms to his theme. Everyone else looks doubtful.

'Where would we have it? At home?' Betty asks. She likes parties, but she isn't sure she wants to organise one.

'No, we'll hire a bar, get a DJ, make it a proper party. Invite everyone we know, not just married couples that we have dinner with, but single people too. People we've lost touch with. It'll be like a reunion.' Johnny has been thinking about the email he received that week and how out of touch it made him feel.

'Do we know any single people?' Betty asks. Her tone indicates that single people might be contagious, but no one notices.

'Of course we do. We just haven't seen them for a while.

There are my friends from university – some of them must still be single – and work. I'll start searching for a venue.'

'What's brought this on?' Betty asks, concerned. Johnny rarely makes any suggestions about their social life. He normally lets Betty organise it. She has a feeling that he is bored, and that thought terrifies her. *What if he's bored with her*?

'Mid-life crisis,' Matt quips, hitting Betty's nail on the head.

'No, I just fancy doing something different.'

'I think it's a great idea,' Alison agrees. She likes the idea of a party, she likes the idea of getting drunk, dancing and maybe even flirting with the single men that Johnny is talking about. Only harmless flirting, naturally.

'That's settled. I'll start organising it next week.'

Johnny looks happier; he has almost forgotten about his golf defeat. Betty is happy for Johnny to go ahead and organise a party as long as it makes him happy. Matt likes the idea of a party for the same reason that Alison does. The only thing worrying Betty is the idea that Johnny really is having a mid-life crisis. But as he leans over and kisses her, placing his hand on her leg under the table, she knows he isn't. He just fancies doing something different and there is nothing wrong with that. An image of Grace pops into her head, although she isn't sure why, and she desperately tries to evict it. It's about ruts, that's all, sometimes it's easy to fall into a routine, and before you realise it that routine has become a rut. She resolves that that will not happen to them, or if it already has, then she will rescue them and get them out again. The party will be a start, but maybe Betty will organise a weekend away for them, for starters. Again, Grace re-enters her mind, but this time she is ready for her. This has nothing to do with Grace, and Grace has no bearing whatsoever on her marriage. Why she should think otherwise, no matter how fleetingly, is a mystery.

Chapter Eight

A week after the lunch with Betty, Grace is preparing to read the proposal from *Modern Woman*. She is sitting upright in her little office. The proposal is lying on the small glass desk, partially obscuring the keyboard. The computer is on, but showing only a blank screen. Files are neatly piled in one corner: pending jobs in red folders; completed jobs in blue. Grace is wearing an old tracksuit, and her hair is scraped off her face. She is idly fiddling with a pen as she stares at the front page of the proposal. No matter what, she can't shake the feeling that reading it will take her to a place she doesn't want to go. The irrational fear that somehow this proposal, lying across her desk, is going to disrupt her life. What she really thinks, though, is that it isn't the proposal that is such a threat to her equilibrium, but the author of the proposal. The smug, posh, married journalist who obviously hated her on sight. Reluctantly, she turns the covering letter over with her newly painted bright red nails, and she begins to read.

The Honey Trap feature and interview with Grace Regan

The feature will cover a total of four pages, and at the moment is set to run in the October issue of *Modern Woman*, which will be on shelves at the beginning of September. This is subject to change. There will be photographs but those photographs will not be of the interviewee and that will be made clear.

> As well as a case study and a 'week in the life' of Grace Regan, there will be a general description of the occupation, some statistics (gleaned from Grace), and a short interview with a woman who has hired a honey trapper.

Grace stops reading for a second. It all seems quite straightforward. As she finishes the rest of the proposal she feels a little bit of trepidation. She tells herself she is doing this for Nicole, who loves the idea of publicity, not for herself. She calls Nicole, and reads it to her, just to ensure that Nicole thinks it is all right. They have a pros and cons discussion, which involves Grace outlining her reservations, and Nicole telling her that they are unfounded.

'But I really got the feeling that Betty didn't like me. What if she reflects that in her article? It'll make the business look bad.'

'Don't be ridiculous. What's not to like about you? Grace, if they do try to make you out to be anything other than you are, I will sue them. They wouldn't dare risk that.'

'But what if they make us out to be home wreckers? They might do.'

'No way. Because we're not. We save these women from a lifetime of lies and misery. We're more like Samaritans than anything.' Nicole really believes this.

'What if I say the wrong things?'

'You won't.'

This discussion carries on for about half an hour, before Nicole, wearily, terminates it: 'Grace, you will do me proud. Bye.'

Grace puts the proposal on her desk and turns her attention back to her work. Betty will get the call she wants, but she won't get it straight away.

She goes through her files of the jobs that she has done this week. She had four jobs: all of the men proved themselves to be cheats, or wannabe cheats. She shakes her head. The only problem this week was Mark, a boyfriend and a very sexy man. She almost slept with him, but she changed her mind at the last minute. Sex isn't in short supply; she doesn't need another man. But he was attractive and she was tempted. It isn't often that her libido makes an appearance when she's working, so when it does, it takes her by surprise. She turned him down but she did so reluctantly. Because it was the right thing to do. She might 'chat up' men for a living but she isn't a slut, and therefore she works strenuously hard to prove that. Although she is a young, modern, single woman, she overanalyses her behaviour and stops herself from doing things that she sometimes wants to do.

The job tonight is unusual for her. A wife suspects her husband of cheating and has overheard him on the phone making an arrangement to meet someone. When she questioned him he said it was one of his old friends, but she didn't believe him. Nicole doesn't normally use Grace for these jobs, but for some reason she seemed keen that she should do it. Grace agreed, without questioning Nicole's motives. She didn't have to talk to him and she would be well paid. A thought that appeals.

After finishing her work, she picks up *Modern Woman*'s proposal again. Then she puts it back down. She will call Betty the following day and not before. Unsure exactly why she wants to make her wait, she does, because she knows that when they start, the confident journalist will probably run rings around her.

Betty knows that Grace will have the proposal and she wonders what she is thinking. When she ran it by Fiona, Fiona was overexcited about the whole thing, so Grace has to agree. Betty's career is relying on it. She knows that it is Grace's boss who wanted her to do the feature, so she is trying to be relaxed about it, but there is a niggle in the back of her mind. Betty thinks Grace is the type of woman to play games, and this worries her. What if Grace does that to her? Although Betty can handle most things, and most people, this slightly worries her. She has a feeling that whatever the outcome, this woman could cause serious problems and she cannot rationalise the feeling, or shake off the fact that she doesn't like it. She wills Grace to hurry up and put her out of her misery, then she can get on with things, including organising the party that Johnny has roped her into helping him with.

Johnny is like a child with a new toy. He has found a venue, Vermin, a new club with a private bar downstairs, which he hired for a sum of money that Betty doesn't want to think about. Johnny seems to be more than happy to throw money at the party. More money than Betty thinks is healthy. He is using their savings, and although they both earn good money, they are not exactly flush. She shakes her head and tries to stop being so sensible. She never used to be so boring, she tells herself. Johnny wants fun and she should want it too. It is just that she doesn't see fun in that way any more.

As well as the venue, he has secured a DJ. Where Johnny found a dance music DJ from is a mystery, but he did and the man is booked. The drinks are going to be free up to a certain amount (Betty balked at this), and then after that people will have to pay for their own. Betty is in charge of invitations (that is all she is in charge of).

She calls the printers that they use at the magazine and does a deal. At least the invitations (all two hundred of them) are going to be relatively cheap. The venue takes one hundred to a hundred and fifty people, so Johnny wants to invite two hundred because not everyone will come. Betty hopes that not everyone will come.

She stares at the phone, willing it to ring. She wants Grace to say yes, she wants to get on with the story, she wants it to be over. She wants to go back to making up embarrassing sex stories, which she mentally promises she will never complain about again.

Grace pulls off her shoes while leaning against the wall. She made a mistake wearing high heels to her job, because when she got there she realised she would have to stand all night. The seats (and there weren't very many) were all taken, she had to find a space near the man she was targeting and stand.

She spotted him straight away. Although he looked older than he did in the photo, he was unmistakable. Grace often wonders why wives send in photos that make their husbands look better than they do. Nicole always emphasises the importance of an accurate photo – after all, it is the only thing they have by which to identify the man – yet some wives still send photos that are years out of date. It makes no sense.

Grace tried to keep out of the way while she waited for his companion to turn up, but of course, she isn't the most inconspicuous person in the world and she ended up having to fend off quite a few men. Her target didn't notice her, though, which was good.

Sure enough, he met a woman. A young woman, younger than Grace. The way they greeted each other left little doubt that this wasn't a friend, and Grace moved closer so she could hear their conversation. Her client had asked for photo evidence, so Grace wore a tiny camera built into a large brooch on her top, one of her favourite gadgets. It was made for her, and although the diamonds are fake, the camera is not. It also records sound perfectly, although with the noise level in the bar tonight she wasn't sure how much of the conversation they would get. By the way the pair were acting, the pictures would tell his wife all she wanted to know. On a job like that, Grace feels like a proper detective, and she enjoys it, even though she's still spying on a cheater.

The husband had his hand on the young woman's buttocks

within half an hour. She was pressing her small breasts into his chest. They had been there an hour when they left. Having heard the conversation, Grace knew they were going to a hotel. Picturing the scene, she knew that they would be tearing each other's clothes off as soon as they got into the room. She felt sorry for his wife, the poor thing, and she had to call Nicole.

Grace hailed a taxi and called Nicole from her mobile. She promised to have the tape ready to courier over first thing in the morning.

She picks up her shoes and hobbles to the sitting room. She lays on the sofa, too tired to move, watching the fish, and drifting off to sleep.

The buzzer wakes her and she feels disorientated for a while, unsure of where she is. Then she realises and answers the intercom, surprised to hear Oliver's voice on the other end.

'You're looking hot,' he says when he's at her door, kissing her on her lips.

'I fell asleep. Have I got cushion marks on my face?'

'No. So I guess you've been working.'

She nods. 'I had a job.'

'So which poor sucker did you seduce tonight?'

'None, I just had to spy.' She smiles. She likes the idea of being a spy, although not in a James Bond sense; in a far less energetic way.

'So why did you dress up then?' he asks, assessing her short, tight, black dress with a suspicious look on his face. He knows that he isn't her only man, although she will not tell him exactly who he has to share her with. In his worst fears it is any number of men, although he hopes that really she just says that to keep him at arm's length. He is constantly confused by Grace, and he knows that she needs that. But still he cannot walk away from her because he knows a few truths about her. One is that she isn't a bad person, she has the biggest heart, it's just not fully functioning. Another is her immense vulnerability. She hides it well, but at times, if you look hard enough, you see it. And lastly is the fact that he loves her and he believes that, deep down, she loves him.

'Don't know, force of habit. What are you doing here?' Finally she is fully awake and she realises that Oliver has committed a cardinal sin. He has turned up unannounced.

'I did call you, but your answerphone was on and your mobile was off.' She must have been in a deep sleep not to hear the phone.

'But it's so late.' She is still scowling.

'Yes, and you work late. Look, Grace,' he sounds cross, 'I was at an album launch in the area and I wanted to pop in on the off chance. Not to upset you or to bug you, or to catch you out, but because I wanted to see you. I'm off to New York tomorrow for a while and, well, I just thought that it would be nice to see you.'

Grace stops scowling and smiles. She cannot help herself. 'Sorry, I didn't mean to be so grouchy. You know how I am with surprises. Let me get you a drink and you can tell me all about your trip and when I will get to see you next.' She smiles warmly. She must stop being so hard on him, and on herself.

Betty is stirring some pasta and wondering if it's ready. She tastes it but is still unsure.

'Johnny, can you test this?' she shouts to him. He walks into the kitchen, his hair slightly messy from where he has been laying on the sofa. He is wearing an old pair of jogging bottoms and a rugby shirt. He fishes out a piece of pasta with a spoon, blows on it and eats it.

'It's done.' He pats her on the bottom. Betty dishes up and they go to the sitting room to eat.

'I haven't heard from the honey trapper,' she says, playing with her pasta.

'Give her a chance. Now, how are the invitations going?' Johnny is obsessed with his party, and visibly not too interested in Betty's story.

'They'll be ready by the end of this week. Have you made a list of who you want them sent to?'

'No, I thought we'd do that tonight.'

'Johnny, do we know two hundred people?'

'Well, probably not, but we can give Matt and Ali a few to distribute.'

'So we're going to have a party full of strangers?'

'Those, my darling, are the best kind.' He tucks in to his dinner and Betty decides to do the same.

'You are all right, aren't you?' she asks as he finishes.

'What, you're not buying Matt's mid-life crisis theory?'

'No, I'm just asking if you're all right.'

'I'm fine. I just fancied doing something different. And after this party maybe we can think about going on holiday.'

'Yeah, we could go with Alison and Matt.'

'Or we could go on our own.'

'Now, I like that idea. Maybe if Grace ever calls me and I do a good job on that feature, I can ask Fiona if I can do a travel one. Then we can get the magazine to pay for the holiday.'

'Oh yes, and go somewhere really exotic.'

'Like the Caribbean?'

'Or Bora-Bora. I've always wanted to go there. Will she go for it?'

'Well, we have a travel editor, but maybe I can persuade them.'

'Do your best.' Johnny leans over and kisses her. She knows she is the world's luckiest woman.

Grace has a job getting out of bed, following Oliver's crack-of-dawn departure. Finally she does, and after she showers and dresses she is ready to call Betty.

'Betty Parkin.'

'Hi, it's Grace.'

Betty says a silent thank you. 'Grace, how are you?' The jovial tone in her voice is perhaps a bit over the top. She mentally kicks herself for her reaction, yet again.

'I'm fine, Betty, how are you?' Grace knows her voice is a bit higher than usual and the brightness she is trying to inject into it perhaps a bit too much.

'I'm very well.' Betty tries, and fails, to sound more natural.

'I've signed your proposal, and I'm about to post it back to you.'

'That's brilliant.' She still sounds like a bad TV advertisement for washing powder.

'So, when do you want to start?' Grace is a little puzzled by the tone of Betty's voice, and also by her own.

'How about next week?'

'That's great. It'll give me time to organise myself.' Grace giggles, she has no idea why.

'Right. But you must remember that I want a normal working week with you.'

'And that's what you'll get.'

Now Grace feels annoyed. As does Betty. She worries that Grace, in her control-freak mould, will put on a show for her. She sounds as if that is what she intends to do.

'I'll call you later this week to arrange the details?' Betty proffers.

'I'll look forward to it,' Grace replies, unsure if she will or not.'

Betty puts the phone down and tries to give herself a talking-to. She is a professional; she's been doing her job for years, so she must not let Grace unbalance her. She feels like a set of scales that is being messed with, or perhaps broken. She must stop that from happening. Next week she will be spending her working hours with Grace, and the least she can do is to try to get on with her – or at least not let herself, or the magazine, down. She resolves to do that. She can disapprove and her mind will not be changing, but she will hide that disapproval. She does not expect to enjoy the assignment but she does expect to write a brilliant feature.

Grace tries to work out why she feels so unsettled by Betty. Part of her is genuinely looking forward to doing the feature, she really is, but part of her is still afraid of Betty and her perfect composure. She decides to call Nicole.

'Nicole Harding's office. I'm not available to take your call. Please leave a message after the tone.'

Grace sighs. She very much wants to speak to her.

'Hi, it's Grace. Call me.' She hates speaking to machines, although she knows that is irrational.

Disappointed not to be able to share the news with her boss, Grace decides to check her appointments for the week that the feature will begin. Because of the nature of the business, they often book in cases about a week in advance – any longer than that and the woman who is hiring her would probably go mad. She does have some jobs pencilled in, but most will be arranged in the next few days. She makes lists of what she will do when she is at home, to give Betty a good idea of what her job involves. In reality, she doesn't actually do too much during the day. Grace's job is a night job. It is more to do with her nature than necessity that she even has an office at home. Most of Nicole's other women have a laptop. Nicole told her that. However, she does have to do research on some of the cases. She had one case that was complicated. The wife wanted her husband caught but the only place she really knew to track him down was on the golf course. So she paid for Grace to have golf lessons before she started. That would be a good story to share with Betty. But apart from that, research is mainly used so she can talk about the men's professions and their hobbies, not actually partake in them. She uses the Internet to do her research and she has the files provided by Nicole. But – and this is her fear – she doesn't have enough work for the day. Her working day is normally a couple of hours, her working night begins by her getting ready at four or five, then leaving the house any time after that. It is usually finished by midnight. Writing up reports after jobs takes about an hour, as does getting any evidence ready for Nicole. So there is a huge part of her day that needs filling and, unbeknown to anyone, the way she fills it is by playing computer games. She sits in her office all day, so she feels like a normal working woman, but she is not working, she is usually blowing things up.

She knows that Betty wants normal but she can't have it. Not during the day. She needs to find things to do and makes a list of what she can do that will be interesting and realistic. She perhaps can show her the gadgets she uses and how she uses them. She can show her wigs and disguises, which are normally only used if the woman hiring her gives the agency a specific 'type' that the husband will go for. The only other use she has for them is in private, in the bedroom, if one of her lovers deserves a special treat. She quickly pushes that thought away. She can take Betty to the spy shops that she goes to, but she is still worried about filling the days. She wishes Nicole would call her back. She will know what to do. All Grace knows how to do is panic.

Betty is worrying that she will not be able to hide her true feelings from Grace. She knows that being judgemental is not part of her job description, but she can't help but feel that with women like Grace in the world, marriage is being trivialised, relationships are trivialised, and that worries her. She knows that she is unable to voice these feelings to anyone in the office, and even Johnny seems to think she is overreacting. Perhaps she *is* overreacting and perhaps she should worry less. She turns her mind instead to thoughts of holidays and looks up Bora-Bora on the Web. As she is imagining herself and Johnny on the white sands, Hannah shouts over that Fiona wants to see her.

'Hi, boss.' She launches herself into the chair.

'Betty, how are you?'

'Fine.'

'Good. How are the preparations going for the honey-trap story?'

'Well, I emailed you to tell you she agreed.' Betty is perplexed. Fiona normally lets her get on with things, but on this story she has been almost pressurising her every step of the way.

'Which is great. Now do you think you're fully prepared?'

'What do you mean?' She is beginning to feel a little insulted.

'Nothing. I just want to be sure that we are one hundred per cent on top of this.'

'Fiona, I'm always on top of things. Why are you so concerned with this?'

'No reason.'

'I know there is.' Betty doesn't often stand up to Fiona, but this time she feels a need to know.

'Not at all. It's just as I said: I wish I'd known about it so I could have used it with my ex. That's all there is to it.' Fiona turns away, indicating she has finished with Betty. Betty leaves, knowing that if there isn't a specific reason Fiona is so concerned with the article she will eat her hat.

Grace is watching the phone when Nicole calls her back.

'What's up?'

'I agreed to the article.'

'Cool. So when does it start?'

'Next week. Nicole, there is just one thing.'

'What?'

'Well, this woman is going to be shadowing me day and night, and, well, I don't do an awful lot during the day.'

'Um, hadn't thought of that. Why don't you call her back and just get her to follow you in the evenings?'

'Well, I did think that, but then if she does she is only going to see me in action, and that will be all she'll write about. I want to give her a fuller picture, make her understand all that is involved. Otherwise I'm not sure she'll be so favourable towards me, or the job.'

'I know, you can do my job too.'

'What?'

'Well, I can set up meetings with clients. I could get you to talk to some of them – you know, pad it out a bit.'

'Oh, would you let me do that?'

'Sure. Otherwise you're right, she'll only have the trapping part in the article. We need to show how sensitive it all is. Besides, you'll be brilliant with clients.'

'Thanks, Nicole.' Grace feels massively relieved.

'Any time, honey.'

With Fiona's words ringing in her ears, Betty prepares a list of questions. She is ensuring that every eventuality is covered. She will give her boss the best feature ever, because that is what she wants.

Grace feels happier as she prepares a list of answers to the questions she believes Betty will ask. She is ensuring that every eventuality is covered. She will give her boss the best publicity ever. It is the only way she can repay her for her support.

Chapter Nine

Day One.

Grace wakes at seven, a ridiculously early hour for her, but then this isn't a normal day. Betty is due at ten to start the week-long case study and Grace is nervous. She takes a leisurely shower and dresses in jeans and a white jumper. For some reason, she doesn't want to be wearing her tracksuit when she works. She even wears make-up and puts shoes on, something she never does, but at least she looks better. She knows that this is meant to be an honest representation but she wants to be portrayed in a favourable light. The woman who wears a tatty tracksuit and no make-up during the day, and then transforms herself into a babe for the evening, isn't the way she wants to be described.

She tries not to feel nervous, but she does. For a reason she cannot fathom, her emotions are behaving like 'first' emotions. First day at school, first exam, first day in a new job, first date. Pull yourself together, you idiot, she tells herself. If you stop behaving like a moron you might actually enjoy it.

Day One.

Betty wakes at seven and while Johnny catches a few minutes of extra sleep, she stares at her wardrobe, wondering what to wear. She isn't due in the office – all she has to do is go straight to Grace's flat – but she wants to create the right impression. In the end she opts for some light brown trousers and a tight black jumper. She wears her high-heeled brown boots, and spends an extra ten minutes taming her hair. She doesn't want Grace to look down her nose at her; and she believes that she will, given the opportunity. Stop being so pessimistic and make a bloody effort, she tells herself. After all, it doesn't matter what she thinks. Her boss wants this article and therefore she has no choice.

Betty gets a bus to the address that Grace has given her and is immediately annoyed at the upmarket nature of her neighbourhood. Her mansion block is really quite sophisticated and smart, and when she goes to the intercom, she notices that everyone else in her building has smart names. Double-barrelled names. Poncy names. She buzzes, waits a few moments, then Grace's voice floods out.

'Hello.'

She sounds self-assured, Betty thinks. 'It's Betty.'

Why does she have to be so confident? Grace thinks.

As Betty enters the building her resentment increases. So many buildings where there is more than one flat have shabby communal areas, but not Grace's. The floor is parquet and polished to within an inch of its life; there are plants; the post cubbyholes are shiny silver; and the doors to the other flats are smart. The stair banisters are again polished, and the carpet that covers the stairs is sumptuous and expensive. What annoys Betty most of all is that Grace got this apartment by wrecking marriages, and Betty knows that the fact that this profession seems to have made Grace rich, or at least affluent, makes it even worse.

Grace's smile is fixed to her face with glue as she stands at the door waiting for Betty's appearance. She hopes that she looks OK, but has no time now to check, although the amount of time she has spent in front of the mirror is ridiculous. She tries once again to tell herself to be calm. She tries to believe that her nerves are really excitement, and she is happy to be welcoming Betty into her life.

Betty sees Grace at the door, standing with one arm holding it open and the other on her hip. It is a typical stance of someone with too much confidence, she thinks, and she plasters her smile on her face, when her heart is telling her to turn round and run away. She wonders how Grace manages to look so gorgeous in just jeans and a plain top. She notices how expertly her make-up has been applied and immediately feels dowdy in comparison. Her clothes are smarter, but Grace looks better. Mind you, Grace looks better than most people.

As Grace steps aside to let Betty in, she wishes she had dressed differently. Her jeans look so scruffy (even though they are new, designer jeans) in comparison to Betty's smart trousers and jacket. She wishes she knew as effortlessly as she assumes Betty does, what to wear during the day. Evening attire is easy, but daytime, that is another matter altogether.

'Hi. Come in.' She sounds breezy.

'Thanks.' Betty shakes her hand.

'I'm not sure where you want to start, but I made coffee.'

'Lovely. That would be great.' Betty wonders why she sounds so false around Grace. She is behaving like a bad soap opera actress with even worse lines. 'Could I look round? I'm sorry but I'm so nosy.' She smiles and feels better. She can be friendly; Grace is working with her and she has to remember that.

'Sure, help yourself. I'm the same. I'm always really curious about people's living environments.'

'I always think it tells you so much about a person.'

'Me too, although maybe I shouldn't let you look round. God knows what you might think.' They both laugh, surprising themselves with their genuineness. They both relax a bit.

Grace pours coffee, while Betty looks around her flat. Grace knows it won't take her long. The flat is laid out on one floor – a living room, a bedroom, the office (which was really another bedroom), a bathroom and a kitchen. But Grace loves her flat, and she hopes that the verdict is good.

Betty starts with the bedroom, surprised by how tidy it is. A large wooden bed dominates the room, with built-in wardrobes along one wall. She feels she might be crossing the line, but she opens one to see rail upon rail of suits and dresses. Grace's working outfits. There is something quite characterless about her bedroom. It is neat, but it says very little about her. The large mirror and dressing table maybe reveal a little, but nothing more than vanity. Betty chastises herself for that thought: her own make-up takes over most of the bathroom.

She moves next to the bathroom, which is modern, with blue mosaic tiles covering the walls of the bath and the shower. She notes the expensive products and, again, thinks of affluence.

Next she moves to the living room. The floors throughout the flat are wooden, with the exception of cream carpet in the bedroom. The living-room floor is oak. The cream couch, which is a kind of mock-suede effect, is only big enough for two people and there are no other armchairs. She sees the fish immediately but deliberately looks away, determined to check out the rest of the room before being distracted. She notes the small television tucked into a corner, where you would hardly notice its presence. A small glass coffee table, which has a copy of *Tatler* sitting on it, is directly in front of the sofa. Behind it is a round glass dining table and four chairs. In the middle of the table is an orchid. Betty presumes that Grace isn't huge on entertaining, although she is unsure why she has come to this conclusion. She thinks of how the flat screams 'single woman', and how her house, all cosy, screams 'marriage'. For the first time she feels slightly sorry for Grace. She wonders if she feels her life is as empty as her flat.

Finally she allows her attention to turn to the fish. At once she is mesmerised. As they seem to dance around the tank, with wonderful different colours, she can't help but watch.

This is something that she was not expecting: Grace Regan has pets.

'They're amazing, aren't they?' Betty turns and sees Grace carrying a tray, which she places on the table.

'Yes, are they tropical?'

'Yeah. I don't know why I got them really. I just think they're relaxing.' She doesn't offer further explanation.

'They're beautiful.' Betty surprises herself. She looks at Grace, who seems equally surprised, and she remembers what she is here to do. 'Right, shall we get started?' She ignores the look that passes over Grace's face, but she recognises it as hurt or at least disappointment.

'Of course.' Grace decides that Betty is too bossy and she doesn't like it. Just as she thinks she might be human after all, Betty takes that feeling away.

Betty takes the lead and sits down on the sofa. She balances her coffee on her knee and reties her hair. She looks at Grace as she, too, sits, her hair flowing, her long legs crossed, and Betty wishes that she were equally as composed. She can tell Grace's type a mile off. Or she believes she can. Making quick judgements about people is a part of her Betty isn't proud of, but she does it none the less. Grace, she believes, had a privileged upbringing, probably spoilt rotten by her parents and told how beautiful she was by everyone else. She never felt insecure about anything. She knew she looked good all the time; she probably never had a spot, or if she did, she would know what to do about it. What Betty can't bear, apart from the fact she is a honey trapper, is that Grace had the sort of upbringing that Betty wishes she had. She is so sure about this that she doesn't need to ask. Grace screams effortless life. Unlike Betty. Instead, she was riddled with insecurities, always trying so hard to be liked, and although she had loving parents, she still always felt awkward. She was definitely a misfit. Betty has worked hard over the years to stop feeling this way; Grace reminds her of it all over again. She sees Grace as the popular girl at school and herself as the one Grace bullied. She knows that to make such assumptions is dangerous, but she needs to do so; she just doesn't know why.

Grace feels her eyes contract as she studies Betty. Betty, who can balance a cup of coffee on her knee while sitting on a cream sofa. Betty, who can retie her hair effortlessly, when it really doesn't need doing. Betty, who was probably always the most popular wherever she went. Betty, who reminds Grace of everything she's not.

Grace believes she knows Betty. Grace made certain decisions about her when she first met her. She knows she probably shouldn't be so quick to judge, but she cannot help it – not when she believes Betty to be so transparent. Married, happily, with a gorgeous husband no doubt. Brought up in a rich, or at least affluent, house. Probably went to private school, where she was always the ringleader. Always managed to be noticed. The opposite of Grace. Grace with her five siblings, crowded together in a four-bedroom council house. Grace with a father who lost the will to work before she came along, and had taken root in front of the television. (Grace rarely saw him anywhere other than in front of the television so that is where she believes she was conceived.) Her mother was distant, obviously driven mad by having six children and a husband who never moved, so she lived in her own little world of multi-coloured rabbit jellies, and not much else.

Grace was not the oldest, nor the youngest. She fitted somewhere in the middle, which was the best place to be ignored. She wasn't close to her sisters and brothers, but they were generally civil to each other. There was enough bullying at the rough school they attended – no one wanted to do it while at home. Grace imagines that Betty had the happiest of childhoods whereas she herself did not. And although she is thankful that she was never beaten, that she did get fed, and that despite their shortcomings her parents probably loved her, she wishes that she had been brought up in a way that gave her Betty's inherent confidence rather than an innate feeling of inadequacy that she battled for years to get rid of. Betty brought it all back to her and she instantly disliked Betty for that reason, although she knows she was being irrational.

'Where would you like to start?' Grace asks, deciding that as the small talk is definitely over they might as well get on. She also determines not to let Betty push her around.

'Well, I thought that first you can tell me what your job entails. I've done some research but I'm after your interpretation. Then we can talk about how you got started, what made you want to do it. Then when I've got some background, you just carry on as normal and I'll take notes.' Grace nods. 'I'll get my Dictaphone and pad and we'll start.' Again, Grace nods. Betty gets up and goes to the hallway where she left her massive bag. She tells herself, for the last time before starting, not to be judgemental and then she returns.

'I thought we'd go into the office. It'll be better there.' Grace gets up and leads the way.

She has put a dining chair in there for Betty. Grace sits down on her desk chair and swings it round to face Betty.

'Fire away.' She smiles and hopes that she isn't about to sound like an idiot.

'How did you first get into honey trapping?'

'Totally by accident. I'm not sure it's the sort of job that you would actually aim for, and I don't mean that in a derogatory sense, it's just that it probably wouldn't occur to you to do it. Anyway, I met a private detective one evening and he tried to chat me up, but when he told me what he did, I was more interested in that than in him. So we talked and I asked questions and at the end of the night he told me that I would make a great detective. I pushed him further. After all, I was thinking James Bond and he clearly wasn't – more Pussy Galore.' Grace stops and laughs; Betty does too. 'But when he explained that I would be hired to check out the fidelity of men, I must admit I was intrigued. At first I wasn't sure, but I took his card and then I thought about it. I hated the job I was doing at the time, so I called him and asked for another chat. There I explained my doubts and he cleared them up. I don't know what made me finally decide, but I think it has something to do with the fact that I can't bear men who cheat.'

'But surely if you're honey trapping, you're not so much catching them out, but tempting them?' Betty's voice is level; she manages to keep condemnation out of it.

'No, not really. If a man was going to be faithful he would be, no matter what.'

'But you're stunning. You go up to a man, show him some interest and he's bound to be so flattered, and maybe, just maybe, he will be so flattered he falls. It doesn't make him a serial cheat.'

'It's not about how I look. I work on a number of different levels, sometimes even in disguise. I need to know about the man, how to approach him. It's not just about looks.' Grace knows she is being defensive but Betty has already hit on her Achilles heel.

'Tell me about your clients.' Betty notices the defensive tone in Grace's voice and thinks that she protests too much, but she decides to take a gentler route.

'Fine.' Grace takes a deep breath. 'Mainly I am hired by women who suspect their partners of cheating in the first place. I'm not testing guys without foundation.'

'And can you tell if they're paranoid or if they have genuine grounds for concern?'

'Women aren't paranoid. They act on instinct, intuition, and I believe strongly in that.' Grace again has snapped, unnecessarily. She smiles by way of apology.

'Right, well, let's say that they do have suspicions, wouldn't it be better to catch them in the act rather than becoming the act?'

'Some women want to know if their husbands are cheating, others want to know if they would cheat. I serve both purposes for them. It's a quick way of giving them peace of mind.'

'Or sending them out of their minds.' Betty regrets the words as soon as they have left her lips, but she seems to have little control over her mouth in front of Grace. She briefly thinks of Fiona and being sacked, and vows to stop.

'It's their decision to hire me. I don't force myself on anyone.' Grace is confused about how and why they are where they are. One minute she was talking about how she began working in her profession, the next she is defending it. She looks at Betty; she is confused and angry.

'Right, well, we seem to be going off the track. Sorry. Can you tell me what it was like when you went to work for this detective and how you trained, et cetera?'

Betty is still cross with herself for betraying her feelings so quickly. She vows, again, to be professional from now on. But as she looks at Grace, she clenches her fists. It is not going to be easy. For some reason she feels an urge to attack every time Grace speaks. Which doesn't make sense. First, she is a professional, and secondly, she is secure in her marriage. It cannot be that she is threatened by Grace. Can it? Betty grew up being totally insecure. She was bullied and teased and she felt awful about herself. She thought that by being a successful journalist and a successful wife, she had finally conquered the irrational fears that insecurities lead to. Perhaps she hasn't. Maybe they stay with you for ever.

She feels guilty for the way she is treating Grace. In her world, Grace is like a client and should be treated as such. Betty knows that Grace has done nothing to deserve her contempt.

'I did have training, you know.' Grace realises her tone is a little bit sharp, but she is still upset. She tells herself to calm down and be more professional; she doesn't want Betty to write vile things about her because they had a spat. 'At first, I learnt a bit about spying techniques, what gadgets were involved and the basic principles. It was more general than just fidelity testing. I learnt how to follow someone, how to bug a phone, all sorts of useful little tricks. Then I learnt about the actual testing part. The woman who taught me is a fidelity tester herself. She has a psychology degree and she showed us how important it is to use psychology when working. For instance, you have to socially engineer the whole meeting, while making it look like the man is the one doing just that. Anyway, we were sent on test cases, which, of course, were set up, but they evaluated your performance. God, I was so nervous when I had my first one, I made such a fool of myself.'

'How come?'

'Well, obviously we use assumed names when we're working, and I forgot the name I'd given myself – my mind went totally blank, which was really embarrassing. It just went downhill from there. But I got better, luckily.'

Both women laugh. Then they look at each other and, remembering where they are, they stop.

'We also learn, which is very important, how to deal with the clients. The women are our priority and it's a very disturbing and emotional time for them, so we need to be sensitive, and also we often have to listen to them when they're upset and try to help them.' Although this is Nicole's role, not Grace's, she hopes that it will make Betty more sympathetic to what she does if she claims it as hers.

'Like counselling?'

'Sort of, but that's all part of it. I'm often giving them news which signals the end of their marriage or their relationship. That needs sensitive handling.'

'So, how long did you train for?'

'I went on my first job after a month. I didn't think I was

ready, but once I got there, instinct seemed to take over and I did it. I was jubilant, which is awful, I know, because this guy propositioned me and he shouldn't have done. But, you know, it was sort of like a performance and I was just relieved that I didn't mess up. I always thought if on my first job the man had turned me down, then I would have felt that it was my fault.'

Betty is scribbling furiously, but she stops and gives Grace a funny look. Grace thinks she has said the wrong thing. She waits for Betty to attack her again. Betty thinks about saying something, but manages to change her mind. She is so desperate to put Grace down for her last comment, but she is also trying to remember who she is and why she is sitting in Grace's flat. She is also picturing Fiona's face. That helps.

'Do you enjoy your job?' she asks in a non-condescending way.

'I think "enjoy" might be the wrong term. Do I get job satisfaction? Yes, actually I do. I believe that I am helping women, getting them out of situations which are hurting them. Heartbreak is hard, but it does go away.' She scowls and remembers that she is not here to witter on. 'It's not always easy, that's for sure, and some nights, after I've been on a job and a horrible man propositions me, I get home and feel, not depressed exactly, but a bit sad. It isn't an easy job, that's for sure.'

Betty feels that Grace is being totally honest with her, and she can't help but respect her for that.

'Tell me about your disguises.' Safer ground.

'Well, sometimes men like blondes, and you can see I'm not exactly blonde. So I wear a wig. Also, if I am going back to an area or a bar that I have been in before, then I think it might be safer to wear a disguise. It's amazing how easily you can transform yourself by changing your hair colour or style. I'll show you later. I've got loads of wigs.' Grace smiles. For a moment it feels like fun; Betty concurs. 'Also, sometimes it's easier to be in disguise because then I become someone else. Does that make sense?' Grace is surprised by her candidness, but not as much as Betty is.

'It does.' Betty checks that the Dictaphone is still whirring, and she makes notes while listening intently. 'How do you know where to find the man?'

'Sometimes it's easy. They are where they tell their partners they'll be. Other times, the client will narrow it down to a few bars and I'll have to search. That can be a bit hit and miss, but normally we find them. If they really have no idea – after all, the fact the man might be a cheater shows that he is capable of lying – then someone will follow them from work or home, and then they'll let me know where they are.'

'Is it always in a bar or a pub?'

'Mostly, but not always. I've had a job in a gym. That was horrid – I hate gyms. Once I was supposed to be testing a tennis coach, so I had to have tennis lessons, and I was dreadful.' Grace laughs at the memory.

Betty laughs along with her, noting how animated Grace's face becomes when she laughs. At first she thought she was expressionless, hard-faced, but when she smiles it is as if someone switches a light on in her face and everything comes to life.

Grace continues, 'The worst job, really, was at a golf club. I had to learn to play golf, follow this guy's game and catch him at the bar afterwards. I hate golf.'

At the mention of golf, Betty immediately thinks of Johnny, and her dislike of Grace, for what Grace represents, comes flooding back tenfold.

'Right, well, that's good background. I can fill in the gaps as we continue. What if you go about your normal day-to-day routine and pretend I'm not here?'

Her tone is sharp, and Grace flinches as if she has been attacked. As if that would be possible, Grace thinks, and she reaches over to pick up the phone.

Grace tries but fails to ignore the presence of the woman whose scrutiny she can physically feel; whose disapproval she is aware of and who she really wants to leave her flat. At times, they almost seem companionable, but others, it feels as if they are enemies. She is glad that Nicole has given her a list of people to call, and is bombarding her with emails. At least she can bury herself in work.

Betty takes notes and tries to fade into the background. She listens intently to Grace's conversations, reads her emails and watches her closely, noting everything. She can't help but feel sorry for the women who use Grace – perhaps, she thinks, because of how scared she is of losing Johnny. She knows that she trusts him – there is no doubt – but insecurity isn't always rational, that much she does know. She would give anything not to feel it, but still she does. As do the women that Grace deals with. The one who is going to meet her, the one who is rushing out to put a photo of her husband in the post, the one whose husband Grace will be tempting that very evening. Those poor women have no idea exactly what sort of honey trap they are setting.

At half-past one Grace pauses. 'I thought I might make some lunch now. Would you like some?' She is running out of work to do, so she decides to break for lunch and then spend the afternoon going through gadgets.

'We could go out.' Betty feels claustrophobic.

'I've got a fresh loaf of bread and some tuna. I could make us sandwiches.'

Betty doesn't see Grace as the sandwich-making type, but she has probably offended her enough for one day. 'Sure, sounds great.' She follows her into the kitchen and watches her make lunch.

'Can I ask one more question?' Betty is no longer in control of her voice. There is a battle going on in her head, one voice versus another. The one she is trying to quash is stronger. She is afraid of it.

'You can.' Grace has her back to Betty.

'Do you ever sleep with them?' The voice wins and Betty feels shameful. Whatever happens, Grace doesn't deserve that. Betty tries to pull it back, but has no idea how. There is a silence for a few seconds as she smarts from going too far and Grace is desperately trying to stop her cheeks from burning.

'No. I'm not a whore.'

Despite Betty's attempts to apologise, which are genuine, lunch is a frosty affair. As soon as they finish eating, Grace makes a decision. She does not want to have to spend all day and all evening with Betty and her condescending manner. She has had enough. Betty's last question is still simmering in her head.

'You know, Betty, I normally don't work in the afternoon. I probably should have told you before, but I didn't think. I do all my calls and admin in the morning, then I normally take the afternoon off to do personal stuff and then work again in the evenings, when I'm on a job. Tonight, for example, I'll probably start getting ready about four, because the man I'm meeting is going to be going out straight from work. I think I know where he's going – it's one of two places anyway – and I like to get there early so I can observe him first, before speaking to him.' She realises she is gabbling but she knows that she wants – no, needs – some time without Betty.

'OK.' Betty tries not to let the relief she feels become audible. She is unsure how much more she can take. She is angry that she asked that question, but at the same time, she is angry that Grace is so easily offended. After all, journalists are supposed to ask probing questions and Grace should know that. Betty has her justification and convinces herself that she has done nothing wrong.

'Why don't you meet me back here at five?'

It is after two. Betty calculates that if she leaves now, she can go home for a couple of hours before heading back, and she can type up her notes there.

'Sounds perfect.'

Grace closes the door and feels she can breathe again. Betty made her feel claustrophobic in her own home. She was polite, helpful, interesting even, but Betty made her disapproval crystal clear. Her voice was steeped in it. When she asked Grace the question about her sleeping with clients, Grace wanted to burst into tears. She felt dreadful; she felt bullied. Grace is sensitive to that feeling more than any other because it is what she remembers most of her childhood: people taunting her, teasing her, condemning her for things she didn't do, just because they could. Betty made her feel like a child being picked on in the school playground, and that was something that not only made her want to cry, but also made her feel sick. It is something she thought she left behind in her old life.

She composes herself and goes to her office to use the phone.

'Nicole, it's me,' she says when she is put through.

'Is the journalist there?' Nicole is whispering although Grace has no idea why.

'No, I asked her to go for a couple of hours. She's oppressive.'

'Really, in what way?'

'She doesn't approve of what I do. That's the bottom line. In every question she asks there is an undertone of disapproval. In every answer I give, she looks as if she is going to argue. She even asked me if I slept with the men I'm testing. She thinks I'm nothing more than a common whore.'

'Oh dear.' Nicole is the mistress of understatement.

'I can't do this.' Grace hopes she doesn't sound as if she is having a tantrum.

'Fine. I'll call her editor.'

'What, just like that? You're not going to persuade me to carry on?'

'Grace, did you call me so you could let off steam, did you want me to persuade you to keep going or did you want me to tell you it's OK to quit?' Nicole is also the mistress of wrong-footing.

'I don't know.' She feels like a baby, a blubber baby.

'Look, I wanted this because of the publicity, but if she is upsetting you, then we'll forget it. I don't want that.'

'You know, sometimes she's really nice. And I don't know if it's because she's a journalist or what, but I find myself being really honest and opening up to her. But then she seems to change and almost turns on me.'

'Does she feel threatened by you?'

'Maybe. She's made no secret of the fact that she's happily married to this guy who sounds like Superhusband.'

'She probably just feels that you and her are in different worlds and could never get on.'

'Probably. So what should I do?'

'Did you speak to clients today?'

'Yes, it was really good. I spoke to the woman whose boyfriend we're going after tomorrow night. Then I made an appointment to see another woman the following day, like you said. I thought it would be good for the story. But now, I'm not sure. Umm. I told her to come back here at five today so she could go and watch my job tonight. Maybe I'll see how that goes.'

'That's a very good and level-headed response.' Nicole offers praise like a mother and Grace basks in it.

'Nicole, if you had told me you wanted me to carry on I'd have probably called you selfish and stopped it.'

'I know.'

'You're a great boss but you're sneaky.'

'Speak to you later, Grace.'

*

Betty sits on the bus, enjoying the sensation of non-crowded travel. She is replaying the morning in her head. She knows she overstepped the mark, but again, desperately doesn't want to think that she is at fault. She was only asking what everyone would want to know. That is her job. She is a journalist. Fully justified, she turns her thoughts to what to wear that evening. She wants to prove to Grace that she is comfortable, and the only way she can do that is to be herself, rather than a sad woman desperately trying to compete with Grace. She decides that she will put on her scruffy jeans and a sparkly top, and so look trendy rather than smart. That was the mistake she made today: in trying to be someone she wasn't she didn't feel totally comfortable and Grace sensed that. She nods at herself in satisfaction.

Her thoughts stop abruptly when she realises the bus is pulling into her stop. She ticks herself off for nearly missing it. Then she smiles to herself and gets off.

The first thing she does when she returns home is to pull out her chosen outfit. Then she spends some time looking for Cyril, who seems to have gone out for the afternoon. Feeling loving, she leaves a note for Johnny, telling him she misses him. Then, finally she decides to call her editor and tell her, honestly, how her first day has gone.

'It's Betty. Can you put me through to Fiona?'

'Betty, are you with her?' Fiona is whispering for some strange reason.

'No, of course not. I'm at home, changing before this evening's job.'

'Oh, how exciting. Very James Bond. Are you going in disguise?'

'No, I'm just observing. Fiona, are you all right?'

'Sorry, just getting a bit carried away. Anyway, how is it going?'

'Not brilliant. She doesn't like me.' Betty tries not to feel guilty, because it's not really a lie – Grace *doesn't* like her – but that is probably Betty's fault.

'Why on earth doesn't she like you?'

'I don't know. She's very defensive, you know. I ask her a question and she goes off. It's going to be difficult.'

'But you're going on a honey trap tonight?' Fiona sounds unmoved.

'Yes.'

'Well, that's good, isn't it?'

'I suppose. But, Fiona, it's going to be really hard to work with someone who doesn't like me.'

'I know, but, Betty, I also know you can do it. In fact, I'm relying on you to do it. After all it's only a few days. Keep up the good work.'

There is no way out.

Betty is standing at the buzzer. It's five minutes after five. Grace's voice flows out from the intercom, announcing that she will come down. Betty reties her scarf. It's not that cold, but the scarf adds to the overall effect. She fluffs her hair a bit, thinking that her thick, unmanageable mane is actually looking quite good for once. Then she rolls her eyes; anyone would think she is going on a date. That is the way she's behaving. The hours spent poring over her outfit and the hours spent on her hair and make-up – she is almost angry with herself about it.

Grace opens the door and smiles. All her earlier hostility has been left in the flat. She decided, after speaking to Nicole, that she would do whatever she needed to do to be nice to Betty. She is a little taken aback by Betty's outfit. She is wearing amazing jeans, which although scruffy, look as if they are supposed to be that way. They are the sort of jeans that Grace has only seen in magazines. On her top she is wearing a red sparkly thing, which crosses one shoulder and ends at different places around her midriff. Again, this is the sort of top that Grace would never feel confident enough to wear. Finally she notes the denim scarf that matches her jeans almost perfectly, and her bright red high-heeled boots. Grace is still smiling whilst taking all this in, but inside she feels horribly inadequate. She feels both old-fashioned and old, whereas Betty looks like she is young and going clubbing.

'I like your hair,' she says, not sure how to comment on the rest of the outfit.

'Thank you. You look great.' Betty is being polite; she doesn't sound truly natural although she does mean it. Betty thinks that Grace does look great. She might not be trendy, but she knows how to make the most of her many assets. She is wearing a suit, a suit that on anyone else would look just ordinary, and perhaps boring, but it flatters Grace. The jacket seems to cling to her shape, the skirt rests above her knees, showing only a glimpse of her thighs. The high-heeled shoes with ankle straps make the outfit a bit naughty. Betty is impressed (even if she doesn't want to be) at how Grace has put the outfit together. It says so much without being obvious. She has to concede that she does not look like a whore, more like a businesswoman.

'As it's after work, I am posing as a businesswoman.' Grace reaches into her handbag and pulls out a pair of glasses, which she puts on.

'Don't tell me, a prop?' Betty cannot believe that Grace still looks just as sexy in glasses. It makes her think of her own glasses at school, thick NHS ones, which made her look anything but sexy. She feels angry with her again.

'Yeah, I like them, though. I know it sounds silly but when I'm getting ready to go out and I'm doing that business-woman-in-town-for-a-few-days thing, I like to wear glasses. I have no idea why.' Grace starts to walk down the street, while Betty tries to decide how to process that last piece of information.

Grace hails a cab and Betty gets in. She immediately pulls out a notebook and starts writing.

'Do you feel as if you're acting?' she asks.

'Yes, but there's no script and there's much more than a director's reputation at stake.' Grace smiles, and Betty marvels at the way she sees her life, but can't help a tiny bit of admiration creeping into her thoughts. It doesn't last too long. 'Here's a photo of the man I'm looking for. He's a forty-five-year-old accountant. He's divorced and living with his current girlfriend, who was his mistress before the divorce. Now, it seems she's had a huge attack of paranoia that he will do to her what he did with her.'

'Sounds like that's what she deserves.' In Betty's world view, mistresses are worse than honey trappers.

'Maybe, but that's not for me to judge. I am simply going to see if he is the cheating type. Then she can make up her own mind what she wants to do.'

'But, surely, it's obvious: once a cheat, always a cheat.'

'I don't know. Maybe he married his wife because he thought he was in love and then really did fall in love. You don't choose who you fall in love with.'

'Maybe you don't,' Betty concedes. 'Anyway, who would want him? He's got more nasal hair than anyone I've ever seen.' With that they both laugh, and almost relax.

They arrive at the first bar and Grace walks in. Betty waits outside for five minutes. She is going to watch Grace in action from a distance and she certainly doesn't want to be sullied by getting involved. When she walks inside, Grace is standing at the bar, positioned in the middle. She is flirting with the barman, who seems to be delighted to be flirting back. After a little bit of banter (that Betty can't hear) the barman presents

Grace with a glass of champagne. Betty is sitting at a table and, watching Grace take a sip, she realises that she doesn't have a drink, so she goes to the bar. She stands next to Grace, who smiles. Betty requests a tomato juice (no drinking on the job for her), and she makes a mental note to ask Grace about the champagne later.

'He's not here yet,' Grace whispers. 'I'm going to give it half an hour and then we'll try the other bar.' Betty nods surreptitiously, and looks at her watch. She can't help but feel a little bit undercover, and as such she also feels a tiny fleck of excitement. Not that she would ever tell Grace that.

It is nearly six. She takes her drink back to the table that luckily still belongs to her. To pass the time, she pulls out her mobile phone and sends Johnny a text message, checking the bar every now and then for activity. After half an hour and about one hundred messages she notices Grace walk past her, gesturing for her to follow.

Once outside, they speak.

'I think we should go to the next bar. If he's not there, then we'll wait and come back here later. It's all we can do. If he doesn't turn up, then I'll have to call my boss and let her know. It does happen sometimes.'

'Are you sure it's OK for us to be seen together?' Betty is getting more into the cloak-and-dagger routine.

'Well, you can follow me if you like.' Grace looks amused as she gives Betty directions to the next bar and sets off before her.

The first thing that Betty notices as she opens the door to the bar is how crowded it is. The second thing she notices is Grace pushing her way to the front of the bar. Thirdly, she sees a group of five men: the victim is one of them. She cannot help but feel a slight thrill as she makes her way to the bar, and decides on the way that perhaps she could have a glass of wine. She isn't the greatest drinker, but one or two glasses she can take. She tries to catch Grace's eye at the bar, unsure if Grace knows the man is there, but Grace is resolutely refusing to look her way. Betty watches her take her glass of champagne to a ledge located near the group of men, but not too near. She is probably going to observe him for a while, the way she said she does. Betty finds a space to stand, but nowhere to sit. She is wishing she hadn't worn her boots, because they are beginning to hurt, but she has a good view of both Grace and the men, and she settles herself to watch.

After what seems an eternity, Grace approaches the group with an unlit cigarette. She says something, and four men all reach into their pockets and pull out lighters. The victim does not. Grace takes a light from one of the men, but establishes eye contact with the victim. Betty shuffles forward a bit, intrigued by the way she works.

Conversation is happening. Grace seems in the middle of the group, and although Betty has no idea what she is saying, she hears the men laughing. Then she starts to move away, but turns round as someone says something. Betty realises that one of the men (but not the victim) has offered to buy her a drink. Grace has her drinking companions for the night. She stands with them for a long time and finally, after two more drinks, she seems to be talking to the victim. Betty wishes she could hear what is being said, but she cannot risk moving nearer. Two of the men leave. There are three now, and it is nine o'clock. Betty can barely believe how quickly the time seems to have gone. She still hasn't drunk her glass of wine, she is so absorbed in observing.

She looks around the bar, and sees that it has emptied without her noticing. She finds a seat, and her feet are grateful. It is so smoky that her eyes are beginning to sting, but she barely noticed that before. People are definitely merry by now – the after-work crowd that always go for one and stay for several. She knows that Johnny sometimes goes out after work and comes back plastered, and she wonders if he would be in a bar like this.

She pulls her attention back to her honey trapper. Grace is now talking only to the victim. The other men are looking the worse for wear, but are still trying to muscle in on the conversation. She sometimes lets them, other times she does not. Betty can see that she is totally engineering the situation, though she still cannot hear a word she is saying.

He whispers something in her ear. She nods, then walks away. She goes to the ladies. She returns later and Betty almost misses it, but sees her put something in his pocket. She immediately thinks it's drugs, and feels confused. Then to her surprise, Grace says goodbye to the men, allowing her look to linger on her victim and walks past Betty out of the bar.

After a few minutes, Betty gets up and follows her out, but can't see her. Then she notices a black cab, stopped a few feet away. She walks to it and gets in.

'What happened?' Betty desperately wants to know. Her curiosity is genuine and she has forgotten to be judgemental.

'It's normal when there are a group of men. He whispered to me, asking me if we could meet later when the others weren't around and asking for my phone number. I realised that while he didn't mind his friends seeing him flirting with me, he didn't want them to know that anything more was going on, so I went to the ladies, scribbled down my phone number and slipped it into his pocket.'

'You gave him your real phone number?'

'Of course not. I should have explained. Each job is different, but I keep a couple of pay-as-you-go mobiles, and take them with me. If further proof is needed then I'll give the man the number. Tomorrow it will be in the bin. I charge it to the client, of course.'

'But isn't it proof enough that he asked for your number?'

'No. I need him to call me and ask me to meet him. That is

what this particular client wants.' Grace pulls out a mobile and starts to dial.

'What if he's trying to call you?' Betty asks. In answer, Grace pulls out another phone and lays it on her lap. She still feels adrenalin pumping from the job, as, surprisingly, does Betty.

'Nicole.'

'How did it go?'

'I gave him a number. He was with some colleagues and didn't want them to know. If he calls me and asks to meet, is that enough?'

'Yeah. If he doesn't call you, then there will be a happy client. But if he does, then the job is done.'

'I can go home and wait then.'

'You might not even make it that far.'

'I'll call you later.'

'Sorry. I don't know where you live.' Grace turns to Betty.

'About two miles away from you. If we go to your flat, I can take the cab on.'

'OK.' Grace shrugs.

Just before they reach Grace's street, her second phone rings. Betty almost jumps out of her skin.

'Hello, Susan speaking.' This is news to Betty, who has no idea who Susan is. 'Oh, hi, you ditched the others then?' Grace's voice is syrupy sweet. 'Well, it is very late. I'm not sure. Oh, what the hell, I'm only in town for a couple of days. Will you come to my hotel?' After a while, she hangs up.

'But you're not going to meet him?'

Grace looks at Betty, then instructs the taxi to pull over outside her building.

'No.'

'But you told him you would.'

'Well, I like to give them an extra present. The idea of the scumbag standing in the bar at the Great Eastern Hotel, waiting for me, gives me a kick.'

'I suppose it serves him right. Why that hotel?'

'I told him earlier that that was where I was staying.'

'What did he say to you?' Betty is still interested in the details, to Grace's surprise.

'He asked me if I'd meet him because he wanted to fuck me, actually.'

Betty looks horrified, as Grace pays the taxi driver and, without another word, she gets out.

Chapter Ten

'She is such a bitch.' It's midnight on day two of the assignment. Betty is at home with Johnny, who has waited up for her. He is wearing his dressing gown and nothing else. The plan was to jump on his wife the minute she walked in the door, but she has other ideas. 'I know I was a bit out of order, giving her opinions, but I'm a journalist and I could argue that I was playing devil's advocate. But she gives me this spiel about how she is doing a job and it's the women who want it otherwise she wouldn't offer it. She makes out she's a fucking saint.' If there was tension on day one, it had nothing on the second day. In fact the first day now looks positively rosy.

'Christ, I don't remember seeing you this riled.'

'Well, you spend two days and two nights with that woman and then you tell me I shouldn't be riled.'

'I didn't say you shouldn't be, I just said it was unusual.'

'Well, it's not unusual because she's a marriage-wrecking bitch who revels in ruining women's lives.' Betty is amazed at how strong her feelings are. She can barely believe that one person could make her feel like this, but Grace has managed to get to her in the worst way.

'But they request her.'

'Yeah, that's what she says. Anyway, it doesn't matter who asks for what, she is a bitch.' They have come full circle.

Johnny manages to get Betty to come to bed, but she continues talking about the honey-trap woman. Johnny realises that he is out of luck and because of that, he almost hates her himself.

Betty turned up at Grace's flat at ten o'clock as agreed. Then she asked her all the questions she wanted to ask after having seen Grace in action. She was polite and tried to keep their relationship professional.

'How comfortable are you flirting, because that's a big part of your job?'

'To be honest, I only flirt so easily because I know I am doing a job. Otherwise I'm hopeless.' Betty didn't believe her, but she didn't say anything.

'There were five men, how did you ensure that you got the right one's attention?'

'Eye contact, mainly. He wasn't the one who was making the moves initially. It was someone else who lit my cigarette, someone else who offered me a drink, but by using eye contact, I managed to get him to chat me up.'

'You were in control the whole time.'

'Absolutely.' The questions were fair, and the answers honest, but things started to go wrong when Grace made a call to a woman whom she was working for that evening. Betty heard only half the conversation, but that was enough.

'I can't believe you just said that,' she said when Grace put down the phone.

'What?'

'You said that she wasn't to worry, you'd be blonde, and you'd talk about stocks and shares.'

'So?'

'Well, you're not testing his fidelity, you're presenting him with his ideal woman, which is a different matter.'

'It's what his wife has asked me to do.'

'Why not just go as yourself, talk about soap operas and if he still falls for it, then you'll know.'

'That is not my brief.'

'I think it's wrong.'

'Betty, no offence, but you're not in my flat to give me your opinions. You're meant to be here as a journalist.'

Betty apologised, and Grace accepted, although it was obvious that neither woman was happy. After an awkward lunch, and a strained hour following lunch, Grace suggested that Betty leave and then, as she had the previous evening, meet her at a bar near that evening's job. Betty felt as if she was being forcibly evicted, so to save face she said she had to go to the magazine office. Betty was relieved to be out of the flat, but not as relieved as Grace was to have her out.

When she got to the magazine she went straight to Fiona's office. She had a plan.

'Didn't expect to see you.'

'Well, Grace is sleeping this afternoon,' Betty lied.

'Right, so how's it going?'

'Fine, really. But I'm not sure I need to spend the week with her. I mean, after yesterday and today I already know her routine and I'm going to watch her on another job tonight, so I was wondering if we should leave it at a couple of days.' Betty believed this. She had seen Grace both make and take calls and she guessed that that was her normal day, and the rest of the week would be the same. She vehemently didn't want to spend more time with her than necessary.

'Maybe, but I want you to see her in action more than twice, so we know about different aspects of her job. I think that you'll get a more complete picture if you stay.'

'Fine. It was just that I thought I might be able to work on other things, as well as this.'

'Nah, I think you need the full five days on this. I want you to write a bit about her personality as well and you can't know that so soon.'

'I suppose not . . .' Betty wanted to argue, but felt it unwise.

'Good. What's the case tonight?' Fiona rubbed her hands together, relishing the tackiness of the whole thing. Betty hated it.

'It's a man whose wife thinks he's cheating on her, and she has asked Grace to do the full tempting thing. Apparently the clients say whether she should approach them, or if she should wait for them to approach her. And this one wants her to make the first move. Oh, and she's got to tape it.'

'Excellent. This is going to make such a good story.'

Betty smiled weakly and then left.

She went home to change before going to meet Grace at a bar round the corner from the bar where she'd be working. She wondered if Grace would be doing the 'businesswoman on a business trip'. Although there was no way she would be standing next to Grace, it became paramount to her to look good. Schoolgirl rivalry was afoot.

She was early. This annoyed her because it made her feel as though she had lost all her cool. First she had worn a short black skirt and chiffon blouse (an outfit that she looked incredibly sexy in). Then she had put on her highest heels (Grace was taller than she and would be wearing heels), then she had spent an hour applying her make-up and painting her nails. She didn't look as trendy as she usually did, but then trendy was last night. Tonight was sexy. When she left the house, she didn't look like Betty – a comment Johnny would make later.

She ordered a mineral water, deciding that she would allow herself a glass of wine later. She was working, and wanted to be professional (even if she looked more like a high-class hooker than a journalist). She sensed Grace's presence before she had appeared. There was the smell of expensive perfume, surrounding her like a force field; there was the click, click of her heels; there was an aura. Betty could almost feel everyone looking their way, a reaction she had not managed to get alone. Finally and reluctantly, she looked up.

Whatever Betty had done it wasn't enough. Blonde Grace looked like something off the cover of *Vogue*. Again, Betty felt anger ripping through her. How would any man (apart from Johnny) resist her? It just wasn't right. The whole premise of testing men like that – being paid to test men – was wrong, and it was certainly wrong for Grace to ensure she looked as stunning as she could. She obviously had an ego to support and that ego meant that she had to prove that no man could resist her. Betty felt her anger well up once again.

'Hello,' Grace said, as if butter wouldn't melt. She had decided, once again, to ignore Betty's earlier outbreak, putting it down to the fact that Betty was not only a bitch, but that she felt threatened by Grace's job. She wondered if her husband had cheated on her, or if she was scared that he would. Perhaps she was not the self-assured person that Grace saw. However, she still found it hard to have any sympathy for her.

'Do you want a drink or shall we get going?' Betty replied, in a friendly manner.

'We can go. He should be there by now.' They smiled weakly at each other as they got up to leave.

They walked in silence. It was only five minutes away, but the silence seemed to increase the distance. As Grace opened the door, Betty noted that the place seemed to be full of the same type of people as the bar had the previous night.

'Are they all like this?' she asked, as if she were looking at an army rather than a random collection of people.

'This bar serves a number of city businesses, that's all. This is the after-work trade. Most leave by about ten.'

'Have you seen him yet?' Betty couldn't help but feel caught up by what they were there to do. Even though she disapproved, she still felt a tiny bit excited. It was the same feeling that she'd had the previous evening, when she had been so absorbed by what was happening. However, because it was against her principles to find honey trapping anything but dreadful, she ignored her interest.

'Not yet. Why don't you sit down first, and I'll go to the bar?'

'I thought I was going to observe you and pretend I didn't know you.'

'No, new plan. You're here with me, my friend, and you will be a part of it.' Betty was surprised but she didn't get a chance to argue, and Grace went to the bar and ordered two glasses of champagne. Betty found a table quite easily; the people in the bar seemed to prefer to stand.

'OK, he's leaning at the bar with another man. He's wearing a grey suit; the friend is in beige chinos and a white shirt.'

Betty looked over at the bar and spotted the man in grey. 'So what now?' She was nervous and worried.

'First, we drink these. There's no rush.'

Betty eyed the 'victim' again, and noticed that he was already glancing in their direction. But then so were most of the men in the bar.

'He's looking over.'

'They often do.'

'What, because of you?' Again Betty's voice was too harsh.

'No, because we are the only two women in this bar without male companions, and that makes us a spectacle. That was all I meant.' The frosty atmosphere between them resumed. 'And normally I am on my own, which draws more attention,' Grace continued.

Betty sipped her champagne. She felt uncomfortable; she should walk out. But for some reason she stayed.

When their glasses were emptied, Grace went to the bar and arranged for drinks to be sent over to the 'grey man', as she had christened him. She told the barman to give him another drink of whatever he was drinking, and the same for his companion.

'You did what?' Betty screamed when Grace told her. Although Grace had outlined her plan, Betty didn't believe she was serious, especially as now she was embroiled in the situation.

'Well, obviously I would have done the same if I was on my own, and if they had come over then I would have made it clear who I was interested in. It's just that now you are here and I thought that maybe you could help. It will make it far more interesting for the article.' Grace couldn't help the slight smirk on her face. That would teach Betty for condemning her.

Betty realised at that point that she truly hated Grace.

'Honey, it's just work. Next week you'll be chasing another story and you'll have forgotten her.' Johnny strokes Betty's hair, and holds her. He is bemused because she is normally known for her tolerance.

'I have three more days of this, three whole days. Shit, I'll end up killing her, I just know I will.'

'Eddie, she's a bitch.'

Grace called Eddie and persuaded him to come over; she wanted to vent her anger. Eddie didn't take much persuading.

'What did she do?' He pours two whiskys.

'Oh, she's just so high and mighty. You know, at first I thought we might be friends. Friends, some hope. It wasn't long before the superior comments were spewing forth.'

'Grace, calm down.' He is pleased that she called him, but he knows that, yet again, she isn't after his body.

Grace continues to seethe. The day was a disaster. Betty was so judgemental, and instead of asking questions she seemed keen to offer opinions. Every time Grace decided to ignore this and carry on, there would be another dig, or another thought, or a question that overstepped the mark. What hurt more than anything was that at times Betty seemed to be genuinely interested. She changed more often than the British weather, and that was something that Grace couldn't understand. It hurt; it was bewildering.

That night, when Grace walked into the bar she couldn't believe what Betty was wearing. On the first night she was surprised by the trendiness of the outfit. It seemed a little over the top for observing, but Grace deduced that Betty was trendy: that was just her. But that night she was all done up like a dog's dinner and Grace couldn't understand why. Trendy was one thing, but this was something else. She was sexy; or she looked sexy; or her clothes were sexy; or all three, and there was no call for that. Grace knew that had she not been working, but observing like Betty, she would have worn something comfortable, something that would enable her to slip into the background. But the way Betty looked – well, she was dressed as if she was going to be doing Grace's job. This is why, in a fit of anger, Grace decided to make Betty her partner in crime. Teach her to have her own private agenda.

She knew there was a risk involved, a huge risk. Grace had no excuse: she lost her cool and put a job in jeopardy. Betty could blow the job and then Nicole would kill her, but she went ahead anyway. Grace hated to think of herself as vindictive, but she had to accept that that was exactly how she was behaving. She was ashamed, but she was also determined.

It was worth it to see the look on her face. After Grace had sent the drinks over, they waited ten minutes before the men came to their table. Grace was pleased that the man she was hired to trap sat down next to her; she tried not to be too amused at the way his friend was drooling over Betty. He was truly a slimy human being, even more hideous than 'grey man'. They all made small talk – apart from Betty, who sat rigid with shock. Anyone would have thought she had never seen a man before, and despite the fact that she was working and this was probably the most unprofessional job of her life, Grace was enjoying every moment. As she was taping the event, she was actually quite grateful for Betty's silence, although she had already decided to tell Nicole that Betty had wanted to help. Serve her right for her comments. How dare she imply that Grace was a tart and a marriage wrecker? How dare she imply that she enjoyed foisting misery on her clients? How dare she look down her snooty nose at her? Well, now she was being taught a lesson and Grace felt empowered. She was not being bullied.

Grace knew she was probably being oversensitive, but she disliked Betty's type: the smug woman who has a fabulous job, wardrobe and man. Everything Betty said to her felt like a criticism and Grace didn't know how to deal with that.

Finally, after lots of flirting on everyone's part except Betty's, the men suggested dinner. Betty looked as if she was going to cry. Grace had been steering the conversation with the client's partner, while trying not to laugh at Betty. The man drooling over Betty had been talking to her whilst undressing her with his eyes, and seemed delighted with her monosyllabic answers. But Grace knew she had a job to do, and fun as it was tormenting superior Betty, she couldn't do it any longer.

'Sorry, but we really must go. Maybe some other time?' Grace said. To say Betty looked relieved is a huge understatement.

'Are you sure I can't tempt you?' 'Grey man' had his hand on Grace's leg and was stroking her thigh. Grace leant in close. She had his proposition on tape, but clients usually preferred to have a bit more than a dinner invite.

'Personally I would love nothing better, but unfortunately we really must go.' Despite the fact that grey suit was a major sleaze who was trying to cheat (Grace believed that thigh stroking constituted cheating), she was a tiny bit turned on. Whether that was a combination of what she had done to Betty and the feeling standing up to bullies gave her, she did not know.

'Can't you take her home and then come and play?' He

whispered this in her ear, but luckily her wire would pick it up.

'Well, maybe I could.' Grace winked at Betty, who couldn't hear their conversation. 'How about I drop you home?' Grace was looking at 'grey man' seductively as she said this. She needed him to proposition her properly. 'So, where do I go after I've dropped her off?'

'How about home?'

'Sure, I could go home.'

'And I could meet you there after dinner.'

'Sounds perfect.' He was still running his hand up and down her thigh.

'Give me your address.' Grace gave him a fictional address in a different part of London. She didn't want to risk bumping into him again. Then she left, blowing him a kiss goodbye. Yet another cheater caught.

They left and hailed a cab.

'I didn't like that,' Betty said. Grace deduced this was an understatement.

'What?' Grace felt as if she'd had some revenge. She smiled generously.

'Being made to feel like a piece of meat.' Betty was a petulant child.

'Betty, it's my job. You're shadowing me. You need never get involved again. Next time just watch me from a distance.' Grace felt a tiny bit guilty. 'I thought you might enjoy it, or not enjoy it, but I thought it would give you more of an idea of what I do. A proper insight.'

'Oh, it gave me that all right.'

'Anyway, at least you didn't have his hand on your leg.'

'No.' Betty lost her fight.

'No, you didn't, and I was being paid to catch him out which, Betty, is what I did.'

Betty nodded, as the taxi pulled up outside Grace's block.

'See you tomorrow then,' Grace said as she got out, giving

Betty money. Her mind was already on Eddie, whom she intended to see, to get Betty out of her head.

'I'll be looking forward to it,' Betty lied.

Later, as Betty tries to sleep, tossing and turning while Johnny gently snores next to her, she cannot get the honey-trap woman out of her head. And over in her flat, Grace is watching Eddie, who didn't try to have sex with her and is now asleep, and she is wondering if she really is the bad person that Betty thinks she is. Does she deliberately drape herself over the men? Is she nothing more than a tart? Looking at Eddie, and thinking of Oliver, Grace, in the midst of sleeplessness, can only conclude the answer is yes.

Chapter Eleven

Day Three.

Betty gets out of bed with far less enthusiasm than on the previous days, which means none. She looks out of the window and sees it is raining. Johnny has already left for work, and she knows she should be going too, but she feels lethargic so she goes to make herself a coffee and she drinks it in bed. She is later than she should be, but she doesn't care. She is sure that Grace won't be eagerly waiting for her. And if she is, after last night's stunt, then she can wait.

Grace nudges Eddie awake. She forgot to set her alarm and she notices that it is already nine o'clock. Although Betty isn't due until ten, she still feels late and disorientated.

'Eddie, wake up.'

'Why?' He looks adorable as he snuggles into Grace.

'Because she'll be here soon.'

'How soon?' He yawns and then he reaches over and kisses Grace.

'An hour.'

'Now, I don't know about you but I don't call that soon.' Grace's protests are drowned out by his kisses.

Betty stands at the door, pressing the buzzer with one hand while negotiating her bag and umbrella with the other. She feels damp and cold, even though the rain is quite warm. Her mac makes her feel dowdy, and her hair is wilting. She knows that once it has dried again, it will frizz up and she'll look pale (her make-up has evaporated in the rain), with a bad Afro hairstyle. She feels depressed. Even more so than earlier.

'Shit, she'll see you here.' Grace wakes to the sound of her buzzer. She had fallen asleep again. She jumps out of bed and shouts at Eddie, 'And you're naked.'

He is amused.

'Shit.' Grace grabs her bathrobe and runs to the door. She is angry with herself. Not only is she behaving in a totally unprofessional manner, but she is also giving Betty more fuel for disapproval. Worst of all is the fact that she cares about what she thinks. She didn't want to.

Betty is pressing the buzzer again, getting angrier, but praying that she never answers the door, when Grace answers the intercom.

'Sorry,' she says, breathlessly, letting her in. She opens the door and prays for a miracle.

'Hello.' Betty looks at Grace in surprise, which Grace assumes is mocking.

'I'm sorry. I overslept.' Grace is at a loss as to what to say, and she has no idea why she feels as if she has been caught doing something she shouldn't. This is her flat, it is her profile, she is doing Betty a favour – her new mantra, developed last night when trying to sleep. But she still feels as if she is in the wrong.

'I tell you what, shall I put some coffee on while you go and get dressed?' Betty is delighted. She never thought she would get to see the perfect Grace looking much less than perfect. Even with her rain-ruined look, she knows that her appearance is far better. Grace is not wearing a good look.

'Thanks.' Grace goes back to her bedroom, while Betty whistles her way to the kitchen.

*

'You're going to have to sneak out,' she says.

'Why? I need coffee. Anyway, I'd quite like to meet this woman. The woman who can send the unflappable Grace into a spin. I'm already late for work, might as well be a bit later.' Eddie's face is filled up with his grin.

'Stop teasing. Please, just go quietly,' she begs. Grace is nervous. She is trying to get ready quickly, but is all fingers and thumbs. Although he finds this amusing, she finds it disturbing.

'No way. Anyway, who cares what she thinks?'

'I don't,' she lies.

'Then, you'll let me meet her.' He is dressed in seconds and before she can protest further, he disappears to the kitchen, leaving Grace wondering if this week can get any worse.

Betty is still whistling by the percolator when he walks into the kitchen.

'Hello.' He stands by the door. Betty turns round. At first she looks startled, but her look turns quickly to one of amusement. She knows that Grace will hate this; she stifles the desire to laugh.

'Hi, I'm Betty.' She flashes her best grin. The day is beginning well.

'Eddie. Pleased to meet you.'

'Would you like coffee?'

'Love one. Milk no sugar. So you're a journalist?' He is standing behind Betty.

'Yes.' Betty looks surprised at him knowing this. But then she remembers she has no idea who this man is.

'Grace told me about the article. How's it going?' It's Eddie's turn to be amused. Although he hasn't seen them together, he knows, because he knows Grace, why they don't get on. He can see, from minor mannerisms and body language, that the woman Grace professes to hate is actually quite similar to her. He cannot help but find this funny.

'Really well,' Betty lies. 'So how do you know Grace?' Just before he gets a chance to answer, Grace walks into the kitchen. She had the quickest shower she could and pulled on her clothes without drying her hair. She hates the idea of Betty and Eddie talking alone. About her. She shudders from the cold.

'Is the coffee ready?' The brightness in her voice is fake, but she is trying to put the bad start to the day behind her.

She is sure she sees Betty smirk as she turns round and hands her a cup. Grace begins to feel hatred rise up. Betty started it all, with her comments, Grace believed she had finished it last night by making Betty speak to 'chino man' for most of the evening, but obviously not. Looking at Betty's smirking face, she knows they are at war and it will only be a matter of time before one of them climbs out of the trench and starts firing.

Betty is happy, smug even. Not only does she find Grace with a man, but also she has caught her on the run, looking dreadful (or as dreadful as Grace can). She feels Grace deserves this for the humiliating experience she subjected her to last night, although she is still not quite satisfied by the revenge. She needs more. She just has to figure out how to teach her a lesson whilst not losing her job.

Eddie leaves after what seems like hours to Grace, but actually was only another ten minutes.

'As I'm running late, let's go straight to the office.' Her voice is curt; cold even. This only serves to annoy Betty further. She thought the least Grace could do would be to offer an apology for what happened last night. But none is forthcoming.

'Fine,' she snaps.

Grace has a meeting with a client that day, the meeting Nicole arranged to show different sides to the job. Unbeknown to Betty, Grace is already feeling apprehensive about this, and Betty's presence doesn't help. She doesn't normally deal with clients; that is Nicole's job. Although she has been briefed, and she knows what to do and say, she desperately doesn't want to come across as incompetent. She can imagine how happy that would make Betty. She can already hear her sharpening her pencil.

They are going to the client's home. The client is nervous and requested a face-to-face meeting before deciding to proceed. Nicole told Grace that at some point she normally meets the client. It is rare that a woman is happy to do the whole thing over the phone.

'Remember I have to go and meet a client in an hour.' She is still upset with the way the day has started, and although she is trying to be kinder, her voice seems unwilling to oblige.

'Oh good, then I can see that side of your job.'

'Yes you can.' Grace feels uneasy; what she doesn't know is that Betty feels the same.

Cold war breaks out in the taxi. Grace sits with her arms folded across her chest, pretending to read notes about the woman whose house they are visiting. Betty sits as far away from her as possible, unsure what to say but determined not to let Grace get the better of her. The humiliation she still feels from the previous night is burning her inside. Even if Johnny thinks she is overreacting, she cannot help it. Betty knows that if women like Grace didn't exist to fuel paranoia and insecurity in women, then the world would be a better place. Relationships would be a better place.

'Eddie is a bit . . . a bit old.' Betty isn't normally a bitch, but Grace brings out the worst in her.

'Not really, he just looks it,' Grace lies. She has no idea why.

'Been together long?'

'Yes, actually.'

'How long?'

'No offence, but I would rather keep my personal life out of this.'

'I'm not asking for the article, I'm just asking to be friendly.' Betty knows that she is doing anything but.

'Really?' Grace's voice is dripping with disbelief.

'Yeah. I mean, you know that I am happily married and have been for two years. Johnny and I have been together for five.' Betty smiles at Grace. The tactic is to wrong-foot the enemy.

'I was going to get married once.' Grace surprises herself with this response. She has no idea what made her offer that information.

'What happened?' Betty is wondering if Grace is trying to wrong-foot her.

'He left me. Well, he decided that he was too young, or something. I guess you could say that I was jilted.'

'Another woman?' Betty is intrigued. Perhaps there is something in that last sentence that explains why Grace does what she does.

'Not as far as I know. He probably did have someone else – most men do – but that wasn't the reason he gave me. He thought we were too young and he wanted to see the world. I let him go. I was too scared to do anything else. Now I know that it was the right thing to do. We were far too young for settling down.'

'How young were you?'

'Eighteen.' Grace has said it. She has told of another life, one that she barely acknowledges exists. A different Grace. The Grace who at sixteen started going out with Dave. Dave, who lived nearby and had known her all his life. Dave, who was two years older than Grace and known on the estate as a good catch. He was the first man who bought her presents; the first man to take her to places, not just to the bedroom or the back of the car. The first man she thought she was in love with.

Ask Grace what love is and she will shrug her shoulders. It was lucky that Betty didn't ask her that question. She believed at the time she was in love with Dave, but it didn't hurt as much as she thought it would when he left her, so she realised that that wasn't love. Her next love affair she believed really was love, and it did hurt when that went wrong, but still, the hurt faded fast. She concluded a long time ago that she would never feel love, and that she probably never has.

Dave had the same background as she: they knew each other's family, they lived on the same estate. She remembers her younger sister, Kathy, being jealous. Dave drove a car (a battered one but it was still a car) and he was training to be a carpet fitter. He was also very handsome.

The old Grace had her life mapped out for her. The only escape from her parents' overcrowded house was to get married. As quickly as possible. Her younger sister (by one year) had the same idea, but unfortunately her strategy was a little bit screwed up. Kathy would sleep with every man she met straight away; Grace would make them hold out. Dave waited patiently for eight months until he told her he was in love with her and she let him have his prize. Grace was the brightest of the Regan children; she was also the best-looking. It was a wonder to her that the best assets had been bestowed on her, although one of her brothers had a great sense of humour. She used her assets to her advantage and she earned herself the coveted engagement ring from Dave.

However, just as she thought she had earned her escape, she learnt that getting the ring wasn't the hardest bit. He said he wanted to wait until they could afford a decent wedding, so they saved. Grace got a job in a factory, in the office, where she did the filing and eventually learnt how to type. Her exams from school had been good enough for her to stay on, but she needed to work, to earn money, to marry Dave.

Then he said that they should also save for a deposit on a house. They saved. Then after two years of saving, he emptied the joint account and left her a note saying he was too young to settle down and he was going to travel. Half on her money. It was the hardest lesson that Grace ever had to learn. Harder than the loneliness of childhood, the awkwardness of her teenage years. Harder than the lack of attention, the feeling of isolation. Harder than the bullying, the taunting and the feeling of not belonging anywhere. Her escape from her family home and the memories of growing up had been Dave. Her escape had escaped.

Kathy got pregnant. Seventeen, single and pregnant (and the gossip on the street was that it could be any one of a number of men's). She got herself on the housing list, but had to live with her parents until a flat came up. Although she didn't have a man to help her out, Kathy was happy. She had always been tougher than Grace; always a survivor.

Her brothers and younger sister were luckier, she guessed. Michael joined the army as soon as he turned sixteen. Escaped. Lee got married to a woman who, like Kathy and Grace, needed to escape. He became an electrician. As far as she knows Peter and Hope are still at home – they were when she left anyway – but she isn't sure. Neither does she know the sex of her sister's baby, or if she had any more.

Grace left, ran away, made her own escape. She was heart-broken (or so she thought), she was angry with Dave for taking their money and she felt claustrophobic. Her family's answer to Dave's desertion was for her to go find another man. They didn't seem to have the energy to give her advice. Her father was too tired from watching television, her mother was too tired from working and looking after (in the loosest sense of the word) the family, Kathy was too tired from having sex with as many men as she could, and her brothers and Hope were too wrapped up in their own lives. Grace had no option but to rely on herself for her escape.

She left a note, telling them she had gone to stay with friends and get a job in West London. She called them once to tell them she was all right but her mother sounded more relieved that she wasn't there than worried about where she was. She told Grace to take care and have a good life. That was it: the last contact with her family. She didn't miss them at all.

She had only limited money, having had her savings cleared out, but she had enough in her current account to survive for one month. She went in search of a job and found one as a secretary to a fashion buyer. It was through an agency and Grace knew she was lucky. She didn't get the job straight away – her agency sent her to ten interviews before she was successful. She was just pleased that it was the fashion industry that she got a job in rather than a bank.

And that was how it started: the reinvention of Grace Regan. What she calls the dignification of her life. It wasn't massive, it didn't happen overnight. Grace had always had a timid voice, and she learnt how to speak nicely – not like a posh person, but without a hint of an accent. She concentrated on not dropping her Ts or her Hs, until it became second nature. She had always had her looks, but she learnt how to make them work for her by dressing nicely, by using the right make-up, and styling her hair. She didn't turn from the street kid into the queen, but she did feel that she had made improvements.

She likes her confidence, even if it doesn't come as easily as it seems. She likes the way she speaks and the way she walks. She likes the way she dresses and she likes the way that she has control over her life. The most important lesson she has learnt is that you can control your life. She never knew that that would be possible, not while she was growing up, not while she was engaged to Dave. However, it is, and now she is living proof of that.

Betty is thinking about Grace being engaged. It surprises her, although she doesn't believe the sob story about being dumped. She thinks that Grace probably broke his heart. No man would walk away from her.

She wonders how she managed to get herself engaged so young, and presumes that he was a richer man, one of her set, someone who went to private school and drove a nice car given to him by his parents. Grace was probably the school flirt, every boy's wet dream but unobtainable to all except the man with the best car. He was probably also the best-looking.

When Betty was at her secondary school, a rough comprehensive, which was large, grey and anonymous, she was not popular with the boys. Actually, she was universally unpopular. She was geeky, unsure of herself. She wore National Health glasses, her hair was wild and untameable, and for a while she had to wear a brace. She was frightful. Not like Grace. The other children were cruel. They would call her ugly and not care about how that could hurt. The girls would tease her, the boys would call her names and it hurt her to the core. It stopped when she moved on from her GCSEs and went to do her A levels at the local tech. Her brace was off, her teeth nice and straight, she got a part-time job and paid for smart glasses, and eventually contact lenses, and even her hair seemed to behave. Everyone was more grown up at the tech, and she met her first boyfriend there. After the age of sixteen she began to feel normal but she would never forget the feeling of inadequacy that she experienced prior to that, or how long it took to get rid of it.

Although her parents were loving to their only daughter, Betty never told them how unhappy she was; they would have blamed themselves, and Betty knows it wasn't their fault. But she resents Grace, for having the life that she coveted so badly when she cried herself to sleep every night, and felt lonely every day.

'Pull in here, please,' Grace says to the taxi driver. She gets out and pays him, and Betty follows.

'It's a shame that your fiancé left you,' Betty says, as Grace is paying the driver. She sounds mean as she says it, but she is unsure why.

'I just hope your husband doesn't wish he did the same to you,' Grace bites back.

Betty stares at her. The cold war is over; hostilities have commenced.

'Mrs X, I'm Grace Regan. This is my assistant, Betty.' She smiles warmly at Mrs X. Betty is still reeling from Grace's last comment. She can feel her cheeks heating up, the rage threatening to overcome her. That is the worst thing anyone could ever say to her. The very suggestion that Johnny might leave her is far too horrible for her to contemplate.

'Hi, good to meet you. Sorry it couldn't be under nicer circumstances,' Betty says, instantly regretting it. She sticks her hand out to shake Mrs X's, telling herself not to misbehave in this meeting. Grace looks horrified, but plasters a smile to her face.

'Please come in.' They follow Mrs X to her living room. The house is in an expensive part of London, and would have cost a fortune. Grace might have come far but she can only dream about a house like that. Mrs X is in her late thirties and is very attractive. Grace cannot understand a husband wanting to cheat when he has such a lovely home and such a lovely wife. She has no idea if they have children.

Grace and Betty sit on the brown leather sofa in silence while Mrs X goes to get coffee. Mrs X is obviously nervous, but so is Grace.

'Here. Please help yourselves to milk and sugar.' Mrs X puts a tray down on the coffee table.

'Where would you like to start?' Grace asks after the coffee has been poured.

'Well, it's a bit difficult really.' She looks at Grace and Betty, then she looks into her coffee cup.

'You only have to tell what you want to,' Grace says.

'We've been married for ten years. Everything was perfect, or so I thought. We've got two children, Molly and Henry, and, well, as a family we were doing really nicely. Then things started changing. He works hard, he always has, but his hours are getting longer and longer. When he is at home he seems distracted. He practically ignores the children, and he totally ignores me. It's a bit embarrassing . . .'

'Don't be embarrassed. I've heard a lot in my time,' Grace coaxes.

Betty bites her lip. Mrs X is too busy staring into her coffee cup to notice.

'We haven't had sex for a year and I have tried. But he always makes an excuse. Then there's the phone calls. I can't believe he thinks he's being so clever. He sneaks out of the house, says he needs fresh air, and I see him in the garden with the mobile phone stuck to his ear. Of course he has the bills sent to him at the office so I will never have proof.'

'Do you think he's been cheating for a year?'

'Yes I do.'

'But you don't know who with?'

'No. I don't even know if it's the same woman. You see, that's where you come in. I thought, although I'm not sure, but I thought that if you chatted him up he would either fall for it, or tell you he was happily married, or tell you he had a mistress. You might be able to get me proof and stop me from going insane.' She lets out a hollow laugh. She looks as if she will crumple in tears.

'You're sure?' Betty asks. Then she looks shocked at the fact that the words were said aloud.

'I'm not sure about anything any more,' Mrs X replies.

'Have you thought about confronting him? Just asking him

straight out,' Betty continues, horrified that she is still speaking but unable to stop.

Grace restrains herself. She almost blames herself. She should have known that Betty would pull a stunt like this. It is all her fault. She has to rectify the situation.

'Of course you could do that. But just one thing: in my experience they deny it, which is fine, but without conclusive proof you have nothing.'

'That's true. If he is cheating he's bound to deny it. I mean, if he is cheating then he's being devious and so another lie won't mean anything to him.'

'But what if he's innocent?' Betty asks. She has stopped thinking, and she's lost control of herself. She is just a mouthpiece for the part of her she has been trying to suppress.

'Well, I don't think—'

'Then I will find that out for her. Which would be wonderful really.' Grace's smile is almost cracking her face.

'Yeah, but what if he's not cheating and then he meets you and he propositions you? Then he'll be seen as a cheat, but he wasn't cheating before.' Betty digs her nails into her palm, but that doesn't seem to help.

'The chances are that if he does proposition me, he has cheated before. Why would he, otherwise?'

'Mrs X, excuse me but have you taken a good look at her?' Mrs X appears confused, but stares at Grace. 'She is simply stunning, isn't she?' Mrs X nods. 'Well, I don't think that it's any reflection on you if a woman like Grace turns up, looking amazing, and starts flattering your husband and he falls for it. Most men would. I am not saying that you shouldn't find out for sure, but you really think sending her in is a good idea?' Betty knows that she has just signed her own death warrant. She is angry with herself but she is still unable to stop. All her frustrations about Grace's job come tumbling out, along with anger at the previous night. She is a slave to her emotions.

'Well, I really don't . . .' Mrs X tails off and Grace feels totally inadequate. She knows she is not the most intelligent person in the world but she never thought that anyone would run rings around her the way Betty is doing.

'Yes, but that isn't how it works. There has to be suspicion. Suspicion, if it's genuine (which in this case I can tell it is), has to be caused. It doesn't just appear and it always has foundation. Now, it might be that he is having problems at work that he isn't telling you, but that is what I will discover.'

'I just don't think that you should put your family at risk,' Betty says, unable to see how that will rectify the situation but hoping it will, somehow.

'Betty, shut up, please,' Grace replies angrily.

'Because it is a risk, as I discovered last night. You turn up in your sexy outfit, and you let the men drool all over you while you flatter them and pander to them and then you say that they are the cheats. You're the cheater. Agent provocateur.' Betty looks at her shoes; she is almost cowering from her words.

'How dare you? How dare you?' Grace is on her feet, Betty is as well. The client sits and stares in shock. Suddenly Grace remembers where she is.

'I am so sorry. Mrs X, this is unforgivable, not to mention unprofessional behaviour. I'm sure you wouldn't hire me in a thousand years after that little tirade, so we'll leave now.' Without giving the open-mouthed Mrs X a chance to reply, Grace roughly grabs Betty by the arm and marches her out of the house.

'How fucking dare you?' she screams when they are on the pavement. She had plenty of fights when she was younger, screaming and physical ones. She actually is something of an expert.

'How dare I? How dare you? Firstly you try to turn me into the same sort of tart as you last night, then you pretend to be sympathetic to a woman who has a nice home, a husband and two children just so you can wreck her happiness.'

'She doesn't seem very happy, does she? Last night was because you were being so superior. I heard the condescending tone in your voice, the disapproval dripping out of you. Well, you can afford it, can't you, with your perfect marriage, but did it ever occur to you that others aren't quite as fortunate?'

'And did it ever, ever occur to you that you should leave people alone to work out their own problems?'

'It's so easy for you, isn't it? The world you live in, people are nicer to each other. They don't cheat or bully. But not everyone has it that way.'

'You know nothing about me.' Grace is stunned by the intensity in Betty's voice. Her words are ringing in her ears. *Marriage wrecker*. She looks at her and wonders why she hates her so much. Was it really the chino man? She suspects it is more than that. The old Grace is making a brief appearance. Here for one time only. She squares up to Betty. 'And you know nothing about me.' She pulls her arm back and slaps Betty hard round the face.

Grace has not hit anyone since she left school, and then it was only to defend herself. Betty has had her hair pulled, been called thousand of names, but she has never been slapped. The rain is getting heavier as they both stand there, shocked, surprised, unsure of where to go now.

'You bitch,' Betty hisses, choking back tears.

'You deserved it,' Grace replies. She is also close to crying. She is no longer going to be bullied. Never again. They stare at each other for a few moments before turning on their heels and walking away in opposite directions.

Grace turns the corner and leans against a wall. She feels winded, and she has no idea what happened. She knows that she looks a sight, dripping wet and almost hyperventilating, so when she spots a coffee shop she goes inside and orders an espresso. She sits down, still shaking with rage and cold, and pulls out her phone.

'Nicole,' she says before the tears get the better of her.

She finds a taxi. Nicole talked to her as if she were a child, and although that was unfamiliar, it was comforting. She arrives home and goes inside. Ten minutes later, the buzzer goes and Nicole is there.

'I'm sorry,' Grace says, and she tells her the whole story.

Nicole does not have children, but she has maternal instincts. As Grace is recounting the full horror of her week with Betty, Nicole manages to run her a bath, get her to take her wet clothes off, and then put her in the bath. She sits on the loo seat next to her, listening.

'When you called me that first day, I should have talked you into calling it quits.'

'I didn't know this would happen. Anyway, I should never have done what I did last night.'

'No, you shouldn't, because you were working, Grace, and that comes before getting your own back, but I understand. I can't believe she asked you if you slept with the men. I can't believe she called you a marriage wrecker.'

'And a slut.'

'And, what else was it?'

'Agent provocateur.'

'That's quite funny. Sorry, Grace. Anyway, there is no need to worry. We're pulling out and I've a good mind to sue *Modern Woman* for the lost job.'

'I should have been able to save it.'

'No, you shouldn't. Now stop beating yourself up. It's over. *Finito*. Now get out of the bath before you turn into a prune, and I'll get some coffee.'

'I'm sorry to drag you away from the office.'

'Oh, for God's sake, stop apologising. It's a quiet day in the land of the spies.'

Later, when Nicole gets back to her office, she calls *Modern Woman* and informs Fiona that she will no longer do the profile. And she tells her why. Leaving nothing, especially her anger, out.

Betty makes her way home, desperately trying to find a cab. Typically, they are all full on a rainy London afternoon, so she hikes until she finds a tube station. It takes her forty-five minutes to get to her stop and she is feeling wretched and uncomfortable. As soon as she gets in, she takes a hot bath, she puts on her dressing gown and she crawls under her duvet where she cries herself to sleep, ignoring Fiona's angry voice on her answer machine.

Chapter Twelve

'I can't believe it,' Johnny says when Betty tells him what happened that day. 'I mean, why did you lose it so badly?'

'Firstly I was still angry at her making me part of her job, and then you should have heard her. She was advising this woman to get her to honey trap her husband. The woman had two kids and had been married for ten years. *Ten years*. She suspects him of having an affair and I just suggested that she should confront him rather than hire her.' Betty is trying to justify to herself, and to Johnny, her outburst.

'Baby, you're supposed to be doing an article on this woman and honey trapping, not ruining her business.'

'But she has been so awful.'

'I know, but it's not professional.'

'I could lose my job.'

'Don't be silly. Fiona won't fire you.'

'But there is no way we can continue this article.'

'Look, persuade Fiona to get someone else to do this one and you can do another feature. I know how much you resented having to do it in the first place.'

'You know it hasn't always been easy for me, not the way she said, but since I met you, well, everything's been so perfect.'

'I love you so much, Mrs Parkin.'

'I know, and I love you too.'

*

'You hit her?' Eddie (who has been called over as an emergency comforter) looks horrified. He is seeing more of Grace than ever, but he is not sure he likes the reason behind it.

'She deserved it. She told a potential client not to hire me.'

'Oh.'

'Yes, oh.'

'But what did you do to her?'

'Nothing. I was perfectly civil.'

'Grace.'

'Well, she was so high and mighty. Flashing her wedding ring around all over the place, being condescending, and making out that I was nothing better than a slut. I think she was getting revenge for me making her join me on that job.'

'Probably.' He knows better than to argue that she is also to blame.

'Well, you know, I thought that maybe it might teach her not to look down her snotty little nose at me.'

'Grace, what if she writes a really awful piece about you?'

'She won't. Nicole called her editor and told them that I would not be taking part any more.'

'I've never seen you so rattled.'

'There's always a first time.' Although they are sitting on the sofa, and the fish are happily swimming in front of them, Grace is swinging her leg and fiddling with her hands. She is clearly disturbed by events. Eddie is seeing a new side to her and it actually makes him think that maybe she is more human than she lets on. He shouldn't feel happy when she is miserable, but he does a bit. She has proved to him that she needs him over the last few days, and this makes him feel pretty good.

The following morning Betty wakes up with a feeling of dread in the pit of her stomach. She looks round the room: everything is the same. The striped yellow and white wallpaper, the large wooden bed, the pale blue curtains and duvet. Everything is exactly the same as it was yesterday, but it isn't. Because today she may not have a job. Fiona sounded so angry on the hundred or so messages she left.

She looks at Johnny, sleeping beside her. His hair stuck slightly to his forehead. His arm hooked over his body. His breathing, quiet but audible. He is truly beautiful. She kisses the top of his head gently. She may not have a job but she will always have Johnny – of that she is sure. This makes her realise that she will always be better off than Grace the marriage wrecker, because she has an unwreckable marriage.

It is early, but she knows that sleep isn't going to happen, so she gets up and makes a cup of coffee. She will go into the office to face Fiona, although Fiona won't be there much before nine thirty, so there is no rush. She also has the party to prepare for that Saturday night – Johnny's party. It means so much to him that she will not ruin it. Even if she is sacked from the job she loves so much, she will make it the best party ever for the best husband ever.

She thinks back to her first meeting with Grace. How had their relationship deteriorated so fast? She didn't like her before she met her, but she had once interviewed a woman who would only sleep with married men and she'd managed to remain civil. Betty wonders if she has been too childish, but then she shakes the feeling off. Grace is a woman that every woman should be wary of. She has merely told her exactly what she needed to hear. With luck, Grace will think next time she is destroying someone else's marriage.

She makes a cup of coffee for Johnny and takes it upstairs to him. She almost feels sorry for Grace, because despite her sugar daddy, and the fiancé that abandoned her, she blatantly has no idea how to love.

Grace wakes and hears him snoring gently next to her. She gives him a tiny nudge and it wakes him.

'What?' he says.

'You were snoring.'

'I was?'

'Yeah. Sounded like an earthquake.'

'Could you make me some coffee?'

'Yes, sir.'

'Well, I do have to go to work.'

'Fair enough, and I did keep you up moaning for hours last night.'

'I could say something about that, but I won't.'

'Good bloody job. You know what I mean.' Grace stops and bites her lip. 'Eddie . . .'

'Yes?'

'Thank you. I do appreciate it, you know.'

He gets out of bed and kisses Grace on her forehead. 'Any time, Grace, any time.'

Betty looks haggard as she goes into the office. Despite all the reassuring pep talks she has been giving herself, she still feels sick with nerves. She wishes she had never set eyes on Grace and she is unsure how she is going to get out of this mess.

'Fiona wants to see you.'

Betty smiles at Hannah although she is clearly grimacing. 'Right.'

'Betty, what have you done? She's been screaming for you, and I did try to call.'

'Sorry, Hannah. I've been a bad, bad girl. Anyway, I'll fill you in later. For now I'd better go to my execution.' She swipes her arm across her neck and manages a smile.

'You'd better hurry up.'

'I'm on my way.' She dumps her coat on the chair with her bag and goes up to the headmistress's office. She knocks before she goes in but doesn't wait for Fiona to respond. She opens the door, feeling nervous. It does unfortunately remind her of being a schoolchild and that is something else she blames Grace for.

'Hi, sit down.' Fiona's face does not betray anything. But then she never does. She has the same expression on her face when she is happy or angry, which infuriates all her staff. Betty sits down.

'I had an interesting call yesterday.' Fiona stares straight at Betty, who flushes and looks away. 'Nicole, the boss of Grace Regan, our very lovely case study, said that not only did you insult her, you also sabotaged a potential client.'

'I think sabotage is a bit of a strong word.'

'Really? But you did lose her potential business?'

'Sort of.' Betty begins to squirm.

'She threatened to sue.'

'She won't.' Betty prays that she won't. It is one thing to annoy Grace, but quite another to annoy Grace's boss, whom she hasn't thought about at all. She feels even more uncomfortable.

'How do you know? Betty, she is furious with us, with the magazine. Because of you and the way you behaved. What on earth were you thinking?'

Betty is catapulted back into childhood, when she was always in trouble for things. That was what happened when you were ugly and awkward. The pretty, confident girls would only speak to you to get you to do things for them that no one else wanted to do. The humiliation still burns. '*Betty, go and steal a lipstick for us*', '*Betty, go and buy us some fags, don't be so wet*', '*Betty, go and put a drawing pin on Miss's chair.*' Of course Betty did all these things, and more because she thought, just for a minute, that it might make her accepted, and it might make her popular. Of course, it never did, and she always got caught, got into trouble. The line, 'What were you thinking?' said by a thousand different people for a thousand different reasons is tattooed on her memory. It will never ever go . . .

'Betty, are you with us?' Fiona's sharp tone snaps her out of her daydream.

'Sorry.' She is not sorry, but she is not feeling very bold. 'Fiona, I don't know what I was thinking. It's just that she's so awful. I saw her in action. The men she was supposed to be testing didn't stand a chance. Not only is she stunning but she dresses like a high-class hooker. Then she flirts for England. If a man had never ever been unfaithful in his life, he would be with her.'

'So you're saying that any man would fall for her?'

'Yes, which is why what she is doing is immoral.'

'What about Johnny?' Fiona is glad she remembers his name correctly. She is so adverse to talking to anyone about marriage that she had to retrieve it from the back of her mind.

'Not him, no way him.'

'Betty, you're not making any sense. You hate this woman because even if a man wasn't unfaithful he would be with her, but Johnny wouldn't be.'

Betty flushes crimson. 'Johnny is different. But other men aren't as strong as him.'

'Don't give me that bull. Betty, if a man wants to cheat he wants to cheat. Johnny is not an exception. He is not unique. You can't apply one rule to him and then another to the whole of mankind. Grace is hired by women to see if their husbands are cheats. Most of them are. But she is only hired by women who are suspicious and usually have reason to be suspicious.'

'She acts like a tart and she enjoys wrecking marriages.'

'She said that?'

'Not exactly, but you should have seen her when the man we were testing propositioned her. She looked so smug. His wife was sitting at home waiting to hear if she still had a marriage or not and Grace was smiling. Happy. She just made me so mad.'

'Right, but this is all personal and you were supposed to be doing a job.'

'I know.'

'So, what are you going to do about it?'

'She made me get involved. She chatted up this man while his friend tried to chat me up. It was awful. He had too much saliva and it was pouring down his chin, and he had this smirk which made me feel sick. I swear he was a psycho. I could have been killed.' Betty hopes that her vast exaggeration of the truth does the trick.

'Rubbish. It sounds like fun.'

'Well, it wasn't. She just did it to humiliate me. And it worked. This man was drooling, and he tried to touch me and, oh, it was so horrible and she could have stopped it but she didn't.'

'So I guess the lecture to the potential client was your idea of revenge.'

'I guess.' Betty is so sure that she is right, but it just isn't coming across that way.

'I don't know what to say. You have worked here for years and you've always been the most reliable writer. Your work is always good. But now, well, I just don't understand what happened.'

'She hit me.'

'She did? Hard?' Fiona is tiring of the conversation.

'Yes, hard. Fiona, I can't explain it any more. We just didn't like each other from the word go. She told me that she thinks all men are cheats and I told her that I didn't agree and it went downhill from there. Fiona, I've got some good stuff here, and I've done loads of research. We could salvage a story from what we've got.' Betty conjures up hope.

'No way. I want a real profile of a real honey trapper and Nicole has told us in no uncertain terms that Grace is not a part of it any more. Which leaves us with a problem.'

'You want me to find another honey trapper?' Hope starts to fade.

'No.'

'Oh, right. Well, what then?' Hope turns to fear.

'Apologise.'

'I am sorry.'

'Not to me, to her. You have to apologise to Grace and get her to agree to finish the story. I realise that this will probably mean we have to add on a bit of extra time, but that's not a problem.'

Betty is white; she feels faint.

'I can't do that. Fiona, why don't you put someone else on the story? They can talk her round. There is no way that she will ever accept me again.'

'That's what I thought at first, but then I realised that she will – if you persuade her you really are sorry and you mean it. Be sincere. Beg. Do whatever, but, Betty, you are going to finish this profile if it's the last story you do.' Fiona's face looks the same as always but her voice conveys that she means business.

'Or?' Betty's fear is wrapping around her intestines. It is here to stay.

'Or, I am going to demote you. Not officially, of course, but you'll be writing the worst features for the rest of your working life. You will cringe every time you see your by-line rather than be proud of it. You will never get a promotion and I personally will ensure that your working life is a misery.' Fiona smiles after delivering her very calm speech.

'Don't you think you might be a bit harsh?' Betty is truly terrified. And astounded. She cannot believe that Fiona is taking this so seriously. Her job really is under threat.

'No. I do not. We are this close to being sued and if you cast your crazy mind back you will remember that it was my idea to do this feature and my idea to use Grace. The boss is always right, Betty. You should know that by now.'

Betty realises that there is no way out. Fiona is stubborn, and she assumes Grace is too. She wants to burst into tears, run away, but she's not a kid any more and she can't behave like one. She thinks of Johnny and wonders what he would say. She knows that he would tell her to apologise to Grace and then finish the story. She doesn't want to be writing boring stories for the rest of her life, nor does she want to lose her job. She knows, however, that Fiona does not dish out idle threats.

'Fiona, please don't be angry. I just want to clarify the situation. Either I apologise to Grace and get the story back or you'll ruin my life. I don't suppose there is a third option?' As she says this she cannot look Fiona in the eye so she reties the lace on her trainers.

'No. Apart from quitting. If you want to resign I would be very sad but I'd accept it.' Her deadpan face makes it impossible to gauge if she is joking or not. Part of Betty is sure that she doesn't mean it a bit, but there is another part not quite brave enough to find out.

'OK, OK, so I apologise. But what if she refuses to carry on with the story?'

'Then you persuade her. Bribe her. Do whatever you have to do. But get her back.' Fiona turns to her computer screen and picks up the phone, indicating to a very green Betty that the conversation is over.

Grace feels quite strange now she isn't expecting to be watched. She goes back to wearing a tracksuit and no make-up. She spends an hour watching her fish in the morning after she's fed them, rather than going straight to the office. When she does go to the office she picks up her emails and arranges her calendar. She has another job that evening. A job that the hateful Betty will not be attending. She smiles because although she was quite excited about being in print, she feels free. Free from condemnation. Free from the judgemental journalist. She feels bad for Nicole, who she knew was looking forward to the publicity, but then she feels good for herself, because she felt dreadful, insecure, and nervous when Betty was around.

She wonders if she has a mark where she hit her. She feels ashamed of that. Betty did push her too far but she hasn't hit anyone since before she was sixteen years old. To behave the way she did showed an immense lack of control. Ever since she left school, no one has made her feel as bad as Betty did, but she still can't quite work out why she allowed her to get so under her skin.

She wonders how Betty's day is going. Then she puts her out of her mind and calls Nicole. She wants to work harder, to make up for any disappointment she might be feeling.

'How are you today?' Nicole asks.

'Better. Thanks for yesterday. I shouldn't have lost it.'

'We all do. Anyway, I trust you, Grace, and I know that this woman must have pushed you to make you feel that way.'

'I'm sorry about the article. I know you were going to get huge publicity out of it.'

'It's not worth it, especially if she had spent the rest of the week driving my clients away.'

'But I want to make it up to you. I want you to give me more work to do.'

'Grace, you already work harder for me than anyone else.'

'Then I'll work harder.'

'You don't need to feel guilty.'

'I know. The trouble is that I do and, Nicole, I really want to make things better.'

'They're fine.' Nicole laughs. 'Grace, you're too sensitive at times. I am not angry with you, I'm angry with this Betty woman and I told her editor that.'

'What did she say?'

'She wanted to know if there was anything we could do to salvage the situation.'

'And you said?'

'Probably not. I told her that it was no longer anything to do with me, it was your call.'

'You want me to go back and continue?'

'No, I don't. If yesterday is anything to go by, I want you to forget about it, pretend you've never met her. But I know that Fiona sounded determined, so don't be surprised if they try to persuade you otherwise.' Now Grace laughs. 'In fact, Fiona seems to be more than a little concerned with this story. She said it was because she thinks that fidelity testing is a statement of feminism and she wants to run the best feature on it before any of the other magazines do. I didn't tell her that it has actually been documented before, but I think she's going to pull Betty by the hair and make her grovel or something.'

'Maybe that could be fun.'

'Grace, what are you thinking?'

'I don't know. I just know that for some reason she really got to me and I'd like to do something about it.'

'Honey, as I keep saying, it's up to you.'

'I'll have a think and let you know if I get any inspiration. Whatever happens, this isn't more important than the job.'

'Exactly.'

They turn their conversation away from Betty and towards the job that evening. It's not one that Grace relishes, because it is slightly unusual, and although morals don't score that high when catching cheaters, when testing men who haven't cheated, they do bug her. The woman who has hired her is a divorcee who has been dating the man in question for only three months. She does not think he is cheating but she thinks he would do, and that thought is tearing her apart. Nicole has had numerous conversations with the potential client before she would agree to the job. Her conclusion was that the woman really needed to do this, otherwise she would destroy her relationship before it got off the ground. They both hope that he turns her down; that would make Grace's day. Any man that turns her down would do that.

She thinks back to the second time she thought she was in love. It was after she started working in her secretarial role. There was a girl there, another secretary, called Helen, who took Grace under her wing and took her out. Helen was her best friend for ages. Her first ever best friend. She took Grace to a wine bar (it was the first time she had ever been to anywhere other than a pub or a nightclub, although she didn't betray this) and Grace met Ben.

Grace left many things behind when she left home. One was the upbringing. Although her accent was not exactly polished, she listened to people speaking and she thought about her words before she enunciated them. Now she comes across as well-spoken but that took her a few years to master. Helen (a girl from a middle-class background) taught her about hair, make-up and anything else she needed to know.

When Grace met Ben, she was a different Grace from the one who had been engaged to Dave. She still believed her personality was the same, if not a little more composed, but everything else had changed. Ben was gorgeous, with curly brown hair that flopped over his face, big hazel eyes and an 'orgasm' smile (Helen's evaluation). Grace believed she fell in love at first sight. He was wearing a smart suit, and it turned out he worked in the same industry. Helen went over to him and his friend and started speaking to them, leaving Grace, amazed at her confidence, speechless. However, they were invited to join them, and finally Grace found her voice, although it was still on the quiet side.

Helen discarded Ben's friend after a week, but by then Grace had submerged herself in her feelings for Ben. She had never met anyone like him. He was educated, professional, had been to private school (or it may have been public, but Grace did not understand the difference), he had lived in the country, and now had a well-paid job, a nice car (BMW), and was only twenty-six. He also was the first man to treat Grace in that way. He took her to dinner (and not the Harvester) and he sent her flowers – huge, huge bouquets rather than carnations from the petrol station. For her birthday (they had been together for six months) he bought her earrings, expensive earrings, and he took her for her very first trip abroad, to Paris.

She was so excited about travelling abroad and she made so many lists that she packed three times before she was satisfied. However, she had to hide the way she really felt behind a cool exterior. Grace had never managed to stop feeling ashamed about where she was from, so she didn't tell. She made her life out to be average, so people wouldn't ask too many questions. She longed to jump up and down, and shine on the outside the way she felt inside, but she didn't. She maintained an aura of cool.

She realised many things about herself when she was in a relationship with Ben. The first was that she was actually quite a snob although she had no grounds to be. When she was younger, she always fantasised that she was swapped at birth by accident, and although she was not the type of child to imagine that her parents were really the king and queen, she did think that they had only one child and they lived in a house with a garden. She was convinced that this was the case because she never felt as if she fitted in to her family, not the way her sister and brothers did. She always felt different and she believed she was. When she met Ben, although her childhood fantasies had long fled, she still knew that for some reason her new life was more natural to her than her old one ever had been.

She believed with all her heart that she loved Ben and she would do anything for him. She often did – cooked, cleaned, had the most imaginative sex, wore sexy underwear, bought him porn. She was the perfect girlfriend. Which is why, after a year, when he finished their relationship, she thought she was going to die.

It felt different from how it had done with Dave. There were no parallels to be drawn. There were two different girls and two different relationships. This was total despair, complete desolation, incomprehension and grief. She was beside herself; she had no idea what to do. She panicked that her old life would be coming to get her because Ben wasn't just a man, he was a symbol of the new improved Grace. Ben had ended their relationship for no good reason. He just decided that he didn't want commitment. Grace retracted into herself and wondered what was wrong with her. First Dave stole her money, and then Ben broke her heart – what was it with her? No matter how much Helen tried to reassure her that that was men for you, Grace refused to believe her. She believed the problem was her. The only thing she could do was to protect herself, so she covered her heart with a suit of armour and she started thinking about herself again.

What annoyed her was that she had achieved so much in the post-Dave period, and then she lost herself again with Ben. She was determined not to become a bitter, cynical woman, but she was also determined to make her life good for herself. The reality was, of course, that she didn't believe she would ever love anyone else but Ben. It did not take her long to realise that she did not love him, but what he was, but instead of liberating her, this realisation made her even more depressed.

So she worked hard, and ignored her misery for two years. Then it resurfaced, and instead of having a man as a culprit she left her job and became an infidelity detective.

Ben was her last serious relationship. She couldn't trust men, she didn't understand them, she wasn't good enough. All these reasons kept relationships, meaningful relationships, away. Also, she believed that Ben was the first real love and was up there on the top of her podium. He wasn't going anywhere. Especially as he gave her the perfect excuse to keep other men out.

Her phone rings and she answers it.

'Hi, it's Betty.' Now Grace could have predicted a number of people that might phone her today, but Betty would not have been on the list. She smiles because it is a surprise and she is in the mood for surprises.

'What do you want?' Just because she is smiling does not mean she needs to be civil.

'I need to talk to you.'

'About what?' Grace hopes that Betty is squirming. Betty hopes that Grace burns in hell.

'What happened between us. I really regret it.'

'Do you?' Grace tries to sound bored.

'I do. Can we talk?'

'Well, I'm a bit busy at the moment.'

'Can we meet? It might be easier face to face.'

'I'm not sure that's a good idea. Remember what happened the last time we were face to face?'

'I know. That's what I need to talk to you about. Please, Grace.'

Grace likes the begging tone that has entered Betty's voice. Meeting up might be fun. 'Sure.' She figures that if she capitulates quickly, Betty will think she is so reasonable. Lure the enemy into a false sense of security.

'Really? When?'

'Tomorrow. Meet me for breakfast.' Grace rattles off the name and address of a café that she likes and hangs up.

What a turn-up, she thinks, Betty grovelling for a meeting. After her conversation with Nicole, Grace expected this. She didn't expect it quite so soon, however. Betty's boss has made her do this, and she probably hates every minute of it. This makes Grace love every minute of it. She is going to enjoy herself. After all, she deserves it.

Betty's face is so red when she replaces the handset that Hannah is giving her a funny look.

'What?' Betty screams.

Hannah goes into a mock cower. 'You look like you're about to explode.'

'Well, I fucking well might fucking explode. Shit, it'd be easier than having to apologise to that bitch.'

'So why do it?'

'I have no choice. Either I apologise or rot in crap story hell.'

'Ah, not much of a choice.'

'No, hell or hell.'

'Is she really that bad?'

'Worse. And the thing is that she is going to enjoy this. Shit, I haven't been this humiliated in years.'

'Just think, though, as soon as you get this story, then you will never have to see her again.'

'True. It's just a shitting shame that Fiona is so set on this. God, I wish someone else was covering it.'

'Betty, you're turning red again.'

'I'm going to get some water. Maybe I'll drown myself while I'm at it.'

'You couldn't do that. What about Johnny?'

'No, you're right. I might be having a bad time but at least I have him.' Betty smiles. 'And we've got this party at the weekend, so maybe I can get over myself long enough to enjoy it.'

'Well, I'm looking forward to it anyway.'

'So am I,' Betty lies.

She was fine about the party last week. She and Johnny were having fun organising it, and she spoke to people she hasn't seen since her wedding. But all seems tarnished now. And she blames Grace for that.

A breakfast grovelling and then finish the story and never see her again, just as Hannah said. That is a positive thought, and one that she will hang on to as tightly as she can.

Then her life, the life she is so happy with, can go back to how it was pre-Grace.

Grace carries on without giving Betty too much thought. But when she does, it is with frustration that she realises she still has no idea what she will do to get her own back, or even if it is worth it.

Chapter Thirteen

It is raining again as Betty leaves and she begins to see that as a characteristic of her time with Grace, a kind of extra punishment, although she feels she is being punished enough.

Last night she told Johnny about her meeting with Fiona and he, characteristically sensible, told her just to swallow her pride and do it. However, at the same time he was supportive and said that her feelings were more important than any job. It had made her feel better about what she was about to do.

She loves features, and she loves *Modern Woman*. She wanted to be doing what she is doing since she was eighteen, so she has actually achieved her goal. Despite the fact that her parents weren't sure that she should go to university ('they're not our type of people'), she went, she grew in confidence, and for the first time in her life she thought she knew who she was. It was hard work; it was frightening. Leaving the small town, taking the train to London. Living in the city, the huge city that always threatened to engulf her. She worked from the minute she got there, on her course, her popularity, everything. Then she fought afterwards to get the job she wanted. It didn't fall into her lap. She made sacrifices, her parents being one. She didn't have time to visit them and the cynicism of their limited world scared her. She never had proper relationships with men because she was too terrified that they might distract her from her goal. Now, she is reaping the rewards for those years, and she isn't going to let one woman ruin it. She has worked hard and she has always been sure she is in the right job. Her conflict about being Modern Woman and Married Woman has nothing to do with it. The reason she feels any conflict at all is because although she loves being married more, she still loves *Modern Woman* a lot. What worries her is what is happening to her now. The two are crossing over and that isn't something she can control. Like water-divining poles they are gravitating towards each other, meeting in the middle and the result is something that Betty is scared of. She has always been scared of water.

Grace worked the night before and is tired. She is also disappointed. The man she was testing was all over her like a rash in minutes and she didn't even approach him; he'd approached her. Yet another cheater, yet another one to add to her generalisation. All men are cheats. They either cheat or leave you. Still, Grace believes he is out there, not just one of him but a number of them. The men that are faithful. She just doesn't get to meet them.

When she started being a honey trapper, her boss told her that the most important thing is for her not to be cynical and bitter, especially as it's the sort of job that could ruin her private life. Grace did not tell him that her private life had already been ruined, and although she wasn't bitter she was certainly cynical. She soon learnt what he meant. The number of men that were willing to cheat surprised her, to say the least, and could easily have turned her into a man hater, so she worked hard for it not to. Nicole has become her role model in this: her marriage is happy, therefore there is hope. Anyway, just because she knows she will never be able to fall in love, that doesn't mean she doesn't like men or find them useful. So she plays it as a game. One day a man will resist her and when that day comes, the game will be won. But that doesn't mean that at times she doesn't feel down in her boots about the men. She just has to make sure that she soon pulls herself out of it, because otherwise it will surely send her mad. Whatever, it is her job and it is important to her. Betty should not be allowed to try to ruin it. Grace won't let her.

As she opens the door to the café she sees Betty, almost cowering in a corner, and cheers up. All thoughts of last night forgotten, she decides that today is going to be a good day – unfortunately not for Betty.

'Have you ordered?' Grace asks, sitting down. She hasn't rehearsed the meeting in her head and has no idea how it is going to go.

'No. I thought I'd wait for you.' Betty smiles. She has done nothing but practise what she will say. She thought it through, and rehearsed it, but she is terrified it might go wrong. Grace picks up a menu and hides behind it.

When the waitress comes over, Grace orders coffee and toast. Betty follows.

'Look, I don't want to waste your time or beat around the bush,' Betty says, once the waitress is out of earshot.

'Good.'

'I'm here to apologise.'

'Right, and it's that simple?' For once, Grace really is enjoying being with Betty.

'No, I know it isn't. I was wrong. I was supposed to be shadowing you, not judging you, and as for the thing with the client, I know that I should never have done that.'

'You lost me a job.'

'I'll pay for it. It's only fair.' Betty can feel her insides churning and she also feels hot. Humiliation is physical. It is also uncomfortable. She has no idea how much money a job is worth. She hadn't got that far.

'No. I don't want your money.' Grace is having a fine old time. She has the upper hand and she likes it.

'What can I do to make it up to you?'

'Nothing.'

'But there must be something?'

'Betty, tell me, why are you apologising?'

'Because I was wrong.'

'And not because your editor told you to?'

'How do you know?'

'It's obvious. We haven't really got on from the moment we met. There was always this twang of disapproval in your voice and a fleck of it in your eyes. You wound me up, I made you do something you didn't want to do; I embarrassed you. Then you lost me a client. So, by my reckoning it's my turn.'

'I'm sorry you see it like that, but I deserve whatever you have in mind.' Betty detests being humble. She detests Grace for making her so, and also Fiona, because it is all her fault.

'Simple, I'm not going to do your article.'

'But, Grace, we have so much good stuff already.'

'Yeah, and I'm pulling out. Also if you use any of this "good stuff" you have, then I'll sue you.' Betty opens her mouth and closes it again because the waitress approaches with their coffee.

'Can I have an orange juice as well?' Grace asks.

'I'm not sure there is any point to me staying any longer,' Betty says.

'Fine, go then. I'm still going to finish my breakfast.'

Betty starts to get up, but then she sits back down again and tells her temper to behave.

'Can we talk about it?' Betty's practice has proved useless. She is feeling desperate, and panic about her job is very real.

'I thought we had.'

'Look, Grace, I really need to rescue this. I can't take back what I've done, but I wish I could. I need to finish the feature and my editor wants a case study of you in order to do that.'

'Well, that sounds to me like we're even. You lost me a client, I lose you a by-line.'

'It's more than one by-line. If I don't do this then she's going to relegate me to all the shit stories.'

Grace laughs.

'It's not funny.' Betty hates the way her voice sounds, all whiny and babyish, and she thinks she might cry.

'Yes it is. You bullied me, and you bullied my client. If it's one thing I can't stand it's bullies. You got what you deserved.'

'You hit me.' Anger is welling up again.

Grace laughs again. 'After you called me a slut.'

'Well, you made me talk to that slimeball of a man all night.' Betty's voice is raised, her earlier grovelling forgotten.

'Because that's my job. I was trying to get you to understand more what I do.' Grace knows that this isn't exactly the truth.

'Oh, I understand it perfectly.'

'Look how quickly the mask has slipped. "Oh, Grace, I am so so sorry." Are you hell? You still feel exactly the same.'

'So what if I do?' Betty spits.

'So, it looks like your job is going to be a bit shitty from now on.'

They are shouting again. War is raging. Betty realises that she has blown it. Grace is still having fun.

'I'm sorry.' Betty calms herself down.

'So you keep saying.' The toast arrives with the orange juice. Grace looks at them both. 'I don't think I'll bother.'

Flashing a large smile at Betty she grabs her coat and her umbrella and she leaves the café. She gets to the door and looks back once. Betty sits there with her head hung dejectedly. Grace, one: the smug married bully, nil.

Chapter Fourteen

Being cowardly, Betty goes back to the office and sends Fiona an email saying that Grace isn't quite ready to forgive her. She practically cowers under her desk for the rest of the day, but to her surprise Fiona doesn't respond. She then sees her leaving the office without so much as a glance her way, and she wonders if, after all, Fiona will let the story die. She prays that she will as she carries on with her work.

Grace is sitting at home, having completed her work. She feels a final sense of relief at Betty being out of her life, knowing that no matter what she says she will not let her back in. She doesn't ever want to see her again. She feels bad about Nicole, and the lost publicity but not bad enough to contemplate working with 'that woman'.

She makes herself some lunch and a cup of tea and takes it into the living room where she switches on the television, something she rarely does. She finds a soap opera, one that she doesn't recognise, and she watches it while she eats. Getting totally caught up in a plot she can barely fathom, she almost jumps out of her skin when the buzzer goes. She prays that it isn't Betty, but she goes to answer it anyway.

'Hello,' she says into the intercom.

'Grace, it's Fiona.'

'Who? Oh, yes, of course. Betty's boss.'

'What are you doing here?'

'You think I could come in and explain?'

Grace shakes her head and buzzes her in. She has to admit, as she stands with her door open, that she is curious.

Fiona smiles at her, and immediately Grace understands Betty's desperation for forgiveness. With her designer clothes, her heavily made-up face and good jewellery, Fiona does not look as if she is to be messed with. For a moment, Grace feels intimidated, until she remembers that Fiona wants something from her.

Without speaking, Grace leads her into her living room, where Fiona sits down, uninvited, on her sofa.

'Grace, thank you for seeing me.'

'How did you know where to find me?'

'Your address is in our file. Betty's file.'

'Well, I told her that I have no intention of going back to the feature, my boss is happy with my decision, so if you've come here with the intention of changing my mind, you won't.'

'Um, Betty said as much. But I didn't come for that.'

'You didn't?'

'No, I came to apologise.'

'Apologise?'

'Yes, for Betty. I know what she can be like and after hearing what she said about you – well, I feel terrible that I, or the magazine, subjected you to that.'

'What she said?'

'Yes, you know, about you being a marriage wrecker and a slut and all those other horrible things.'

'She said them about me to you?' Grace knows Betty's views, and she isn't really surprised that she has said things to Fiona, if only to save her skin.

'Yes, well, me and the rest of the office, actually. She's terribly indiscreet. Anyway, I thought it only fair that I apologise.'

'She's been bad-mouthing me to everyone at your magazine?' Grace is losing her calm and anger is welling up.

'Yes, and her friends and her husband, although I'm sure you knew that already. She's not been very fair to you.'

'That's an understatement.'

'It is, I know. But, Grace, I want you to know that I don't hold with her views and I am dealing with her.'

'I hope you fire her.'

'Um, well, I can see you might want that, but I can't. The employment laws in this country are a joke. It's impossible to fire people without paying them. Anyway, you can rest assured that she will be punished by me.'

'I wish I could get my hands on her.'

'Oh, I don't think that would be a good idea. I hear you had a little fight.'

'She lost me a client, she judged me constantly; I couldn't help it.'

'Quite right. I'm sure I'd have done the same in your position. She really, really hates you.'

'Well, I thought it was more that she hated what I did.'

'Oh, yes, and that, of course. But she took against you quite severely and I have no idea why.'

'Neither do I.'

'Anyway, I can see that you're not a stuck-up bitch.'

'She said that?'

'Oh, I didn't come here to tell you that. I'm sorry.'

'What are you going to do to her?'

'Well, I'm going to give her a few horrible articles to work on.'

'That's it?'

'What else can I do? I mean, I'm her boss and I can't do anything that isn't professional. I know she was wrong to describe you as a vulture picking the eyes out of women—'

'What? What the hell does that mean?'

'Oh, you know, how you hover around men, taking them away from their women and then discarding them, and even making them pay. I know that isn't how it is, but Betty, well, as I said, she's very judgemental.'

'I don't believe this. I knew she hated me, but to be saying this to everyone . . .'

'I know. That girl needs to be taught a lesson. Oh well, I've said what I came to say, so I'd better leave you.'

'Hang on. You came here to apologise and you've made me angrier. I'm not continuing with the feature, you know.'

'I wish I could persuade you otherwise.'

'You can't.'

'Um, how about if you could get your own back on her?'

'Fiona, I'm angry but I'm not vindictive.'

'I know, but, well, I think that you should definitely do something about her.'

'Why?'

'Because she is slandering you all over town. That's why.'

'The bitch.' Grace is beginning to get caught up in Fiona's web.

'Exactly. You know what? If I was you I'd do something.'

'I just want to forget her.'

'Of course, but you won't. I know these things. The problem is that she's going to haunt you unless you do something.'

'You think so?'

'She needs to be brought down a peg or two.'

'I agree with that, but I don't see what I can do.'

'Honey trap her husband.'

'What?'

'A bet.' Fiona stands up, jangling her jewellery as she does so. 'Betty thinks her marriage is so perfect that she has the right to look down her nose at you. So, you propose a bet whereby you try to seduce her husband and in return you let her finish her feature.'

'Don't be ridiculous.'

'Fine then, leave it. Let the perfect wife haunt you for the rest of your life. Let her win.'

'But she hasn't won because I refused to do the feature.'

'You believe that? Actually, Grace, by refusing to do the feature you have just given her more fuel to bad-mouth you.'

'I have?'

'Which, believe me, she is doing. What I would do if I were you would be to challenge her to this bet. She gives you some time – say, three months off the top of my head – to try to seduce her husband. That way, she learns properly about what you do, and how serious it is, and she will also think twice before belittling you.'

'I don't see how that would work.'

'Well, it's simple. She thinks she has the perfect marriage, you and I know that she's probably wearing rose-coloured glasses, so you prove it to her.'

'And if he refuses to be seduced?'

'Well then, she will still have endured the agony of not knowing and she'll think twice about treating you badly in the future.'

'That's evil.'

'Yes, but she is being evil about you. Anyway, I really ought to go. I've got a magazine to run, after all.'

'She's really been horrible about me?'

'I'm afraid so.'

'To everyone?'

'Yes.' Fiona moves towards the front door.

'You think this would work? I mean, you think she'd stop being such a bully?'

'I do, but it's up to you. Give me a call.'

Before Grace has the chance to question her further, she has gone.

Chapter Fifteen

Grace is enjoying an evening with Oliver, who got back from New York earlier than expected. He turned up at her flat with champagne and a hamper from Fortnum's, and although she was expecting him, she was almost overjoyed to see him. They take the hamper to the living room and eat on the rug, just like a picnic, although Grace insists on plates.

'This is so nice,' she says, leaning over to kiss him.

'Glad you like it. I knew better than to try to get you to go out.'

'Good. I've had a shit week.'

'Work?'

'No. Remember the journalist that was supposed to profile me? Well, we had a row and I walked out on her story.'

'Tell me more.'

Grace does. She tells Oliver the whole story, omitting the part about Fiona's visit. She hasn't quite processed that information herself yet. Oliver, who usually finds everything bar his business boring, looks intrigued. 'God, this woman disapproves of what you do and she actually said so in front of a potential client?'

'Yes.'

'Well then, I'd sue her.'

'Nicole threatened to, but I don't think that's the best course of action.'

'What do you have in mind?'

'I thought I'd teach her a lesson.'

'How?'

'I don't know. But I'm sick of people like her, you know, middle-class, safe people, never taken more of a risk than wearing odd underwear once or twice, looking down their noses at me.' She thinks it might be a good idea to test the water with Oliver, although deep down she knows he will advise against it. For now, she decides to keep the details to herself, until she reaches a decision.

'That's what she's doing?'

'Undoubtedly. She practically called me a whore, actually I think she might have done. So I am going to teach the smug married cow a lesson.'

'How?'

'I have no idea.'

'Well, let's look at it logically. This woman hates you because of what you do. And you hate her because of who she is.'

'Where is this going?'

'I'm just trying to think. Grace, do you want to be doing what you're doing for ever?'

'What has that got to do with anything?'

'Just humour me.'

'OK, well, no, because when I'm grey and old and have saggy tits and my false teeth fly out whenever I try to talk, I don't think the men will fall for me.'

'But before then?'

'I don't know.'

'You know how we always talk about love and you tell me that you can't fall in love, which is why you'll never marry me?'

'Yes, but I didn't want to talk about us.' Grace feels defensive when Oliver brings up the question of their future.

'Are you sure you don't just feel threatened by her?'

'Why would I?'

'Because she is everything you're not.'

'You mean, she's normal.'

'Gracie, don't be so defensive. Look at it like this: you are both sitting on opposite sides. You are happy not being married, she is happy being married. She's the anti-Grace and you're the anti-her. It's simple. She probably feels threatened by you and you feel threatened by her.'

'I do not. She's just vile, that's all.'

'But you never normally care what people think about you.'

'Well, I do now. I must be getting sensitive in my old age.' Grace stands up, abandoning the hamper food for a moment, before she decides that having a row with Oliver would just be silly and, besides, she is still hungry. Oliver smiles.

'Let's not row. I haven't seen you for ages.' He leans over and feeds her some pâté.

'OK, let's forget about *her* and have some fun then.' Grace looks at him seductively and he is a fallen man.

Betty is getting ready for her party. She still hasn't heard from Fiona, and she doesn't want to think about Grace any more. She hopes, in the wilds of her optimistic imagination, that on Monday she'll receive a call from Grace, agreeing to resume the profile. But that is only in her dreams. Now, she still has a major problem on her hands: how to get Grace to agree to let her run the story. How to pacify her rapacious boss, because it is only Fiona's greed for a good story that is causing her all these problems and now not only is Grace a villain but so is Fiona. Betty feels as if her mind is slowly slipping away.

'What am I going to do?' Betty is wailing at Alison. She is trying to decide what to wear at the same time as trying to figure out what she is going to do about Grace. Johnny has banned her from talking about it as part of his plan to get her to enjoy the evening. However, Alison knows nothing of the ban. Johnny and Matt have gone to the bar to set up, leaving Betty to discuss her dilemma with her best friend.

'Firstly, pick an outfit. You're making me dizzy with all this indecision.' Betty is finding it hard to focus on the party. She would rather be staying in and trying to figure out how to salvage her career. But she refuses to let Johnny down, so she is trying to make an effort. She is also trying to stop herself from moaning, but that isn't proving easy. Eventually she settles on a pale pink dress and some strappy sandals. The final effect is good.

'I love that dress,' Alison says wistfully. She envies Betty's style, which is straight off the pages of her magazine. Alison is far too scared of looking silly so she keeps her clothes simple. When Alison first met Betty, she was fashionable but not overtly so, but she has seen her transform. Now, Alison contents herself with being in her friend's fashion shadow.

'Yeah, well, I am trying to look good even though I feel like shit.'

'Betty, are you sure you're not exaggerating the seriousness of this?'

'No I am not! Fiona, who is not coming tonight, thankfully, said that if I don't persuade Grace to do the profile she'll demote me.'

'Can she do that?'

'Well, not officially, but she can make me do all the worst stories for the rest of my life.'

'Oh. Well, you could get another job.'

'I shouldn't have to. I love my job. Normally I do.'

'Oh dear, you really have to get her back on side.'

Betty looks at Alison but decides to be nice; it is not her fault she is being completely unhelpful.

'Yeah, I do, and I have no idea how.'

'Flowers?'

'I think it might take more than that.'

'Fine, but it's a start. Why don't you go to her flat, take flowers and refuse to leave until she talks to you.'

'I'm not trying to woo her.'

'I know, but what else can you do? If you call her, she'll just hang up. Are you sure you can't just tell Fiona that you won't do it?'

'No. I really can't. I know what she's like. When she wants something she never lets up and she always, always gets her way. I know what she'd do. She'd put one of the junior writers on to it, just to humiliate me. Shit, I hate her.'

'Fiona?'

'And Grace. I hate them both.'

'So you're going to turn up to her flat with flowers?'

'I guess I will.' Could life get any more shameful?

Betty leaves for the party with the intention of not talking about Grace. She has always managed to work things out; that is the reward for her hard work. She will sort this out; she has to.

Grace sits upright, having just experienced divine inspiration She has been unable to sleep and she's made her decision.

'Oliver, are you awake?' She knows he is not, but also knows he soon will be.

'What?' he mumbles, his voice drunk with sleep.

'Oliver, wake up. I know what to do.'

'Is there something wrong?'

'No, the opposite. I know what to do about smug Betty.'

'And you felt you had to wake me to tell me. What is the time, anyway?'

Grace looks at the clock: it is four a.m. She decides not to share this information.

'I didn't tell you everything. Betty's boss came to see me and I've been thinking about it all night.' She is indignant that Oliver seems disinterested. Although, he is interested, it's just he's more afraid of the obsession that she seems to have developed.

'Well, tell me then.' He knows that the only chance of sleep is if he hears her out.

'I'm going to seduce her husband.'

'Grace, that is evil. You're not a nasty person normally.' Oliver is tired and angry. Things are going too far and he does not understand why she is being this vindictive. What he loves most about Grace is that she really is genuinely sweet. Not in a weak way, but in a lovable, amusing, beautiful way. As a character evaluation it is partly true. Grace is not malicious; she is amiable, desperate for approval from those she cares about. But there is another side to her that Oliver, and the other people in her life, do not see, and that is the determined, ambitious side. Not ambitious in a career sense, but in a personal one. In her desire not to have to face the past, and certainly not go back to it.

'Fiona suggested it. She told me that Betty has been telling everyone who'll listen how awful I am, and she suggested teaching her a lesson. That's exactly what I'm going to do. I'll challenge her to a duel.'

'Am I asleep? Am I dreaming?' Oliver rubs his eyes, but he knows that he has lost. Grace is alert, manic, even. She is living her plan and there is nothing he can do to reach her.

'Not a real duel, but a figurative one. What I am going to do is this. I will agree to do her profile.' A smile appears on Grace's lips. Oliver gives up trying to get the story over and done with quickly and, wide awake, sits up to face her.

'Explain.' Grace explains Fiona's idea to him.

'I can't believe it. Hell, Grace, it's horrible – worse than horrible. It's evil.'

'Which will serve her right, because she was evil to me. Oliver, I don't expect anyone has ever picked on you, told you you were useless, stupid, boring, that you'd never make anything of your life. Well, that happened to me all the time, and the worst thing was that I nearly believed them. All of them. Whenever I was called a name I thought they must know something I didn't. My childhood consisted of me being stripped of my entire confidence, and my adulthood has consisted of me trying to build it back up. She tried to take it way again and I can't let her.'

Grace has tears in her eyes and Oliver is startled by her outburst. But he still can't believe that this woman deserves what Grace is suggesting.

'Then don't go near her again. Grace, this is madness. You are going to get yourself into trouble.'

'Relax, it'll be fine. A bet, a bet to end all bets.' Grace's composure is back, as if the outburst had never occurred. Although she was reluctant, she has finally seen that Fiona is right.

'What if she says no?'

'Then she'll be in trouble at work. You see, I really can't lose.'

'Why is ruining this woman's life so important to you?'

'She treats me like dirt and she condemns my job.'

'But a bet to seduce her husband? That's really low.'

'Oliver, I didn't ask for your approval and if you really want to be like that then you can get out of my bed.'

'Grace, don't start fighting. We'll talk in the morning.' Oliver turns on his side and shuts his eyes, unable to figure just who the woman next to him is.

Grace faces the other way, worrying that she is doing the wrong thing. She finally falls asleep.

They both sleep well into the morning. Oliver wakes with a start. He feels disorientated and when he looks at the clock, he feels even more disharmonious. He never sleeps past eight in the morning and it is ten. He remembers the argument with Grace, or the near-argument, and he pokes her in the ribs.

'Ow.' Grace sits upright for the second time.

'I overslept. I have to get going. I've to get home, pack and catch a plane to Frankfurt this afternoon.' His tone is colder than normal and Grace feels it.

'Finc, go then. Leave me to sleep.'

'Like you did to me last night?' He gets out of bed, pulls on the clothes he has folded neatly on Grace's chair and dresses. 'Grace, I really think you're making a big mistake here. You could ruin her life, sure, but how will you live with yourself?'

Grace refuses to respond. She tucks her head deeper into her pillow like a child. She hates him for being uptight about what she is doing. She wishes she had never told him.

'I mean it, Grace, this will all end in tears.'

Oliver leaves the house without looking back. Angry with her, angry with himself for being angry with her. Unable to do anything about it and unsure of why he feels the way he feels.

Grace sleeps for another hour and then gets up to feed her fish. She is still angry with Oliver. She doesn't need Oliver to tell her she is doing the right thing. She is independent and as such has learnt to be responsible for her own decisions and her own actions. She cannot expect everyone to understand her; after all, she keeps too much back. But she knows what she is doing, and she knows that it is right. What is most irritating is that Grace has not let anyone get under her skin for years, and now that is exactly where Betty is. All Grace's men are kept at arm's length, so that even Oliver storming out will not hurt her – not properly – but Betty is in there, inside, and Grace wants her out.

Although it is Sunday, she calls Nicole.

'Hi, Gracie, what's up?'

'You sound more like a gangster rapper every day,' Grace says.

'If I knew what one was I might agree, but I don't. Why are you calling me? What's wrong?' Nicole asks.

'Well, I wanted to apologise for the fuss I made about the *MW* journalist. I overreacted a bit.'

'Well, she did lose us a client.'

'I know, but I did sort of provoke her by making her get involved in the case.'

'Yeah, that was naughty. So you're going to do the feature now?'

'Well, I am, but she has to agree to something first.'

'What are you doing?'

Grace explains about Fiona's visit and her realisation that the bet is the way forward. When she finishes, she hears Nicole take a sharp intake of breath.

'My God, that girl *has* upset you. I'm not sure; are you sure?'

'Absolutely, and Oliver has already fed me the lecture so if you want to do the same, then don't.' Grace knows she is being a bit sharp with Nicole but she is tired and defensive.

'I wouldn't dream of it.' Nicole actually likes it when Grace stands up for herself, but it also worries her. 'But I would say be careful. And if you really are sure then you have my blessing. But you should question Fiona's motives for suggesting it and think carefully about it.' Nicole hears the determination in Grace's voice and is undecided how to talk her out of it without alienating her.

'I wasn't sure you'd approve.'

'I'm not saying I approve, I'm saying I understand. Now, you need to set rules of the bet.' Nicole also knows that she might be needed at some point to pick up the pieces. She curses Fiona and wonders just what sort of boss she really is.

Grace takes the piece of paper Fiona left her with her mobile number on it, goes to the study and dials.

'Hello.'

'Fiona, it's Grace.'

'Hi, Grace. So have you had time to think?'

'I have and I agree.'

'You agree to doing the feature?' Fiona's lips spread into a greedy smile.

'And the bet.'

'Good girl. Now here's what you need to do . . .'

Fiona outlines the plan that she has carefully formed, and Grace accepts everything she says. She doesn't even know if she is doing the right thing but she knows that she is going to do it anyway.

Grace calls her at three o'clock, the details of her plan now fully formed. She is actually quite excited; Fiona managed to fire her up. She also managed to get her to agree to keep Fiona out of it and make Betty think that the bet was all her idea. Here is the potential challenge her life needs. The challenge no longer offered by her job.

The phone is answered straight away.

'Hello.'

'Betty, it's Grace.'

'Right.' Betty sounds confused.

'I hope you don't mind me calling on a Sunday, but I thought that perhaps we should talk.'

'Great, great.' Betty cannot inject the enthusiasm she feels into her voice because a storm is raging in her head. Grace doesn't notice; she is too caught up in her plans.

'Can you meet me for breakfast at nine tomorrow morning? Same place as last time.'

'Of course. Have you changed your mind?'

'We can talk tomorrow.'

'Right. Can you . . .'

'Yes?'

'Can you give me a clue what it's about?'

'All I want to do is to sort things out so we're both happy.' Grace smiles as she puts down the phone.

'Who was that?' Johnny comes up behind Betty.

'The honey-trap woman.'

'What did she want?'

'To meet. She said that she wanted to sort things out and that we would both be happy.' Betty tries very hard to smile, but is unable to, due to the fact that her head feels as if it is going to fall off.

'I can't believe how awful you look.'

'Thanks. Don't you just know how to make a girl feel good?'

'Sorry, honey, but you did go a bit far last night.'

'I got drunk at the party that was your idea. So it's all your fault.'

'I didn't hold your head back and pour the alcohol down your throat.'

'You may as well have done.'

Betty cringes as she tries to remember what happened at the party, but past about ten o'clock she cannot. Johnny, always one to remember everything, told her that she ranted about 'the honey-trap bitch' to anyone who would listen. She has no idea if she fell over and she has a horrible feeling she was sick at some stage. But she does not want to ask about that, just in case. Thirty-one, and behaving like a teenager.

She woke that morning with a head that felt as if it had been repeatedly hit with a heavy object. Her mouth felt dry and rough, like sandpaper. Nausea bubbled away in her stomach. She was fully aware that she had the hangover from hell. And worse than that, the hangover from hell followed her being drunk as a lush, leading to extreme memory loss and an acute sense of embarrassment.

It led to a row. Johnny told her that she hadn't made an effort, wasn't sober enough to talk to all the people she hadn't seen in ages. He accused her of letting 'this woman' take over her life, and sulked all morning until she felt well enough to apologise and try to explain.

'Johnny, you didn't know me when I was younger. I know I told you about it, but you didn't see me,' she said. 'The thing was that I was really ugly. Bad hair, bad teeth, bad eyes – I had the whole package. You know when we watch those American teen films and they always have the class geek? Well, they make me want to cry because I was like that, and I got treated like shit.' Despite her throbbing head, her words were managing to perform. 'When I was about sixteen, my teeth were fixed, I discovered and could just afford contact lenses and I grew in confidence, but I could never quite get rid of the chip I felt. I remember when I first went to university, and when I met Alison I was so serious, determined to succeed, but really chippy about my past. I was defensive and, well, actually I was a bore. Alison taught me to let go of the past and enjoy the fact that I was liked. You see, I'd never been liked before, so it was this huge novelty, and at the same time I couldn't quite believe it. Anyway, she takes me back there, that's all. She takes me back to the ugly unconfident, unpopular girl, and I vowed I wouldn't go back there.'

'But how?' Johnny softened and stroked her hair. He knew how hard Betty had found it – she had been candid with him about her insecurities when they first met – and although he didn't often see her as someone who would be bullied, there were times when the scars were still visible. He found it hard to be angry with his wife at the best of times, but especially when she was vulnerable.

'She just does. Her confidence, her poise, her job, destroying people's lives – only someone arrogant would ever think they could do that. Her upbringing was perfect; she has always been beautiful. She was the type of girl that made my life a misery, that meant I had to rebuild myself. I don't fully understand, but she's there, inside, trying to make me feel the way I used to feel and I can't, Johnny, I am terrified of being there again.' Betty cried and cried and Johnny held her.

*

Johnny makes tea after the phone call.

'I'm never drinking again.' Betty utters the overfamiliar statement that no one ever truly means.

'Of course you're not.' He pats her bottom, and hands her a cup.

'Did you enjoy the party?' Despite the hangover, she is relieved. Yesterday she believed her career was over, due to Grace, which is why she drank so much, but now there might be a chance to save it. She hates Grace even more for making her wait.

'Yeah, it was good to catch up with everyone. We should make more of an effort.'

'But time is a commodity in short supply.'

'Blimey, hung over and still able to utter wise words.'

'Shut up. You know what I mean. There is no way that we could see everyone, even if we wanted to.'

'Not all the time.'

'Anyway, are you so unhappy with our lives?'

'No. I just think it's a shame that we don't see people we used to be close to. I know it's inevitable, but it's sad.'

'Being a grown-up isn't easy.'

'Well, maybe that's why you weren't one last night.'

Betty swipes at Johnny. 'For that, you can take me out for pizza.'

'My God, all you've done today is eat.'

'Well, I need it. Besides, I need to keep my strength up for tomorrow's breakfast meeting with the bitch.'

'Are you sure? I mean, if she gets to you that much is it really worth it?'

'You know how I feel about my job.'

'Yes, but you know how I feel about you. I'm worried.'

'Don't be. I won't let her in any more. The marriage-wrecking whore will not hurt me, will not make me feel bad about myself.' Betty smiles. She will not tell Johnny how threatened she feels by her. That is one piece of information she will keep to herself.

'What I love about you is that you have to grovel to her but you're still slagging her off.'

'Oh, darling, you have to be willing to be two-faced in my business.' She kisses him on the cheek, determined to show him that she can handle it, that she will not take it seriously, and she leads him out of the house.

Chapter Sixteen

Grace tries to push her reservations away. After all, this is part of her revenge. It makes perfect sense. It's a long time since she has felt so strongly about anything. The rage from her past, she thought she had buried. But it must have been simmering and now has resurfaced. Betty was the trigger, that much she is certain of. That is why she must do this, although at times she feels ashamed; she thought she was bigger than she is. It's not often that someone like Grace is given the opportunity to get one over on someone like Betty. That is how she justifies it, so she is determined to be in control, and she is determined that this will be fun, although she knows it probably won't be. She is caught up in her contradictions, but there is no going back. Whatever the outcome of the bet, this will restore her belief in her self-worth. The same self-worth that Betty is trying to steal. Despite her feelings, she is trying hard to believe that she is doing the right thing.

She wears a pair of jeans and a plain white shirt for her breakfast meeting. She is smiling like a clown as she makes her way there. She giggles aloud on the bus, prompting strange looks, but she feels better than she has in ages. For once she is taking control, and defending what is important to her. She is no longer scared of the bullies.

If Betty's husband is as devoted as she makes out, then the bet will be one hell of a challenge. Grace gives herself a fifty per cent chance of success, which is an evaluation based on her general experience of men and what Betty has told her about him. Although if she fails, Betty will be even smugger, she will definitely have experienced doubts and insecurity, and therefore will not be so quick to judge in future. The other point is that if he turns her down she will have met a man who doesn't cheat because he loves his wife, and that will restore her faith in men. It may even remove the figurative block she has that prevents her from falling in love. Which is why the fifty per cent chance of failure makes her just as happy as the fifty per cent chance of winning.

Either way she will win. Betty does not need to know that. That information belongs to Grace. All she has to do now is to get Betty to agree to it.

They face each other in the café, waiting. Betty looks nervous; her face is twitching. Grace orders coffee and then takes her time choosing breakfast, even though she ends up ordering just toast. Betty is trying to smile but her face feels as if it is going to crack from the effort. She can see how much Grace is enjoying herself and all Betty wants to do is to jump across the table and smack her in the mouth (a very un-Betty thing to do). But instead she tries to break through the pain that her smile is causing her and she sits on her hands, just in case.

'How was your weekend?' Grace asks.

'Great, thanks. Yours?' Betty has entered a world where small talk happens only to mask the real reason behind such false conversation. A world where the anticipation of the pain gives pleasure to the administer of the pain. When Betty was younger she always believed that dentists were sadists who would make everything last longer to prolong the pain. As she grew older she switched the accusation to the beautician who waxes her bikini line. Now it is Grace.

'Oh, it was all right. I had a row with my lover.' Now Betty is stunned. Grace is offering her personal information. She needs to tread carefully. If she lets her defences down then she will be in trouble.

'The one I met?' Polite, but wary.

'No, another one. Anyway, I won't bore you with the details.' The coffee and toast arrive and both women stare at each other as it is placed on the table in front of them. When the waitress leaves Grace waits for Betty to take a bite of her toast before she speaks.

'I'll do your profile, but I do have a condition.' Betty stares at her with her mouth full. She cannot speak, which was Grace's intention. 'Because you hurt my feelings, really. You tried to make me out to be cheap and I'm not. So, in order to do your little story, you have to agree to a bet.'

'A bet?' Betty has discarded the rest of her toast, she can see that it is being used to keep her at a disadvantage. She begins to hate the toast. She glances longingly at her mug of coffee but doesn't dare to take a sip. Just in case.

'Yes, you know, a wager.'

'I don't understand.' Betty is confused and Grace is playing with her.

'A gamble, Betty.'

'Gambling what?'

It is time to put her out of her misery. Grace smiles. 'You give me three months to seduce your husband. Of course, if he's as devoted as you make out, he won't be interested, but if he isn't, then you will perhaps look differently at me before you judge me.'

Betty laughs. She laughs loudly. She has never heard anything more ridiculous in her life. Her fake smile and politeness have fled in disgust.

'You have to be joking. You're mad, mental, completely insane. There is no way, in a zillion years, that I will even consider anything like that.' She laughs again, loudly. She has never heard anything more ludicrous in her life.

*

'I accept your bet,' Betty says.

She is in the office, on the phone to Grace a few days after the breakfast. She has tried everything to avoid agreeing, bar speaking to Johnny about it, and she can barely believe the words she hears herself saying. It has been nothing short of agonising, and her hatred of Grace and what Grace stands for has intensified. She has swung between deciding to quit her job, to crying because she doesn't want to. She is officially in hell.

She left the café in disgust and went straight to work. There, she requested an urgent meeting with Fiona and was kept waiting for an agonising half-hour.

'So?' Fiona started as soon as Betty walked through the door.

'Fi, we've had loads of stories go wrong – why is this so important?' Betty sat down, when she was eventually granted an audience.

'I love this story. It's like women taking control of the cheating bastard husbands or boyfriends. I think the idea of being a honey trapper is fascinating, the job, everything. I think this Grace woman is interesting and I want this as a lead story.'

'When?'

'I've booked it in for three months.'

'Three months,' Betty repeated, remembering the last time she heard those words.

'Look, we work hard to get good features, you know that, and I want something different from the "how to give good head" stories that we seem to have had rather too many of lately. Fucking hell, Betty, we're not struggling with our circulation but we will be if we don't keep on top of it. So I want really interesting features about real people who do unusual things. Grace Regan is one of them. The first and, in my view, the most important.'

'So there is no way I can convince you to drop this story?' Betty felt desperation creeping into her whole being.

'Nope. Unless you can get me a feature on something so amazing that I'll replace it.'

'Like what?'

'Can't think of anything, can you?'

'No.' Betty had felt a flicker of hope, but it died. 'There is no way I can do this profile.'

'Of course you can.'

'Fiona, I've just been with her, with Grace. She said the only way she will agree to it is if I let her try to seduce Johnny.'

'What?' Fiona looked stunned. She betrayed no sign of knowing anything about the situation.

'Exactly. She wants a bet whereby she gets three months to try to seduce my husband and that is her condition. Fiona, surely you can see that I can't agree to that.'

'Well, I suppose so. Would you like some coffee?' Fiona only offers coffee to people visiting her office if she wants something from them. Betty felt her heart sink. She nodded and tried to think, but she couldn't. She felt as if her hangover had returned. Fiona called her PA and asked for the coffee, then she smiled. Betty prepared herself for the worst.

'Betty, I would never force you to put your personal life at risk for your job, I hope you know that.' Betty nodded with a sinking feeling. 'But you and Grace, it's more of a hate relationship, isn't it?' Again, Betty nodded. 'Well, I think this is your perfect opportunity to get your own back on her and get a great story.'

'I don't follow.' Betty didn't want to be there, and she didn't want to hear what Fiona was going to say.

'Well, you know that Johnny wouldn't look at another woman, even Grace, and therefore you agree to her bet, although I'm not sure that three months is a bit much. Anyway, you agree, and then when she fails miserably, you will win.' Fiona smiled as if she had discovered the meaning of life.

'Or I could agree to the bet and tell Johnny about it, so he'd know all along.'

'I don't think that is such a good idea.' Fiona hadn't thought about that barrier.

'Why?'

'Because you have to prove to Grace that she cannot wreck marriages, and the only way to prove that would be to let her see, genuinely, that she cannot wreck yours.' Fiona prayed that this logic would work.

'Fiona, it would mean me lying to Johnny.' Betty felt sick.

'Oh well, yes, I can see how difficult that would be. Did you tell him how much your Prada shoes cost?'

'No, I said they were in the sale.'

'Exactly.' The triumphant smile had reappeared.

'Fiona, no offence, but this is a bit more serious.' Betty rolled her eyes. It was getting ridiculous.

'Well, yes, I suppose it is, but what I am saying is that Johnny need never know, and the only people who do are me, you, Grace, and, I assume, her boss. Betty, you know as well as I do how much this job means to you, and you also know that if you told Johnny he'd refuse to go along with it. If the only option is keeping this from him, then I think we might have to do that.'

'I really don't want to do this.' Fiona was a control freak and a bitch and Betty wanted to cry, even though she isn't the crying type.

'Why not? You trust Johnny, you have no doubts, and you said yourself that this woman needs to be taught that she can't just wreck any marriage she wants.'

'So you mean that I win this and I get to destroy her.'

'Something like that. Maybe you could have a condition, take back control. Oh, this will be such fun. You tell her that if she loses (and we know she will) then she will agree to give up her job.' This was Fiona's trump card.

'You think she would do that?' Seeds of doubt began to

plant themselves in Betty's head, along with thoughts of revenge.

'She'll have to if she wants her little bet. Think about it.' Before Betty even got her coffee Fiona ushered her out. Betty could see in Fiona's face the determination of a woman who was sure that she would get what she wanted. Betty's heart told her to say no at all costs. To refuse and face the consequences. To tell Grace where to stick her bet and tell Fiona to stick her feature up her arse. But her head knew she would do neither; Fiona and Grace had won. She would accept the bet.

Albeit reluctantly. This is the first real secret that Betty has ever kept from Johnny (apart from the shoes). She has always been completely honest with him, always totally open, never even wanting to keep anything important from him. Yet here she is with a situation (she refers to it as a situation) that she would do anything to keep from him. She feels guilty, she feels as if she is betraying him, she feels that she is a rotten wife and, most of all, she is scared to the quick that perhaps her job is more important to her than her marriage. She can't believe that. She has always known that Johnny is the most important person in her world; he *is* her world.

Her head was whirring after her meeting with Fiona, so she quickly called on Alison for an emergency meeting. She went to Alison's office and told her very surprised-looking best friend that there was a crisis.

After she told her the story, Alison looked at her in total surprise. Finally she found her voice.

'Johnny adores you. He'd never cheat, even with this supermodel woman going after him. But you know that; you don't need to test that.'

'What about my job?'

'I know, but I just don't think it's fair to put temptation in front of him like this. And the fact that I know she's trying to seduce him, I know she's going to fail – I know it, but it feels wrong. Most of all you'd be lying to him. Betty, you can't lie to him.'

'Well, ordinarily I would say it is wrong, but I love my job and I've worked hard to get where I am, so this is the only way, and we all know that she's the one who'll lose.'

'That would be satisfying, but still definitely not worth it.'

'Ali, Fiona made it clear that I have little choice.'

'It sounds to me that you've already made up your mind.' Alison clearly disapproved.

'No. Yes. I feel rotten, really I do, but I'm not sure I can walk away from my job.'

'She won't sack you, you're too good.'

'But I can't risk that.'

'Can you risk your marriage?'

'But it's not at risk.' They were in danger of going round in circles.

'Is it just one night?' Ali asked.

'She wants three months.'

'What?'

'I know.'

'It's ridiculous.' Alison had never been angry with Betty before, but she was now.

'Alison, I need your support.'

'I'll try, but don't think I agree with you.'

'Fair enough. I'm not sure I agree with me either.'

'It's not just your job at stake, it's your pride.'

'It's not that simple. I trust Johnny. That's the one thing that isn't at risk in all this. My marriage is rock solid and I will have the last laugh. Please say you'll be there for me.'

'Of course.'

'Ali, it's a big ask, but do you think you might be able to keep this from Matt?'

'Only because if I tell him then your marriage will be over.'

'So you don't mind not telling him this.'

'I didn't say I didn't mind, but it wouldn't be fair because he's Johnny's friend and would probably feel he had to tell Johnny. I think it's best we keep this just between us.'

'You're a good friend.'

'I know. But then so are you.' Alison wasn't happy, but she was resigned to the fact that she couldn't get Betty to change her mind.

'Well, that's fantastic,' Grace replies to Betty's acceptance of the bet.

'Is it? We need to talk about the details. I have some terms of my own.'

'Fine. I'll draw up my terms and then we can discuss it when you come to interview me or profile me or whatever you call it.'

When Betty puts the phone down, she is convinced that Grace is sick. How could she take pleasure from this? It is all beyond her, but she has no way of turning back. She feels sick, angry and scared. But it is too late to change her mind. She has to think that she will win and Grace will be left with more than egg on her face.

Grace calls Nicole to impart the news.

'I can't believe she agreed,' Nicole says.

'Well, she did.'

'It's just that I thought she'd turn you down and there would be an end to it all.'

'Oh.'

'It's not that I don't approve, I just don't think it's worth it.' Nicole has been thinking about the bet quite a lot. She personally wants to get hold of Fiona and wring her neck. She has a feeling that Fiona is playing with both Grace and Betty, although Grace won't accept that.

'But it will make me feel better.'

'Just as long as it does.'

'But I do have your support?'

'I told you you did. But I have conditions. You don't fall apart over this. She's hurt you enough as it is. Second, you keep working as normal. You need normality and I don't want this bet taking over your life. And last, I need your assurance that you won't physically harm her.'

Grace laughs. 'Promise. Nicole, I am going to be all right.'

'Of course you are.' Grace smiles as she puts the phone down. Everything is going to work out.

That night, as Betty snuggles into Johnny as much as she can, and she sniffs to smell him, to feel his warm, soft skin, she feels overwhelmed with love for him and she knows that he is her life – but then again so is her job. She tells herself that she is not jeopardising him because she would never lose him. He loves her; she feels that. It's physical. Their relationship is the strongest she knows.

Grace wants to torment her but that can work both ways. She will torment Grace, she will watch her fail and humiliate her. She will make her quit her job. The boot is on the other foot, and it feels so much better there.

For a moment she thinks again about telling Johnny, but she knows that Fiona is right. There is no way he'd play along and therefore she really does have no choice.

Grace watches her fish and smiles. There is a new chapter in her life. She would never tell her but she has Betty to thank. The hostility, the superiority, the feeling that she has been bullied by her has given her a much-needed kick. She never used to believe in revenge – she always thought it was braver to turn the other cheek – but not any more. Betty pushed her and now she is going to push back. It might not make her a nice person – she understands that – it might not make her a better person, but it will make her feel stronger, and at the moment she needs that.

After the bet, she will start to put her life back together again. She will become a normal person, she will have normal relationships, not like her current whirligig ones. She will discover if it is possible for her to fall in love. She will try to laugh more. She will cut back on her job, not working so much so she has a social life. She is looking forward to that, to the new Grace, but first she has a bet to win. And she is really looking forward to that too.

Chapter Seventeen

Betty arrives at Grace's apartment, ten minutes late. She tried to be later but public transport proved unusually efficient. She presses the buzzer and waits. Grace answers almost straight away and lets her in.

'Hi.' Betty feels a mixture of nervousness and resentment.

'Come in.' Grace is behaving as if Betty is sunshine. Grace points her towards the living room where a tray of coffee is waiting for her. Grace pours it, still smiling.

'Why are you smiling?' Betty asks. She is suspicious of Grace being nice.

'I'm really glad you agreed to it.' For some reason, ever since Grace agreed to proposing the bet, she has embraced it. She doesn't think of it as harmful, but just an opportunity for her to get Betty to not condemn her so much.

'But you might not win.'

'No, I might not. But I think it's worth the risk.' Grace is definitely behaving as if she has the upper hand.

'Really?' This confuses Betty. She wonders when exactly it was that Grace took the upper hand and kept it safe in her pocket.

'Yup. I don't even mind if I lose.'

'Then why do it?'

'Because if I win, as you put it, then I will have taught you a thing or two about me, and if I lose, as you put it, then I will still have taught you not to be so judgemental. To be honest, finding a man who doesn't cheat would be such a novelty.' Grace is playing with Betty; it is written all over her face.

'You really are a bitch.' Now Betty has agreed to the bet she feels she can behave however she wants. She has done everything Fiona wanted, she has agreed to risk something that she knows, deep down, she should never risk, but she did it because she loves her job and has a misguided loyalty to her boss. But she can draw the line at being nice. That way, she can claw some, at least a tiny bit, of self-respect back.

'Um, and you're a pussycat. Anyway, would you like to hear my terms?'

'Sure.' Betty sips her coffee and wonders how on earth they are going to make this work. She has to listen to a woman who is going to try to seduce her husband, and write about her. She wonders if she is dreaming or something, because all of a sudden life doesn't feel very real. She wishes that Grace weren't real.

'Firstly, as I already mentioned, we set a deadline of three months. You give me information about your husband and we'll take it from there.'

'I want a review at two months. And I am not sure that I should tell you anything about him. I'm not helping you.'

'Fine, but I have no idea what his name is or what he looks like. So without your help, I have no way of getting to him. I'll agree a two-month review, if you give me the information I need.'

'OK, I'll tell you his name but that's it.'

'And hobbies, and where he works. You have to give me some information.'

'And if I don't?'

'Then the deal will be off and you lose your job, I guess.'

'Fine, but I'll only give you limited information.'

'Does he know my name?'

'What?'

'Well, have you been slagging off "Grace Regan" at home?'

Betty thinks. 'I haven't actually mentioned your name at all. To be honest I call you the honey-trap woman.' Or the bitch, she adds mentally.

'How sweet. Fine, then I will use my name so if he starts talking about me, you'll know. Also, I won't talk to you for the first two months.' Grace smiles a smile dripping with insincerity.

'Oh, so there is a good side to this.' Betty returns the false smile.

'Ha ha. Anyway, we won't communicate because it's easier that way. The start date will be when you've finished my profile. But I won't allow you to publish it until the bet is over because otherwise you might cheat. I explained that to Fiona and she agreed.'

'Wouldn't the profile be better done after the bet?'

'No way. Betty, you don't want to write about the bet because Johnny would find out, and also I think that you might be more inclined to be mean to me depending on the result of the bet. I want it finished and approved before we start.'

'Fine.' Betty is trying not to smile. She is not sure why she feels like laughing, but all of a sudden this whole thing sounds like a joke, or a bad TV show.

'Well, I think that's it. Unless you have anything to add?'

'Oh, I do. You see if I didn't agree to this bet, then I would have had serious problems at work, and in agreeing to it, I might lose my marriage. I don't think I will, but I might. So you should have something to lose.'

'What do you mean?'

'If you lose the bet, then you should sacrifice something.'

'What?'

'Your job.'

'Don't be ridiculous.' Grace is incredulous. But then she thinks about it and knows that there is no way she will actually have to give up her job if she does lose. Grace is prepared to cheat.

'Right, so I should be happy to sacrifice everything but you won't give anything up.'

'OK, I'll give my job up if I lose, but then I might have to double my efforts to get Johnny.' Grace smiles. She just told Betty that she didn't care if she lost, and now she has a vested interest in winning. She wonders if Betty is stupid.

'But you're not as determined as I am.' The gloves are on; the fight is starting.

'Should be a good fight then. Shall we get back to the profile?'

Grace is no longer shocked by Betty's demand, and she almost respects her for it. She is quite willing to agree. She thinks that if she does seduce Betty's husband, Betty is the sort of woman that will forgive him and carry on as if there is nothing wrong. She knows that because, she believes, that is the root of why she disapproves too strongly of Grace's job. She belongs to the 'turn-a-blind-eye' brigade, and in Grace's job there is no room for that. She wonders if Betty knows what she is letting herself in for, but if she doesn't she soon will. And anyway, it makes a change for Grace to have something challenging to do. If she has opened a can of worms, then that will prove exciting, because danger can be exciting too.

They call a truce after agreeing the terms of the bet, and they continue the profile with Betty slipping quietly into the role of observer and Grace successfully ignoring her. Grace wants to get the profile over with and the bet started. She can't wait.

Betty knows that she should have been quiet in the first place and just played out the week, as was her brief. She would have avoided the bet, and avoided having to have Grace in her life for any longer. She is paying the price for her judgemental attitude and her inability to bite her tongue. She sighs as she takes more notes and hopes she has learnt her lesson without having to lose the man she loves.

Chapter Eighteen

On the last day of the profile, the weight of the bet is upon them, but somehow both women find it easier to work together, neither being able to understand why. Betty's questions are more professional and her judgements tucked firmly away in her mind; Grace respects Betty more and doesn't try to compromise her in any way as she had done before. They are sitting in the office, facing each other, with the Dictaphone between them.

'So, you've finished the report for the job last night. Can I see it?' Betty asks.

'Sure,' Grace replies, handing it over. For a moment there is silence as Betty reads and Grace watches her face, looking for disapproval.

'You handle it sensitively,' Betty says, when she's finished reading.

'Thank you.' Grace is taken aback and also suspicious.

'I mean it. You could have made it sound as if the man was drooling over you, but while you say he propositioned you, you make it easier for her.'

'That is my job.'

'I didn't think of it like that.' They smile at each other. It's a breakthrough of sorts.

'Betty, tonight is the last job you'll come on. I just want you to know that I won't pull any stupid stunts.'

'Then neither will I.' They smile again, amazed at the lack of tension between them.

Grace puts herself in another position. She wonders, if things had started differently, whether the two women might have been friends. Betty thinks the same, although she doesn't want to. Because always there, in the back of her mind, is the thought that Grace will be trying to win Johnny away from her, and also, in the back of her mind, is the awful, horrible thought that he might let her.

'I'm done,' Grace says, when she has finished her work for the morning and Betty has listened and taken notes without engaging in any altercations.

'I'll leave you to it then, and meet you tonight.'

'That sounds fine.' Grace is pleased that Betty didn't suggest lunch and knows better than to do so herself. The morning went too well for her to risk prolonging it. As Betty leaves, they arrange to see each other again that evening, and they part on good terms.

Grace goes to the window and watches Betty walk away with mixed feelings. She wonders why they hadn't been able to behave this way when it all started. It would have made life so simple. For a minute, she also feels guilty about the bet. She is unsure now why she agreed to it so easily, why she didn't stick to her guns and just finish the whole situation. She thinks of Fiona and wonders why she would do this to Betty. Fiona isn't someone to be messed with, that much she knows, and she also found it impossible to say no to her. But she agreed and that she will have to live with. Not only is she putting herself in a position to mess with Betty's life, but she is also lying to her about the origin of the bet. She questions herself and her motives but finds she has no answers.

Betty feels lighter as she goes to get her bus. The morning was easier than any previous one. They established the working relationship that they should have had from the start. If only she had done that, she wouldn't have to go through with the bet. She thinks about whether she should broach that with Grace, suggest that now they are being civil they should call the whole thing off, but she can't quite bring herself to because maybe that is why they are behaving the way they are. She cannot shake off the thought that somehow the bet has made everything better between them and allowed them to work together, even if potentially it might ruin her life.

She doesn't think too much about her outfit as she gets ready to meet Grace. She tries not to think too much about anything. Although 'if only' keeps popping into her mind, she brushes it away with efficiency. She has learnt a good lesson and she hopes she will not learn any more. She still feels confident that Johnny is immune to Grace's charms, but she is nervous about him spending time with her in any way. He is hers, after all, and even though he won't fall for Grace, she is jealous at the thought of them even having a conversation. Although she fully trusts Johnny, she still doesn't trust that she is good enough for him. Even after all this time. And that is her problem with Grace – with everything. A woman as perfect as Grace shouldn't be allowed near others' husbands, because no woman can compete. Again, Betty pushes this thought away. She has to believe in Johnny's love, just as she has to believe in her career, because those two things are all she has to maintain her self-esteem.

Grace meets Betty in a wine bar in Kensington. They are there slightly later than usual because this isn't an after-work case but an after-gym one. In Grace's experience too many men use the gym as an excuse to go out and pull. She has lost count of the number of men she has tested who have had their gym kits lying by their feet.

Betty is waiting at a table near the bar. Grace nods at her and smiles. Betty returns the gesture. Grace goes to the bar, immediately spotting the man that she has been hired for. He is with two other men, clearly fresh from the gym, with slightly wet hair. She goes to the bar, orders her drink and engages the barman in a conversation, letting the men notice her.

Betty watches Grace and grudgingly admits she is a professional. She is standing at the bar, innocently, and the man that Betty saw in the photo earlier is already eyeing her up – not the behaviour of a happily married man, or not how he should be behaving. She realises that Grace is bait, and she won't stop thinking that, but the predatory look in the man's eyes says everything about him. Grace is the meat and he wants his dinner.

Betty glances at her watch and realises that it took him twenty minutes to approach her. Grace's brief is not to approach him, and both of them were hoping that Betty would get to see a man ignore her presence. But not this time. Although she couldn't hear what he was saying, she could see him clearly. The way he leant his head in close, the way he ordered a drink for her, the way he whispered something in her ear. Grace accepted but, Betty had to admit, she wasn't throwing herself at him. Again, that isn't the brief. Instead she was receiving him with only the smallest amount of encouragement, so small you could almost miss it. Betty noticed how the man's companions were looking over at Grace and how he turned to face them, giving them a victorious smirk. Betty hates that man. She feels sorry for his wife. She even feels sorry for Grace.

Grace is conscious of Betty watching her and she hopes that she isn't seeing her as a tart. She is trying her best to do her job, but also to leave Betty with a positive image of her. The man, she knows, is one of the worst. He approached her so quickly, he offered to buy her champagne, and ordered it before she had a chance to answer him. He is so sure of himself. Grace noticed the way he looked over to his friends and she felt anger well up.

There are times when she hates her job and this is one of them. She wonders if she should tell Betty that. She glances over at Betty but doesn't see any disapproval in her eyes, which annoys her. It could have been like this from the start. She is finding it hard to concentrate on the man, but is determined not to blow the job.

He is doing all the talking, a man who loves the sound of his own voice. She knows that this won't take long. He isn't the sort of man who has much time and he doesn't want to hide it.

'Can we go somewhere?' he asks.

'Where?'

'Dinner, your place . . . ?' She knows that dinner was thrown in but not meant.

'I have flatmates; it's difficult.' She has told him that she lives locally and is in here because her flatmate has her boyfriend over and she felt in the way.

'We could go to a bed and breakfast.' He smiles, she returns it. She should have guessed that he's cheap. Not even a hotel, but a seedy B&B. Something needs to be done about these men.

'How about we take a rain check? Give me your number and I'll call you.'

'It might be better if you give me yours,' he suggests.

'No. Either I have yours or nothing.' She is just wrapping it up, her job done. All the wife wanted was for him to approach Grace and proposition her. She wants to leave now; she's had enough. Reluctantly he scribbles his mobile number down, and she doesn't even look at him as she takes it and walks out.

Betty waits for about five minutes before following her out.

'Are you all right?' she asks as she meets Grace outside.

'You know what? I could really do with a drink. Care to join me?'

'Yes, I would.' They both look surprised, briefly, before Grace leads Betty to another bar.

The wine bar she chooses is fairly empty, the rain outside

putting people off. They find seats and Grace goes to the bar, returning with a bottle of wine.

'Never thought I'd see the day when we share an after-work drink,' Betty says.

'No, me neither.' They both smile.

'So tell me what happened.' Betty pulls out her notebook, reminding them both of why they are there.

'He was a sleaze, just as we suspected. He asked to come back to my flat, I took his number. That's the job done.'

'You don't seem your usual self.'

'To be honest – and, Betty, I don't want this in the article – it depressed me. He depressed me.'

'At least you're not married to him,' Betty answers cheerfully.

'I'll drink to that.'

They stick to the subject of Grace's job for the remainder of the wine, knowing that tension could reappear at any time.

'I guess we ought to get home,' Grace suggests when the bottle sits empty on the table.

'Yeah, I guess.'

Betty gets into the first taxi, at Grace's insistence. She sits back and thinks about things. About Grace. About Johnny. About honey trapping. And she feels that so much has been left unsaid, but she doesn't know how to change that.

Grace lets Betty get into the first taxi, an act of kindness she wants to do. It is as if she is unable to convey to Betty how she feels. How sorry she is that the bet is going to start. How she would like to take it back, but can't quite bring herself to. How she would like to start again and see Betty differently. The real Betty, not the one that she made assumptions about. But, as she gets into the taxi, she knows that it is far too late for that.

Johnny is snoring as Betty gets into bed. She throws her arm over him and snuggles into his warm back. She cannot get Grace out of her mind. She wishes she knew the real woman, not the honey trapper. She feels bad for thinking she had a perfect life, assumptions she made without any right. She wishes she hadn't accused her of being a whore. But as she radiates in Johnny's warmth she realises that she will never like Grace. Because Grace, despite the niceness, is trying to take her husband away, and she cannot like anyone who would do that.

She feels apprehensive all of a sudden, because the day, the evening, seemed to take reality away for a while, but now it is back. The profile is over. She has spent the last day in the company of Grace and the bet is about to start. Reality is back with a vengeance.

Grace gets into her cold, empty bed and feels alone. Her emotions are mixing themselves up and she doesn't normally let them do that. She thinks about Betty, in bed with her husband, and then she thinks about the bet. She tries to imagine what Johnny will be like. She is convinced he will be tall, dark, handsome but boring. She hopes that is what he'll be like. It will make things easier.

Betty can't sleep, so she mentally writes the final feature up, something she often does when this occurs. But with every line she writes, the bet pops into her head. Grace will be getting ready to seduce Johnny, her Johnny. Betty's hands feel clammy, her head begins to pound and she is unable to think straight. What has she done? Is she crazy? She must be barking mad.

She puts it to the back of her mind, pushes it away. She refuses to worry; she has nothing to worry about. Abandoning the feature she is writing in her head, she decides that she will take him out to dinner the following night. That is what she will do. She will dress up and take *her* husband out to dinner.

Chapter Nineteen

It is the first official day of the bet. The day after Betty walked out of Grace's life, and Grace walked into hers. Into her home life. When Grace wakes, she feels a new sense of purpose, and she remembers why. No matter what anyone says, she is going to enjoy this. Enjoy the revenge, enjoy the feeling of being in control, enjoy seeing smug Betty get what she deserves.

As soon as she gets up she turns to her preparations: organising her schedule and making appointments. She has given herself a week to prepare, because she is busy at work and she needs to get things ready. She cannot just storm in. Preparation, as usual, is required.

She has lunch with Nicole, who helps her gather financial information, and who insists on feeding her and giving her a pep talk. Grace knows that Nicole is only helping so she can keep a close eye on her, but she accepts this because Nicole will come round in time. They sit in a small bistro while Nicole hands over papers and they both look at each other, waiting for someone to talk.

'Grace.'

'Nicole.'

'I am going to help you, you know that, but I am not sure that you should go through with this.'

'I have to.'

'Grace, it's me you're talking to. Stop being all serious and uptight.'

'I am not uptight.' She knows she is.

'Betty isn't your best friend, I know that, and I don't like what she said to you any more than you do, but this – this could hurt everyone. Including you. Especially you.' Grace relaxes at Nicole's words. She is only worried, and that is welcome.

'Oh, Nicole, I know you worry about me and that means a lot to me, it really does, but I know what I'm doing.'

'Do you really?'

'Of course. I'm planning it carefully. Step one is to meet him. I'm making an appointment to see him as a financial adviser. That way there is no chance he can be suspicious. Then I'll take it from there. How on earth can I get hurt?'

'I don't know but I just feel that you will.'

Grace laughs at the look on Nicole's face. Her tough cop act has been replaced by maternal concern.

'I'll be fine. This is my job, remember. I'm a professional, and this is going to be a very interesting project, I really believe that. Also, I can't lose, as I've told you. The best bet in the world is one you can't lose.'

'There's no arguing with you, is there?'

'You already tried it, Oliver tried it, and no, there's no arguing with me.' She smiles and, reluctantly, Nicole smiles back.

Betty wakes Johnny up with kisses. She knows that it is the first day of the bet, although she is unsure if anything is going to happen.

'Morning.' He smiles at her, her favourite smile: his sleepy smile.

'I've got a busy day at work today, so I've got to go, but if you want I'll bring you up a cup of coffee.'

'Really? That would be nice.' He snuggles back under the duvet and she stares at him for a second before she goes to put the kettle on and take a shower.

In the shower she thinks about things. She is going to go to work. Write up the honey trap feature. Have lunch with Fiona, as a reward – although God knows she hardly sees lunch with her boss as a reward – for getting the story finished. She laughs as she thinks about the stakes. She had to agree to have Grace try to seduce her husband in order to get her story. Fiona made sure of that. And she agreed to it. That is way above and beyond the call of duty. Unless, of course, her husband was unseduceable. Which, of course, he is.

She gets out of the shower, and wraps herself in a towel. Then she goes to make some coffee, which she takes to her sleeping man. She pokes him in the ribs, which stirs him.

'Ow,' he says.

'Coffee,' she replies, and, whistling, she goes to get dressed.

After Betty has finished writing the feature, Fiona calls her and tells her it is time for lunch.

'Oh, who's special?' Hannah asks, teasing her.

'Me,' she replies, beaming. She feels good today. There is no way that she can feel any other way. Grace is going to learn the lesson of her life. She is going to learn that she cannot wreck all marriages, and she won't even begin to wreck hers. Johnny wouldn't fall for her in a million years. That much Betty is sure of.

Fiona has booked a table in London's newest, trendiest restaurant. As they are led to their seats, Betty realises that it is crowded, full of trendy people, either famous or wannabes, and it is also really noisy. That might not be a bad thing. She isn't sure she can sustain a conversation with Fiona for very long.

'So, how is the feature?' Fiona asks as soon as they are seated with their Bloody Marys.

'Done. I'll email it to you this afternoon and you can let me know what you think.'

'Perfect. I've decided that as a reward for your dedication – and, Betty, I really do appreciate your loyalty to me and the magazine – I am going to give you more responsibility.' Fiona smiles, and Betty begins to feel scared. She is not sure that that sounds like a reward.

'How do you mean?'

'More stories, better stories. You can also have more input into what you write about. We are still a fairly small magazine but we can grow and you can grow with us.'

Betty wonders what book Fiona has been reading. It really isn't her style to talk like that. She also finds her motives questionable.

'Great,' Betty replies, reading between the lines. More responsibility means more work, more stories means more work, more input means loads more work. 'And I guess that means more money?' Betty smiles as Fiona suddenly looks a bit flustered.

'Not exactly, but you will reap the benefits of it, though not immediately. I haven't got the budget but when the new one comes up, I'll make sure you are considered.' Fiona knows she is pushing a bit hard, but Betty needs more responsibility. She decided as soon as Betty agreed to the bet that she owed it to her to keep her busy, distracted.

'Fiona, did you bring me to lunch to tell me that I'm going to do more work for the same money?' As Betty has been so loyal to her boss, she feels that she can say what she thinks – just for a while, anyway.

'Yes, but you'll benefit in the long run.' Fiona smiles again but looks a little confused and Betty resists the urge to laugh.

'Brilliant,' she says, with a mocking tone that she knows Fiona will ignore.

'I think so too,' Fiona concurs, relieved.

They distract themselves by ordering and Betty is glad that she will have more work to do, for the next three months, anyway. It will take her mind off the bet – off Grace and the bet. She isn't worried, of course she isn't, but she knows that she is only human and she will be thinking about it at times.

'It's nice to have lunch, don't you think?' Fiona says.

'Absolutely.' Betty wonders if Fiona means lunch with her, or lunch in general. She isn't sure.

'How are you, Betty?'

Now Betty really does want to laugh. Fiona doesn't like to concern herself too much with the welfare of her staff, unless it is necessary.

'I'm fine.'

'Are you sure?'

'Yes.'

'It's just with the bet . . .' Ah, finally Betty understands what the lunch is about. Fiona, or her of no compassion, is feeling guilty. Betty sees the second positive aspect about the bet. One, destroy Grace; two, get her boss's concern.

'Fiona, I know I was reluctant at first, but you made me see how much this could benefit me. I've got a lot to thank you for.' Fiona chokes on her drink and Betty smiles sweetly.

'Well, yes.'

'It was a great idea. Cheers, Fiona. You really are a wonderful boss.' She raises her glass, and Fiona, reluctantly, follows suit.

'So you're quite happy?' She is still a little puce from the choking incident.

'I can honestly say that I've never been happier.' And for a moment, looking at her boss and feeling truly that she has the upper hand, Betty means it.

Grace is at home, preparing for a job. She has a message on her answerphone from Eddie and she is unsure how to respond. If he wants to see her, she will not be able to hide the bet from him – or maybe she will. Maybe she will keep quiet and he won't know anything is wrong. She doesn't want everyone to desert her. She has only Nicole, Eddie and Oliver. Oliver is already angry with her, Nicole barely approves, and if Grace loses Eddie . . . She shudders as she realises how she wouldn't be able to cope with that. Perhaps she is selfish but she needs him. Perhaps she is the bad person Betty thinks she is. She shudders again. For the millionth time she is having doubts about the bet. There might be more at stake than she first thought: her friendships as well as her job. Maybe she didn't think it through properly. She let Fiona steamroller her into it. Why? She is losing sight of why she agreed. Maybe she will suffer the way Nicole said. She might get hurt. And is it worth it? She has no idea.

The thought won't leave her; the idea of a big mistake is staying with her. She doesn't know who to talk to about it. Nicole would welcome her doubts and persuade her to act on them. Oliver, would do the same. Eddie is ignorant. She has an irrational need to speak to someone: her enemy.

'Betty Parkin.'

'It's Grace.'

'Grace? What do you want? I thought we weren't allowed to speak for two months.' Still on a high from lunch, Betty is surprised but pleased at the call.

'I just thought you might like to know that I haven't contacted him yet.'

'Why would I want to know that? Grace, I would only want to know that if I was remotely worried about you contacting him, and I'm not.' She beams her smile down the receiver.

'Good, I just thought . . .' Grace has no idea what she thought, or what she is thinking. She wishes she hadn't called. She curses her stupidity.

'Well, not to worry about me. I'm surprised you are worried about me. After all, you don't like me much.'

'But that's not the point. Look, this bet, it's not going to be easy.'

'No, it won't be, you're right. My husband wouldn't look at a tuppence tart like you, not even once, let alone twice. So calling me up with these stupid platitudes is a waste of your time and mine. So, if there's nothing else . . .'

'Nothing. Let the bet commence.' Grace is now pleased she called. Everything is back in perspective.

'And may the best woman win. Oh, funny, I think I will.' As Betty's laugh rings in her ears, Grace hangs up.

She isn't angry after the phone call: she feels an immense calm. Betty really is as evil as she thought and now she can prepare for the bet without any of her earlier hesitancy.

She prepares her file. Well, her notebook. She knows that Betty is trendy and thinks that maybe that is the way forward for her. Or perhaps the fact that she is not like Betty might be to her advantage. Why would he fall for someone who is similar to his wife? He loves his wife, according to Betty, so that would make sense, but Grace has a feeling that that isn't the best way here. She resolves not to wear disguises, but to present him with her as she is. Her character will be moulded, it has to be, but her looks will be her own. With that in mind she picks up the phone to her hairdresser. Then she makes an appointment with the beautician. He will see her, all right, but a little modification never hurt anyone.

'What is with you?' Hannah asks as Betty sits at her desk chuckling out loud to herself.

'You know this bet?'

'Yes. It's all I've been hearing about.'

'What do you mean? I haven't been going on about it, have I?'

'No.' Hannah colours. 'It's all round the office. Fiona told Michelle and you know what Michelle's like.'

'Tell me, Hannah, oh devoted assistant, are they taking bets, by any chance?' Even the idea of this doesn't upset her.

'No. Well, not officially, with odds or anything. Most people are sure that you're going to win.'

'I am. Grace called me. She's already riled and I think she knows that she's made a mistake. There is no way she can win this and she knows it. That's why I'm chuckling.'

'Good for you.'

Betty sends Alison an email, thinking that it is all very good for her.

That evening as Grace leaves for her job, she wonders when the right time to see Johnny is. She decides that she will stick to her original idea of a week. A week to prepare herself and her plan of action, and also to tease Betty a bit. No matter how confident she sounded earlier, Grace knows it won't last. She is one hundred per cent sure it won't. She decides to number the days of the bet from the first day she meets Johnny. And this week is preparation week. It will still all fit within the three-month deadline. In fact, the more she thinks about it the more she decides she won't need that long. Three months is too long. Again, she wonders at the reason behind Fiona's deadline. She wonders at her motives – hers and Betty's. Grace knows, believes, that if she had a husband she loved and who was faithful, she would never ever test him. She shrugs all those thoughts off. The bet is underway and any musings about motive aren't necessary any more.

She walks into a private club to do her job. It is a sumptuous club, all large leather sofas, expensive art and men dressed in a similar uniform of Savile Row suits. She sits down at a table, giving her a good view of the bar, and she studies the faces. A waiter is with her in seconds to take her drinks order, and she requests a glass of champagne. When he is gone, she spots the man. Tall, greying, posh-looking. They are all the same, she thinks as she takes a breath and waits to make her move. All the bloody same. But maybe Johnny will be different. With this dangerous thought she receives her glass of champagne and drinks a toast to it.

Chapter Twenty

Fiona lives up to her word and swamps Betty with work. On day two of the bet she gets to work to find more emails than she wants and more assignments than she has time for. She thinks about arguing, but although Fiona is feeling guilty, she still doesn't like being argued with. Betty shakes her head as she realises she is stuck. She pushes away an irrational thought that Fiona is deliberately trying to keep her away from Johnny so Grace can win. Fiona doesn't like her being married – this she has made clear – but although she can be a bitch at times, she wouldn't do that to her. Would she?

At the same time, Fiona is sitting at her desk, composing another email to Betty. She isn't the sort of woman that suffers from guilt. She is vindictive, she knows that, ambitious to the hilt, and alone. She hasn't always been that way. When she started out in journalism she was like Betty. Just like her. She had a husband she adored and she worked hard and happily. She pulls her compact out of her handbag and looks at herself. She sees the person she is now. She used to look like Betty, a smile on her face and a twinkle in her eye. *He* came first. *He* always came first. Then he destroyed her. One man took the twinkle and the smile and left her with the hardness that her face now lives with. She can't bear to see Betty go through the same. When she first met Betty, Fiona was a features writer for the magazine, and Betty was her work experience girl. She adored her from the first moment she saw her. She saw herself in her and she promised herself that Betty would be successful. She delivered. Somewhere along the line, Fiona lost *him* and became bitter. She began to let her ambition take over, because it was all she had left. She climbed up to the top, but she left her smile behind as she fought the competition off. She would never let a man take over her life again. The scars lasted too long.

Betty is like her – she knew that, she was convinced – which meant that Betty would get hurt. Sometimes Fiona thought her conviction about this was irrational, but she believes it. That was the reason for Grace. She didn't necessarily want to prove herself right, she just wanted Betty to find out for sure. She knew that Betty would hate the assignment – she herself would have done back then. She knew that Betty would feel threatened by Grace and what she stood for. She knew that she had to introduce the bet.

The idea came to her after the dinner party. It wasn't just about the feature, it was about Betty. She wanted to know – correction, she wanted Betty to know – that her man was either rock solid or like *him*. She needed Betty to find out now before it was too late. She did it because she had promised, from the moment Betty started working for her, that she would take care of her, and she was merely keeping that promise.

All she had to do was to find an opportunity to suggest it. No, she didn't suggest it – she knows that – she made it happen. Betty gave her that opportunity. She didn't know that Betty and Grace would fight the way they did; she hadn't seen that coming. But it provided her with the opportunity she needed to do what she had to do. That is what she believes.

Hannah delivers coffee and perches herself on the corner of Betty's desk.

'Hannah, I know how this office works. I know how much they love to gossip and I love it too, but if they are using you to get them regular updates they'll be disappointed.'

'Oh.'

Betty smiles indulgently. She would have done the same. 'Well, maybe I will let you in on the situation and then you can go and be fawned over as the fount of all knowledge.' She smiles again. 'But at the moment there is nothing to report and I have so much work to do, I don't know when I'm going to think about it. But I've got a mountain of research I need you to help me with.'

'OK. But you will tell me?'

'As soon as there is anything to tell.'

'Good. Betty?'

'Yes?' She sips her coffee.

'I made an appointment for you to get your hair done. And your nails. Just to be prepared.' Betty feels shocked. It hadn't occurred to her that she had to do anything. But then, having her hair done and everything else can't hurt. It's only what she normally does anyway.

'Good thinking, Hannah. Thanks. Oh, and maybe you could add a bikini wax as well.' Her assistant goes back to her desk with a smile on her face. Not only will she be the most popular member of staff for the next few weeks, but she also has her boss's favour.

Betty cannot think about the bet for the rest of the week, because she is too busy working late and not even getting to see Johnny herself, let alone knowing if Grace has met him yet. They are existing on phone conversations and when they do see each other she is too tired to speak and he is too tired to ignite conversation. She swings between wanting to kill Fiona, and feeling grateful for the distraction. She is unsure which. Part of her still believes that Fiona is trying to split her and Johnny up, but the other part of her can't believe that she would do that. She hasn't got enough time to let them debate it.

She determines that, work or no work, she will devote her

time to him at the weekend. On Friday, she skives off early to keep the appointments that Hannah has made for her. Her first stop is her hair.

'Highlights?' Beth, her hairdresser, asks.

'Why not?' Beth normally knows what is best for her and Betty is almost too tired to think about it.

'Any occasion?' she asks when Betty is sitting down, having her hair painted.

'Not really, just due.' She doesn't want to have to discuss the bet with anyone else. The office gossip is bad enough, as are Fiona, Hannah and Alison.

'Just want to look nice for your man,' Beth says, which is fairly near the mark.

'And for myself,' Betty replies, remembering that she is Modern Woman.

When she has an amazing head of hair, notably shorter, but also notably sleeker, she gets her nails done, and then an incredibly painful waxing. Of course she is doing it for Johnny, but she is also doing it for herself. She praises herself for the sensible way she is behaving. She has barely given Grace a second thought.

As preparation week draws to a close, Grace feels an immense excitement building up. The anticipation that the week has provided has given her even more of an appetite for the bet.

She goes to the hairdresser, a smart salon, one she has never been to before. What is amazing about it, apart from the prices, is that as someone does her hair, someone else does her nails (hands and feet), and she feels as if she is receiving a proper pampering.

'Any occasion?' the man doing her hair asks.

'No, not really. Just thought it was time.'

'Well, darling, with your hair, you must come here more often. It's a joy to work with.'

'Thanks.'

'I mean it.' Grace is tempted to tell him the truth – she's getting her hair done to seduce another woman's husband – but she stops herself. Enough people are judging her right now; she doesn't want to add to the number. Especially as she knows that she is right. She has to be.

Back home, as she admires her new haircut, looks at her beautifully manicured nails and picks up the all-important notebook, she knows she is ready. And she is going to win this bet.

Chapter Twenty-One

It is the first day of the bet proper. Grace wakes with a smile on her face, which Eddie, who is lying beside her, thinks is for him. Unexpectedly she gets up, and makes him coffee before packing him off to work.

'Just like a wife,' Eddie says.

'Not quite,' she replies.

Once her flat is hers again, she follows her usual routine. On day one of the bet, she has an appointment to see a financial adviser at eleven. Which gives her ample time to choose the right thing to wear.

She goes to her office and picks up the bet notebook. Inside she has his place of work and his phone number along with what she knows about him. All that, she memorised last week. His name is Johnny Parkin. He is thirty-three and a financial adviser for STN, which is near the City. He likes golf, football and *Carry On* films. She still has no idea what he looks like because Betty refused to give her a photo, but as she has a professional appointment with him, she doesn't need one.

She has headed a page 'Phase One'. Under 'Phase One' is today's date and the time of her first appointment. She is looking forward to writing a description of that meeting when she gets home. She is treating the bet as a business transaction, a normal job, even if it is anything but.

*

Betty wakes feeling funny. At first she is unsure if she is ill, but she feels a bit wobbly, unhinged and uncertain. Then she remembers that the bet has been going for a week and she has no idea if Grace has even seen Johnny yet. She looks at the still-silent alarm clock, and sees that it is about to jump into life. Then Johnny will, and then she will have to, in order to go to work. She wonders again what Grace is doing, if she has arranged to see him. How is she, Betty, going to cope with not knowing? Ignorance is bliss, Alison said, spouting the old cliché, but Betty is not sure that she can submerge herself in it for two months. She knows she will win. She is still as confident as she was last week. However, she must stop these recent habitual visits of anxiety. She must shake those feelings away.

The alarm goes off. Johnny opens his eyes. He looks sleepy but beatific. Betty plants a kiss on his forehead. He looks at her, slightly startled, still in a half-conscious state.

'Good morning, my dream girl,' he finally says, reaching over to her.

'I love you so much,' she replies. She looks around the room: everything is the same, nothing has changed. 'I really do love you, you know,' she says, and she kisses him.

Everything is going to be fine because they love each other. No one can penetrate their relationship.

Grace has managed to limit her outfit dilemma by choosing a role for the bet. She is going to enjoy the drama of the situation. Of that, she is determined. When she thinks back to the reason she is doing this the humiliation wedges itself around her, tightening itself with huge screws. She thought that Betty might be a pain but she certainly didn't expect an enemy. She doesn't think she deserves one either. Betty made her feel worthless and in Grace's world, in the carefully constructed life she lives, no one is supposed to do that. Betty cannot think she is better than

Grace; she shouldn't be allowed to think that. She is luckier than she is, that is all, but not better.

She pulls her thoughts back to the task at hand. After a week of planning she is ready for her new challenge. Johnny Parkin. It is as if a light has gone on in her head. Maybe it is a game, maybe it is more, but she has a role to play and therefore she must throw herself into it.

She settles for a conservative beige suit. She looks good, as she always does, but she also looks like a character – the character she is playing. Grace Regan, divorcee, legal secretary, vulnerable damsel in distress. She will melt hearts with her sorrow, and then she will attract hearts with her resilience. That is the Grace that Johnny will meet. He does not stand a chance.

Betty has finished the second draft of the honey-trap story. The first draft, according to Fiona, was too full of 'blatant disapproval'. In the second draft she doesn't write a bad account of Grace, but the fact is that her disapproval of the industry (is it an industry?) is more subtly apparent. She questions lack of trust; she points out that for any relationship to stand a chance, trust has to be visibly employed. She trusts Johnny. Her faith in him is unshakeable, which is why this bet isn't really bothering her. At worst she is just angry about it, ashamed she is lying to Johnny, and unhappy about Grace cropping up in his life. After all, look what she did to hers. She is as disruptive as the winter wind, that much she knows, and she wants to get the bet over and done with and move on. The end of the bet will get Grace out of her life once and for all. For ever.

Fiona has the story again and will let her know if she wants changes. Betty has four other stories on the go now. Her workload is ever increasing and she is not quite struggling but almost. Even so, she can't help wasting time speculating about Grace marching into Johnny's life and trying to steal him like the common thief she is, but then she is only human.

*

His office is on the seventh floor. It is one of London's many characterless, huge glass spaces. Grace would hate to work in one like it. For some reason it reminds her of the soulless homes she grew up in, built by the council, obviously a council house, using the most depressing grey cement rendering to remind them that they weren't quite worth anything else. She chastises herself for such thoughts. Those thoughts are banned in her new world; she must remember that.

She gets out of the large empty lift, checking her reflection one last time, and walks into the reception area. It is small but the furniture looks expensive. The sofas are red with chrome legs, the coffee table is glass and chrome, and the reception desk matches. It feels a bit like a furniture showroom, with choice paintings on the walls (canvas) and wooden floors sprinkled with rugs.

She announces herself to the receptionist (a woman who looks as designer as the furniture), feeling adrenalin kicking in. She is slightly nervous about messing up, or giving herself away, but that is normal in her job. That slight lack of confidence makes her good at what she does; arrogance makes mistakes.

She sits on the sofa and flicks through *The Times*, not really concentrating as her eyes dart from the pages to the door leading from reception. Finally, she sees him walk towards her.

For a minute everything is in slow motion. She instinctively knows it is him, although he looks nothing like she expected. He is tall, with hair so blond it is almost white. He looks slightly serious; a frown decorates his forehead. His suit is immaculate but not in a sleazy way, not the way she associates with her usual bastards. His face is perfect, as if someone knew what they were doing when they lovingly put his features together. Her heart speeds up; she does not move. Everything is still for a minute. He has a word with the receptionist, and then moves towards her. She feels her hands become clammy. She is unsure why she is having these feelings; she tries to slow them down. It is just nerves, she insists to herself. There is, after all, so much at stake.

'I'm Johnny Parkin,' he says, his hand outstretched.

Grace looks at him, smiles and stands up, feeling shaky. 'I'm Grace Regan,' she replies. Although she still feels slightly light-headed, her inexcitable nature is returning.

She follows him to a small meeting room where a cafetiere, a teapot and two cups greet them. He gestures for her to sit down, and she obliges. He sits opposite her. She studies him. He looks honest, his face is open, and his smile is delicious. For a split second something in her head tells her to run, but she doesn't run. She stays and refuses to listen.

'Are you OK?' he asks.

She wonders what he must be seeing, what she must be showing him. She sternly tells herself to behave.

'Sorry, I'm just a bit nervous,' she replies truthfully.

He establishes what she wants to drink and pours her some coffee. She adds the milk, concentrating on not letting her hand tremble. She shakes her head as he proffers the sugar bowl.

'How can I help?' he asks, and she gets an urge to tell him the truth, but she doesn't. Of course she doesn't.

'I'm in a bit of a mess.' Her character clicks in, and starts working, much to her relief. He is looking at her intently and she feels naked. 'You see, my husband – well, ex-husband now – left me almost a year ago and he dealt with things. I thought it was time I took control. I have no idea what to do.'

'Where do you want to start?' he asks, looking surprised.

He *is* surprised. He has noted how beautiful she is and wonders why her husband left; how any man could leave some-one who looks like her. He is cross with himself for being so sexist. And unprofessional. She could, after all, have a really horrible personality.

'I have some money, not a huge amount, but some. And I

have a job, and I have the flat. I didn't bring all the details because I didn't know what you'd need. But I want to make sure that I'm going to be all right. I probably need a pension and, well, you see so much about mortgage deals and I'm hopeless with all that. He did it, you see – took care of it.'

'I'll probably need to see everything before I can advise you.'

'Of course. I should have brought them, but I was feeling a bit nervous, out of my depth. I have got details of my earnings here, so a pension should be a start, I suppose.'

'How old are you?'

'Thirty-two. I suppose I should have all this sorted already.' She allows herself another look at his eyes. They really are spectacular.

'Not everyone does.' He is being kind. Grace hands him some papers that Nicole helped her prepare. Although Grace knows she doesn't approve, she is being very helpful. They have details of her earnings from a fictional job, and also details of her savings. When she phoned up to make the appointment, she spoke to Johnny's assistant, who told her to bring as much information as she could. However, she realised that if she brought everything he would require, then there wouldn't be the excuse for the contact that she was planning.

'I can get everything else to you. I just find finance baffling, to be honest.'

'Grace, the number of times I've heard that, please don't worry. What we'll do is collect all the information I need, and then I will go through the options, leaving out all the technical terms and making it simple. It is simple, but we don't like people to think that. We like them to think that we're really clever.'

Grace likes him. She wasn't expecting to like him – after all, she cannot stand his wife. This surprises her and scares her. Finding the men devilishly attractive is acceptable, but she isn't supposed to like them. Even if this man isn't one of her normal jobs.

They spend the rest of the meeting going through a few financial details, until Grace tells him, unprompted, that her ex-husband had been a serial philanderer and had left her devastated. He looks on with sympathy as she describes six months of despair before she pulls herself together. It is all part of the plan. When she gets ready to leave, not only have they made an appointment for Friday of that week, but she also has his much-needed direct line number, which he offered. It is early days but it all seems to be working like a dream. The only thing bothering her are the lies. Lies are second nature to her, but for some reason she is feeling ashamed.

'Johnny, I'm sorry if I bored you with my story. I shouldn't have burdened you with it.'

'Don't be silly, it's fine. Look, don't worry. I know that it feels like the financial wilderness, but I'll sort you out, promise.' He is so incredibly lovely, she can barely believe that he would marry someone like Betty.

She takes his outstretched hand and shakes it, holding it for slightly longer than she intended.

'See you Friday,' he says, smiling.

Grace returns the smile and walks away. She hopes she can feel him watching her as she leaves; she can.

Johnny returns to his office thinking that it isn't often that he gets a client who looks like that.

Betty is conducting a phone interview with Nessa O'Neill, a relationship therapist, a woman who is paid to sort out people's romantic lives. As she asks the questions and listens to the answers, she gets a strong feeling that she could do with one. Despite it being only the second week of the bet and despite her confidence that she will win, a tiny particle of worry has managed to lodge itself under her skin. When she feels unbalanced she often looks around her to check that everything is normal and it is. But then she knows that Grace is out there, somewhere, trying to seduce her husband, and that is not.

'Nessa, do people come to you on their own if they feel their relationship is under threat or just as couples?'

'They come for all sorts of reasons, but yes, that has happened.'

'And what do you say?'

'I say that if you love someone, and they love you, you have to believe in that. If you don't, then there is very little else.' Betty smiles as she relays that to herself throughout the afternoon. Nessa made her feel better. She vows to give her a great write-up. Fiona emails her to ask about the bet, as does Alison. She is fine about it, but she soon won't be if everyone else keeps on. She doesn't share those thoughts with her boss or her friend but sends them curt emails telling them that as far as she is aware it isn't even happening. Not quite the truth, but almost. Most of the time she is managing to ignore it. Only sometimes she thinks of it and worries.

By the end of the day, she is desperate to go home to Johnny. To see him, to see if he shows any indication that he has been 'Graced'. When it is finally time to leave, she calls him.

'Hi, babes,' he says. He sounds the same as normal.

'Hi. I'm leaving work now. What time will you be home?'

'Ah, well, Matt just called. He wondered if I wanted to go for a quick drink in the City, before we brave public transport.' Although this is a normal occurrence, immediately Betty feels threatened. She cannot speak. 'Is that all right?' he asks.

'Sorry. Yes, of course. I was just thinking that maybe I'd go for a drink with people from here. See you at home later?' She curses everyone. Look what they've done. They've made her paranoid just over a week into the bet. And now that she is paranoid because of them, not because of her trust in Johnny, she is going to start driving herself mad.

'I'll be back by eight.'

She hangs up, grabs Hannah, and drags her to the nearest

wine bar. As she buys a bottle of wine, Hannah looks at her questioningly.

'Betty is there something wrong?'

Betty takes a large gulp of wine. 'Absolutely not.' Everything is fine, nothing is wrong and if she doesn't pull herself together, she knows that the next few months will destroy her.

She loves him and he loves her. He is not going to start an illicit affair, he isn't underhand. She can trust him, she should trust him; he deserves nothing less. Grace can no more tear them apart than she can bend metal. Betty hopes that she can't actually bend metal.

Grace returns home from her first meeting with Johnny to find a message from Nicole on her answer machine. She calls her back.

'Grace, I wanted to talk about the job tonight. The wife has panicked about where he is going to be, so I've got Tony following him from home. Apparently, he is going to play squash, but she doesn't think he is. Anyway, she's a wreck and doesn't know if she's coming or going, so I think that having him followed is best.'

'Fine. I'll make sure I'm in the area, and Tony can call me.'

'Oh, and can you wear a video wire? She wants to see everything.'

'I feel sorry for this woman.'

'You and me both. Honestly, she is in a bad way. I tried to persuade her to postpone us until she felt a bit better, but it's the idea of him cheating that's making her like this. So, did you meet him?'

'I did.'

'And?'

'He's very kind.'

'Kind? What kind of description is that? I'm kind, for God's sake. What does he look like?'

'Oh, he's very nice-looking. Well groomed, but not in a smarmy way. Lovely eyes, and I get the impression that out of his suit he's probably quite trendy. But then his wife is, so that would figure.'

'You didn't hate him?'

'No, actually I didn't. Nicole, he was so nice to me and I know I was spinning a yarn, but there was something quite special about him.' Grace stops and blushes. She has lost track of what she is saying; she's said far too much.

'Grace, are you telling me you fancied him?'

'Oh, come on, I'm not a teenager. Anyway, this is business. I have his direct line number and I've made a second appointment, and then at some point I'm going to have to lure him from the office.'

'You told him you were a lonely divorcee?'

'Yup.'

'Look, I know I said that I didn't approve but as I'm already helping I might as well continue.'

'Go on.'

'Talk about something you used to do with your husband, an innocent activity, and I'm not talking sex. You need to ensure that said activity is one of his passions.'

'Um . . .' Grace pulls out a folder that Betty had given her with details about Johnny in it. Along with his work details is a list of hobbies. 'He likes golf,' Grace says, 'and *Carry On* films.' She frowns, she never got *Carry On* films. Too many ugly men and blonde women with big breasts. Disturbing.

'Bingo. Look, I can get you in to one of the most exclusive golf courses in London. What we need to do is for you to have more contact. Then we'll get you a membership card. You say you've got no one to play with, and because it is such a hot course, he'll be sure to offer to come with you, or he'll tell you how much he likes golf, and you ask him. Brilliant. And if you need more time with him then you take him to see a film.'

'I haven't played for ages and I hate those films.'

'No, but you got quite into it. I'm sure it's like riding a bike, and, anyway, you being a bit rusty will fit nicely into the whole story of not playing for ages. As for the films, you just laugh at every other line and he'll never know.' Nicole can barely believe how helpful she is being.

'You're a genius, Nicole.'

'Yeah, but it's a bit soon to be asking him for golf. Leave it until maybe the end of the month. I'm not sure why I'm telling you what to do. Anyway, I'll get you a membership card.'

'Excellent. Anyway, I already know my next move.'

'And it is?'

'I'm supposed to have a second meeting this Friday, and I'm going to cancel.'

'You really are the best, honey.'

'Nicole?'

'Yes.'

'Am I doing the right thing?'

'How on earth is anyone meant to know that? Trust your instinct, Grace, that's all you've got. That's all anyone has.'

'He has the sexiest smile.'

'Shit! You do fancy him.'

They both laugh, while Grace protests too much.

Grace changes for her evening job but can't get her mind off the bet. Her next move will be to take the rest of her finances to Johnny. She is giving him the true story. The savings account, which sits there getting fatter but doesn't do much else. The dwindling mortgage, which she knows isn't the best one for her. The credit cards, the receipts for clothes, the household expenses, the insurance policy she took out on a whim – she is giving him her financial life. And, who knows, he might even sort that out for the better, which is an added bonus. But she is in charge of timing, so when she goes back to her notebook and fills in details of the meeting, she writes underneath it: 'Hard to get.' Because although they are not dating, that is her first tactic. Johnny might not be trying to 'get' her, but he will be by the time she has finished. She leaves for her job, knowing that the next move is in hand. Go for the tried and tested. It nearly always works.

Betty walks through the door, annoyed that Johnny is not there. She stumbles slightly as she bends down to pick up the mail.

'Bugger, how did I get drunk?' she asks herself. She is sure she only had a couple of glasses. She goes to the sitting room, sits on the sofa and turns on the television. Maybe if she doesn't move, Johnny won't notice. The screen is helping her focus, although she is having trouble with double vision, so she closes one eye.

She hears the door open, and tries to sit up straight. Johnny walks in and goes to kiss her.

'Betty, is something wrong?'

'Nah, why?' She is perfecting nonchalance.

'Because you are sitting here with your coat on and your handbag still over your shoulder watching football.' There are flaws in her plan.

'Am I?'

'Are you drunk?'

'Are you?'

'No, I've had two beers. Betty, come on, I'll help you out of your coat.'

She stands up, amazed at how well she can do it, and shakes her coat off.

'Have you eaten?' Johnny asks.

'Nah. Not very hungry, actually.'

'Betty, it's OK for you to be drunk, although it's a bit early. Anyway, stop trying to pretend you're sober. I'll make us something to eat.'

They eat in near silence, because Betty's head is stretching all over the place and she cannot think of a single thing to say. She tells herself that she is behaving this way because she feels guilty for lying to him, not because she is worried.

Later, in bed, she feels sober again. Sober and silly. If she continues being Betty the lush, that will only drive Johnny into the arms of another woman.

'Johnny, I'm sorry about tonight. I'm not sure what came over me.'

'A bottle of wine on an empty stomach, by the look of it.'

'Yeah, but I don't normally do that. Sorry. It's been a shit evening, hasn't it?'

'Don't be daft. Now go to sleep and hope that you don't have a hangover.' He kisses her gently, and as warmth and sleep wrap themselves around her, she forgets to worry about Grace. She is in his arms and that is where she belongs.

Grace opens the door and throws her shoes off. They are killing her, but she should know better than to wear that particular pair. She goes to the kitchen and finds a bottle of whisky. She pours a glass, gets the ice tray and throws in some ice cubes, drinks it down and repeats the motion. It was a horrible night, with a horrible man, and the most horrible thing of all is that she couldn't stop thinking about Johnny. He was with her all evening – she couldn't shake him off. His image is stalking her. She managed to get her job done, but at times she felt herself losing it. She was angry with herself. This is her bet, her idea and she is in control. But despite the angry words she has with herself, when she goes to bed that night, he is still on her mind, and in her dreams.

Chapter Twenty-Two

On Thursday, Grace calls Johnny to cancel their second meeting, as per the plan. She is a little bit miffed to find that she doesn't want to cancel, but she pushes that away. She might have developed a tiny little crush on him after their first meeting, but only because of his eyes. And his smile. It is utterly manageable; she is still in control.

'Johnny, it's Grace.'

'Hi, how are you?'

'Fine, but I have to cancel our meeting tomorrow. It's work, you see. I'm swamped.'

'Do you want to rearrange, or maybe you can send me the papers so I can look at them first?'

'No, the papers are messy. It's probably best I explain them, and, to be honest, I don't trust the mail. I'll call on Monday to rearrange. Should I call your secretary?'

'No, call me, I am quite good at looking after my diary.' He laughs, kindly.

Grace giggles.

Johnny doesn't know why, but he puts the phone down and feels disappointed. He tells himself that it is because none of his other clients is quite as attractive as Grace, but nothing more than that. Then he ticks himself off for sounding like a horny teenager. He is a happily married man with a beautiful wife. He doesn't need beautiful clients.

Grace replaces the receiver and smiles. He is so sweet. She

almost feels disappointed that she won't see him, but she brushes that away. Lucky Betty, she almost hates her more now she knows just how lucky that woman is. As per Phase Two of her notes, five minutes after hanging up from Johnny, she picks the phone up again.

'Sorry, it's Grace again.'

'Hello.' He sounds confused.

'I was thinking, can we rebook another appointment now, I'm just a bit fed up of having all this hanging over me.'

'Sure. When do you want to come in?'

'Next Wednesday. Hopefully I should be able to get away in the afternoon.'

'Say three o'clock?'

'Perfect, I'll be there. Have a nice weekend, Johnny.'

'Thanks, you too, Grace.'

Make sure you think of me, Johnny, she silently adds, although it might be a bit soon for that.

Betty has arranged for their friends Sarah and Will to come for dinner on Thursday night. It is all part of the normality of life that she is determined to maintain. They are friends of Johnny's that she knows because of him, which she believes makes them safer than any other couple. Johnny is in charge of cooking. Betty is in charge of making the house, and herself, look nice. She is delighted with her control over the bet. She has barely given it a second thought. She isn't going to let Grace mess up her life; she has done too good a job of messing up her own. She won't sink to her level, or play her games. Her marriage is rock solid and there is nothing Grace can do to penetrate its walls.

'Um, something smells good,' she says, creeping up behind Johnny and putting her arms round him.

'And someone looks delicious,' he replies, turning round.

There is no way that Grace can come between them. There is no space.

'Oliver, what a surprise.' Grace could have sworn that he wouldn't be calling her again.

'How are you?' He sounds formal, stiff.

'Fine, you?'

'Busy as always. I wanted to ask you something, I wanted to ask you if you went ahead with that bet.'

'I did. I am doing. I know your feelings on it, which is why I didn't expect to hear from you.' She feels defensive, but at the same time she would really like to talk to him about it.

'Grace, I care about you. I want you to stop this and be with me, properly.'

'Hardly the most romantic-sounding proposition.' She has no idea how to respond. Together with him 'properly' – the thought terrifies her. She doesn't love Oliver, she doesn't love anyone, and she can't be with anyone 'properly' unless she finds her heart. She also realises that she is talking to Oliver but thinking about Johnny. No, there is no way she can be with him. But she still doesn't want to let him go. What's wrong with her?

'I know, but it's my best. Listen, Grace, I'm not doing this any more. I'm not dropping in and out of your life. Either we do this, or we don't. I can't do half-measures any more. I love you, Grace, and you're driving me crazy.'

Grace is surprised to find she is crying. She will miss Oliver. He is one of her best friends. She also hears the hurt in his voice and hates that she inflicted that. She doesn't want to miss him, that much she knows, but how can she communicate it?

'Olly, I'm sorry, but you know I can't.' She wants to say more, but all she feels is a hole opening up inside her. She wants to stop him from leaving her but she doesn't know how.

'I'm always going to love you, Grace.'

'Oliver, please, don't do this.'

'Give me one good reason not to.' He sounds so sad and she feels sad. She could stop him going, but she can't. She hates herself, and she wants to make everything better, but she can't. She isn't equipped for normal relationships, normal life. She is just going to have to let him go, but she doesn't want to.

'I care, Olly.'

'That's not enough any more, Grace. I need more. Give up the bet, think about quitting your job. Move in with me.' He doesn't sound as if he's begging, he's so matter of fact, as if he were offering her a job.

'I can't.' For a split second she wanted to. She wanted to give it all up for him, to be with him, to find a life that doesn't leave her vulnerable. But then she remembered: it would do exactly that. If she relied on him then she would be exposed and she couldn't risk that.

'Then, Grace, I can't do this any more. I don't want to but I have to finish this.'

'Can't we carry on as we are?' She knows it sounds lame, she knows that he will say no, but she says it anyway.

'You know we can't. Grace, I'm going to go now.'

'Oliver, please . . .' She cannot find the words.

'I'll always love you, Grace.'

She regulates her breath, and tries to stem the flow of tears, but when she realises that he has just gone, she cries harder.

If anyone could see me, see what I do to people, they'd lock me up. Or stone me, or worse. I destroy lives. Maybe Betty's right. I destroy people's happiness.

'So, Betty, how's work?' Sarah asks as they are tucking into the starter.

'Great, as always, although my boss is getting more insane. I've got about five stories on the go at the moment, and it'll be her fault if they get mixed up.'

'My boss's like that. He's piling on the work. I can't bear it.' Sarah has some high-flying City job.

'Oh, Betty, tell her about the story that upset you so much, the honey thing. What was her name?' Johnny prompts.

'Gr— Griselda.' Everyone laughs, Betty reddens.

'Was she really called that?' Johnny asks, racking his brain for any memory of her name.

'No, really she was called Helen, but Griselda suited her better.' Betty has made a startling recovery and she goes on to entertain them all with the honey-trap story; omitting a few major details.

'What are you up to this weekend?' Will asks, over dessert.

'Nothing, I think. I'm going to try to get away with playing golf.' Johnny reaches over and kisses Betty's cheek.

'Well, we thought we might try for a last-minute break in the New Forest, maybe somewhere with a golf course.'

'Isn't it a bit late?' Johnny asks.

'No, it's off season. Anyway, if you're interested I'll see what I can do.'

'Count us in,' Betty says quickly. 'But only if you find somewhere with a golf course.'

They will go away, Betty knows that. They will spend time with their friends, in the New Forest, eating pub food and drinking pints and walking, maybe, even if it is only for a couple of days. They will be together, and where will Grace be? Alone, like the Griselda that she is.

Grace recovers and takes a phone call from Eddie.

'It feels like ages,' he admonishes.

'I'm sorry, but I've been working so hard.'

'Then I don't suppose you'll have time to come away with me at the weekend?'

'Where?'

'Bath. I've been invited to a restaurant opening. It's an old friend's place, so I thought I'd book a nice hotel and make a weekend of it.'

'Bit last minute – surely you knew before now.'

'I did, but I thought if I asked you at the last minute, then you wouldn't be able to wriggle out with an excuse.' She laughs at his accurate evaluation. Just as she is about to turn him down and find one of her lame excuses, she thinks better of it. A weekend away might do her the world of good, and Eddie doesn't hate her like Oliver does.

'That sounds lovely.'

'Really?' He can't help the surprise edge into his voice.

'Really. It's going to be great.'

She is smiling when she puts the phone down, as is he. She is delighted with events, because maybe they will take her mind off Johnny. Or maybe they won't. Whatever, she will enjoy herself with Eddie because he deserves it, and if she can make him happy then maybe she won't be such a bad person after all.

On Friday afternoon, after she has packed her weekend bag and fitted an automatic fish feeder to her fish tank (purchased for such occasions but never used), she calls him again. This is the last stage in Phase One and it is a bit of a gamble.

'Johnny Parkin.' His voice makes her shake; she is nervous.

'It's Grace.'

'Hi, how are you?' He sounds puzzled by her call.

'I feel really silly calling you, I hope you don't mind, it's just that my solicitor is away and I can't talk to my boss. I didn't know who else to turn to.'

'What's wrong?' He is concerned, she can hear it in his voice.

'It's silly really, but my ex-husband called me. You see, I bought this flat with the divorce settlement, and now he says I owe him. I think he's facing financial difficulties. Can he take my flat? It's all I have.' She sounds upset. And although part of her feels guilty because Johnny is genuine and she is using that

– exploiting it – the other part of her feels it is necessary. She has to play the charade, but she is playing it almost too well.

'No way. You bought it when you were no longer married to him. It's in your name, there is no way he is entitled to it. It sounds to me as if he is trying to scare you into giving him money.'

'If it wasn't for you, he might have succeeded.'

Johnny is incensed. Poor, hapless Grace being bullied by her ex-husband is almost too much for him to bear. She is so, so, undeserving of such treatment.

'Grace, please don't listen to him.'

'I shan't, I promise. I'll ignore him. I wish he'd stay away from me.'

'You're not in any danger, are you?' He is worried about her vulnerability.

'No, not physically, if that's what you mean. He's just a bully, but he won't come near me. But thank you for your concern.'

'Hey, you're about to become one of my best clients, I have to take care of you.'

'See you next Wednesday, Johnny. Have a great weekend.'

'You too, and don't worry.'

Johnny replaces the receiver just as his mobile rings. He sees it is Betty and answers it.

'Hi, darling.'

'Johnny, I tried your line but it was engaged. We're meant to be leaving in an hour – are you ready?'

'I'm leaving now. Sorry, work shit.'

'But you are leaving?'

'Five minutes, I promise.'

He puts his mobile into his jacket pocket, locks his filing cabinet, and shuts down his computer. Then, just as he is about to walk out the door, he turns back. He picks up the desk organiser and opens it to a certain page. He feels an overwhelming desire to call her, he has no idea why. He is worried about her but he has to stop. She's survived without him and she will continue to. He chastises himself for being so soft. He has a weekend to go to and he can't afford to worry about his clients like this.

Grace is smiling to herself, but the guilt is growing, because he is a nice guy and she has made him worry about her. The phone call she made was so calculated; she is playing with his kindness, but again, she can't help herself. Yes, the move was planned, but she needed to hear his voice, wanted desperately to hear his voice. She knows that everything is complicated, and although she is not proud of her behaviour, she also can't change it.

'*Walk away,*' a voice says. '*I can't,*' another replies. She is sunk.

Grace has no idea why it's happening but it is. She doesn't know if there is some grand plan. Betty came into her life, upset her, led her to the bet, which in turn is working on defrosting her heart. It could be fate or something, or it could just be coincidence. Whichever, when she decided to get her own back on Betty she had no idea that it would be like this: that she would feel like the bitch Betty thought she was one minute, and like the happiest person in the world the next. The kaleidoscope that are her emotions have changed from black and white, back into colour.

On Saturday, the weather in the New Forest is wet, putting an end to Johnny's idea of playing golf with Will, and Betty's idea of romantic walks. Instead, they sit in a pub all afternoon, getting drunk, watching sport and eating packets of crisps.

'Not exactly what we had in mind,' Sarah says, as she opens yet another packet of cheese and onion.

'Me neither. Maybe we can go back to the hotel for an afternoon nap,' Betty suggests. She isn't drunk, but a little bit merry, and she wants her wicked way with her husband.

'Good idea.' Johnny winks and they set off after finishing their drinks. Despite the weather, they feel relaxed. Just being out of London does that for them. Betty's mind is completely empty of thoughts of Grace, although Johnny's is not. He is worried about her; he can't help it. He knows that he should be concentrating on his wife and his weekend away but he cannot help but fear for her. She has no one and the fact she turned to him proved that. He is just being a good Samaritan.

Although it was only a short walk from the pub to the hotel, they are all a bit wet when they arrive in reception. Both couples make their way to their respective rooms.

'Let's get you out of those wet clothes,' Betty says, winking suggestively.

'OK,' Johnny replies.

Betty marvels at how attractive she still finds him after all this time, and she hopes, prays, he feels the same. Despite her resolve, Grace has crept into her head again.

They make love and Betty gives it everything. She feels a need for intensity so he understands. She loves him, and lying to him is making her feel guilty. She hates lying to him.

He feels the intensity and returns it. He wants his wife to feel safe and secure, not like Grace. He realises that he is worrying about her still, despite the fact that his naked wife is next to him, and he hopes that it is just because he is a nice person and not because he is a bad one.

Grace is enjoying Bath. It is trying to rain but she doesn't mind because it is so nice for her to be somewhere different. Ed drives her round, they look at the Georgian architecture, she falls in love with the Royal Crescent, and then they go back to their hotel for an afternoon nap.

As they make love she is thinking of Johnny. Is he worrying

about her? Her assumption that he is thinking about her is not vanity. It is because she knows that he is a nice person and she was upset. He is going to worry about her, but that is all. She does not expect him to want her yet. Soon, but not yet.

Eddie feels that she is distant but that happens often when they are making love. He has no idea where she is and he knows better than to ask. There is a down side to dating Grace, but there are also up sides, the main one being that she is not demanding. He holds her while she sleeps, secure in the knowledge that she is not dreaming about him.

Chapter Twenty-Three

'I am going round the fucking bend.' Betty picks up her glass of wine, looks at it and then puts it down again. She is angry, most of all with herself.

'Betts, calm down.' She is in a bar with Alison. It is the beginning of the fourth week of the bet and the pressure is beginning to get to her.

'I have no idea if he's seen her or not. But he said he's going for dinner with "a client" tonight and when I asked which client, he said it was a rich guy that he needed to keep sweet. What if he's lying to me already and he's going out with *her*?' Her cool confidence has slipped, mainly due to the barrage of questions everyone is throwing at her about the bet.

'He goes out with clients. That is part of his job.'

'Yeah, which was fine before the bet. It's been three weeks – that's a quarter of the way through. What if it is her he's having dinner with?' She hates how wet she sounds, but she feels wet. She is trying not to be, she is trying to be nonchalant, but it isn't working.

'Call her.'

'What?'

'Call her and ask her if she's seen him.'

'What, and give her the satisfaction of knowing how edgy I am?'

'Betty, this is stupid. More than that, it's ridiculous. When you agreed this bet you trusted Johnny one hundred per cent, but you seem to be losing percentage points on a daily basis. He hasn't changed in his behaviour towards you, and you have no reason to be suspicious. You don't know if, how or when she contacted him, which, if you ask me, is the problem.'

'You're right. You know, I thought I could do this, but the paranoia is taking over. I'm going to call her. I'll stop being so pathetic and call her, making sure that she knows that I'm not a bit worried or upset whilst at the same time finding out anything she knows. That's what I'll do.'

'But not now.'

'Why not?'

'Because she will probably be working and if she's out, which she will be, and Johnny is out, which he is, then you'll put two and two together and come up with five.'

'Is that a saying?'

'I don't know. Betty, please, relax and finish your wine.' Alison is taking on a motherly role with Betty, which is confusing because previously Betty always took charge. Alison feels ill-equipped for the part. Lying to Matt, lying to Johnny, pacifying Betty – it is all taking its toll.

'OK.' Betty sighs. The bet is turning her into either a nervous wreck or an alcoholic.

Betty's fears are founded – not the one about her beloved having a torrid affair with the honey-trap woman, but the one about them having dinner together.

They met on the Wednesday of the third week as arranged, and she gave him all the papers he requested.

'You've got a good nest egg here,' he said.

This much Grace knows. 'I want to ensure that I'm looked after when I get old, as I seem to be doing rapidly.'

'Nonsense, you're a mere youngster.'

Grace was doing some blatant, old-fashioned flirting. She was wearing a slightly short skirt, and a low-cut top. Her long legs were emphasised by her high-heeled, knee-length boots. She moved rapidly from the sombre divorcee to the coquette. Her flirting was subtle, but she noted it was being well received; Johnny was flirting back. It wasn't just in his words, but in his look and his actions. And all the time Grace was falling deeper and deeper into his eyes. A body language expert would have found it obvious.

Phase One had been the initial meeting, Phase Two had been vulnerability and playing hard to get, figuratively speaking, Phase Three was flirting. And he was flirting back.

'Thanks, but, hey, that I know isn't true. Every day I wake up and find a new wrinkle or a new grey hair. I might need you to set up a savings account for plastic surgery. Anyway, I don't want to dominate your time too much. What happens now?' She looked at him directly, with a slight smile. The problem was that flirting had ceased to be a put-on; she was flirting for real.

'I am going to take this away, study it and come back with some options.' He couldn't help but admire her. She was not only beautiful but warm and friendly. He pushed those thoughts away.

'Excellent. When?'

'Well, how about Monday?'

'Monday is fine. No, wait, next week is a bugger. I've got a really tight schedule. Maybe you could post something to me. No, that wouldn't work because I probably wouldn't understand a word of it.' She giggled and leant towards him slightly.

'You haven't told me what you do.'

'I'm a PA for a very demanding lawyer. I think it's because he lost his hair when he was young that he's so grouchy. It's dull but, as you can see, it pays quite well.'

'It does. I should become a PA.'

'Because he's so difficult, he has to pay me to stay.' She laughed. 'Anyway, how about the following week?' She was playing with time, which was dangerous because it was running out. Slowly, slowly. She will get her man. Patience would get her her man.

'We could meet after work. I don't mind that.' Johnny was not sure why he suggested that. He normally only met long-standing clients after work, and that was client entertainment. Grace wasn't yet a client and would never be in the league that demanded dinners. He told himself that he was worried that if he didn't make the next appointment she might go somewhere else and he didn't want that. He had no idea why he felt that way. It was business, and in business Johnny liked to play with big money. This wasn't big money; it wasn't going to make him rich. He told himself that it was because he felt sorry for her; her vulnerability and fragility were blatantly apparent to him. He felt the need to take her worry away. That was all.

They arranged dinner on Monday evening (Johnny might have thought that he had suggested dinner without thinking, although perhaps his subconscious was thinking more than he realised), and Grace left to go back to her fictional demanding boss.

'See you Monday,' she said, smiling. The smile, which lasted awhile, was a triumphant one. Phase Three had worked.

'Who was that?' Dan, Johnny's colleague, walked into his office after Grace left.

'A potential client.'

'Can I have her?'

'What?'

'Johnny, you're happily married, I'm unhappily single. I should get all clients that look like that.'

'Like what?'

'Oh shit, are you blind? She is only one of the most gorgeous women I've ever seen.'

'I hadn't really noticed.' Dan laughed; Johnny had turned red. 'Well, maybe I noticed but I'm married, not blind.'

'Exactly. Come on, I'll buy you lunch and you can tell me all about her.'

Johnny went home that night feeling disturbed. He had met this woman twice and she unnerved him. He put his feelings down to sympathy, although he definitely found her attractive, for some reason that made him feel guilty. But he really had nothing to feel guilty about. He was married, not blind.

When Grace left Johnny on Wednesday she realised something. She had never felt it before, of that she was sure. Whatever she was feeling was new. Not only was it new but it was also wonderful. It was exciting, and made her feel wanton; free. Whatever it was, she was enjoying it. She was still in control of what she was doing, but barely.

Perhaps it was going to be easier than she had first imagined. He suggested dinner; she was going to ask him for lunch the following week. She was euphoric, but, as she explained to Nicole, only because she was winning. Nothing more. He was good-looking, he was funny and kind. But it was only about the bet. That was all. And all the fuzzy feelings, the central heating that had been switched on inside her, that was only because of the bet. Nothing more. Because, as she had written in her book, Phase Four, the dinner date, was in the bag.

Just as Grace was making her way home, Fiona summoned Betty to her office.

'I thought I'd find out how it's going.'

Betty looked at her. She couldn't tell if she was being kind or she just wanted the gossip.

'Fine, as far as I know. Johnny still sleeps in my bed, anyway.'

'But what about her?'

'I don't know. Remember one of the conditions of the bet

was that we don't speak until the two-month mark.' She looked sharply at Fiona. This was all her idea and she was sitting there, unaffected.

'So, you can only guess what she's doing?' Fiona saw a flaw in her plan. She was uncomfortable with Betty's ignorance. It was making her edgy.

'Yes.'

'Doesn't that make your imagination run wild?' Fiona knew hers was. She genuinely wants Betty to win this; she wants Johnny to turn Grace down, because then she will know that Betty isn't like her and has a rock-solid marriage. Yes, sure, it will make her jealous as hell, and she knows that deep down in the vindictive part of her brain she would like Betty to lose him, to prove to Fiona that all men are shits and it's not just Fiona who can't hold on to her man. However, the nice part of her, which is buried beneath the rubble of the divorce, wants her to win.

'Fiona, I don't need to worry. This is Johnny we're talking about, remember.' But Betty knew then that she was slightly worried. She believed this was a sign of human nature, not a sign of mistrust. She was just acting as any normal wife would if she thought that a gorgeous woman was trying to seduce her husband.

'Of course you don't. I'm just feeling a bit responsible.'

'What?' Fiona never, ever took responsibility for anything.

'Well, it was my idea. I'm just checking that it isn't driving you mad.' Fiona was frustrated. If she had known that the bet would be dredging all these tiresome emotions out of her, then she might have thought twice before suggesting it.

'Absolutely not.'

'Well, then, I was right to persuade you to do it.'

'Eh?'

'You'll thank me in the end.' Fiona felt better.

'I will?'

'Especially as you have no doubts about him and you don't feel a bit insecure. Well done, Betty. I am proud of you.'

Betty left the office feeling insecurity fly on to her shoulders and follow her out.

Johnny has booked a large, bright, Italian restaurant near his office, and near where he believes she works. He is there first, nursing a Bloody Mary and feeling guilty. Although the dinner is technically work, he has lied to Betty for the first time in their marriage. He told her that the client was male. He doesn't know why, because he has nothing to hide – this is strictly business – but the fact is, he lied. He could have told her the truth, she wouldn't mind, and he doesn't feel proud of himself for not doing so.

He sees her approaching. She is wearing a black trouser suit. Her body looks amazing in it, and Johnny notes how everyone in the restaurant turns to look at her. Again, he finds it incredible that her husband left her. He must have been mad. Another thought flashes into his head: he feels proud to be meeting her. He knows that everyone else is envious of him and that makes him feel good.

'Hi,' she says, sitting down and placing her handbag on the floor and the napkin on her lap.

'How are you?' He is rigid – nerves rather than intention.

'I think I'll be better with a gin and tonic inside me.' She smiles, and he orders. The flirting from Phase Three is being carried over to Phase Four.

'So, how was your day?'

'Johnny, that's the sort of question my husband would ask. Actually, not my ex-husband because he didn't give a fuck about anyone other than himself.' She laughs to show him she is teasing. 'But it was hell. I really think we should probably not talk about it, otherwise you'll have to endure an evening of me ranting. Why don't you tell me about your day?'

Her voice seems to be having a physical effect on him. He looks a little flustered.

'How about we order and then I will bore you with all this wonderful information about how to make you rich?'

Grace wonders if she is the only person aware of the chemistry. She is sure she can sense something in his eyes, in his face, in his tone, that suggests he is fully aware of the situation, even though there isn't really one. Two meetings and a dinner. It hardly constitutes infidelity; betrayal. She fancies him, of that she is sure. Like a heady teenager, she wants to be bullish about it, to storm him, knock him over, keep him there with her. But she cannot, because that would only scare him off. She is embarking on a dangerous mission because her feelings are already intertwined with the bet. She thought about many possibilities before she decided on her favoured revenge against Betty, but this was not one of them. Not that she would get personally involved. Not that she might end up hurt. And certainly not that she might end up caring that she hurt him. But she does. Her feelings are clear. Despite the brevity of their acquaintance she knows this is not just fancying.

She has never been as alone as she is without him in her whole life. She spent the weekend with Eddie, thinking about Johnny, his face, his voice, his manner. She knows little, but she thinks she is in love.

'What's your wife like?' she asks him. She knows that that seems an idiotic move – one that will make him aware that he is married for the rest of the dinner – but Grace knows what she is doing. She is two Graces at the moment: the professional seducer and the terrified little girl. She is trying to ignore the fear and go with what she knows, the seasoned 'provocateur', because that doesn't instil her with panic. For a minute after she asks the question, Johnny seems taken aback.

'She's a journalist for a woman's magazine. She's lovely, a bit dizzy at times; like you, hates finance. That's how we met.'

'You don't mind me asking?' Grace notes how Johnny looks flushed and is fiddling with his tie.

'No, no, I just didn't know that . . .'

'Wedding ring.' She winks at him.

'Of course, I should know by now that women are more observant than men. You don't wear yours any more.'

'I'm not married. I have no intention of wearing that pig's ring. Sorry. Tell me about how you met your wife.' He starts recounting the story, and Grace sees love in his eyes. She can gauge the way a man feels about his partner by asking him, and then looking. She is in no doubt that Johnny loves Betty; she is also painfully aware of how lucky Betty is. They are interrupted by the waiter, and they order. Grace asks Johnny to order the wine, and then gestures for him to continue.

'I'm not sure about all this love-at-first-sight stuff. I thought she was attractive but, well, she pursued me quite relentlessly. That's what I liked, really – the fact that I didn't have to do the running.' He laughs to show he is joking, but also serious.

His eyes shine with love for his wife, but he feels uncomfortable talking about her to Grace. She has all she needs to know.

'Well, I'll tell you how I met my ex. I was playing golf.' Her professionalism is back as she prepares herself for a future phase.

'Sorry to interrupt, but you play golf?'

'Yes. Why are you surprised?'

'I don't know.' He blushes. Grace loves his blushes. They make her want to stroke his face.

'I know, it's a man's sport. Anyway, I love it, although I'm a bit rusty. Do you play?'

'Avidly. Go on.' He is still slightly red-faced from her teasing but he is enjoying it, which is, of course, the idea.

'Right. Yes, well, I was playing golf – with a boyfriend, actually – and the ex was in front of us. But the game was really slow and I wasn't having a good day, and when we were at the last hole, actually finished the last hole, he said that I could do with some lessons and he'd teach me. Told me he was a golf coach. Anyway, my boyfriend scowled, but he gave me his number and I called him. He wasn't a coach, by the way, he was a sales manager, but that was that. We married after six months. It was a whirlwind. What do they say, marry in haste, repent at leisure? I'm doing that.'

'Do you still love him?'

'No. You know, the awful thing is, the longer it goes on, the more I realise that I never did. I was hurt by his betrayal, my ego is still bruised and my self-confidence is living in my shoes, but I don't think we were in love. Isn't that awful?'

Johnny doesn't answer as the food arrives. He is thinking, and his thoughts are entering his brain at one hundred miles a minute; travelling too quickly, and he feels constricted. He is not doing anything wrong; he keeps telling himself that. It is not a crime to find a woman attractive if you're married, or to find her interesting, intelligent, funny. It is human to care that she is obviously very hurt and it is human to want to help her mend that hurt. But he feels he is being mentally dishonest; to Betty and to Grace. It is not business, he knows that – he is enjoying her too much for it to be business – but he doesn't love his wife any less; he adores her. He has no idea why he is feeling the way he is, but he can't help it. Can't do a damn thing about it.

The rest of the dinner passes in talk of golf and Grace's fictional boss. It is nearly eleven, when they order coffee and realise that they haven't talked about Johnny's proposals.

'I'm sorry, I shouldn't have yapped on so much,' Grace apologises.

'No, it's my fault.' Johnny is now furious with himself. He has never been so unprofessional in his life. He enjoyed talking to her, listening to her voice, looking at her big hazel eyes. He hates himself for behaving as if he is having an affair when that is the last thing on his mind. But it was meant to be a business dinner and he was happily distracted from talking about finance at all.

'I'll come to your office. It's easier for me not to gabble on there.'

'Really, Grace, it was my fault.'

'Don't be so polite. Now we'd better hurry up and get you back to your wife before she thinks you've turned into a pumpkin.' She winks. Phase Four is complete. Mission accomplished.

Betty watches television when she gets back from her drink with Alison, but she finds only trash on offer. She feels restless and a tiny bit merry. She goes to the fridge and pours herself a glass of wine. She then pulls out some work to do, but she finds herself unable to concentrate.

The weekend they spent in the New Forest enters her mind. Wonderfully restful, pub lunches, overindulgent dinners, making love with an intensity they normally reserve for when they are away – it was perfect. But there was a nagging feeling that Johnny wasn't always there. Nothing major, just a little tiny fleck of doubt. She has no idea if it is her or if it is him.

She promised herself she wouldn't get paranoid, but now she admits she is. She is going to call Grace, but until then she is alone with her suspicions, which seem to be eating her from the inside out. *Is* it paranoia or are her instincts right?

She sips her wine as she again blames Fiona for unnerving her. Then she blames Alison. It was her idea to call Grace. Then she blames Grace. Then she blames Johnny, because he might be interested. Finally she blames herself because she agreed to the bet. But she will not let it defeat her.

Betty is in bed when Johnny gets home, but she isn't asleep.

'How was dinner?' she asks.

'Dull. Sorry I'm so late, he wouldn't stop talking.' He baulks at his lies.

'It doesn't matter. Night, honey.' Betty shuts her eyes and prays that he is not lying.

Johnny shuts his eyes and tries to get rid of the image of Grace that seems to be tattooed to his eyelids.

Grace feeds her fish, with a smile. As the fish food melts in the water, she realises that her heart has started to melt, and once it starts there is no way she can stop it. She does not know if she is in love, but if she is then it feels wonderful. Most of all she feels liberated from herself.

Sleep dances around, eluding her, teasing her, as her thoughts are fully on how she will win Johnny. It is not the bet she wants to win now, but the man. This makes it very dangerous for her, for him and especially for Betty.

She is torn, utterly confused. If she really cares about him the way her feelings were telling her, then she would let him be. She wouldn't lie, or try to confuse and upset him. It is nothing to do with Betty, although it is, because now she knows how special he is; she knows that she would destroy Betty if she took him away and she doesn't want to destroy her. Her anger against Betty has ebbed away. There is only a trickle left and she is no longer involved to hurt her or teach her a lesson. However, Grace cannot leave him. She wants him. She must do because she has never felt so glued to anyone in her whole life.

She also knows that even if he thinks he has feelings for her (which she believes he is developing like a slow rash), he won't have when the truth emerges. The idea of the bet was for her to seduce him and then walk away, but she cannot walk away, not while he will let her be with him. If she seduces him once, she will want to keep doing so. She wants him, properly, as Oliver would say, properly in her life.

And if in the next month and a half she achieves this, what is going to happen? She will lose him. Either that or she will always have to be Grace the divorcee legal secretary. She cannot do this. Whichever way she looks at it, she has boxed herself into a corner. She has to play out the bet. She can't but she will, and that is all there is to it.

The first thing Grace knows is that Johnny loves Betty. She also knows that he finds her attractive. Johnny invited her to dinner and he let her distract him from business the whole night. She knows that he doesn't think he is doing anything but being a kind, financial adviser or a typical man who can't resist a damsel in distress. Especially when that damsel is wearing a short skirt. But there is something about her that he is drawn to, and although she knows that he is the type of person who will hate himself for it, she knows that she is already somewhere under his skin. It just remains for her to ensure that she stays there. Seductress Grace is now in charge.

Progress, for just over three weeks, is very promising, but for what reasons she is unsure.

Chapter Twenty-Four

Betty is in Fiona's office. Fiona is out at a conference, so Betty has commandeered her office to make the phone call she has been thinking about all night, which meant she didn't get much sleep. The stupid bet is in her head, under her skin, everywhere, and it will drive her insane unless she takes a stand. Trust, she has discovered, is not as easy to believe in as she thought. This is a weakness in her rather than in Johnny. She hates herself for it; she has no idea how to get rid of it. There is a battle going on, and she knows that she is responsible, no one else. She was trustful, he was trusty. Now she is feeling suspicion and insecurity, and he is still trusty. Isn't he?

She sits in Fiona's chair and rests her head on her desk. She needs to put her thoughts in order. There has been only one night when he was out, and that was the previous night. If she has seen him, which Betty is sure she has, then it must have been during the day, and if he was lying, then last night. But Johnny doesn't lie, that much Betty knows. He was with a client, but he specified that the client was male, so he couldn't have been with Grace. Because if he was with her, he would have said that his client was female. Betty isn't a jealous monster; she knows he has female clients and that's fine. The trouble is that if Grace is posing as a client, which Betty believes she is, then she is not only a female client, but a female client intent on seducing him.

Why did I ever agree to this? she asks herself, but the answer upsets her as much as the question. Is her job more important to her than her marriage? Or is she just more sure of her marriage than her job? That would be a good answer. She agreed because she knew, and everyone else agreed, that she had nothing to worry about. Johnny is her husband, her best friend, her lover. He is the one person in her life that has never let her down. She is unsure now why she felt even the tiniest bit of doubt.

However, she still picks up the phone.

Grace is woken by the phone ringing. She looks at the clock. It is half-past ten. Because sleep teased her all night, she has slept late. She thinks about ignoring the phone, but then she gets out of bed and goes to her office, mentally making a note to get another phone as she stubs her toe on the door in her sleepy state.

'Hello,' she says, rubbing her toe and suddenly realising how cold it is. She is wearing only a T-shirt.

'Hi, it's me.'

'Betty?' She blinks and wonders if she is still asleep.

'Yes. Look I know we agreed that we wouldn't talk or whatever, but I just wanted to . . . to . . .'

'To know if I've fucked your husband.' Now she is awake. She is also in a very bad mood.

'Grace!' Betty immediately feels her hackles rise.

'I'm just teasing you. I haven't, by the way, in case you were worried. The deal was that you don't call me and I don't call you. Until after two months. If you're getting all paranoid then it serves you right. The woman who said she would never doubt her husband is doubting him. Tut-tut, Betty, that's not very nice of you, is it?' Grace's memories of why she dislikes Betty are prominent.

'I am not calling you because I am worried about him.' Betty is remembering what a bitch Grace is.

'Really?'

'I'm not worried, I just feel guilty. You know how it is.'

'I have no idea. I don't have a husband.' Grace knows she is being deliberately obtuse but then she doesn't want to make it easier for Betty. She wants to make it as hard as she can. And she can.

'I trust him, OK? It's just really hard knowing that I've done this to him and that he might be seeing you or might not be. I'm not blaming you, I blame myself. I hate myself for doubting him, really hate myself. And it's only been a short time. I am worried that I won't keep it together for the rest of the month, or the next one.' Betty is trying to stop herself from crying. She is angry with her eyes for even thinking they should be allowed to shed tears.

Grace does a U-turn and feels dreadful for being such a bitch. Betty loves him; she doesn't deserve to be hurt. The problem is that although Grace knows she should let go of the whole thing now, she can't. She can't because she has come alive, and he is her life support. He is the blood that is coursing through her veins. He is her reason. So as much as she feels awful for Betty, which unexpectedly she does, she cannot let go. She is not ready to die again.

'Betty, I am sorry. I shouldn't be goading you, really I shouldn't. I know how much you love him. I can't stop this because a bet is a bet and I need to see this through; we had a deal, after all. But listen to me, the reason I said we shouldn't speak was because I didn't want you driving yourself even madder, or for me to lie to you and tell you things which will make it worse. So, although I think this should be the last time we talk until it's over, I am going to tell you something. Firstly, the men I am paid to test are normally horrible, but Johnny is not. Secondly, he loves you, that is the clearest thing I have ever seen. Thirdly, if you feel threatened at all, then just ensure that he knows how much he means to you. I can't imagine I'll win this, Betty, I really can't.' She is surprised by how nice she is being but she feels guilty herself.

'Do you mean that?' Betty is surprised by Grace's kindness and she doesn't altogether trust it.

'Yes. Listen, you were out of order with the way you treated me, and I am full of anger at you, chock-a-block full. Moreover, although I can behave like a bitch, I'm not really one. Now, I'll talk to you when the agreed deadline is up, all right?'

'Yes, I am now.'

Grace puts down the phone and feels her face. It is wet with tears. She is crying because she has just realised the full extent of what she is doing. Betty sounded desperate, and although she isn't her biggest fan, and despite her recent actions, being horrible isn't her. As she thinks about stopping, she feels even worse. She can't contemplate not seeing Johnny again; she has to see him, she needs to see him again. As sorry as she is for Betty, she is more sorry for herself. Her tears are for her, not Betty. She is ill equipped to deal with her feelings; she is not familiar with them. She is terrified of everything, and she cannot think of Betty. For now, she has to think of herself. For once she is going to try to catch some happiness.

Or, if Johnny chooses, she will melt her frozen heart. The ice queen will learn how to smile. But one way or another she will pursue this. Because she has only just found that she has a heart, she needs to ensure that it is real and the only way she can do that is by feeling it fill with happiness, or by hearing it break. She is prepared for either option.

Betty puts down the phone and banishes the threat of tears. At first, she thinks that Grace is going to lose because she herself admitted that Johnny loves Betty. Then she thinks of the advice she gave her. She takes Johnny for granted, and that is her only danger. Grace will present him with perfection; Betty must learn to compete. There is no rule in the bet that says Betty has to sit back and do nothing. She can try to win too. If she makes sure that he knows how much he means to her, and she treats him like a king, then he will have no reason to go elsewhere. She is taking out extra insurance. Bye-bye, Betty Parkin; hello Betty Superwife. She will not surrender without a fight, nor will she behave in the paranoid way she has been behaving. It is time for her to take control and win the damn bet.

Despite her tears, Grace has to pull herself together and get on with the bet. She mustn't think of Betty; she can only think of herself. This is not yet Phase Five but an appendix to Phase Four. Grace dials Johnny's direct line and, to her relief, he answers.

'Johnny Parkin.'

'It's Grace,' she sobs.

'Grace, what's wrong?' He is surprised to hear from her so soon, and although part of him is pleased, another part feels wary.

'I left my job.' She wonders how many lies are forgivable.

'What?' Why she is calling him with this information? He knows why – because even though they barely know each other, he held out the branch of friendship, and she took it. He doesn't mind her calling – in fact, he is happy to hear her voice – but no matter how many times he tells himself that he isn't doing anything wrong, part of him feels that he is. He has no idea how to stop this guilt without breaking contact with her, and he can't do that: she needs him. He doesn't want to do it, he just doesn't.

'He was so horrible to me, I just couldn't stand it. Oh, Johnny, I'm sorry, I shouldn't be calling you. You're a financial adviser, not a counsellor. I am so sorry.' She sobs harder. The tears are left over from the conversation with Betty, hence their willingness to return.

'Grace, it's OK. You can talk to me.'

'But you're at work.'

'Look, I'm flat out, but why don't you meet me for lunch, in J&J's, the deli opposite my office?'

'Are you sure you have time?'

'I can spare an hour. I'll meet you there at one.'

The appendix to Phase Four is underway. She tries to be pleased with herself but that is becoming slightly difficult.

Betty goes to the fashion department.

'Rich.' She approaches the fashion assistant.

'Yes, darling?'

'I need some underwear.'

'Why are you telling me?' He looks at her in his campest mock horror.

'I wondered, have you got any fancy stuff down here I can nick?'

'Well, there is a baby-blue négligé with a little tiny dressing gown – you know, fifties style. It's over there and we haven't used it. But if you tell anyone I led you to it, I'll shoot you.'

'You're a star. Will it fit me?'

Rich looks at Betty's slim frame. 'Of course, and probably have room for him in there too.'

'That's the idea.'

'You know what you need?'

'What?'

'Those fluffy high-heeled mules. We don't have any here, but you could go buy a pair.'

'I might just do that.' She kisses Rich on the cheek and then goes to steal the négligé.

While Betty was thinking about underwear, Grace is thinking about outerwear. She picks out a suit, one that she imagines is the sort a legal secretary would wear. It emphasises her long legs and tiny waist. She wants Johnny to think she has come from the job she has just quit. Again, she feels a small pang of guilt at the fact she is lying. She is also aware that she is playing a role all the time, one that didn't matter when it was about revenge but does when it is about more than that. She can only hope that he will forgive her, or be too in love with her to care, details that she is not equipped to deal with yet. If he does fall in love with her, then she will address the problem. Now, she still needs to get him to fall for her.

Grace sits in the deli, still wearing her 'work suit'. She is early, so she orders a coffee and waits. Her stomach is fluttering slightly, another new sensation. She is enjoying the experience of each new emotion, although each takes her by surprise. She would like to pin them down, to isolate them, but they are moving too fast for her to catch. She is on a rollercoaster ride, and she is screaming with joy.

'Have you been waiting long?' Johnny asks, concern apparent in his eyes.

'I kind of wandered around after I called you. I ordered a coffee, but nothing to eat.' She gestures to her coffee.

'What do you want? I'll order.'

'Nothing. I'm really not hungry.'

'You have to eat. What about a cheese sandwich – plain, but at least it's something?' She likes the fact that he is taking charge; he hates the fact that he wants to make her feel better. His old friend guilt has returned.

'All right then.' She smiles at him sadly. This is genuine. She doesn't want to be lying to him, she wants to tell him the truth. But if she does she will never see him again. She watches him at the counter with intense fascination. She only ever felt like this when she looked at her fish, but she could watch him for hours. He returns with a coffee and two sandwiches.

'Johnny, I'm sorry I called you. It wasn't fair.'

'What do you mean?'

'You're trying to sort out my finances, not my other problems.

It's just . . . well, it's embarrassing but I don't have anyone. I trust you.'

'What, no friends?'

'Not many. By the time I married I'd whittled all my friends down to mutual ones. When we split up everyone found it easier to side with him. It's hard for me to trust people, but for some reason I trust you.' She casts her eyes downwards.

'Why?'

'I don't know. People I thought were my friends weren't. I learnt not to rely on people.'

'That's awful.'

Johnny is thinking about his group of friends. Despite the recent party, most of their friends are couples, who somehow or other are mutual friends. There are a couple of guys at work that he is friendly with, but socialising is limited to an occasional after-work drink. He wonders what would happen if he and Betty split up, then he brushes that thought away. They won't split up. He has no idea what is happening to his head, but thoughts are entering it that he should never allow. He finds it hard to breathe. He looks at Grace, and wonders if she has put a spell on him. He knows that now he should walk away, go back to Betty and tell Grace she will have to find another adviser. He opens his mouth to tell her as much. It is for the best.

'I can't believe fucking people sometimes.' His vehemence takes them both by surprise. He didn't say what he thought he would; he knows he can't. He has no intention of having an affair, cannot believe his head will allow that thought in either, but he can't walk away. She needs him, that's all there is to it, and he is a good person. No, he can't walk away.

'Anyway, I still shouldn't have called you. I know, let's go back to business. I haven't seen your proposals yet and, God knows, I'm going to need to sort something out now I have no income.' She thinks he wants her, but she also senses his reluctance. He is in love with his wife, and she thinks of herself as a distraction for him. She is excitement, versus routine. She knows that he will not have an affair with her. She cannot tell how she knows but she knows. If she wants to win the bet or, more importantly, win Johnny, she will have to get him to leave Betty. Can she get a devoted husband to leave his devoted wife in under three months? And could she live with herself if she did? She has no idea, but one thing she does know is that she is falling deeper and deeper into him.

'Well, you could come in tomorrow.' He pulls out his Palm Pilot and checks his diary. 'About two?'

'Sounds good. I've got nothing else to do.'

'What you are doing now?' His voice is full of concern.

'Shopping, I guess. What all women do when they need to cheer themselves up. Oh, and I'll probably go home and watch *Carry On Camping.*' Grace has decided that if the golf isn't enough she will invite him to a film with her. She has no idea where or how, but sowing the seed now seems like a good idea. *Carry On Camping* is the only one she knows.

'You like *Carry On* films?'

'Love them.' She smiles and so does he. It is incredible that she likes the same things he does. That is the thought he takes with him that afternoon.

Grace doesn't go shopping when she leaves him. She goes home to prepare for her job that evening. But although she is determined to remain professional, she is acutely aware of the lies.

Betty spends an hour shopping. She decides that as she has a work function that night she will thrill her husband the following night to within an inch of his life. She smiles and then laughs. Her confidence is back.

Chapter Twenty-Five

'Unbelievable,' Grace says, when she has listened to him.

'What?' Johnny is feeling nervous about her reaction for some reason.

'I understood. I actually understood! Wow, this is amazing.'

'Brilliant. I must be better at explaining things than I think.'

'Oi, matey, it might be that I am actually secretly a financial whiz-kid.' They look at each other. 'Nah,' they say in unison and laugh.

'Grace, I hope you're all right about your job now?'

'I was upset, but more because of security than anything. But now I feel liberated, free. I feel like doing something really crazy.'

'Such as?'

'A bunjee jump or something – I don't know – but something that I wouldn't normally do.'

'Well, be careful.' He laughs. 'Listen to me, I sound like a stick-in-the-mud.'

The phone rings to announce his next appointment is here. Grace stands up.

'Thank you for letting me disrupt your day.' She smiles and walks to the door. He follows her.

'It was a pleasure,' he replies, still feeling light-headed. She leans in and kisses his cheek, lingering for just a few seconds. He blushes again.

'Goodbye,' she says. The papers he prepared for her are still on his desk, the lipstick mark is on his face. Traces of Grace, both mental and physical, are there.

She is about to get into the lift when someone calls her. She turns to find herself facing a young suited man whom she has never seen before.

'It's Grace, isn't it?'

'Hello, do I know you?' She hopes to God that she doesn't, as the panic of someone who is being deceptive intensifies.

'No, sorry, I'm stalking you. Oh God, that sounds awful. Don't call the police, I'm not really stalking you, but I saw you come in for an appointment and I wanted to talk to you.' He looks flustered; Grace looks amused. A perfect tool for a new phase has fallen into her lap.

'Well, my non-stalker, I'm at a disadvantage. I have no idea who you are.'

'Dan. Sorry, I'm Dan. I work with Johnny. I'm also a financial adviser.'

'Typical, you wait years for one and then two come along at the same time.' Her composure returns as quickly as it had fled.

'What?'

'I'm teasing. Tell me, Dan, what can I do for you, or are you trying to poach me from Johnny?'

'Oh no, nothing like that. No, I wouldn't nick business. I just wondered if you might . . . Shit, I sound like a moron. Of course you don't want to.'

'Meet me at seven at the bar round the corner, what's it called?'

He steps back in surprise. Grace is smiling at him with one eyebrow arched.

'Aeration?'

'That's the one. I'll see you tonight at seven, shall I?'

'You certainly will.'

Grace shoots him a last smile before getting into the lift. She notices the receptionist staring at them, which is good. She just hopes she is a gossip. Just before the doors fully close she catches him still looking at her. He appears so pleased with himself, and he was sweet. Grace feels awful: another life played with, although she is sure he won't suffer too much. A date, a kiss on the cheek, he'll recover. He's just a casualty of her own private war and, unfortunately, as in every war, there have to be casualties.

Grace arrives home and goes to her notebook. Under the heading 'Phase Five' she writes two words: 'jealousy' and 'Dan'. Then she goes to get ready for her date. Perhaps she is going to hurt him, or maybe he's a playboy that picks up women and discards them all the time. Of course, she will not feel bad about him because a man who asks a woman out after just seeing her in his office must be full of confidence, and also a serial philanderer. Just like all the men she works with. But not like Johnny. She may be using him to get to Johnny, but he is using her. So, they are quits and she has nothing to feel guilty about.

Johnny is about to leave when he sees Dan still in his office.

'You're working late.'

'I've got a date. I'm just hanging around, really.'

'Oh yeah? Well, have fun.' It doesn't occur to Johnny to ask who he is seeing and Dan doesn't get a chance to boast to him before he's gone.

Grace chooses a pair of tight jeans, high-heeled shoes and a black chiffon blouse. She looks sexy, but not as if she has tried too hard. She arrives at the bar fifteen minutes late, and immediately spots a very anxious-looking Dan at a table. She goes to join him.

'Sorry I'm late.'

'I thought you might have changed your mind.' He cringes at his keenness.

'No, of course not.' She feels bad now, because he thinks she is on a date with him, but she's not, although she resolves that she will try to be. She will be as charming as she can, and she will try to ensure that he enjoys himself. Then she won't feel so guilty. 'I'd love a glass of white wine,' she says, slightly teasing.

Johnny opens his front door and hangs up his jacket. As he turns towards the sitting room he stops in his tracks. Betty is standing in the doorway, one hand on her hip, the other clutching the door frame. Her hair is wild, she is wearing more make-up than he has seen her wear, ever, and she is wearing a blue négligé and high heels. He has an uncontrollable urge to laugh, but thinks better of it.

'What's this in aid of?' he asks, approaching her. He has to admit she looks amazing in a slutty way.

'You,' she replies, throwing her arms around him. Then, after she has kissed him and made her intentions clear, she leads him to the kitchen, where she makes them even clearer.

Dan returns from the bar with a bottle of Chardonnay. Grace thinks he really is a nice guy.

'Can I ask you a personal question?' she asks.

'Sure.' He looks pleased.

'How old are you?'

'Twenty-nine.'

'A youngster then.' She is smiling in the way she does when she wants to tease.

'I can't be younger than you,' he replies.

'You can. I'm thirty-two. Divorced. Bit of a mess, really.'

'I don't think so. You only look as if you're in your early twenties.' She smiles at his flattery. It is going to be hard to get rid of him, she realises that. Maybe she is wrong and he's genuine. She tries desperately not to think that, because although she is really sorry she feels it is unavoidable.

'How long have you worked with Johnny?' She tries to make

the question sound innocent, although she worries that it is anything but.

'About three years now. I joined the firm, he was already there. He's a good guy.'

'But is he a good financial adviser?'

'He is, one of the best, which is a shame because otherwise you could work with me.'

'Isn't it unethical to take a client on a date?'

'No. Not if you really want to. But it's probably best that you work with Johnny. Then I can't be accused of seducing you to nick all your money.'

Grace cringes. He has made his intentions clear. She is not sure if she sees a way out.

'Do you socialise with Johnny as well as work with him?'

'We go for lunch occasionally, and we go for a quick drink after work sometimes – oh, and he had this party a few weeks ago that I was invited to, but that's all.'

He looks puzzled by her interest, but she needs to keep pressing him. 'You went to a party. I guess you met his wife then?'

'Yeah, why?'

'Well, it's just that he always talks about her and, you know, it's unusual for men to talk about their wives when you want to talk about finance.' She laughs. He relaxes.

'It's the whole garlic and vampire thing.'

'What?'

'Well, you're the vampire – no offence, but you're stunning and he's married – so he talks about his wife, who is the garlic, to ward you off.'

'But I had no intention of jumping over the desk and seducing him.' Even if I really want to, she thinks.

'I know, so does he, but men get funny around beautiful women. Anyway, she's attractive. Really slim, quite boyish, but at this party she was so drunk, Johnny was mortified.'

'Is she a lush?' Grace thinks it would have been worth going to the party to see Betty make a fool of her control-freak self, but then her plan never would have worked.

'I don't think so. Anyway, she's nice. Really trendy and I have never heard him say a word against her. I think he's completely devoted.' That is more than she wanted to hear. He isn't devoted. If he was so devoted why was he paying her more attention than he needed to? She feels cross all of a sudden, then calms herself. She is behaving like a schoolgirl with a crush and she isn't. She never was.

'Are you hungry, Dan?'

'I'll go and get the menus, shall I?'

He smiles, and Grace decides he has a really nice smile. When he asked her out, she saw it as a chance to make Johnny jealous, but she was the jealous one. She must sort herself out, because otherwise she is going to drive herself mad.

'What did I do to deserve that?' Johnny is collapsed on the kitchen floor.

'Nothing. I felt like doing something different.'

'Have you been to blow job lessons?'

'Johnny!' She hits him, gently.

'Sorry, I was joking. Come here.' He pulls her into his arms. 'You are amazing, you know that?' She kisses him, gently this time.

'Are you hungry?'

'Um.'

'I've got dinner ready.'

'You cooked?' The fear creeps into his voice.

'I did. We've got lasagne.'

'That's my favourite.' Johnny can't believe his luck. All his favourite things in one night, and it isn't even a weekend. He just hopes she hasn't burnt it. Or forgotten to put lasagne in it.

'I know.' Betty kisses him again.

'Betty, there isn't something I should know about?'

'Like what?'

'It's not my birthday, is it?'

'Don't be silly. If I can't do something nice for my husband once in a while . . . Anyway, go and set the table. I'll bring dinner in.'

'I really want a burger. Are they good here?'

'They are, but, Grace, wouldn't you rather go somewhere else? The food is a bit . . . you know . . .'

'It's perfect. Dan, I don't want anything fancy. I'm not like that.'

'So two burgers then?'

'Yes, and another bottle of wine maybe.' She arches an eyebrow. 'Let me give you some—' He puts his finger over her lips, a move that disturbs her.

'I'll get it.' When he walks away, she tells herself off again. Poor bloke, thinks that he's Mr Romance when he's nothing compared to Johnny. She tries to think about what she is going to do with him. She even hates herself for her thoughts. She feels miserable. Johnny is with Betty, and she is here with a man who thinks it's sexy to silence her by putting his finger on her lips. She hates that. Just as she thinks she is going to boil over, she calms herself. She is using him, therefore has no right to be cross with him. She wonders what Johnny and Betty are doing. In her mind, they are having dinner, she is blabbing on and on about her day, and he is keeping quiet because he will probably be thinking about Grace. About the way she looked when she was in his office, how he caught a glimpse of her suspender belt (very old trick but it worked; he blushed, boy did he blush), how he would rather be with her than his boring old wife. She is out of control, she knows that now. Her feelings are out of control. She realises, as Dan returns with another bottle of wine, that she has managed to get herself drunk.

*

'That was delicious,' Johnny says, stroking Betty's thigh. He touches her suspender belt and his mind automatically switches to thinking about Grace. How he glimpsed the top of her stocking. How he was shocked, because he expected her to wear tights, although he had no idea why she should. How turned on he was for a few minutes, and the blush that he felt creeping up his entire body.

'Are you all right?' Betty asks, noting the colour he has turned.

'Sorry, darling, I was thinking about what you did to me earlier,' he lies.

'Why don't we go to bed, leave this for morning and have a repeat performance?' Betty leads the way, although, Johnny notes, she really can't walk in those shoes.

'That was delicious,' Grace says, as she finishes the burger and another glass of wine.

'Glad you enjoyed it.' Dan leans in close. He seems to be drunk as well.

'It's late,' Grace says, although she has no idea what the time is.

'It's half-past ten,' Dan replies.

'Bedtime,' Grace says.

'Right.' He sounds put out.

'I meant our bedtime. Where's your flat?' She has no idea where the words came from and she regrets them as soon as they leave her lips. She curses herself for her stupidity. She doesn't want to sleep with him. She's only just met him. What is she playing at? And why does everything lead back to Johnny?

'Ten minutes in a cab?' He looks as if he doesn't believe her, or just doesn't believe his luck.

She doesn't know what she is doing or why. She feels wretched, slightly nauseous, jealous – consumed with jealousy.

She looks at Dan and sees Johnny's face. His face is everywhere, when she is awake and when she is asleep. All she wants is him. Instead, she climbs into a taxi. Dan leans over to kiss her the moment the taxi pulls out, but she distracts him with conversation. Think! she says to herself. Think, think, think. She cannot know what to do. She opens her mouth to get the taxi to stop and for her to jump out but the words don't come. She takes a deep breath. What is she actually doing that is so wrong? She's with a handsome man, she's a free agent, she is going to go back to his place. This is the modern day and she's not doing anything wrong. So why does she feel such a slut?

'I can't do this.' Suddenly the words are out, just before they reach Dan's flat.

'What?' He looks crestfallen.

'I'm sorry, but I can't do this. I'm not over my husband, sorry my ex-husband, and it's unfair to use you this way.' It is a lie, but she hopes it is kind.

'I don't mind,' he replies.

'Dan, I can't. I'm so sorry.' She asks the taxi driver to pull over and she gets out. As she walks away she hears Dan shouting after her, but she refuses to listen. She is not a slut, Betty is wrong. She doesn't try to hurt people, only sometimes she does. But she doesn't try.

Johnny gently extricates his arm from behind Betty's head. He gets quietly out of bed and makes his way downstairs. He goes to the kitchen and fills a glass with water, then he goes to the sofa and sits down.

His head is a muddle. He cannot help thinking of Grace, although he spent all evening thinking of, and enjoying, his wife. It is not that he loves Betty any less, it's just that he wants them both. That is what it is. He thinks of Grace and he thinks of Betty. He wants them both, but he knows that he cannot have that. Nor is he proud of himself for wanting it. Betty is the perfect wife, she is also his best friend, so how can he even contemplate another woman? He vows to get Grace out of his head, and to be nothing more than her financial adviser.

Grace wakes. Her head is throbbing. She looks over at her clock and sees that it's still the middle of the night. She crawls out of bed and goes to the kitchen to get some water and take some headache pills. Then she goes back to bed.

Perhaps she is no different from Kathy, her sister who would sleep with anyone. Although she didn't sleep with Dan, she almost feels worse for that. If she had, at least he would have been happy. Instead, they both are miserable, although he will get over her, surely. He barely knew her and she will try to ensure that she doesn't see him when she goes to visit Johnny. Because this is all about Johnny, and her behaviour is guided by her feelings for him. Shit, she wants him so badly, she has never wanted anything this badly. She is not trying to hurt people, she just seems to be good at it.

Chapter Twenty-Six

'Johnny, can we grab a quick sandwich at lunchtime?' Dan pops into Johnny's office first thing.

'Sure, about one-ish?'

He doesn't think about it until Dan comes back to his office to collect him at the allotted time. They go to the same deli that Johnny went to with Grace, which again makes him think about her, even though he is trying not to. He is not going to think about her, he is going to concentrate on his gorgeous wife.

They order sandwiches and drinks and sit down.

'Can I talk to you about something?' Dan asks.

'Sure.'

'It's Grace.'

Immediately the sensation returns. Everything prickles, he feels uncomfortable. His mind is in turmoil. Why is Dan talking about her? Has he guessed something? He feels like a man with a secret, although he hasn't done anything wrong.

'What about her?' He manages to get the words out, although they feel stuck in his throat.

'I went out with her last night.'

Johnny closes his eyes briefly. He is angry now – jealous, confused. He did not expect this.

'What?'

'I asked her out when I saw her leave your office. She suggested that night; last night. Anyway, we went for a drink after work, had a burger and then she came home with me.'

Johnny is on his feet. He has an overwhelming urge to hit Dan, who looks surprised. Johnny realises what he is doing, and sits down again.

'Sorry, I'm a bit shocked.'

'I was when she said yes—'

'YOU SLEPT TOGETHER?' Johnny shouts, interrupting him, and the whole deli looks over. Dan cringes into his seat. Johnny feels sweat building on his brow. He has no idea how he is going to get through the next few minutes; he feels he might spontaneously combust.

'Please, Johnny, shush. No, we were nearly at my place and she asked the cab to stop and said she couldn't do it because she isn't over her ex and she was really sorry and all that. It was weird. All along she had been flirting, teasing – she's the hottest woman I've ever met – and then all of a sudden she does this U-turn, leaving me high and dry.'

Johnny feels better about the fact that they didn't sleep together, but he is still angry. He feels betrayed, and he feels hurt. But he is also angry with himself for feeling that way. He is married, he loves his wife, Grace is nothing to him. She is a client. He has no right to mind what she does.

'I think you need to give her space. You never know, she might get in touch, when she feels better.' He knows it sounds lame, but he is lost in his thoughts.

'She's not ill, Johnny.'

Johnny doesn't care any more. He's sorry that Dan is sad because Dan is a mate, but he doesn't care because Grace is not going to be with him. It is selfish but it is all he can think.

'Look, give her time, that's all I'm saying. It was only one date.' There won't be any more dates, he wants to add.

'Johnny, you don't understand. She's amazing. The way she looks is enough to make any man fall for her, but that's not even it. She's smart, and she knows how to dress, and when she teases you, it makes you feel like you're the most important man in the world. The way she smiles, you could live and die in her smile. Everything about her is wonderful. I know it sounds really lame, and it's not like me, but I fell for her. I really fell for her. I can't expect you to understand.'

The trouble is that Johnny understands perfectly.

'I can't believe you did that,' Alison laughs, as Betty tells her, over lunch, about the previous evening.

'It was such fun. Honestly, you know I'm not really the role-playing type but I did it quite well. Johnny was putty in my hands.'

'It sounds like it. I guess this is about Grace?'

'Well, I thought if I gave him everything he needed at home he wouldn't go elsewhere. But I like to think it's not just about her. I thought that maybe I take him for granted, you know, and it was time I stopped.'

'I think this is about her.' Alison is looking at her with disapproval, although she is not entirely surprised. She had warned Betty, when she agreed to the bet, that insecurity isn't something that is under control. Although Betty has changed, gained confidence, and become one of the strongest people Alison knows, it hasn't been an overnight transition. When Alison first met Betty, she couldn't figure out if she liked her or not. At first she was very serious, a bit timid, and seemed to have total incomprehension of what fun actually meant. But the more time they spent together, the more Betty showed her real self. It took a year for Alison to discover that the reason she was so loath to show it was because no one had ever been interested in her properly before. Alison was her first real friend.

Betty is complicated; she has simplified herself, but that doesn't change the fact. She still battles with her private 'ugly girl syndrome'; she still blames her parents for her childhood, although even she can't fully explain why. Sometimes she still finds it impossible to believe that she is as successful as she is;

she isn't sure if it is real or not. University gave Betty many things she needed: fun, friends, attention, the means for her to see what her goal is and achieve it. Johnny has given her everything else.

Johnny was the first man that Betty ever asked out. She told Alison when she first met him, that she just had to and she couldn't think about the consequences. Being Betty, she pursued him vigorously before actually asking the question, but her confidence was whole by then; she was whole. Their relationship saw Betty finally shed the last pieces of self-doubt. As they fell in love, she seemed to be the anti-Betty; the opposite of the woman that Alison first met. But insecurity doesn't go away, it just gets buried. And, like all things buried, it has a habit of getting dug up.

'Alison, you haven't met Grace.' Betty concedes that it is to do with her.

'I don't need to. Johnny loves you, and do you really think that by acting strangely around him, that will make it all right?'

'I'm not acting strangely, I'm being sexy. I'm being Superwife.'

'As much as I am sure Matt would love me to do the same, it's not going to happen. Occasionally I put on a pair of stockings, or bring out massage oil – you know, something different – but, Betty, if you do this every day from now on, he's going to know something's up.'

'He'll just think he's lucky and, anyway, I am going to be like this all the time, even when that bitch is out of the way.'

'It's not normal. You hate cooking, and I'm not sure you can afford to order in every night. You'll get bored of blow jobs, and sexy undies, and whatever else you have in mind. Betty, he loves you, he loves you for you, so don't try to be someone else.'

'Your marriage isn't under threat so I'm not sure I can expect you to understand. But I am not someone else, I am me, just the new me.'

'Betty, you work at *Modern Woman* – how many articles have you written about not changing for a man? If he loves you, he'll love you for you – ring any bells? Christ, Betty, this woman will be gone soon and you'll be fine, your marriage will be fine. But only if you stop this madness.'

'I can't. I can't stop it.' Betty is shouting at her friend, but only because she is growing more terrified by the day. She hates herself for that, for not feeling in control, for not being confident, but she cannot seem to stop. 'I am so scared of losing him to her. I didn't think about it before, but now the bet is nearly halfway through and I keep thinking I notice things about him: that he's a bit more distant than normal; that he's thinking about her; the dinner with a client. All those things make me think that he's with her, or he wants to be with her, and I can't lose him, Ali, I can't.' She doesn't like the desperation she hears creep into her voice. She doesn't like a lot of things at the moment.

'I know, honey, but trying to keep him by pretending you're someone you're not isn't the way. He married you because he loves you. You have to trust in that.'

'What if I can't? Alison, the only way I can get through this is by making him think I am so perfect that he won't want to leave me.' Sound logic, or it is when she decides it.

'Betty, do what you have to do, but I don't believe for one minute that Johnny is going to fall for her.'

'I wish I had your confidence.'

Betty's confidence has disappeared and Alison has no idea how to get it back.

'You nearly slept with his colleague?' Nicole looks shocked. They are at Nicole's house, a place Grace visits rarely, but today she needed someone and Nicole was that someone.

Grace nods.

'Have you eaten?'

Grace shakes her head. Nicole leads her into the kitchen

where she opens the fridge, closes it, then goes to the cupboard and brings out a packet of cheese biscuits. 'Haven't been to the supermarket for a while.' She shrugs in apology.

Nicole marches back to her office, where she and Grace began their chat. Grace tries to keep up but at the same time look at her surroundings. Nicole's house has three floors, but the kitchen and office are on the same one. She knows there is a living room as well, but the door is always closed when Grace has been there, as if there is a big secret lurking behind it. Grace knows that Nicole is fond of her, but she also knows that she likes to keep her private life away from her business life.

The walls are all white. It doesn't look cold, it looks modern, and to avoid the rooms looking clinical, Nicole has ensured there are plenty of pictures, a mixture of canvas and photographs, which add colour (the canvas) and warmth (the photos). Grace often wonders if Nicole planned the eclectic layout, or if it was just a random thing. Before she can think about it further, she finds herself back in Nicole's large office, sitting in a leather armchair.

'I feel awful,' Grace says. Nicole looks at her.

'Why? Because of Dan or because of Johnny?'

'Both. Dan was sweet; he didn't deserve to be used. But I justified it with the fact that I'm single, I'm a free agent, I'm still youngish so therefore I can go out with who I want. But the problem is that I didn't want to be with him. I wanted to be with Johnny, and when Dan asked me out all I could think of was that this was my chance to find out how Johnny really feels about me.'

'I see. So Dan tells Johnny today and Johnny either slaps him on the back and doesn't mention it to you, or gets angry.'

'Precisely. But now I feel bad for using him. Because that's what I did. We had drinks, dinner – well a burger, not exactly dinner – and I felt drunk so I told him to take me to his place. Then I freaked out, jumped out of the taxi and didn't even look back. The thing is that I didn't feel like a free agent when I was with him. I didn't feel single. I felt that I should be with Johnny.'

'I knew that this was happening. From the way you spoke about him when you first met him, I knew you were falling for him. I should have stopped you, put a stop to it when I could. Grace, this wasn't meant to happen.'

'I know.' Grace's eyes fill with tears.

'Grace, honey, he's married. And he loves his wife. And even though she is the bitch from hell to you, she loves him. You don't wreck marriages, you always say that. You want them to work. You can't continue with this, you can't take him away from her. Especially as I think that he wants you.'

'What makes you say that?'

'Look at the way he's behaved: dinner, dropping everything to have lunch with you.'

Grace wipes her eyes. 'He's just being nice.'

'No. But I do think he is probably confused. Grace, I'll support you as your boss and your friend, but I'll give you this warning. It is all going to end in tears and someone is going to get very hurt. Either you or Betty, or both. And what I hate is that it might be you.'

'I know. But I can't stop it, Nicole, I can't. The thought of never seeing him again fills me with dread.'

'So you're carrying on?'

Grace nods.

'What's your next move?'

'Golf,' Grace says, and bursts into tears properly.

Johnny can barely concentrate. His head is stretching in different directions, and it's beginning to pound. He is angry, so angry, but he doesn't know why. Every time he tries to clear his head, there are images invading it: Grace laughing with him; Betty in a négligé; Dan and Grace. He doesn't want any of the thoughts in his head, he just wants to get on with his work.

He hopes Dan didn't notice his discomfort over lunch. He feels sorry for him, but he feels sorrier for himself. Did Grace go out with him because she wanted to or because she was lonely? He has to believe it was because she was lonely. That has to be the only explanation. At least, he rationalises, she didn't sleep with him. Was her excuse true? Is she still getting over her divorce? She said that she was over her ex. Was she using that as an excuse to let Dan down gently, or was she still in love with her ex? But she said she was never in love with him and she had a bruised ego – he is sure that was what she had told him. He remembers everything she told him.

Why is he letting this drive him crazy? He looks round his office, at the furniture, the soulless prints on the wall, the wooden floor polished to within an inch of its life, and the glass desk. Modern, expensive, trustworthy. That is the image that he portrayed through his office. But he doesn't feel trustworthy. He has taken his professional life and turned it inside out. He is involved with another woman, yet he has not kissed her or expressed a desire to do so. He is being mentally unfaithful yet he still loves his wife and was making love to her only the night before. He can't get Grace out of his head, and that is something he has no idea how to address. Betty is his life, that much he knows; he can't imagine being without her. Grace is a threat to his certainty but she cannot be any more than that.

So why am I so consumed with jealousy? he asks himself, just as his telephone shrills at him and his wife announces herself.

'Johnny?'

'Yes, darling?' He feels his insides twisting as he tries to sound normal. Will she detect the confusion in his voice? Will she know that something is wrong? Maybe she'll know what it is more than he will. He feels as if he will explode.

'I just wondered what time you'll be home tonight?'

He feels ill equipped to answer a mundane question, and as he thinks about the previous evening he knows he cannot face a rerun. He was having sex with his wife while Dan was with Grace. That thought is haunting him.

'Normal time, but I thought that we'd have dinner with Alison and Matt.' He needs to ensure that they are not alone.

'Oh.' Betty is disappointed and Johnny notices, but he cannot worry about that. He has to keep himself together, in one piece and he is unsure how else to do it.

'I suggested it to Matt and he seemed quite keen,' he lies.

'Funny, I had lunch with Alison and she didn't mention it.' Despite the conversation with Alison, Betty has a plan for the evening. It involves her in a tiny G-string, an apron (a cooking one), very high heels and a chicken stir fry. Now Johnny wants to share her fantasy with their friends.

'You know what Matt's like – he never tells her anything. Anyway, we're going for Chinese. We haven't had Chinese in ages.' He picks up a pen and scribbles on a Post-it note. The first line reminds him to call Matt as soon as possible, the second tells him to bribe him if necessary.

'What time?'

'About seven. I'll meet you there.'

'But you haven't said where?'

'Oh, meet me at Barnie's and we'll go from there.'

'OK, see you later.'

'Love you.' Johnny replaces the receiver and feels the sweat on his forehead. He was never made to lie, he certainly couldn't ever have an affair; he doesn't want to be unfaithful. But he admits he is in a mess as he picks up the phone to call Matt.

'Matt speaking.'

'It's me.'

'What's up?'

'Well, I thought we'd have Chinese tonight, out. Meet in Barnie's at seven?'

'OK. I better check with the Missus, but sounds fine by me.'

'Matt, listen, trust me on this. Please act as if I asked you this morning.'

'But you didn't.'

'I know, but pretend I did. It's just that Betty wanted me to do something tonight that I really didn't want to do, so I fibbed.'

'Oh, probably talking about curtains, eh?'

'Something like that.' Johnny rolls his eyes and wonders what Matt's marriage must be like. A conversation about curtains he could handle. Being alone with his wife is the thing he can't.

'Seven. Barnie's.' He hangs up.

Betty is replying to an email, and trying to work out if she is all right or not.

'How was dinner last night?' Fashion assistant Rich perches on the edge of her desk.

'Well, the starter was outstanding,' she jokes. 'Even the lasagne was pretty damn good. I got the recipe from the food department. It certainly was foolproof.'

'You know what I think? I think that all women can cook, but because if you do you're seen as a mumsy homemaker type, you all pretend you can't.'

'Rubbish. I really can't.'

'But you made a lasagne.'

'Yes, but that was beginner's luck.'

'I tell you, you'll be threatening Nigella's crown in no time.'

'If I ever get that good, I promise I'll invite you for dinner.'

'Really?'

'Believe me, it'll never happen. Now, are there any other hot tips for me?'

'I made you a list.'

'A list?'

Rich hands Betty a piece of A4 paper. She starts reading it and bursts out laughing.

'"Chocolate body paint. Flavoured condoms. Whipped cream but must be in a can." Is there anything here which won't make me fat?'

'They're not high in calories. Sperm is very fatty, though, I think.'

'Yuck. How on earth do you do number five?' Betty's eyes open wide and Hannah leaves her efficient workstation to come over and read.

'Ah, that takes a bit of know-how. You first of all have to practise using your teeth not your hands. I can teach you.'

'How long will it take?'

'About a month if we practise every night.'

'No, I don't have time for number five. Let's see. Three in a bed? I am not inviting some hooker over just to spice up my sex life.'

'OK, well, if you won't do that, then it'll have to be lesbian porn. Buy him that and he'll be in heaven.'

'Do I have to?'

'You want to prove to your husband that you are the best possible woman?'

'Yes.'

'Then I'm afraid so.'

'How do you know so much about it? You're not a woman and you're not straight.'

'Darling, we both sleep with men, that's how I know. Now, have you got time to skive and go shopping?'

'Oh yes, especially as there is a feature in all this somewhere. Or that's what I'm telling Fiona.'

'Good. I'll meet you downstairs in five.'

'Rich.'

'Yes?'

'Will you ask for the porn?'

'Yes, and the massive vibrator. I'm not proud.'

*

Grace is tidying her flat, and trying to forget about Johnny. Nicole's advice keeps swimming around her brain. She should break it off – not that there is anything to break off, not yet. She goes to her office because maybe, just maybe, she will be able to think there.

She has no job that evening. The one that was planned has been cancelled at the last minute. She is relieved, although she didn't share her views with Nicole.

She has lost enthusiasm for work. She doesn't want to see these men, she wants to see Johnny. Maybe she will call him tomorrow and ask him to meet her, and then she will put an end to it. She could explain that she is in love with him. On the other hand, would that prompt him to question his feelings? No, to be fair to him and to Betty she will say that she has family in Australia and has decided to move there. That may be the coward's way out, but it is the most attractive option.

She picks up the golf membership that Nicole gave her and remembers when she saw it as a game. How could so much change in a month? She thinks about how she behaved with Dan, and feels ashamed; she was wrong. She went too far. All this trying to beat Betty is pathetic and people are getting hurt along the way. She is angry with herself, she is not seeing any sense in her behaviour. She will put an end to the bet. She thinks briefly of Oliver. He told her that it was a bad idea, although he didn't anticipate this outcome. She wishes she had listened to him instead of losing him. She wishes she had never set eyes or ears on Fiona.

This past month Eddie has been still very much on the scene, even if she has barely seen him. The weekend in Bath was enjoyable, but she knows that her heart isn't with him any more. Although she still thinks he is attractive and he is her friend, she cannot keep sleeping with him because that makes her feel like a harlot, a fake, a whore. She never minded having two different partners, because everything was honest, but now it makes her feel dirty. She has to stop because she is unable to change her feelings. Bizarrely, she feels she is being unfaithful to Johnny.

She resolves to tell Eddie. She will end the relationship, she will lose her friend, but she will also stop playing with him. It is not only better for her but it is better for him. Of that much she is sure. The sense of liberation that that decision gives her shocks her. She has never thought of herself as trapped within her relationships, but she probably is, or was. She used the men to protect her from loneliness; she used them because she wasn't in love with them. Love, she knows, now she feels it, is more dangerous than anything. With that momentous decision made, she goes to the living room, curls herself up on the sofa and watches the fish.

Half an hour later, her mobile phone rings, making her jump. She gets up and goes to answer it.

'Hello.'

'It's me.' Her heart speeds up at the sound of Johnny's voice.

'Hi.'

'Grace, I need to speak to you. Can you meet me?'

'OK.' She feels uncertainty fluttering around.

'Can you meet me now?' He can't keep the testiness out of his voice. She wonders if it is about jealousy and prays that it is.

'I guess so.' She has lost control of everything and now he is calling the shots.

'Where?' he asks.

'Where what?'

'Where can I meet you?'

She thinks about it, but doesn't know where to suggest.

'Come to my flat,' she blurts out before thinking.

'Give me your address.'

She shuts and locks the office door, tidies the already immaculate flat, and then paces up and down the living room. She doesn't know why he is coming over or what he wants. She knows he didn't sound happy, but then she is not happy, so why should he? She will break it off now, no more delays. Not that they're having an affair, but she will tell him that she is leaving the country in a week. Can you arrange to emigrate in a week? She doubts it, but she can say she is going on holiday. Then he'll forget her, go back to life with Betty and Grace will be alone again. But alone knowing that she has a heart that's in full working order.

But the problem is that you only love one person, don't you? Yes, that's what it says in all the women's magazines. 'The one', not 'the three'. As she now knows she wasn't in love with Dave or Ben (although she was, it was just a different kind of love), and she isn't in love with Oliver or Eddie, then Johnny is 'the one'. Her first love. Therefore her last. So she can love but she can only love him and therefore she will have to go back to having a heart of stone. Why is it all so difficult?

If she thinks back to her last rationalisation, Betty came into her life for a reason, to give her her husband. It almost makes sense. Doesn't it? Can she really let them fall apart? Can she really let him go? Just as she is trying to decide, her buzzer goes.

They stare at each other for a few seconds before Grace invites him in. She looks at her watch. It is six o'clock.

'You finished work early,' she says for want of something to say.

'I left. I had to see you.'

'Right.' There has been no small talk. No tour of the flat, although it is the first time he has been there. He hasn't noticed the fish tank or anything. He is just looking at her.

'Why did you do it?' He sounds cold.

'What?' She knows, but she also fears this conversation. On paper it is far more straightforward than in real life.

'Why did you go out with Dan?' He doesn't know what he is doing there, but he knows he has to ask. He picked the phone up a hundred times before he finally found the courage to dial. He has no right to ask, he knows that, but he feels that he does. He should not be there, he shouldn't have left work. He seems to be filling his life with doing things he shouldn't and that he doesn't understand. Everything is a contradiction.

'I don't have to answer that.' *I did it to make you jealous, you buffoon,* her inner voice shouts. She doesn't know whether to be angry or flattered; she is both. She almost slept with Dan because she wanted to know how Johnny felt about her. It seems to have worked, although now she doesn't want to answer the question.

'I just want to know.'

'Why?' She is going to put it off; he has to give her a gift first, the premise that her sister Kathy always used to work on. One boy gave her a massive box of Milk Tray once and he got rewarded handsomely. Grace is after something more, now, though.

'I don't know.'

Finally he sits down on the sofa and she perches on the other end. They are both consciously trying to keep their legs from touching. It is such a small sofa and they both have long legs. They sit in silence for a while.

'What's happening?' Johnny asks finally.

'I don't know. Dan took me by surprise when he asked me out. I've never even seen him before. And I don't normally go out with anyone who asks. It's just that, well, I thought of you, and how you'd be with your wife and that made me feel miserable. I feel awful for it, if that makes it any better.'

'Do you like him?' He knows he sounds like a child, but he feels like one.

'He's a sweet guy. I told him that it wouldn't happen again.'

'You jumped out of the taxi on him.'

'I see he filled you in on all the details. Saves me from doing so.' She is visibly annoyed, but really she is scared.

'Don't blame him, he was upset. I'm upset.' Johnny is angry again.

'You're upset because I left him in a cab?'

'No, I'm upset that you went out with him.'

'Financial advisers have expanded their brief, haven't they?' She sounds bitchy, which she wouldn't have done in her role, but her role is fading.

'What's that supposed to mean?' he snaps. For a minute he thinks they sound like a bickering couple.

'It's supposed to mean that you have no right to be upset that I was with him.'

'I know.'

'And I have no right to be upset that you're at home with your wife every night.'

'Grace, what's happening here? I barely know you but I feel as if my world is being shaken.'

'Like a snowstorm?'

'What?'

'You know, those snowstorms that you shake and the snow comes down.' She looks dreamy, because she is imagining a life, a life never lived, where she was the woman that Johnny married; she was his wife. She wants to be that woman.

'I don't give a fuck about snowstorms but I do care about you.'

'I care about you too.'

'But . . .'

'But you're married and you love your wife.'

'Yes. I do. Grace, I don't know what to do.'

'Neither do I. I was going to tell you something today, but I didn't.'

'What?'

'Actually I was going to call you tomorrow, and I was going to tell you that I was leaving the country.'

'But you aren't?'

'No, I'm not. But I thought that if I walked away now, then it would be best all round.' She looks at him and slightly relaxes her legs. Her knee brushes his and she feels as if she is on fire. How can she walk away from him? Then she lifts her head and she sees that he is staring at her as if he is boring a hole into her.

'I shouldn't have come.'

'No.'

She is glad that he has, and she has decided that she will do whatever it takes to get him. She has to, otherwise the only conclusion she will draw about herself is that she hates herself. She doesn't and she loves him, and that is worth fighting for. She told Betty to fight, and now she will tell herself the same. If she can get him on a Saturday, then it will only be a matter of time. Phase Six is going into action: spending leisure time with him is tantamount to a love affair. People will think they are a couple, and he will begin to think he wants them to be a couple. He is confused, she knows that and it breaks her heart, but she loves him, and there isn't anything she can do to change that. She should walk away but her legs won't take her.

'What next?'

'Golf.'

'What?'

'You said you like golf, and I love it. I've got membership of the Python Club.'

'No one can get membership there.'

'I can, and I have. Play golf with me, Johnny. It'll clear our heads.'

'You think?'

'Saturday. Play with me then. We'll have a round of golf, some lunch, and then we'll talk about what to do.'

'Betty?'

'She lets you play golf occasionally, surely? Anyway, you're not doing anything wrong.'

'I feel that I am.'

'Johnny, we're not having an affair. Golf, yes or no?'

'Yes.' He wants to say no, but yes comes out instead. He cannot help himself, but he tells himself that after that, they will stop. Grace isn't putting pressure on him; she isn't trying to draw him into infidelity. If she was doing that, then he'd know. And he is afraid of that, because if she took her clothes off, or kissed him, then he is unsure he is strong enough to say no. 'I should go now,' he says. It is half-past six.

'OK.' She smiles.

'But I don't want to.'

'OK.'

'Can we just talk a bit or something?' He doesn't want to be physical, but he doesn't want to leave.

'I know, can you play rummy?'

He nods and Grace goes to get the playing cards.

Betty goes home after her shopping trip and puts the bags into the wardrobe. Then she decides to unpack them, although she feels a bit dirty. She has never got involved in things like that before, not really. Sexy underwear, a tiny bit of role playing, but nothing like this. She feels naughty and she giggles as she takes everything out. She pulls out the vibrator and hopes that Johnny won't be intimidated by its size. She giggles. Then she unpacks the rest. Body paint, handcuffs, different types of pleasure condoms, porno videos, blindfold, a game where you have to perform sex acts as forfeits, and crotchless undies. She decides that she will keep them hidden until the weekend, and then she will bring Johnny breakfast in bed, and keep him there all day. That will spice things up nicely. She hides everything in her wardrobe. Johnny never goes in there.

They have never had a boring sex life, and there has been no indication of either of them going off the boil, but it doesn't hurt to introduce new things. Just in case.

She is also taking more care over her appearance. She used to get in from work and change, but now she keeps her work clothes on, even the high heels (her feet hate her but they'll forgive her). She reapplies her make-up and she ensures the house is spotless when he gets home. Superwife is here to stay. She goes to the bathroom to do her hair and fix her make-up before leaving for the bar. It is not pathetic to want to please your man. No one can say that it is.

'Where the fuck is he?'

It is half-past seven, and Betty, Alison and Matt are all sitting at a table in Barnie's.

'Maybe he got held up.' Matt thinks he is being helpful and he doesn't notice the look of disdain in Betty's eyes.

'Why isn't he answering his phone?' She is snappy, angry, her evening is ruined. She knows where he is: he is with *her*.

'Because he's probably been held up on the tube.' Matt smiles, and Betty scowls at him. He retreats as if she will spit.

'Matt, hon, why don't you go and order another glass of wine each for us?' Alison notes that Betty has finished hers, and as they didn't expect to be waiting for long they didn't order a bottle. Without protest Matt gets up and goes to the bar.

'He's with her.' There is so much rage inside her. Betty spent all afternoon buying lesbian porn to keep him happy and now he's with *her*. Well, Betty decides, she is not giving up. She will fight to the death for her husband. Grace doesn't stand a chance against her and her lesbian porn.

'You don't know that.' Alison prays this is true, but she has a bad feeling. There is no denying that Johnny's behaviour has changed; but then so has Betty's.

'He'd phone normally. You know that as well as I do.'

'But Matt is probably right for once. He might be stuck in a tunnel.'

'Or he might be with her.'

'Betty, you have to put a stop to this. Call Grace, tell her to stuff the article, and call the bet off.'

'I can't. Fiona would kill me.'

'This might kill you anyway.'

'Alison, it might be all right. He might not be with her.' Hope is fading fast but she has to pull herself together.

'That's what I told you. Don't let her do this to you.'

'Grace Regan is a fucking bitch,' Betty says, as Matt returns to the table.

'Who the hell is she?' he asks, having caught the sentence and been surprised by the anger in it.

'No one, just something to do with work,' Alison says quickly, while Betty turns red.

'Don't mention her to Johnny. I've been going on about her a bit and I think he's fed up.' Betty hopes she sounds convincing. She is becoming a competent liar.

'No worries. Anyway, how can I? He's not even here.'

Alison swipes him, Betty stares into her glass and Matt rolls his eyes. Sometimes he can never say anything right.

'Grace, where did you grow up?' Johnny looks from his cards to her. They both know that the game is just a façade, a façade to stop them from ripping each other's clothes off. That is what Johnny thinks and he is grateful for the protection the cards are offering. It makes him feel safe. They are his armour against the ever-growing temptation. Grace is about to tell him her invented story, the one that makes her feel as if she is the person that she wanted to be, not the person she is, but somehow with Johnny, her words are not under her control.

'In a council estate in East Sussex.'

'You don't sound like that . . .' Johnny turns red. He expected a tale of the middle-class home, a bit like his, not a council estate.

'I know. I changed. There were six of us altogether. My dad

didn't work; I never saw him go to work.' She tells Johnny about the chair. He is the first person who she has told in London, the only person to be allowed a glimpse into her real background. She tells him about her mother, her sisters, and her brothers. She tells him about Dave, and the abandonment. She tells him about moving to London to escape and find a better life.

'I had no idea. That's an amazing story. Shit, Grace, you've been through so much.' For once, Grace sees it as the truth. 'And then to marry that bastard.'

Grace looks shocked. Johnny looks angry. She realises that mixing fact and fiction isn't easy; she fills up with guilt. A tear rolls down her cheek.

'I didn't mean to make you cry.' The concern in his voice ensures that another tear is evicted.

'You didn't.' But he did, not because of her background – she has long since come to terms with that – but because of the reality. She has lied to him, and she wishes that she hadn't because that hurts her more than anything her background has done.

'Do you ever see your parents?'

'No. Never.'

'But surely you must feel something towards them, even if it's curiosity.'

'I don't.' This is almost the truth. She thinks about them sometimes, but when she does she squeezes those thoughts out of her head and keeps them out. 'Johnny, I've never told anyone this.'

'What, about your family?'

'No, or what I'm about to tell you.'

'Go on.' He wants to hold her because she looks so vulnerable, so hurt. He wants to take it away. He thinks of Betty, her self-composure, and how she fought against her background. Betty he loves, but she is capable. Grace, he feels something for, and she needs him.

'I don't love my family. There, I said it.' She crumples in tears. This is the first time she has ever admitted this to anyone else. She means it. There is no phase attached to this declaration, no motive behind it.

'Do you mean that?'

'I do. I don't feel anything. I don't miss them, I don't want to see them. I just want to obliterate them from my memory. I don't want you to hate me for that.'

'I would never hate you.'

'But you think I should visit them?'

'I don't know. I think you should do what you think is best, and I can't tell you what that is.'

'It's a horrible declaration. Even those people who get treated so badly by their families feel something, but I don't. I must be a freak.'

'No, you're not. You've had to do everything on your own. I think that makes you more self-sufficient. Stronger, more independent. I think they'd be proud of you.'

'Thanks, Johnny.'

'For what?'

'For not judging me.' She smiles at him, and he smiles back. They both quickly turn back to their cards.

'Oh shit, it's half-past eight.' Grace jumps up, scattering her cards everywhere.

'You're joking?' Johnny prays she is joking.

'No. And you are probably supposed to be elsewhere.' He blushes.

'And I was winning,' she teases, and they both smile.

Johnny leaves with a promise to play golf on Saturday, and he arranges to pick her up from her flat. He feels relaxed in her company, which was the aim of the card game, he guesses. She says goodbye, deliberately avoiding any physical contact and thinks that she will miss him. He is thinking the same.

Johnny hails a cab and switches on his mobile. He has a large number of missed calls. Instead of listening to his voicemail, he calls Betty's mobile. He is flustered as he thinks about what he is going to say. Lying doesn't come naturally to him.

'Hello, is that you?' She sounds annoyed.

'Yeah, I'm in a cab. My tube got stuck, there was a passenger emergency so I had to wait for ages, and then we were told it wasn't going anywhere, so I've just managed to get a cab. Sorry I didn't call before but there was no service.' Thank fuck for the inefficiency of London's transport system, he thinks, otherwise he would be in trouble.

'I thought it was something like that,' Betty replies, relaxing. Matt shoots her a look. Alison shoots him a look. 'He'll be here soon,' she informs them as soon as she's hung up. Betty desperately tries to believe Johnny is telling the truth.

'Grace, it's Eddie.' Grace looks at the answerphone but does not reach for the handset. 'I haven't seen you in ages, and I'd quite like to. I'll try your mobile.' Grace picks up her mobile to make sure it's switched off. Does she want to see him? Not really. She doesn't want to kiss him, to make love to him, to imagine he is Johnny. If she does she will feel like a slut. She knows that she is hurting him, despite her resolve not to, but she cannot face him yet. She went out with Dan to make Johnny jealous; she is not going to sleep with him to make herself feel wanted, because she will end up hating herself. She already hates herself enough.

She puts her hands over her ears as the phone rings again and her answerphone clicks. She will not wreck any more lives, starting with Eddie's.

'Sorry I'm late.' He kisses Betty's cheek, and then Alison's. Betty has forgotten to be angry, because Matt, being Matt, has plied her with drink.

'Shall we go and eat straight away?' Matt says. 'I'm starving.'

'OK.' Betty stands up and grabs hold of Johnny.

'I do love you, you know,' she says, into his ear, but loudly enough for everyone to hear.

'I love you too,' he replies, pretending to ignore the fact that she is once again drunk. He thinks of Grace. They drank at dinner, but she didn't get drunk. He cannot imagine that she would ever get drunk like Betty. He feels immediately guilty at the unfair comparison.

They go to the nearest Chinese restaurant where they order set meals because they all want to try everything. Matt feels the tension but ignores it as they all eat. Alison knows about the tension and is starting to doubt Johnny. Betty is oblivious to the tension because she is properly drunk, and Johnny is drinking too much, which is not usual for him. Matt is looking a bit puzzled as he concentrates hard on his food.

'What's going on?' Matt asks Alison when Betty and Johnny have both staggered to different loos.

'Nothing,' Alison quickly replies, but she knows. Even she is lying. She begins to think that Matt is the only person who is innocent.

'We're having dinner with two fucking drunks. Betty normally gets pissed really quickly but Johnny doesn't.'

'I know. We'll probably have to take them home.'

'Who wants another bottle of wine?' Johnny asks, sitting down again, and when no one replies, he orders one anyway.

Grace pours herself a brandy. She sits in the dark, thankful that she does not have to work that evening. She replays the events, trying to figure out what she is doing. She had decided to walk away, but instead she bared her soul to him. In return she felt as if he was giving some of his to her. But not all of it, because he wasn't a cheater. Grace has finally met the man she has been searching for. The one who doesn't want to be unfaithful. She just wishes that she hadn't fallen in love with him.

What is he doing now? Is he holding her hand, kissing her, looking into her eyes? It is almost too much to bear. Jealousy is not one of Grace's downfalls. She rarely envies others because she believes in getting what she wants. However, she is being eaten from the inside out by her jealousy. Betty was horrible to her, and Grace hated her for that, but now she just feels pathetic because she wants to be her. She wants to kill her and fill her shoes. She wants to hold the door open to Johnny when he gets home from work, pour him a drink, cook him dinner, curl up on the sofa with him, have his babies. Finally she laughs at herself and her new insanity. Grace has never felt remotely maternal. She saw her parents make such a mess of being parents she is far too terrified to try. But the thought of Johnny and her and a child or two feels right. It won't be like her life; it will be perfect. She is sad but she is happy at the same time.

'Who's coming back to ours for brandy?' Johnny asks, as he signs the credit card slip.

'I'm a bit tired, actually,' Matt answers, desperate to get away from his friends for once.

'Nonsense. Let's go,' Johnny insists. He has discovered that when he is drunk he cannot think and that is his new favourite discovery. Alison raises her eyebrow and shrugs. Then as Johnny marches out of the restaurant, she grabs hold of Betty and helps her up.

'I feel like I'm taking my pissed teenagers home,' she says, laughing.

'Only worse,' Matt replies, running after Johnny.

When they get back to the house, Johnny pours four brandies, rather generous measures, while Alison goes and checks that the cat has food. Alison comes into her own in a crisis and she sees this as one.

She grabs Matt, and drags him into the kitchen.

'I'll talk to Betty, while you ask Johnny if there's anything on his mind.'

'Why?'

'Because he's acting strangely and he might tell you.'

'Fine then,' he sighs. He would much rather be tucked up in bed with his arms around his wife than questioning his drunk friend. Matt doesn't really like problems because he never knows how to deal with them.

Alison coaxes Betty into the kitchen and sits her down on a stool.

'Do you want some water?'

Betty purses her lips and shakes her head. 'Yes,' she replies, sounding almost together.

'Come on, I'll get some.'

Alison hands her a glass of water and decides to put her to bed. 'Come on, upstairs.'

'Johnny?'

'He'll be up in a minute, he's talking to Matt.' Betty obeys and walks upstairs, with Alison on her heels. She manages to get her to take her make-up off and clean her teeth. Then just as she has removed her clothes, Betty pulls Alison over.

'Ali, look,' she says, opening the wardrobe.

Alison can barely believe her eyes as all sorts of things tumble out. She looks at Betty, and decides to leave it. She bends down and starts putting them back, shocked at what she is actually handling. Body paint she can cope with, handcuffs and blindfolds she can accept, but *Lesbians from Outer Space* and *Lesbian Mud Wrestling* she has a slight problem with.

Finally, after Johnny has accepted their suggestion to stop drinking and join his wife in bed, they leave.

'Did he say anything?' Alison asks, as they start the short walk home.

'Nothing that made sense.'

'What did he say exactly?'

'Well, he talked about golf and rummy, for some reason, and Dan, he doesn't like Dan but it's not Dan's fault. Christ, Johnny never gets drunk like that.'

'That's what worries me.'

'What are you talking about?'

'Matt, you don't think that Johnny could be having an affair, do you?'

'Don't be ridiculous.'

'Would you know if he was?'

'Of course I would. Even if he didn't tell me, I'd know. We've been mates too long. We can't keep secrets from each other. He's not having an affair. Of course he isn't.' But Matt has his doubts, because if Johnny were having an affair, that would explain his behaviour perfectly.

Chapter Twenty-Seven

It takes two days before Johnny's hangover truly lifts. He has guilt as a lodger, but he cannot stop thinking of Grace. He also thinks of his wife, and feels twisted up inside. But one minute he smiles, and the next he scowls at his behaviour. He is angry with his feelings, but he is also aware of the positive way they make him feel. He blames the hangover but knows the true culprit is himself.

Betty, being used to hangovers, recovers sooner. She forgets about how strange Johnny seems to her, and concentrates on arranging a perfect weekend in bed. She buys more underwear, goes to the beautician for a top-to-toe makeover, and reads all the sex tips that her magazine has ever written. She intends on ensuring that by Monday, Johnny will only have thoughts for her.

Their friends, however, are still having a few problems with the evening. Although one of them knows more than the other, they are jointly insistent on sorting things out. Without confiding in Matt, Alison resolves to get Betty to put an end to it all with Grace. Without fully understanding, but being increasingly convinced that Johnny is having an affair, Matt prepares for confrontation.

Grace goes out shopping for a new outfit, suitable to play golf in. She can't help herself, although she is unsure of the outcome – whether it will leave her happy or in total despair. She has a couple of jobs before Saturday, but she does not mind because she is too consumed with happiness.

Nicole is worried about Grace. Not because of work, her professional life is fine, but she is worried about her personally. The more she thinks of the admission that she is in love with Johnny, the more she blames herself for allowing her to make such a bet in the first place. She should have known better. Nicole was upset when Grace told her how she'd been treated by Betty. She took it personally because Grace is special to her, but she knew that there was so much risk involved in Grace's plan. Everyone was going to end up hurting. Things were falling apart.

Nicole decides to talk to Grace, face to face, about what is happening and put an end to the bet properly.

Alison emails Betty.

> Betty
>
> Let's go shopping on Saturday and for a nice girlie lunch. I need to get out of the house and spend some money on myself before I go mad with decorating chores.
>
> Ali xx

It isn't strictly true, but Alison wants to make out that she needs Betty, not vice versa. However, she hopes that Betty doesn't see through the decorating lie – Alison has never worried about decorating in her life – but she desperately needs to do something.

Matt sends Johnny an email.

> Mate
>
> A good game of golf on Sat is in order. Can't bear to spend the day shopping for carpets, which is what the Mrs wants. Let me know.
>
> Matt

Matt hopes that Johnny doesn't remember that they got new carpets only a couple of months ago.

Nicole sends Grace an email.

> Grace
> How about a day out with your old boss on Saturday? My beloved is away and you know how terrible I am at being on my own. We'll have a fun girlie day, and it would be doing me a real favour.
> Nicole

Nicole believes that a day will be all she needs to talk Grace out of continuing with the bet.

Betty reads the email. She sees through it straight away, and is immediately reminded of that drunken night when Johnny was late and they both ended up a bit worse for wear. But she is no longer worried. She has everything under control. Johnny isn't seeing Grace, she is sure of that, and they will spend the whole weekend under the duvet.

She fires an email back to Alison, saying sorry but she and Johnny have plans. She smiles as she presses send.

Johnny reads his email just after coming out of a meeting. He reads Matt's, and wonders why he is wittering about carpets when Alison bored them all to death discussing it a few months back. He thinks of the planned golf game, and finds himself smiling at the thought of seeing Grace. He makes a mental note to buy her a gift, to say thank you for the opportunity to play at London's top golf course. Then he tries to decide what to buy her. Betty likes being given chocolates and flowers – she says she is old-fashioned in that way. He is angry again, because he is thinking of buying Grace a present, but not Betty. Then he tells himself that a thank you gift is very different from a present he would buy for Betty. He calls up a gift service his company uses and arranges for flowers and chocolates to be sent to Betty on Saturday when he will be at golf. Then, with an extra pang of guilt, he adds a bottle of champagne. He then shops on the Internet and decides to buy Grace something connected with golf. He buys her a golfing cap. Totally unromantic.

He forgets about his email, until Matt sends him another one, prompting him for an answer. He replies that unfortunately he has to play golf with a boring client. He crosses his fingers as he sends the lie.

Grace checks her emails. They are nearly all from Nicole, apart from one that Eddie has sent. She reads the message about spending Saturday with Nicole and feels immediately suspicious. Nicole never spends time with her at the weekend; they just don't. She knows that this is about Johnny. Just as she is about to reply, telling her she can't make it because of the golf, she changes her mind. Instead she tells her that she is seeing Eddie. That way, Nicole will not try to hassle her into changing her mind. And she doesn't want to do that. She is looking forward to a day in the fresh air with Johnny.

Betty receives final copy for the profile on Grace and the honey-trapping feature. The issue that it is going to appear in is being finalised already, as monthly magazines are always produced far in advance. She decides to email the final copy to Grace, just for her information. She adds a note saying that she hopes she is well. That way, Grace will know that Betty doesn't feel at all threatened by her.

Grace has just sent an email to Eddie, saying that she needs to talk to him, when she receives Betty's. She thinks that the woman is so transparent. Then she reads the profile and feels angry again. It is not a bad article, but there is Betty's patronising tone running through it, especially in the interview with Grace. She smiles as she realises she no longer cares about that, and she replies saying:

> Love the feature. You have made it so interesting. Glad that you are feeling well and seem calm about the bet now it is well underway. I have to say that I admire your composure. I'm not sure I would be as together as you, with so much at stake.

She smiles as she presses send. That will teach Betty to patronise her.

Betty receives Grace's reply and all her composure melts away. She feels the threat, the distinct threat.

'Hannah,' she shouts.

'Betty, I'm right here. Why are you shouting?'

'Because I am angry. Fucking angry. Can you call Fiona's office and get me a meeting, and also can you pull some strings and get me a hair appointment with Guido?'

'Of course. Are you all right?'

'I will be once my hair looks good.' Fighting talk.

Grace calls Johnny. Upsetting Betty is no longer the goal, but it is looking like an attractive bonus.

'Hi, it's me.' She likes the familiarity that comes with saying that.

'How are you?'

'Not bad. Listen, I just got a call from the club checking our reservation. It made me think that you might have changed your mind.'

Johnny can hear the hesitation in her voice: she sounds worried. He feels a jolt of affection.

'Absolutely not.' Even if he knows that he shouldn't go, he cannot help himself. He needs to see her.

'Good. You're still OK to pick me up?'

'I'll be there at ten. Grace?'

'Yes?'

'I wondered if we should grab an early supper before heading home?'

'That would be lovely.'

'What's up, Betts? We've just finished a great story.'

It is time for Betty to make Fiona realise what she's done.

'I am so glad, seeing as it's going to cost me my marriage.'

'Don't be so dramatic. Only the other day you said it was all fine.' Fiona feels herself heat up at Betty's words. She is beginning to realise that she perhaps shouldn't have done what she did.

'I try to believe that, but when I know that she is trying to seduce my husband and I have no idea how she is doing it, what methods, when she sees him, it's driving me a bit crazy.'

'Betty, darling, you trust Johnny.' Fiona speaks to Betty as if she were addressing a child. Not that she knows much about children.

Betty paces her office. 'I do, but I don't trust her. Would you?'

'I don't have a husband.'

'That's not the point. The point is that the other night I put on a négligé before he came home and I did unspeakable things to him on the kitchen floor.'

'Great idea for a feature. What exactly did you do?' Fiona realises that she just can't help herself as she mentally tells herself to shut up.

'Fiona, please, let me continue.'

'Sorry.' Fiona rarely apologises but she is beginning to realise just how serious it is.

'And then, Rich took me shopping.'

'Oh dear!'

'What do you mean "oh dear"?'

'Well, the last time he took me shopping I ended up buying this really silly tent thing which was meant for meditation and tantric sex. I've never had tantric sex.'

'Yeah, well, I got chocolate body paint, edible undies, handcuffs and lesbian porn.'

'Oh.'

'Yes, oh. Don't you see what I've been reduced to? A couple of nights ago I went out and he was two hours late and I got so drunk worrying. I'm falling apart.'

'Um. I think you're doing the right thing.'

'What?'

'Well, spice up your sex life. Have your hair done – have you done that?'

'Does it look like it?'

'Not really.'

'That's because I haven't. But you know what I have done? I've had everything waxed. I even had a Brazilian. I've got this tiny tuft of pubic hair left, and it was bloody agony. I also had a facial, a manicure, a pedicure, it is costing me a fucking fortune.'

'But it's worth it. Did you consider colonic? I can get you a special deal.'

'Fiona!'

'Sorry, wasn't thinking. What I meant to say was, if you need anything, you know where I am.' She wonders if now would be a good time for her to hide under her desk.

'That's why I'm here now.'

'Oh. Why exactly?'

'Because you encouraged me to do this so I thought it only fair that I rant at you.'

Fiona looks relieved that that is all it is. She is worried that she might have been rumbled.

'Quite right too. Well, I think you are proving yourself to be very resilient. And if you want to borrow my tantric tent, I've never used it and would be quite prepared to give it to you.'

Betty glares at Fiona, who looks a bit scared, a little confused and slightly manic. Then she laughs.

Fiona breathes a huge sigh of relief and laughs too. 'Remember, she will not win. He is yours.'

'You're right. Thanks, Fiona. You've been really helpful.'

'Any time,' Fiona replies, without a clue about what she actually did.

Betty marches back to her desk, feeling refuelled.

'Hannah?'

'Six on Friday night. I pulled every con to get this so make sure he does you proud.'

'He will. You're a star.' And Grace is history, she adds to herself. It is time for her to stop being a wimp and fight properly.

Johnny pays extra for next-day delivery to his office for Grace's cap. A cap, even though it is a funky one, is not a romantic present and it is not too expensive. He feels pleased with himself.

Grace has her new outfit, and is ready to go. All that stands between her and a day with Johnny is a couple of jobs. She just has to wait patiently for Saturday to arrive. It's like waiting for Christmas.

'What are you doing this weekend?' Alison asks Matt over dinner.

'Nothing, so far. I did ask Johnny if he wanted to play golf but he was busy.'

'I know. I asked Betty if she fancied shopping and she said they had plans.'

'That's funny, because he said he had to play golf with a client.' Alison looks at him, feels herself panic, and decides not to let on.

'Oh, I must have been confused.'

'Right . . .' Matt doesn't believe her. Alison never gets things like that mixed up. He feels as if everything is strange at the moment, but he is trying not to think about it. Matt doesn't like to think too much.

Later, Matt is watching a drama on television, so Alison goes into the hall and calls Betty.

'Hi, it's only me,' she says when Betty answers.

'Hi, Ali.'

'I just wanted to check if you definitely can't come shopping on Saturday.'

'I can't. You know, operation handcuffs and porn, that's Saturday,' she whispers.

'With Johnny?'

'Who else would it be with?' Alison quickly changes the subject and wraps up the call soon after.

'I spoke to Betty, Matt, and she thinks that her and Johnny are spending Saturday together.'

'Well, maybe they are then, and the client thing was him being confused.'

'I hope so.' Alison has a bad feeling about everything now, and especially about Saturday. 'But if not, then Betty might want to go shopping.'

'That's fine. I wouldn't mind a day in peace to watch sport.' Matt hugs her extra tight, not something he normally does. 'I love you,' he says, and buries his lips in her hair.

Alison can't help but feel that the bet is affecting everyone, and that Saturday is going to be a turning point.

Chapter Twenty-Eight

Grace never went on day trips or holidays as a child, but she thinks that this is how it would have felt if she had done. She can't sleep with the excitement. Every time she tries to sleep her head whizzes round, but she is so happy that the lack of sleep doesn't upset her. She gives up at five in the morning, lies in bed for another hour, then gets up and goes to have a long, hot bath. She pours in her most expensive bubbles, and lies for as long as she can without wrinkling up. She thinks, thinks, thinks. All thoughts of Johnny. When she gets out, she goes to make coffee, which she enjoys with the fish. It is still too early, so she has another cup before making herself eat some cereal to try to calm her stomach.

She liberally applies her best body moisturiser, and she gets dressed and puts her make-up on. Then she sits, like a child, staring out of the window, even though she has almost three hours left to wait.

Betty is so excited that she can't sleep. She got in late on Friday night after a work do, and Johnny was gently snoring in bed. But that served a purpose because she wants to blow his mind today. She lies awake, planning her outfit, her entrance, what she will do first, what she will do next. She watches him sleep, smiling at the thought that he has no idea what treats are in store for him. At seven she gives up on sleep and gets up. She goes to the bathroom and has a long hot bath, with expensive oils, before covering herself in moisturiser. It is still only seven thirty so she quietly tiptoes to the wardrobe, pulls out the edible knickers, her high heels and the handcuffs. She puts the knickers and the high heels on once she is back downstairs, and she makes a breakfast of croissants (partially cooked, only need heating), orange juice (freshly squeezed) and coffee. He won't know what's hit him.

Johnny has no idea what Betty is up to, but he doesn't want her to know he is awake. He has been awake for a while, thinking of the day ahead and worrying about what he is doing, at the same time as looking forward to it. His head is a fuzzy mess. He notices Betty get out of bed and go downstairs, so he tries to doze. Later she comes back, opens her wardrobe and disappears again. He knows that he won't sleep but he still can't face getting up yet.

He can see the sun seeping in through the curtains and he hopes that it will be a sunny day. He doesn't want the rain to ruin his golf, or his time with Grace. He might be fuzzy but he needs that.

Betty returns to the bedroom with a tray.

'Morning,' she says seductively, causing Johnny to open his eyes and sit up.

'What on earth . . . ?' He looks at her in disbelief and hits the side of his head to make sure he is awake.

'Well, big boy, I thought I'd handcuff you to the bed, and feed you your breakfast. I'm wearing your dessert.' Betty walks seductively up to him but it goes wrong as she tries to balance the tray on one hand and unhook the handcuffs with the other. Although she doesn't drop the tray, Johnny cannot help but burst out laughing. Not his most sensible move.

'What's funny?' She regains her balance and abandons the handcuffs.

'What are you doing? You, you . . . I don't know what to say.' He is astounded.

'I thought we'd have breakfast and stay in bed all day.'

'Nice thought, but you know I have to play golf with a client today.'

Betty puts the tray down on him, hard, and he steadies it so he doesn't end up wearing the coffee.

'I knew no such thing.' She is standing up, half naked and exposed. She still has the handcuffs. Johnny knows that he hasn't told her, but he did that on purpose because of the guilt. He kept meaning to tell her, then backing out. He has had to play golf with clients at weekends before, but this time he is meeting Grace and she still isn't technically a client.

'I did say,' he protests. Lying makes him feel even worse. He is not having an affair, he is not going to, he just needs to see her, which is different. To his surprise, Betty bursts into tears.

'You've ruined everything.' She is angry with him because she knows that he didn't mention golf and she is afraid that it is with *her*.

'What? What have I done? Betty, we didn't discuss your plans this weekend either.'

'I planned to keep you in bed.' She angrily marches over to her wardrobe and pulls out her large brown paper bag. She empties it on top of him, spilling the coffee, which he is powerless to mop up. He gets out of bed and puts the breakfast tray on the floor, then he starts going through what is lying on the duvet. As he looks through Betty's sex toys he doesn't know whether to laugh or to be outraged. He has a strange urge for both.

'Betty, what on earth's brought all this on? Please tell me you're not doing a feature on it.' They have never spoken about the need for sex toys. Underwear is one thing but porn isn't something he believed his wife would ever even watch, let alone buy. The idea of her going into a shop and asking for lesbian porn is enough to make him want to laugh hysterically. He can't picture it with a straight face.

'How dare you suggest that I would only have sex with you with all this for a feature?'

'A French maid's outfit? We've never done dressing up.'

'There's always a first time.'

'Porn? I'm not complaining but you told me that porn disgusts you.'

'I changed my mind. I'm allowed to change my mind.'

'I don't need this.'

'What? What the fuck don't you need?' She is not Superwife any more, she is superfluous.

'I don't need you to do this for me. I love you and I am quite happy with our sex life. I don't need to eat your knickers.' He bursts out laughing, unable to keep it in any longer.

'How dare you laugh at me?' She is stamping her feet and her fists are clenched. He goes to put his arm round her. She shrugs him off.

'Fuck off, fuck off. Go to your client. I hate you.' She gets into bed and pulls the duvet over her head. She is having a tantrum but she doesn't want to look at him. She doesn't want to drive him any further into her arms, but neither can she just let it happen. She wishes Grace were there. She would love to slap her right now.

'I'm sorry.' He touches her shoulder, feeling awful. He just can't get over how bizarre she looks.

'Just go.' She pushes him away. Johnny looks at her, feels awful as he sees her body shaking with rage. He wants to kiss her, to apologise, to make it up to her. But just as he is about to do that, he thinks about where he is going, and torn, feeling ripped in two, he starts towards her, then away, and then towards her, finally going to the bathroom where he has a shower, before getting dressed.

Her head is still firmly under the duvet when he says

goodbye, and despite the fact that he feels wretched, he leaves.

As he walks out of the front door, he acknowledges that he has a big problem and he has to deal with it. Soon.

He is early, so he drives around near Grace's flat, feeling awful and wonderful at the same time. He wishes that his life were not going this way. He is not a cad, has never been, even in his youth. He wants to be happy – he is happy – but all of a sudden his happiness is being questioned, being teased, changing beyond his control.

Grace moves away from the window as the time draws closer. She checks her reflection in the mirror, and she goes through her handbag, making sure she has everything she needs. She reapplies her lipgloss, and tries to feel calmer. Next to the front door, her golf clubs are waiting. She is glad she held on to them. She has pulled her hair back in a ponytail, and she is wearing a pair of loose brown trousers, and a cream jumper. She looks practical, yet still a bit sexy, as the jumper is tight. Her flat shoes go with the outfit. She can't believe they are spending the day together. She can barely contain her excitement.

She thinks back to the first day they met, and how she was going to give him the full Grace treatment. He is getting just that, but genuinely. She means everything she says or does.

Betty lifts her head up after she hears the door close behind him. She feels awful. She looks round and sees that Johnny has packed up all the toys, and removed the tray. All that remains of her humiliation is the fact she is still wearing her edible knickers and her high heels, and she is also clutching the handcuffs. She takes them off and puts on her tracksuit. She takes a deep breath. Was he telling the truth? Is he playing golf with a client? She hates herself for it, but she goes to the hall cupboard and sees that his clubs have gone. She then opens his wardrobe and sees that he is wearing his casual golf clothes (she knows his entire wardrobe). She breathes easily. Until she remembers what it was that set her off when he mentioned golf. Grace once trapped a man playing golf.

She knows what she has to do as she starts ransacking the house, looking for clues. She has to know if he's cheating, or if he's about to. Would Grace have called her if they had already done something, or would she wait? It is nearly the two-month deadline; it is looming so close that she can almost touch it. But she can't wait that long. She has to know. First she goes through his work jacket pockets, but finds nothing. Then she goes through the desk drawer where he keeps his bills, but still nothing. She looks under the bed (irrationally), in his trouser pockets, even in his shoes. Finally, exhausted and with nothing, she picks up the phone and calls Alison.

Grace's buzzer sounds at exactly ten o'clock. This doesn't annoy her, as it would do normally. She feels relieved. She had been worrying that he might not turn up. Grace isn't used to conventional dating, and the fear that sat within her until the buzzer went was immense, and alien. Not that she is dating, of course. But it shook her up. She grabs her clubs, locks her door and bounds down the stairs to meet him, as they arranged.

He sees her coming towards him and he smiles. She opens the door, and he cannot help but plant a kiss on her cheek as he takes her clubs for her. She looks delicious. His mind flips, briefly, to Betty and her knickers, but he banishes it. Whatever happens, he needs this day. Even if it's the last.

He opens the car door for her and she climbs in. She turns to him and smiles, he does the same as he switches on the ignition. Anyone witnessing them would assume they were a happy couple going out for the day. Instead of being locked in confusion.

'I've got you a gift,' he says, handing over a silver bag. She smiles. She wants whatever is in that bag more than she wants anything. She opens it, and pulls out a cap. It's funky but also perfect for golf.

'You're an angel,' she says, kissing his cheek and putting the cap on. Whatever happens, she will always cherish the cap. Her gift from Johnny.

'Betty, will you calm down? I can't understand a word you're saying.' Alison is in bed, on the phone. Matt is looking at her with questions in his eyes and also exasperation. They were in the middle of making love and it annoys him that Alison abandoned him for the phone. His penis is deflating at a rate of knots.

'OK, give me half an hour and I'll be over,' she says finally.

'Great, not only do you abandon our Saturday shag but now I haven't got any chance of a retry.'

'Don't be silly, it doesn't take you half an hour.' She decides to take a leaf out of Betty's book and keep her man happy before she leaves.

Matt stays in bed while Alison dresses.

'So, Johnny isn't there, I take it?'

'No, he must be playing golf, like you said.'

'What is going on with those two?'

Alison colours slightly, and feels angry all of a sudden that she has to lie to him. Matt can be a bit frivolous at times but that doesn't mean he deserves this.

'I don't know, but Johnny is acting strangely, according to Betty.'

'Well, he seems fine to me. Apart from that drunken thing the other night.'

'Matt, do you think he's cheating on her?'

'No, I don't. First of all he's not like that, and second he adores her. Christ, they have the perfect marriage, or that's what it seems like. I don't understand what's been happening lately.'

'Maybe Betty will shed some light now. Are you sure you don't mind me going out?'

'No way. I get a nice peaceful day.' He winks to show he is teasing, and she kisses him and leaves.

'Have you been burgled?' Alison asks, as she walks into Betty's house.

'No. I did this.' She is storming around still. The lack of evidence has made her even more angry.

'You ransacked your own home. Why?' Alison is trying not to be too shocked by Betty's appearance. Her hair is sticking up, as if she has been electrocuted, her tracksuit is one that she normally would wear only to weed the garden, and her face is pale. She looks like a wild woman.

'I wanted evidence that he's with her, that he's having an affair. I need to know. You know, Grace told me once that sometimes you might only have a tiny, tiny bit of doubt in your mind, but that tiny doubt grows and grows, with suspicion feeding it and she says it drives people mad. That's how she justifies what she does. She says it's better to know what's going on than to suspect, because otherwise you go insane. And I argued and told her that trust was the most important thing and what she did was wrong, but look, she was right. I don't trust him any more. I have a tiny doubt and it's taking me over and now I've ransacked my house looking for clues and I am going mad.'

'Then put an end to it.'

'What, the bet?'

'Of course the bet. Look at you. Remember when you told me you were doing this? I told you not to, but you said that you trusted him completely. And for the first week you were fine, but then you began to lose it. First the doubts just because you knew she was chasing him but you didn't know when and where. Then the Superwife thing, which is still going on. Betty, you're right, you are going mad. So for goodness' sake put an end to it, please.'

'I will.' It suddenly makes sense and she feels composure return.

'You'll call her?'

'Yeah, let's do it, let's do it now. But what if she pulls the article?' She can barely believe that, in the state she's in, she is still thinking about the article.

'Then she does. You tell Fiona that you can't do it.'

'But she'll kill me.'

'And that's more important than Johnny?' Alison snaps.

'No, of course not.' Betty remembers how she did all this for her career and realises that her priorities were round the bend. Why didn't she refuse? Was she really afraid of losing her job, or was she, deep down, curious to know if Johnny was a cheater? She is unsure if she wants to find the answer.

'Well then, tell her that she'll have to demote you. You'll get another job if you need to, Betts. Please just stop this and worry about the consequences later.'

'Shall I call her now?'

'Yes! Right now.' Alison is rarely exasperated with her friend, and she is not used to being the sensible, in control one. She wants Betty back, and Betty with Johnny, like normal. The world would be rebalanced.

'Shall we have coffee before we start?'

'Um, yes, please, I'm still half asleep.' Grace yawns to demonstrate this fact, but she is just beginning to realise how tired she is. They sit in the golf lounge and wait for the coffee to be brought to them.

'This place is amazing,' Johnny says, looking around him at the heavily portraited walls.

'Isn't it? I love it here.' It is not quite a lie: she does love it, but she is also seeing it for the first time. She blames it on her sleepiness that she was initially not entirely sure where she was going, but she has quickly discovered the way round and memorised it; something she is used to in her job.

'So, how are you doing? You still haven't given me an answer on my financial proposals.'

'Oh, so that's why you agreed golf with me, so you could get me to sign my money away to you?'

'Absolutely.' Johnny smiles at her, feeling an urge to kiss her. He pushes it away. There is too much of a mess in his head. He is just going to enjoy the day, enjoy it for now. 'But there was the added bonus of playing golf here. I've always wanted to do it.'

'Right.' She pretends to be disappointed, but she can tell from his eyes that he is happy to be with her.

'Oh, and the company isn't too bad.'

Now she laughs, as does he. She finds it unbelievable that their conversations are so basic yet they fill her with joy. There is no intellect needed – not like with the others. With Johnny, just a hello is enough to keep her warm for an hour.

'This coffee is lovely. Johnny, I hate to ask this, but I have to. Did your wife mind?'

'You're a client, or you will be one day if you ever get round to signing the papers. I'm playing golf with a client.' He looks serious.

'I'm sorry, I shouldn't have asked that. I didn't want to, but well, you know . . .' She wants to declare her feelings to him. Not as part of any phase – she has long given up playing that game – but because she needs to. She has to mention Betty to him because she is an issue, and Grace needs to know how he sees her before she opens her heart.

'Grace, I don't know what's happening here, but I'm with you today, and that's all. Please can that be all?'

'Yes, Johnny, that can be all.'

*

Betty dials Grace's home number. It rings until the answer-phone kicks in. She listens to the message, as if it will offer a clue, but she hangs up just before the beep.

'She's not there.'

'OK. Leave a message.' Alison is talking to a child.

'Saying, "Keep your slutty hands off my husband"?'

'We don't know if she has her slutty, I mean, her hands on him.'

'I'll call her mobile.' Betty dials for a second time.

Grace is about to hand her handbag over to the cloakroom attendant, when her phone rings. She thinks about not answering it, but when she sees it is Betty, she cannot resist. She chastises herself for her evil, but there is a devil sitting on her shoulder. It is out of her control. She mouths 'sorry' to Johnny and answers.

'Grace.'

'It's me.'

'I'm a bit busy at the moment.'

'Doing what?'

'I'm not sure I can say.' She looks at Johnny, who smiles back.

'I need to talk to you. It's urgent.'

'Well, I'll call you tomorrow.'

'It can't wait. I need to talk to you now.'

Grace smiles at Johnny apologetically. She realises that there is no need for Betty to know who she is with, that revenge is not her goal, and that Betty doesn't deserve that kind of vindictiveness.

'Look, I'm really going to have to go.' She shrugs in exasperation, which Johnny takes as his cue.

'Grace, come on, or we'll miss our slot,' he says loudly.

Grace freezes, Betty freezes. Grace hangs up the phone and, feeling dreadful, she gives her bag to the lady who has been patiently waiting for it.

*

'Betty?' Alison is staring at her, as she holds the receiver in her hand. She blinks, but does not move. 'Betty, give that to me.' Alison hangs up the phone and leads Betty to sit down.

'I heard his voice,' she says eventually. 'He's with her, and she's won. And I've lost.'

'What's wrong, Grace? You seem a bit preoccupied.' Johnny has barely managed to get a word out of her since they made their way on to the course.

'Sorry. I just didn't think it would be this hard.'

'What, golf?'

'No. Not golf.' She smiles at him sadly, but she cannot walk away. Not yet. 'I know, let's get on with me thrashing you, and then we'll talk over supper.'

'Good idea. Golf and talk don't mix. I hope you're not one of those women who never shut up when they're playing.'

'How dare you?' She pretends to be indignant. 'For that, I'm going to tee off first.'

As they start playing, Johnny is swinging from feeling relaxed. It is a mixture of fresh air, his favourite game and Grace that is doing it. But his composure is being interrupted by a collage of the morning's events with Betty. The breakfast, the handcuffs, the edible knickers. He hits a bad shot.

'Oh dear, you weren't concentrating,' teases Grace, who is on good form despite the fact she hasn't played for a while.

'I thought I'd give you a chance, or something. But for that, I won't. Prepare to be humiliated.'

'OK, Johnny, do your worst.'

The most awful thing is that he can see it now. There are two Johnnys: the one who would now be talking about going to the supermarket with his wife, Betty; would be petting Cyril, and arguing over who does which chore. Then they would have lunch and then he would probably play golf with Matt, or watch sport. Not the most exciting life, but his life, his chosen life, the life he was always happy with.

Then there is the Johnny who would bring her breakfast in bed, because Grace is the sort of woman for whom you have to do that. He can picture himself pulling back the duvet, and kissing her from her ankles, up her long legs. He shudders with that thought. Luckily, Grace is lining up a shot. Then, after a morning of making love, they would get up and do something. Play golf, maybe, go horse riding (although he can't ride), drive to the country. That is what he would do with Grace. She promised excitement and he wouldn't go shopping, do chores – no, because that isn't what Grace represents.

He knows that there is an element of fantasy attached and the reality would be different, but the worst thing, the thing he is losing the ability to cope with, is the thought that he wants to try. To give that life a go, maybe.

He loves Betty, but he believes he loves Grace, and there aren't two of him to go round, so he is clueless as to what to do.

'Nice shot,' he calls, as he realises that the only thing he can do is play golf.

'They're playing golf together, but that doesn't mean that anything else is happening.'

'No, but how do we know they are playing?'

'You said he said that they'd miss their slot.'

'That could mean anything. They could be fucking. "Oh, Grace, put the phone down. I missed your slot." ' Betty realises what she's said and she bursts out laughing, sounding hysterical.

Alison shoots her a worried look. 'That was really crude, even for you. I'm sorry, but you have to do something.'

'But what? I can't ask him, can't let on that I know because he'd never forgive me. I can't speak to her because she's with him.' Betty puts her face in her hands. Tears begin rolling down her cheeks. 'He said that he was having supper with the client as well. Shit, Alison, I'm going to lose him and I have no idea how I'll ever cope with that. Oh, shit. You know what? I'm not letting him go. I can't do that. We need a plan. I know, we can think while we clean this mess up.' They start on the house, putting everything back so Johnny will never know that anyone has been through his things, looking for clues that Betty no longer thinks she needs. She is falling apart but she is still determined to fight; that is keeping her together. Just as they finish, the doorbell rings.

'I'll go,' Alison says. After a few minutes she returns with a bouquet of flowers, a bottle of champagne and a box of chocolates.

Betty looks at them and bursts into tears, for the first time, at the action of her guilty husband.

'I've become a cliché. And I fucking hate clichés.'

Chapter Twenty-Nine

'Can I try some?' Grace asks, putting her fork into Johnny's mushroom risotto and taking a mouthful.

'I didn't say yes.'

'I know, but it is so good. Here, to be fair, you have some of my lamb.' Johnny obliges.

He beat her at golf but she played well. They had a drink at the club before Johnny drove her to a bistro near her flat. He feels tense again as he realises that his need for her is now physical as well. There is only so much you can put down to her attractiveness. It is not about her looks. He is beginning to weaken, to feel that he is unable to resist her and he knows that if she made a move, he would be powerless to refuse her. But she hasn't done anything but give him a peck on the cheek for winning, and lightly brush his hand. He is relieved but disappointed.

Grace smiles at him. She feels truly happy. Whatever happens to her, she resolves that she will remember this day for ever. The day that she let everything good flood her body, because she feels normal, human. She will always remember it, and him. Even if she cannot be with him. She senses his confusion and wants to help him, but knows that only he can decide. And she also feels that whatever decision he makes will be the right one. She trusts him – if he stays with Betty, or if he comes to her. She knows that it is wrong to try to break up a marriage, she knows that, but she is in love, and the fact that they aren't having an affair, or not a physical affair, is important. She is not sure that it is better to have a mental affair, because you still get the mental guilt. She doesn't want him to agonise over it, she doesn't want him to be hurt, but he will be, as will she herself or Betty. They might all be hurt. But she cannot stop it. Not now. She is going downhill and the brakes have failed.

'Thanks, Ali,' Betty says, as she sips a cup of tea, having woken up from a long nap.

'You needed sleep, you're so tense.'

'I know. I feel saner now.'

'It's understandable, but the thing is that you have to pull yourself together. How long left for the bet?'

'Not long.'

'Call it off tomorrow.'

'I will. I'll tell her. She might even understand if I beg. I'm sure that's all she wants anyway. I'm sure she has no use for Johnny – it's all about getting me riled. And she's doing a pretty good job.' Betty feels calm about everything. She will tell Grace that it's over. She'll tell her that she won. Then she'll tell Fiona that she's not carrying on. Then she will address the problem of Johnny. Because if he left her . . . She cannot yet contemplate that.

'But in the meantime if you want to keep him I'd have a shower and do something with that hair, and also put on some decent clothes.' Alison smiles. They giggle at the tracksuit Betty is still wearing.

'He's having supper with her.' Tears are coming back.

Alison is mixed up and doesn't know what to do. She opts for denial.

'Look, I know how tough you are. I've seen it. Get changed, come home with me for supper, call Johnny and leave a message on his mobile telling him you're having drinks with us and for him to join us when he's finished. Pretend he has been playing golf with a client and nothing more.'

'You're right. If I don't feel threatened then I might be all right.' Betty is trying so hard not to be threatened. That way, if she can keep control, she knows she will win.

'Well, you might not go mad.'

'I might not. Thanks, Ali.'

Betty gets up to go and have a shower while Alison starts praying.

'You better not drink any more, you won't be able to drive,' Grace says, tipping the rest of the wine into her glass.

'Thank you, Miss Sensible. I'll get a coffee, just in case.'

'You could come back to the flat for coffee.' Grace realises the minute the words leave her mouth that it sounds like a corny line. She giggles, like a young girl, and that is how she feels. When she works she is so precise in what she says to the men, her chat-up technique is faultless, but now she cannot control her mouth.

'Nice line, Grace. I gave you more credit than that.'

'OK, then how about this? Shit, have you seen how much they charge for a coffee in this place? You'd better come and have some at mine. It's free.'

'Better, but not sure if it still doesn't sound like you're trying to get me into your lair.' He leans in close. Grace is right, he has had a couple too many to drink, and he shouldn't drive. But part of him feels that he is drunk with her, because he is now over the line that he created – finished with self-justification, and lengthy explanations. Now he wants her. If that is wrong, then it is, but he is blocking out right and wrong. He's blocking out Betty. He sees only Grace because that is the world he wants to inhabit right now.

'Actually, I'm trying to save your driving licence.' She knows that this is it. She knows that physically she could have him, and she senses his desperation. But she is not sure that it is the right thing to do. She knows it isn't the right thing to do. She doesn't want him to be unfaithful to Betty. She doesn't want to be 'the other woman'.

The mood is broken, the spell that Johnny is under lifts.

'We're not going to do anything, are we?'

'Apart from have coffee.'

'I don't know what's happening to me.'

'Me neither.'

'I should call my wife.' The way he said it, '*my wife*', is a physical blow to Grace.

He knows that he is playing a game of contradiction. A minute ago he was ready to leap over the table and grab her, and now he is sitting opposite her, making her listen to him calling his wife.

Betty is sitting on the sofa watching the latest reality TV show with Matt. Alison is cooking. Betty looks normal again. She is wearing a pair of jeans and a ballet top. Her hair is tied up, her face made-up. The mad woman, the banshee has vanished.

'Oh, my God, that woman is so embarrassing. How can she think that she's normal?' Betty cringes at the screen.

'The worst thing is that she thinks she's "zany". You know a person's a saddo when they describe themselves as "whacky", "zany", or "mad".' Matt laughs. What he likes about Betty is that she enjoys the same television as he. Johnny hates anything like it, as does Alison. They prefer a good drama, or a comedy, and although Matt likes that too, he also likes trash. Betty and he are often comrades when it comes to viewing.

Betty's mobile rings and Johnny's name flashes on the display. A mixture of relief and fear comes across her, because although she wants him to call her, she is afraid of what he might say.

'Hi,' she says.

'Are you all right?' She thinks back to the heap he left her in that morning. But she is composed again.

'I'm fine. I'm with Matt and Ali. Oh, I meant to say thank you for the flowers and chocolates. They were lovely.' She is all sweetness and light.

'You're welcome. Are you out?'

'No, at their place. If you want to join us at any time, you know, when you've finished your business dinner . . .'

'Yeah, I might be a while longer.' His guilt was growing, he could no longer contain it.

'Just call when you're on your way, to check I haven't left.'

She ignores Matt's questions about Johnny, lost in her own thoughts. Alison is right: she has done this. She knows where Johnny is and who he is with because she set him up. She didn't hire Grace, but she agreed to the stupid bet. She might as well have given him another woman on a plate. He is lying to her, but she is lying to him. She looks at the screen, takes a deep breath and forces a smile. She has no one to blame but herself.

'So, coffee?' Johnny asks, reluctantly. He feels as if she is his addiction. Then he feels silly for behaving like a romantic. He is not. He likes lager and football and golf and sex. He likes love, but doesn't want to go on about it all the time. He is not romantic.

'Yes. Johnny, I am not going to try to get you to do anything.' Grace cannot quite express what she means. What she wants to say is that there will be no pressure from her, no moves. She won't make it more difficult for him than she can see from his face that it already is. She wonders what Betty made of the phone call. She knows he is with her, and that must make her feel awful. Grace feels bad for Betty. She knows how special he is and she is now terrified of not having him there, so she knows how Betty feels. She wonders if that is the case with affairs – if the women who sleep with other women's husbands feel dreadful but can't help it, or if they don't care. Grace does care; she surprised herself with that, but she does. Poor Betty.

'Good, then you won't make me pay the bill,' he jokes, finally getting everything normal again.

'Apart from that,' she replies.

Alison serves dinner. She can see that Betty's equilibrium has slipped a little, but on the whole she is impressed with the way her friend is coping. She suddenly feels angry for Matt. She doesn't want to have to deal with this on her own. She wants to talk to her best friend, but Betty is involved and Matt cannot know. She is torn herself. Part of her would love to confess everything to Matt, knowing that although he isn't a serious person, he will know what to do about it. He will come up with a good solution. Part of her wants to sit in his arms and tell him the story, then let him fix it. But that would destroy everything. Matt is loyal, fiercely loyal, and he would no doubt tell Johnny. Betty would hate her, and she couldn't have that, because Betty means so much to her. She is trapped.

'So, is Johnny coming over, or am I stuck with the birds all night?' Matt asks.

'He'll be here later, as soon as he can get away from his client.'

'Good.'

'Are you worried about your testosterone ebbing away?' Alison teases, determined to keep the evening light-hearted.

'Never. Just wouldn't mind talking about something other than shoes.'

'As if that's all we talk about.'

'It is.'

'Well, would you prefer us to talk about lesbians?' Betty asks, winking at Alison.

'Now that would be good.'

It is Betty's fault. She will sort it. Tomorrow, she will sort it out once and for all.

'Well, there's this movie I've heard is quite good. *Lesbians in Outer Space.*'

Matt's jaw drops as Betty and Alison fall about laughing.

'How are you, fish?' Johnny asks. 'You all look quite happy. Do you enjoy swimming around in your tank? What about food – do you like your food?'

Grace walks in with coffee and catches the conversation. 'No one else normally talks to them except me.'

'Do they talk back?'

'Not really, but they come to the front of the tank sometimes and I like to think they are trying.'

'They're really pretty.'

'I know. I find them relaxing.'

'Were they yours?'

'What do you mean?'

'Sorry, I mean did you have them when you were married?'

'No. I got them when I moved here. For company. Silly, really.'

'I don't think so.'

They sit down and drink coffee.

'Grace, I hate to think of leaving you, but if I stay . . .'

'I know.'

'We could play a game. You know, like rummy. So we can talk but we'll be doing something else and we won't, you know . . .' He is red with embarrassment.

'I'm really good at Trivial Pursuit.'

'Why don't you pour us some brandies and we'll play?'

'Johnny, you're driving.'

'I'll get a cab.'

'Are you sure?' she asks.

He looks at her, she looks at him. Her eyes are so beautiful, big hazel eyes; his eyes are so honest, she thinks, so blue, and honest. She goes to find the board game and she directs Johnny to the brandy.

It is eleven when his phone goes. He is just about to answer a question to get his last wedge. Grace is losing badly. She has no wedges and is drunk. Although not Betty drunk.

'Hello.' He knows it is Betty.

'Johnny, I'm about to go home. I thought I'd tell you.'

'Sorry. Hold on.' He smiles at Grace, and gestures quiet. 'I just wanted to get out of earshot. The client seems intent on making a night of it. I don't know what time I'll be home.'

'Fine. I'll see you when I see you.'

'I better go,' Betty says, when she's hung up.

'I'll walk you,' Matt says, sensing that something is very wrong, but having no idea what.

'I'll come too. I could do with some fresh air after all that food.' Alison is more concerned about Betty keeping it together. She is coping well, but looks a bit manic every now and then; as if the banshee could reappear. Suddenly Alison realises that she is also being furtive, worrying about leaving Matt and Betty alone in case she blabs to him. Whereas this would solve her problem of keeping quiet, she knows that Betty will regret it, and she is trying to be a friend. They are all deceiving each other. Matt is the only one amongst them that is innocent. She hopes. She shakes the feeling off her, physically, as it sinks in just how paranoid and awful the situation is making her feel.

A couple of months ago, they were two couples, friends, best friends, who hung out together but were decidedly normal. Now, one made a bet with another woman that her husband couldn't be seduced; the husband is probably being seduced; the best friend is lying to her husband; he is unsure what is wrong, but knows something is. And, Alison concludes, it is a mess. Which, again, she concedes, is a huge understatement.

'It's turned cold,' Matt says, with a puzzled look on his face.

Alison sees it clearly: that's what it has come down to. You know that something is very wrong when Matt refers to the weather.

'It's not fair. I don't want a history question.'

'But you need a wedge. I've only got one more to get, and then I've wiped the floor with you,' Johnny points out.

'Maybe, but I'm sure you cheated.'

'You said you were good at Trivial Pursuit.'

'I lied.' She laughs. She has played the worst game of her life. She was unlucky with the questions. She couldn't stop wishing that he were kissing her. They both sat at a safe distance away from each other. Their hands did not touch. Their legs did not touch. It was like something from Jane Austen courting days. No touching until you've secured that engagement. But, she wonders, did they have the electricity then that is simply electrocuting her?

'No kidding. You're the worst.' Johnny doesn't want the game to end, but when it ends, then what? He can't let himself touch her. Her smell is intoxicating and it has taken every ounce of strength to keep his nose away from her ear. He feels as if he is a magnet and she is a very attractive piece of metal. He, at times, caught his body moving towards her, and had to pull it back. He's a married man and he loves his wife. He *does* love her. He even missed her at certain points. He thought of something that he would say to her, and she would laugh, but she wasn't there. Grace was. And he wanted to be close to her too. He has no idea what he is going to do, but he is beginning to realise that he must do something. Fast. He is drowning. He is lying. He is unsure of his next move. He looks at Grace, her eyes, so big and bright; they are killer eyes. He doesn't dare look at the rest of her, because she is perfect. He loves Betty, but Grace is perfect. She is everything that any man could desire. He wonders if she is an illusion or if she is real. He never imagined that such perfection existed.

His head is hurting with the confusion that is spinning around. He wants to take her in his arms and he knows that he won't be able to prevent himself doing this for much longer.

'Johnny?' she asks him, having noticed that his face has changed colour a number of times.

'Sorry?' he says. She knows that she has him sometimes, but that she also loses him. She knows that the dilemma plays in his head like a stuck record. She feels bad. She had told herself to walk away a thousand times. If she loved him then she would, surely. Because love is about wanting someone else to be happy, about wanting the best for them. That's storybook love. Grace has only just rediscovered her heart, and now it is beating again she can't walk away. If she does then it might never stop, and she will exist, Miss Havisham-like for her eternity. She is angry with herself for being so selfish. She knows that she is in the middle of a situation that will hurt at least one person. She is not a horrible person. So why does she feel as if she is?

'Johnny, you're a funny colour.'

'Am I?' He looks at her and smiles. He cannot help but smile when he sees her.

'Yes, which I am guessing means you've drunk too much brandy, and I am going to call you a cab before you vomit in my flat.' She is impressed by how light-hearted she is. She is impressed that she is telling him to go rather than jumping on him. But she is unimpressed by the fact that she will be going to bed alone. And that can be cold.

'I'm not sure I want to go,' he says. His lower lip is trembling. He looks like a child. She feels his vulnerability, but will not take advantage of it.

'Just in case that's the drink talking, I'm going to call you a cab anyway.' She smiles at him warmly, and tries to convey in her look how much she wants him to stay, but he knows it already. He feels it too.

He sits in the taxi, wondering if he will see her tomorrow. He said he would call in when he came to pick up his car. She said that she would make him coffee. They looked at each other for a bit longer than they should have done. He sighs. He is drunk, but not drunk in the conventional sense. In one way he feels sober. He is beginning to see clearly. One thing he knows is that this cannot continue. He will not lie to Betty.

Betty, the girl who came to interview him. She was so annoyed at having to do the 'boring' financial feature. He could see it in her eyes – for a second, until he smiled at her and she smiled back. That was it. He thought she was hot, and she was, is, hot. Trendy, quirky, opinionated. Loved her job, was so passionate about it, that he couldn't help but find that attractive. Even if he didn't fall in love at first sight, he soon did when she started pursuing him. Then she was the same about him, which was, of course, what hooked him. She was so vibrant that when you spent time with her you hoped it would rub off on you. When she fell in love with him, she was so enthusiastic about that, that he was. And she kept it up. They hardly ever row because she hates arguments. She always makes him laugh if they are bickering or about to fall out. She has the odd tantrum but afterwards she will take the mickey out of herself, imitate herself being a prima donna and he will forgive her.

They have been together for ages. There is more than a hint of routine in their lives. Maybe that is what he had been trying to break, deep down – the routine of it all. Is Grace his mid-life crisis? No, she isn't. He isn't in crisis with Betty. They have a brilliant sex life; he fancies her. They have spirited discussions, they aren't bored with each other. Just because the glamour of the early days is now buried beneath the mortgage payments and trips to the supermarket doesn't mean that it is over. He still loves her, that much he is certain of.

But Grace. Grace is in there, in his head. He feels he is in hers. Sometimes when he looks at her he thinks he can see her mind, and she can see his. She hasn't tried to pressure him, she isn't behaving like a mistress, although he hates that term and he is not a cheater. He won't cheat on Betty. He will choose, if that's what it comes down to, he will make his choice and live with it, but he won't lie any more. Not to the women he loves.

As the taxi pulls up outside his house, he sighs as he gets out. The decision is edging closer. He fishes his keys out of his pocket and opens the door. The house is dark, but he feels Cyril brush against his leg and he wants to cry. That's his life: his house, his cat, his wife. He has a family. He goes to the sitting room and sinks into the sofa. He doesn't turn on the light. Upstairs is the woman he loves. He imagines her in bed now, in her T-shirt, or, more accurately, his T-shirt, because she always wears his T-shirts to bed. She will be breathing gently and dreaming, he hopes, good dreams. Because that's what he wants for her.

Across London, he imagines her. She will be putting the board game away, taking the brandy glasses to the kitchen. Washing them up, because she told him she hates to wake up to any chores. She will say good night to the fish, the way he always says good night to Cyril. Then she will go to her bedroom and get ready for bed.

He doesn't know what she wears in bed, what colour her toothbrush is, what face cream she uses, if she uses any. He doesn't know how she breathes when she is asleep, whether she snores. He doesn't know if she is still, like Betty, or if she thrashes around. He doesn't know what it is like to kiss her before going to sleep, or wake with his arms fastened around her. He doesn't know what her hair smells like when you bury your head in it. He doesn't know how her lips feel, how they taste. He doesn't know any of these things.

He strokes Cyril as he imagines both of them sleeping. Safely. And as he thinks of the two women, he has never felt lonelier in his life.

Chapter Thirty

Her head feels fuzzy from the drink. She knew that, after he went and she poured herself a large brandy, her last drink, her nightcap, she would regret it in the morning. She stands under the shower trying to wash the headache away, but finally concedes defeat and goes to the kitchen for some pills. She checks that her mobile is switched on, and she even picks up the handset of her normal phone and hears the dialling tone, just to check it is working. She knows that she is not behaving like herself; she is behaving like a normal woman. A thought that terrifies her.

She puts some bread in the toaster and makes coffee. She also drinks a glass of water. The phone rings just as the kettle boils, and she runs to get it.

'Grace, it's Eddie.' He sounds hurt.

Her heart sinks. She hadn't got round to telling him that it is over. She just left him, which makes her feel bad; guilty of neglect.

'Eddie. I'm sorry I haven't called.' She is sorry.

'You haven't returned any of my calls, and I've been calling.' He is angry and a little desperate.

'I know.' She feels ashamed. She isn't married to him, nor has she made him any promises, but that is no excuse for treating him badly. None at all.

'Well, can I see you?' he snaps.

She decides to do it face to face. 'Tonight. Shall we go for dinner?'

'Now I know something's wrong. You never want to go out.' She curses her stupidity. She is becoming more normal every day.

'Well, you could come here, but I've got no food.' She feels tired and the fuzziness in her head intensifies. She doesn't want this; she doesn't need this. But she is doing the right thing.

'I'll come round at seven.' He is still reeling from her suggestion that they go out and she knows not to push it.

'I'll see you at seven then.'

Her toast is cold as she eats it, and the coffee makes her head hurt more. She is a mess. She is breaking off with her friends, and she wonders if she will miss them. She will, she knows that, because other than them she has only Nicole. Unless Johnny, unless he . . . She shakes her head at the thought. She cannot presume that she will be with him. And even if she's not, she has to stop. Eddie sounded so wounded. They had a rule, that no one was to get hurt. They agreed to that rule, but rules break themselves sometimes. The bet had a rule too: that Grace would seduce Johnny and then leave. But rules break themselves.

'Morning, handsome.' She forgets for a minute that he was out until all hours last night with Grace. But then she remembers, and she remembers the horror of the day before, although she manages to sustain the smile on her face.

She must have fallen asleep before he got in, although she had convinced herself that she was so upset she would never sleep again. It was torturous not knowing what time he arrived and if he smelt of her, but as he reaches out for her, Betty cannot smell anything but Johnny.

'Morning,' he replies, and he starts kissing her.

They make love and she feels that he is hers again. He might be confused but he is with her, making love to her and that is the main thing. For now, he is hers and that is better than nothing.

They shower and dress and Betty takes Johnny out for breakfast.

'This sounds weird, but I feel like I haven't seen you for ages.'

'It was one day,' he snaps, without meaning to. He is tired from his nocturnal musings and the fact that he has a slight hangover. He doesn't mean to be defensive, and immediately he feels guilt.

'It wasn't a criticism.' She is hurt. She had him, now she has lost him. Confusion is threatening to bubble over into her mind, as she tries desperately to keep it in check.

'I'm sorry. I'm just tired. Yesterday was a long day. So, if we haven't seen each other for ages, what's new?'

'Nothing, but I think we need a holiday.' Although she might not be able to get him on a plane there and then, the fact that they make a plan for the future means they have a future.

'Good idea. Did you manage to get a freebie?'

'No, unfortunately the travel department don't need me, although they said that if we go somewhere exciting they might use the story, so we'd get paid that way, but unfortunately we are going to have to finance it ourselves.'

'Where do you want to go?' Suddenly the world seems a big place; and without Grace in it, that is not necessarily positive. Betty is also thinking how big the world is. How can she choose a destination that he will love when there is so much choice?

'I'll have a think.' She can sense his sudden reluctance, but she tries to ignore it as she attempts to eat her breakfast. It is making her feel sick. She sips her coffee – coffee that, for some reason, reminds her of Grace. She gets an overwhelming urge to ask him, to confront him, and also a strong desire to scream; but she does neither.

'I'll get some brochures tomorrow. We can look tomorrow night,' Johnny offers, guilt reminding him how to behave.

'Good idea.' She notices how their conversation has changed. She feels insecure, and needs something from him, something more. 'I've been given a feature to write, about infidelity,' she blurts. She notes the pale face that looks back at her, and wonders if she should shut up.

'You didn't say.'

'I forgot. I remembered because Fiona needs some ideas by tomorrow – you know what she's like. Anyway, after the honey-trap story I hoped I wouldn't have to go down that road. I mean, how can we be sure that the signs to spot a man who cheats are the same, or how much of it is paranoia? I might write a feature saying that women are too suspicious and should trust more. What do you think?' Betty can see things in his face, the face she knows so well. He was chewing when she started speaking but now he has stopped. He looks as if he will be sick. He has tilted his head to one side. He opens and closes his mouth, just like Grace's fish. She thinks he is going to confess.

'You're right,' he finally says. 'Absolutely.' And in that he says nothing and everything.

Betty goes to buy the papers on the way home. He trails after her but his thoughts are elsewhere. He is unhappy with himself, and he still has no idea how to resolve the situation. He watches her choosing all the papers. Picking up the tabloids first and putting the broadsheets on top as she always does. He knows that she will read the tabloids first and then save the others until last. He knows that she will pull out the magazines and not get round to reading the papers. He knows most things about her. He has no idea if Grace even reads a paper.

He knows that he has to see her. He cannot go on like this, and it is not fair on anyone. Betty even spoke to him about infidelity – does she suspect him? He needs to sort it out, although he still has no idea how.

'Do you want coffee?' Betty asks as they walk into the house.

'No, I've got to go and pick the car up.'

'Where is it?'

'In some NCP car park, probably costing me a million pounds.' He is lying, but he smiles because Betty should have a nice day. 'I'll only be about an hour, and then we'll do something.'

'I'd like that,' she says, kissing him. 'We could go to a market or something.'

'That sounds perfect.' He kisses her, then leaves.

He calls Grace as soon as he leaves the house. Her phone is engaged. He wonders who she is talking to and realises that he is totally out of control. He feels that he needs her, but he also wants Betty. Just who does he want more?

Betty calls Grace as soon as Johnny is gone. Her line is engaged, and she wonders if she is talking to her husband. She can't go on like this. If Grace has a better nature, Betty hopes she will find it.

After Grace puts the phone down to Eddie, it immediately rings again.

'Hi, it's me.'

'Hello.'

'I'm coming to pick the car up. Can we have a quick coffee?'

'Of course. I'm just mooching around, really. How long will you be?'

'About half an hour, if I can find a cab.'

'See you soon.'

She puts the phone down and it rings again straight away. She shakes her head at her new popularity.

'Hello.'

'Have you been speaking to him?'

'No, Betty,' Grace lies. 'I was talking to a client.'

'Grace, can we talk?'

'Yes.'

'I know you were with him yesterday. He said he was with a client.'

'I know.'

'I'm going mad. I can't cope with it. The fact he lied to me makes me imagine him doing all sorts of things with you and I can't cope at all.' Betty's voice is laced with hysteria.

'Calm down. He might have lied to you but we haven't done anything.'

'What you mean is you haven't had sex with my husband,' Betty spits.

'No, I haven't kissed him. I think he feels weird because we're friends.' Grace isn't sure what to say, but she wants to pacify Betty, for some reason.

'Friends? Is that all?'

'Yes, Betty, that is. You've got nothing to worry about,' Grace lies again. 'He loves you.'

'So can we call the bet off? No winners or losers, just finish it.'

'OK. You don't have to give up your husband, I don't have to give up my job. We'll call it a day.'

'I don't believe you. He's on his way over and you're lying to me.'

'I love him, Betty,' Grace says, and hangs up.

Betty cradles the receiver to her chest. The panic is rising, and she has to concentrate to breathe. She loves him. Those words are repeating in her head. *She loves him.* What if he loves her? She cannot lose him. She must not lose him. But how can she ensure that she doesn't? Suddenly it feels like the biggest fight of her life and she is unsure what her strategy to win is any more. Even Superwife doesn't feel enough.

Grace feels the tears fall and hopes they will stop. She has Betty's words ringing in her ears – not her words, her sound. The desperation in her voice. The pleading tone to leave her husband alone. She thinks of her life, of Dave, who she knows she didn't love; of Ben, who she didn't love like this. Of Oliver and Eddie – again she doesn't love them. She enjoys the sex, she enjoys the company but it isn't love and she only knows that now because she understands. She finally knows what love feels like. And people are right when they say it is the best and worst feeling in the world. Because it is. For a moment, when she woke up and she pictured his face, she was the happiest woman in the world. But now, having spoken to Betty, she is the unhappiest. She cannot do this. She cannot carry on.

Johnny sits in the taxi, unsure why his hands are shaking. Is he going to tell her that it's over? Or is he going to tell her it's just starting? He doesn't know. Panic is threatening to overtake him. He is getting closer to her flat, but he is no closer to knowing what he is going to do.

Betty washes her face and applies her make-up. Maybe he will come back home within the hour, as he said, and if he does she doesn't want him to see her looking such a mess. She picks up the first tabloid newspaper, settles herself on the sofa and reads. Perhaps there is only one way to win, and that is normality. Johnny loves his life with her and he will not jeopardise it for a wild fancy. That is not his style.

Grace can't face it: that much she knows. Her life feels traumatic, which it hasn't done since she was young. She knows that she is seeing Eddie that evening to tell him that their fling is over. But what is she going to say to Johnny? Can she walk away, as Betty has asked her to do? She knows that she should walk away. But can she?

With indecision still flying around her head, her buzzer goes. She answers it and nearly screams when Eddie announces himself as her visitor.

'This isn't a good time. You were supposed to be here tonight.'

'I couldn't wait.'

'Eddie, please, not now, really not now.' She panics.

'I'm not leaving until you let me in. I mean it. I'm not being ignored, like you try to do to me.' He sounds hysterical.

Reluctantly she buzzes him up. He has always been so calm and together. She feels a pang as she realises that she will miss him, but she doesn't want him to be there now.

'I want to know what's going on.' He sounds oddly formal, like in old films, and Grace expects him to call her a hussy at any minute.

'This is not only unnecessary but it's not what we do. You knew when we started that this wasn't going to be one of those relationships where we could put our hands on our hips and demand answers from each other.'

'Yeah, well, maybe I knew that, but you let me fall in love with you.'

'I didn't. I always told you not to.'

'Well, maybe my heart isn't such a good listener.'

Grace feels as awful as she has ever felt. The tears return. She looks at him. He's so dishevelled, yet Eddie is not that type. He looks hurt, and she has caused that hurt. There is so much hurt around that she doesn't even know how they will contain it. Will it ever go away? Then her buzzer goes.

'Who's that?'

'My financial adviser,' she says automatically.

'On a Sunday?'

'We're friends. I don't need to explain that to you. Anyway, I guess I better get rid of him.

'Hi,' she says, eager, despite everything, to hear his voice.

'Hi yourself.' He still doesn't know what he will say when he gets to her door.

'Listen, I should have called, but a friend dropped in unexpectedly. Do you mind if we give coffee a miss?' I mind, she says to herself. I fucking well mind.

Disappointment hits him. He wants to know who she is with. He pauses for a moment.

'No problem. Will you call me? Tomorrow?' He still has no answers, but he was hoping that he would find some in her flat.

'I will. Bye.' She feels as if she has to physically tear herself away from the intercom as she walks back to Eddie.

'Is he worth it?'

'Worth what?'

'Worth sacrificing everything for. Me, whoever else you play around with. Your life.' He is almost spitting the words out at her.

'I'm not sacrificing my life.' It is all too much. She is exhausted.

'Tell me, Grace, would you give up your job for him?' He looks her in the eyes. Everything is still. Time has frozen.

'Yes,' she answers, honestly, as she watches Eddie walk out of her life.

Johnny is by his car, but he hasn't yet got in. He sees a man walk out of the front door, and he wonders if that is the person Grace was with. He looks upset. He could just live there though; he might not have been with her. He feels jealous at the thought, as he reluctantly gets into his car. He considers turning back for a second, but he stops himself.

Betty calls him. If she is going to lose him, she won't do it easily.

'Hello.'

'Babes, it's me.'

'Hi.' He sounds upset.

'I just wondered if you were any way near coming home?'

'I'm in my car now. Took me ages to get a cab. Anyway, I'll be home soon, honey.'

'I'll look forward to it.'

Grace looks out of her window and sees Eddie disappear up the street in one direction, and Johnny start up his car and pull out in the other. She has no idea what happens next, and she doesn't know how to begin to find out. But one thing is clear as she looks around her perfect flat: her life has changed now, and there is no going back. No matter how awful she feels, or how guilty she is, there is no way she can let Johnny go. Betty is irrelevant, almost. Grace needs him, she wants him, she would give up her job for him. No one has ever entered her life and given her what he has given her. No one has ever made her feel the way she feels with him. She hasn't touched him, she admits that she barely knows him, but that is the amazing thing. She cannot walk away – she has tried, but she cannot. The next time she meets him she will tell him how she feels, and she will pray that he feels the same.

He opens the door and plasters a smile on his face. He feels wretched, and is unsure how he will spend a normal Sunday afternoon without giving away that fact that he is consumed with jealousy. He is unsure how he will resolve the situation, but he knows he must. It's not indecision, it isn't, but he does not know what the right thing is. He still loves his wife, but he fears that he loves Grace too. And he can't have them both. He has to choose one.

Betty greets him with a hug. She notices that he looks upset but she ignores it. She will not show him weakness. She will be Betty, Super-Superwife. She leads him into the sitting room, where the papers are scattered, like a normal Sunday. She gently pushes him on to the sofa and she sits down too. She touches his arm lightly. She smiles, straight into the eyes she loves. She will not fall apart and she won't lose him.

'You will not believe what they've printed about that MP,' she says, as she launches into the latest scandal, and he laughs and they discuss it. For a while she has got him back. Her Johnny. She prays with all her might that she will keep him.

Johnny relaxes into the familiarity of the routine. He has always loved Betty's idea of a Sunday. She will read the newspapers, he will read the sports pages, she will regale him with gossip and scandal, and he will discuss it with her. Then they will watch the *EastEnders* omnibus if they aren't going out, while still making their way through the papers. Then, if they haven't gone on Saturday, they will rush to the supermarket before it closes and buy the food for the week (normally ready meals and, of course, cat food). They will return home, open a bottle of wine and have supper. Occasionally they'll attempt a roast, but more often than not they will have lasagne (one thing Johnny likes making), and garlic bread. After supper, they'll again return to the sofa to watch TV, before having an early night.

Johnny kisses Betty on the top of her head. You cannot buy that comfort. You cannot buy the warmth. But you can choose to give it up, if you really think that it's the right thing to do.

Chapter Thirty-One

Grace feels girlish as she dresses, all attempts at sophistication masked by a silliness, a nervousness, a feeling that she is on her first date. That is how he makes her feel. She is doing what Betty asked: she is forgetting the bet. Only, one thing she doesn't know is that she is going to follow her heart. No guilt. Eddie took it badly and she felt wretched for the whole of Sunday. She ended things because it is time for her to do what her heart tells her to do. Her heart tells her to be with Johnny. There is no bet. Just a love affair waiting to happen. She will tell him how she feels, she will let him decide how he feels. She will feel bad if he leaves Betty for her; she will feel worse if he doesn't. But she will take the risk.

She pulls on a short blue floral dress, one which makes her look feminine, because she wants that femininity. She wants to give it to him. Johnny makes her feel this way, and oh how she loves him.

She searches her wardrobe for some strappy sandals, and pictures his smile. Such a gentle smile, such an inviting smile. She longs to kiss him, to feel his arms around her. She has become the heroine of a romantic novel, because that is how he makes her feel.

And tonight is the night. The night when he will tell her that he feels the same. She knows this; feels it in her heart, and in her head. After the disaster on Sunday, he said he had to see her, and the urgency in his voice told her what she needed to know. She has won him, which has nothing to do with winning the bet.

She won't entertain the thought that she has lost him. Grace isn't a person who has always got what she wants – that isn't the reason. The reason she will not think about him not loving her is that she has no idea how she will deal with it. It is easier not to think about it, but to enjoy the feeling she has that it will all work out.

She brushes her hair. It is getting so long, but that makes her feel girlie, and that is how she wants to feel: like a girl falling in love for the first time. That is who she is now. Not Grace the honey trapper, but Grace the woman, the young woman with a huge romance ahead of her.

As she applies her mascara and her lipstick – not too much make-up, just a little, to complement her features because she no longer needs to hide her face behind it – she contemplates her future, with Johnny. Because that is what she hopes she has now: a future.

The taxi drops her outside the restaurant. It is an expensive choice – his choice. Not the sort of place you take a friend. She hopes it is not the sort of place he would take a friend.

She didn't mean to do it – fall in love. That wasn't her choice. In her line of work she knows the hurt and she would never fall in love with another woman's husband on purpose. But Betty told her that love was something she would, could never understand, and Betty was right. She didn't understand, she just *was*. Which is why she now tries not to think of Betty, but, because Grace isn't a total bitch, she does think of Betty. Often. She thinks back to when Fiona came up with the idea of the bet, the purpose of which was either to wipe the smirk off Betty's face, or to find the man so in love with his partner that she would be rejected. At the time, she didn't mind which outcome, but now she wants neither. She wants to be in love with Johnny, she wants him to be in love with her. If that is selfish, or wrong, then she cannot help it. Love is like that.

She knows that he might not feel the same. The fear that that thought evokes is something she has never experienced. When she was younger, the fear she felt at being bullied had nothing on this: the fear of rejection. Without Johnny there is a huge gap inside her, a black hole, one that will grow, without him, until it takes her over. She cannot live without him. She is so sure of that. She is so sure of him. Her feelings have been identified. She is thirty-two years old, not a kid playing with relationships. She knows what she is doing. She knows exactly what this is. For the first time in thirty-two years Grace Regan is in love. Properly, absolutely, totally in love. With someone else's husband.

She pushes the door open and notices that it is a small, dark, intimate restaurant. It is romantic, or it feels romantic. She sees that the small number of tables are seating couples. Some are holding hands, others staring into each other's eyes, some are talking, softly so you can hear a murmur but not what is being said, others seem to be silent. It is where Johnny has chosen to take her and that says more than Grace ever needs to hear from his lips. She is led to the back, where Johnny is sitting. He stands when she approaches the table. He is wearing a shirt, no tie, and his hair is neat. He looks troubled. As the waiter who led Grace to the table stands aside, Johnny leans towards her and kisses her cheek, leaving her feeling warm and tingly. She smiles, and despite the fact that he looks as if he doesn't want to smile, he smiles back. They sit down.

Johnny can see that even though they are in the middle of coupledom, the men are all looking their way. Men normally do when he is with Grace. Despite the fact that he doesn't want to, he feels proud – something he abhors himself for. He is at a loss at what to do, what to say, but he knows that he has to be honest with her; it is killing him. She is the most beautiful woman he has ever met, and so vulnerable, so delicate, so in need of him, and he is faltering. The perfect veneer he believes in so strongly is slipping because he wants her. But then he is only human and there is no man that wouldn't want her – most would want her just after looking at her. At least he got to know her. But there is a huge problem, and that is his wife. He loves his wife. She is his life. So why is he so drawn to this woman sitting opposite him? Is it because he is human, or is it because he is married to the wrong woman? He knows that he is going round in circles. Every decision he tries to make brings him back to the starting point. He is repetitive, and he is also stalled; he is getting nowhere.

He tells himself it has to stop. He tells himself to make a decision. He chastises himself, he beats himself up, but that does not change a thing. He is edging closer but getting further away. The horizon has disappeared. All there is is a vast space. He has to sort it out, he tells himself, but he is not being as obedient as usual.

Grace wishes she could see into his mind. When she works, she normally can tell what men are thinking, they are so transparent. They may as well have flashing neon signs on their heads. But Johnny's eyes are so full of confusion, and she knows that she is on dangerous ground. He is unhappy, she can see that, and she knows that she is responsible. She is vulnerable because although she thinks he invited her here to tell her he loves her, he might have invited her here to tell her that he cannot see her any more. The fear is threatening to engulf her.

'Would you like the wine list?' the waiter asks and, grateful for a break from their thoughts, they both smile.

'Red or white?' Johnny asks. Grace wants so badly to touch his face.

'Red,' she replies.

He gets an urge to kiss her. Johnny orders the wine, and then they both pick up the food menus.

'Johnny . . .' Grace says, then falters.

'Yes?' Johnny looks at her.

'Did you invite me here to tell me that you can't see me again?' There is a silence. Grace didn't mean to ask that question. After all, they are not having an affair. Their contact has been non-physical, and all of a sudden she has suggested something else. But they both know that they cannot carry on, and she has decided to release him, if that is what he wants. She didn't plan it, but she felt it. She desperately does not want to hear the answer is yes. She is so terrified of that 'yes' that she wants to run away as horror inside her intensifies. But she stays.

'Grace . . .' It is now Johnny's turn to falter. Luckily the wine waiter returns, giving him a respite. 'Grace,' he continues after the wine has been tasted and poured, 'I don't know.' He sits back, feeling inadequate. She is relieved. He doesn't know why he feels so guilty but he does – not only for Betty but for Grace. Can you be in love with more than one person? If you can, you are not allowed to be. He briefly wishes he was from a country where a man can have more than one wife. He truly believes that if he could have both Grace and Betty, then he would be complete. But they probably wouldn't be so keen on the idea.

Grace thinks that his not knowing still gives her a chance. He is confused, and that means he feels something for her. She understands that it is so much more complicated for him. He has a wife – a wife he loves – and he doesn't normally cheat; has never cheated on her. This for him is much more than that. She understands, but she also knows that he has no clear decision. She could do the right thing and walk away, or she could do the right thing for her.

'Johnny, I don't want to come between you and your wife.' She does, though. That is exactly what she wants, but only because she loves him. It is no longer vindictive. Love isn't real if it is at all vindictive; that much she has learnt.

'I know. I don't understand what's happening.' He takes a sip of wine. 'Grace, first you were a client, then we became friends, but I don't know where we are now. I love my wife, I do, and I've never pretended otherwise, but you confuse me.'

He looks so sincere that her heart threatens to break. All she has to do now is the right thing. She knows what the right thing is, but she cannot. Bet or no bet, she cannot let him leave her.

'Johnny, I don't need to tell you how I feel, and I certainly don't need to put any pressure on you. To be honest with you, I think I've done enough of that.'

'No, Grace, you haven't.'

'That's sweet of you to say but I know I've been relying on you, on your friendship, and I didn't want to ruin your marriage, I still don't.' She lies again, or maybe not lies exactly, because she doesn't want to ruin his marriage, but knows that unless that happens she will never be happy.

'It works both ways. I enjoy being with you.'

'I know, and I think that perhaps we should stop.' Grace is taking the gamble of her life. She is putting all the chips on red, and she is praying the ball doesn't land on black.

'Stop seeing each other?' Despite his confusion, the thought of not seeing her upsets him. He is so mixed up.

'Just until you know what to do. Johnny, I want you around, you know that, and well, I love you. I hope that we can work out, but I don't know. Maybe if we take a break . . . I'll wait for your call, I won't bother you . . .' She tails off and her eyes fill with real tears.

'Just a bit of space?' he asks. 'A week?' Grace nods. She musters every ounce of strength in her body and her mind, and she gets up from the table. She leans over and kisses his cheek, touches his hand, strokes his hair. Her entire body fills up with feelings. She bites her lip to stop it from trembling.

'I'll be there. You know, whatever, I'll be there waiting.'

Now it is Johnny's turn to nod as she allows herself one last look at him before she walks away.

Grace hails a taxi almost straight away, tears blinding her as she sits and waits for home. She had to do it, that much she knows. If he wants her, then he must want her for her. There is no way that she will manipulate him. There is no way she will try to trap him. She can hope and pray, but that is all she can do.

Johnny decides to finish the wine they ordered. He cannot face going home. The menus that they barely glanced at lie on the table and remind him that he has no appetite and no companion to dine with. He looks to where Grace sat and wonders how he got himself into such a mess. It isn't his style; he isn't a cad, a bounder, a womaniser. He loves Betty; he is terrified he loves Grace. He finishes the wine, and wonders what he is going to do. No answers come, but one thing is clear: he needs to do something.

It is early, only half-past eight, so he calls Matt and begs him that he needs to talk. He knows it might be dangerous talking to Alison's husband, but he is also his best friend and he has no other option, or none that he can think of.

Grace arrives home, feeling lonelier than ever. Her answer-phone is blinking so she presses play. Nicole's voice speaks to her, and also a desperate message from Betty, begging her to call and let her know if anything is happening. Grace has gone from hating Betty to feeling sorry for her, to fearing her. Or maybe she feared her all along. Maybe that was the problem. But since she has ceased all contact with her lovers, she has no one to ask or talk to, because they were her only friends. She can't call Nicole. Despite her friendship, their relationship is a work one, and she doesn't want her boss to see her falling apart.

She thinks that maybe she will call Betty, but then she decides she won't. What would she say to her? There is no way she can tell her the truth, because at that moment she has no idea what Johnny wants. Or if anything is going on.

Betty jumps every time the phone rings, but it is not the person she wants it to be. She called Grace earlier in the evening because the day has been torture. Ever since Sunday, she has felt positive, but now that positiveness has fled. Deserted her. And Grace wouldn't speak to her to tell her. She thinks about phoning her again, but stops herself. If Grace thinks she is as hysterical as she is, then she will only use it against her. She pours herself some wine and realises that if she had only stood up to her boss, she would never be in this situation. It is Fiona's fault. It is her job's fault. It is Grace's fault. It is her own fault.

Chapter Thirty-Two

Johnny sees Matt sitting at the bar nursing a beer as soon as he opens the door. He has deliberately not spoken to anyone about Grace before, but that is about to change. Although Matt can come across as a bit of a joker, Johnny trusts him. He is the only person that he truly trusts apart from Betty, and he can't talk to her. For once. That is part of what is killing him. Betty is not just his wife, from the moment he met her she became his best friend. Keeping things from her is eating him up, as it has been ever since he met Grace. He justified keeping Grace from Betty at first. He doesn't talk about his clients, nor tell her when he goes for lunch with them. But the telephone calls, the games at her flat, the golf, the dinner – they couldn't all be explained as justifiable. Then he wasn't just not telling Betty the truth, he was lying to her. Deliberate lies.

He isn't having an affair, and that isn't what he wants. If he knows nothing else, he knows that he can't sleep with both women, no matter how much he wants to. No matter how tempted he is, he knows he would never do that. But he can't go on the way he is, torn between two women, two women he really believes he loves. He loves them both. Full circle.

'Hi, mate,' Matt says as Johnny sits down beside him. He gestures to his bottle of lager and Johnny nods. He catches the barman's attention and puts up two fingers. In seconds two bottles of lager arrive and Johnny hands over a five-pound note.

'Thanks.' Johnny takes a long drink. He managed to finish

most of the wine in the restaurant but needs more Dutch courage. He is about to voice his biggest fears out loud and then they will be more real than ever.

'You sounded different on the phone,' Matt says, not one hundred per cent sure why he is sitting at the bar, but sure it isn't just because Johnny wanted a beer. After all the weird happenings, Matt is convinced that Johnny is having an affair. He believes that he is about to hear the confession.

'Matt, if I tell you something, will you promise me something?'

'I hate it when people say that. How do I know if I can promise you until I know what it is?'

'What I mean is, I don't want you to tell Alison.'

'Oh, well, that's fine then,' he jokes. They both avoid eye contact.

'I've met someone.'

Matt takes a look at Johnny but he is staring at his lager bottle. Although this is what Matt thought, he is not prepared for how hearing his best friend say it will make him feel. Ever since he met Johnny, he has been jealous of the certainty. He is jealous of his relationship with Betty, and has tried to model his own, with Alison, on theirs. Johnny has been a relationship role model, but this is one road that Matt doesn't want to follow him down.

'You're having an affair?' His voice is shaky. He is unsure if it is full of anger but it is full of something.

'No.' Johnny still stares at his bottle. He is trying to find the words to describe what he is doing but it keeps coming down to the fact that he is lying to his wife and he has fallen for someone else.

'Johnny, mate, you've got to help me out here. What's going on?' The anger has subsided, if that is what it was. Now Matt just wants to get out of the bar and pretend that this evening never happened.

'I met this woman. She's a client, a new client, and, well, she's incredible. Her husband divorced her, and she came to me to put her finances in order. There wasn't loads of money, but she got to me. She's beautiful, I think the most beautiful woman I've ever met, and also vulnerable, and a bit sad – you know, like there's so much sadness inside her it's reflected in her eyes . . .'

'Slow down a minute. Johnny, are you in love with her?'

'I didn't mean to be. But I think I am.'

'And Betty?'

'I love her still. I haven't stopped loving her and wanting her. I'm not having an affair, Matt. I haven't kissed this woman, nothing, but she feels the same, and now I know I have to do something in case it kills me. Or kills her and Betty.'

Matt gestures to the barman for more beers, then changes his mind.

'Two double brandies please,' he says. Johnny doesn't argue. 'I'm not sure I can get my head round this. Johnny, you and Betty are the best couple ever. Everyone agrees you're made for each other. Are you sure that this isn't just a crush?'

'No, I'm not sure of anything. When I see her I feel good – you know, warm and stuff – and when I see her I feel sparks. Is it a crush? Should I just not see her? In fact, tonight she told me that we shouldn't see each other. She doesn't want to be a marriage wrecker.'

'But you both know that there is more to this than a platonic friendship?'

'Yup. I don't want to lose Betty, but I'm not sure I can walk away from this, it's so powerful, you know. I'm being sucked into her and I'm not sure that I can resist. When she left tonight, I thought about how I'd feel if I never saw her again, and I was scared. Look, I'm not good at this talking about my feelings stuff, but this isn't like anything else.'

'No, it's not.' Matt is trying not to panic. He feels inadequate in his side of the conversation, having never encountered one like it. 'Johnny, I guess this is a silly question, but do you love one more than the other?'

'I don't know. The thought of life without Betty is horrific, but so is not seeing her again. Shit, I just don't know.' He downs his brandy, and gestures for two more.

'Johnny, I think, and believe me I have no fucking idea about this, but I think you should take her advice. Have a few days with no contact, try to date your wife – you know, take her out for a change – and then see. If by the end of the week you really feel like you need this, this . . . what's her name?'

'Grace. Grace Regan.'

'If you really feel you need this Grace— Hang on, did you say Grace Regan?'

'Yes, why?' Johnny gives Matt a puzzled look, which Matt returns. He feels a chill sweep through him. The name, why should it bug him? He thinks he's heard it before, recently, but he can't remember. His brain starts rejecting all attempts to coax his memory into action.

'Matt?' Johnny is still looking at him.

'Sorry. It's just that Grace is quite an unusual name. Anyway, where was I? Oh yeah, well, spend a week apart from her, make an effort with Betty, then we'll have a chat at the end of it, and see where we go from there.'

'Thanks, Matt, you're a good mate.'

'Don't mention it.' As they both lapse into silence, Johnny almost feels better. Matt's right: the answer he needs will come to him if he just allows himself some breathing space, and he is also right about spoiling Betty. That is what he will do.

Matt drinks his brandy and tries to think. His mind isn't working but he knows that something is wrong here, and he knows that for Johnny's sake he needs to figure out what it is. Not being strong on intuition normally, Matt tries to brush it away, but this feeling is too powerful to ignore. He just needs to work it out. He is angry with himself for being so stupid, and not doing something before, but he knows that somewhere in his empty head is the answer, and as his head is empty it shouldn't be too hard to locate.

Betty is sitting on the sofa watching a documentary on television when Johnny walks in. He goes over to her and sits down.

'You smell of booze,' she says kindly, wondering in her head where he has been. Grace hasn't called her back, but she is beginning to resign herself to the fact that she has lost. Just how much she has lost she is yet to figure out. She doesn't want to figure it out. Not yet. Not until she has to.

'Sorry, but you know what Matt's like.'

'Oh, I didn't know you were going out with Matt tonight.' She tries to keep her voice level. She spoke to Alison earlier in the evening and she hadn't mentioned anything.

'I wasn't, not at first. I was with a client, then I asked Matt to go for a quick beer. You know what it's like.'

'Of course I do, honey.' Betty feels the anger and the jealousy well inside her. She knows exactly what it's like because she knows exactly which 'client' he was with before Matt. But she pushes the knowledge away because being the perfect wife is not about anger. She is wearing a dressing gown, which she lets slip open to reveal her naked body. 'Now you're home, perhaps you might like to take me to bed?' she says, launching herself at him.

While they kiss, and she tastes that woman on him, or the evening that was with that woman, she prays that he won't leave her, and she tries that little bit harder so he won't. Why would any man leave Superwife? He'd have to be mad. Wouldn't he?

Grace sits in the darkness watching the fish. She is drinking red wine because it reminds her of what she walked away from. She has done with tears and she has work that needs doing. She has to pull herself together.

Tomorrow, she promises herself, tomorrow she will be better. She will get on with her work and be like the old Grace. The trouble is that she doesn't want to be the old Grace any more. But she has to, because that way she can cope if he decides to stay with Betty.

She wonders what he did after she left. Did he drink the wine, or pay the bill and leave? Or did he, and this is the most horrific thought, did he call his wife and ask her to join him?

Tears return as she fills her glass again. Whatever the outcome she is alone and she has never felt lonelier.

'You stink of brandy,' Alison complains as Matt tries to cuddle her in bed.

'Sorry, but you know what Johnny's like,' he replies, slurring his words slightly. He and Johnny left the bar, but instead of heading straight home, Matt stopped at another one on the way. He is still racking his brains for the name Grace. It is in there somewhere.

'I know what you're like,' Alison replies, but she plants a kiss on his head.

He thinks about asking her, but doesn't want to start a fight, and mentioning the name of another woman you can't place can potentially do that. He closes his eyes, with the room spinning slightly, and regrets the last two brandies. He is asleep, but then he is awake. He has no idea what the time is but he sits bolt upright, sobriety has returned, as has his memory.

'Alison, wake up.'

'Umm.'

'Wake the fuck up,' he shouts.

'What? Is the house on fire?'

'No, but we need to talk. Get up; I'll make some hot chocolate.'

'But I want to sleep. I've got work tomorrow.'

'Alison, get up. This is important.'

There are times when you can mention another woman's name to your wife. Those times are when her friend is the one who has used that name and you have a feeling that she knows more than she is telling you.

The kettle has boiled by the time Alison appears in the kitchen. She has her bathrobe wrapped tightly around her, and she is yawning.

'What on earth is this?' she demands, sitting down at the kitchen table. The light is on, which hurts her eyes. She is angry and tired, and thinks that Matt is just drunk. Matt hands her her drink and starts pacing. He has set up an interrogation room in the kitchen, but Alison does not know this. He stops suddenly and turns to face her.

'Tell me who Grace is.'

Alison opens her mouth, closes it again, and blinks. She wonders if she is in a dream, that her subconscious is worrying about the consequences of her keeping things from her husband. But then, as she feels a chill down her spine, the situation feels horribly real.

'Who is she?' Matt asks again.

'I don't know,' Alison lies.

'You do because I heard Betty talking about her.'

'Oh,' Alison says.

'Yes, oh. But that's not all. Johnny was talking about her tonight.'

'What was he saying?' She can see everything crashing around her.

'That's not the point, or not at least until you tell me who she is and how on earth you and Betty know her.'

Alison feels sick. 'She was Betty's honey-trap woman.'

*

Alison tells Matt the whole story, leaving nothing out.

'I can't believe you kept this from me.' Matt looks sad, and a bit frightened rather than angry.

'You'd have told Johnny.'

'And a good job that would have done – stopped all this nonsense. I can't believe you let Betty agree.'

'She needed to. She had to keep her job.'

'Oh, don't be so dramatic. Do you really think she would have lost her job?'

'She might have.'

'And that was worth losing Johnny for?'

'She didn't think that he'd fall for it.'

'Well, he hasn't. Not yet anyway.' It is Matt's turn to tell Alison what Johnny has said.

'He's in love with her?'

'He thinks he is. He thinks he loves them both.'

'But nothing's happened?'

'No, nothing. And you know what? She hasn't pushed him either. Tonight she suggested that they have some space from each other.'

'But that doesn't make sense, not for the bet.'

'Well, Alison, this whole thing doesn't make sense, but the worst is that Johnny is going through agony and it's all a damn setup. How could you not tell me?' He is shaking with rage.

'Betty begged me not to.'

'Has she lost her marbles?'

'I think she might have done. You know, she's been turning herself into the perfect wife for him, so he doesn't stray.'

'Christ. We have to sort this out.'

'How?'

'I am going to tell Johnny.'

'But Betty'll go mad.'

'I don't care, Alison, and I won't mention you. Maybe she'll think I managed to put it together all by my clever self. But don't tell her that I'm telling him.'

'Why? I have to.' It is all getting messier and messier.

'No, because Johnny has to work out what to do, and if you tell Betty what I've told you, and that I'm telling him, then it'll be a bigger mess.'

'I'm not sure that's possible.'

'Neither am I. But promise me, Ali.'

'OK, but you'd better sort it out quickly.'

'I will.'

Johnny untangles himself from Betty and goes back to the living room. He can't sleep, and he feels wretched. That night he confessed to his best friend that he might be in love with another woman, and then he has sex with his wife. He's hypocritical; he's in a huge conundrum. He goes to the kitchen and makes himself a cup of tea. He then sits on the sofa until he manages to fall asleep.

Betty opens her eyes and sees that he isn't there. She wonders if he is downstairs thinking of her or thinking of Grace, a thought that makes her angry and more determined. She regrets starting this, she has regretted it from the word go, but even more so now, because her husband is on the brink of being stolen. A theft that she has almost invited. She tries to get back to sleep before he comes back. If he is ever coming back.

Grace tries to imagine what he is doing but stops herself because he is probably in bed with his arms around *her*. If she had known what this would do to her she would never have started it. Or she might, because at least she knows now that she can fall in love. But she also knows she was right all along: love always hurts. As she makes her way to bed, she realises that she feels more miserable than she can ever remember feeling.

'Maybe, we should go to bed now,' Matt suggests.

'Yeah. I am really sorry that I lied to you.' Alison strokes his arm.

'I just don't think it was the sensible thing to do.' He is beginning to thaw.

'I know, but if you hadn't recognised the name, would you have told me what Johnny told you tonight?'

'Probably not.'

'It's hard having best friends married to each other.'

'Especially if it threatens our relationship.'

'But we won't let it, will we?' Alison feels scared.

'No, Ali, we won't.' But they both feel cold as they climb the stairs because somehow it seems that every relationship has been threatened now, and all because of one stupid bet.

Chapter Thirty-Three

'I feel dreadful,' Alison says when the alarm goes off.

'So do I.' Matt looks at her and kisses her. Not only is he tired but he is also worried. But he has already decided what he's going to do.

'Do you want first shower?'

'No, you go. I'm pulling a sickie.'

'Good idea. I'll join you.'

'No you won't. I'm taking the day off to sort things out and I don't want you around.'

'Oh God, you're going to tell Johnny.' This makes her feel even worse

'I think he has a right to know.'

'But what about Betty?'

'Alison, Betty might be losing him anyway. I have to tell him. We decided that last night.'

'I won't be able to concentrate at work.' Alison adopts her little-girl voice. She wants to pretend that none of this is happening. She is terrified.

'Alison, just go. Please.' He looks at her and she does what she is told. She knows that she should be on probation for lying to him.

While Alison is in the shower Matt calls Johnny's mobile.

Betty is in the kitchen when she hears Johnny's mobile ring. She immediately prickles as she picks it up, but Matt's name is on the display and she relaxes. She hands it to Johnny.

'Hi.'

'Johnny, listen, we have to talk.'

'Hold on.' Johnny is regretting telling Matt, especially as phone calls this early in the morning will only evoke suspicion in Betty. He doesn't want to talk to him all of a sudden, but furtively, like a true adulterer, he leaves the room. 'OK. We can talk later.'

'No, I need to see you now.'

'There's this little thing called work.'

'Call in sick, I'm doing that. This is more important and it can't wait. Don't tell Betty, but be at mine by half nine.' He hangs up before Johnny can reply.

'What did he want?' Betty asks. The problem is that once suspicions are aroused they grow. She is thinking that maybe he put Grace's number into his phone as 'Matt', so she wouldn't know. She feels sick.

'He's mad. He was going on about football tickets. Apparently he had a dream about them and decided we needed to go.' Johnny is not pleased with himself for the way that his lies are like second nature, even if they sound a bit strange.

'Right. Well, I have work.' She kisses his cheek and leaves the house. The burden is on her. The two-month deadline is forgotten. Grace has already broken the rules. Now there are no rules, this is a bare knuckle fight, and Betty has no idea how to throw the next punch.

Johnny phones his secretary at nine and says he has flu. More lies; the foundations of his life are being built on them. Then he has another cup of coffee before changing into his jeans and making his way to Matt's.

Matt has showered and although he feels awful, he has managed to dress. He really is ill, so he wasn't lying. He feels sicker by the minute for what he has to do; the conversation he is about to have.

'This'd better be good.'

Johnny is standing on the doorstep. Matt moves aside and ushers him in. They go into the sitting room.

'Listen, Johnny, we've been friends for years, and I won't see you hurt, not if I can help it, but there is something I have to tell you and you're not going to like it.'

'Well, get on with it then.' Johnny has not given too much thought to Matt's demanding behaviour. He thinks that he will get a lecture from him, a telling off at worst.

'Grace, your Grace, is Betty's honey-trap woman.'

'Impossible. She's a PA, an unemployed PA.'

'Do you remember Betty telling you about the honey trapper?'

'Yeah, but she usually called her bitch. I have no idea what her name is. Oh yeah, she called her Griselda, remember?'

'Griselda, Grace, coincidence?'

'They both begin with G. Matt, are you all right?'

'I heard Betty mention the name Grace Regan a while back. She was with Ali and she said, "That Grace Regan is a right bitch." Well, I didn't think anything of it, until you mentioned her name yesterday.'

Johnny is feeling hot. He still doesn't understand what is happening, but he has a feeling that he isn't going to like it.

'Go on.' He looks stony-faced.

'The name rang a bell, but not a very clear one. I was trying to sleep last night when it came to me. I got Alison out of bed, and I asked her about it. She told me everything.'

'So you're saying my Grace is Betty's Grace?'

'Yes, and there's more. They had a big row, that much you know, and Grace pulled out of the story. Then Fiona told Betty that she had to get Grace to agree to the piece because otherwise she'd be demoted. Well, Grace offered to do the feature if Betty agreed to a bet.'

'A bet?' Sweat is pouring off Johnny's head. He feels sick. The room starts spinning for a minute until he composes himself.

'Grace and Betty had a bet over you. Grace had to try to seduce you. That was the bet.'

'Why would they do that to me?'

'You're the innocent victim, as far as I can see. Grace wanted to get back at Betty so she chose the thing that Betty valued most, you. Betty didn't want to lose her job but she was so sure that you loved her and you wouldn't capitulate that she agreed.'

'They did this to me?' He is feeling odd. Detached, almost. As if he is hearing about someone else. There is no way that this can be happening to him. No way.

'Johnny.' Matt has been thinking nearly all night about what he is going to say, and how he is going to say it, but everything sounds inadequate, especially as he is not good at handling difficult situations. 'Johnny, I am sorry. I didn't know what was happening, and if I had known, I would have put a stop to it. Alison said that Betty tried to pull out a number of times, but Grace – well, it seems that Grace was determined.'

'She told me she loved me.'

'Grace?'

'Yes. And Betty – all that underwear, new seduction techniques . . . Oh God, they were both playing me.'

'I thought that at first, but then I'm not so sure.'

'Really?' Johnny is still having trouble absorbing the information.

'Betty didn't want to lose her job and didn't imagine she'd lose you. Grace must have fallen for you along the way, so when Betty asked her to call the bet off, she couldn't, because she really has fallen for you.'

'When did you get to be such a fucking expert?' Anger has finally arrived.

'I'm not, but Grace offered you a break; she wouldn't have done that if she wanted to seduce you. It doesn't make sense.'

'It was probably part of it, just like Betty being so fucking understanding, not questioning me when I was behaving oddly, because she knew. How sick is that? She knew that I was with Grace and she didn't even try to keep me away from her. Apart from the golf day. Oh shit, this is sick. Twisted. Yesterday I was in love with two women and today I find out I was a game to them.' Anger is here to stay.

'I don't think it was like that.' Matt has no stronger argument, and he is worried about his best friend, who he has never seen lose control.

'I think it was. It was exactly like that. But they're not fucking going to get away with it. The whores. The bitches. How dare they play with my emotions? I cannot believe they'd do that. Love me? How can they love me? They hate me, that's the only explanation. I was this fucking close to fucking her but I didn't because of loyalty to my lying wife. I was going to make a choice, but now there is no choice. None at all.'

'What do you mean?'

'I mean, that yesterday there were two women and today there is none. And you, Matt, are the only person left that I can trust.'

Matt is a man's man, so when his best friend starts crying, he only manages to pat him on the shoulder, although he knows that it isn't going to help.

'What am I going to do?' It is the hundredth time that Johnny has asked that question.

'Talk to them, both of them. Individually. Ask them why.' Matt is quite sure that this is the right advice; it is his only advice.

'I want to kill them.'

'You're not the murdering type.'

'No. But I am angry.' He looks like a lost boy. He is unable to express, properly, how he feels.

'I know, and hurt.'

'I was wrong too, though. I fell for her; I was mentally unfaithful. That's the worst thing. I didn't do anything as bad as they did to me, but then I wasn't exactly innocent either. Even I am guilty.'

'Go and talk to her, phone her.' Matt means Betty.

'I want to talk to Grace.' Johnny gets up and goes to the bathroom where he washes his face. Then he picks his phone from his pocket and dials her number.

'Hi.'

'Grace, it's me.'

'Johnny?'

'I know we said a week but I need to see you. Can I come over?'

'Sure. I'm just at home.'

'I'll be there as soon as I can.' He hangs up.

'Johnny, don't you think you should speak to Betty first?'

'No, I want to speak to Grace and get the whole story before facing my wife.'

'Look, please call me, whatever.'

'I will. I'll come back here when I'm finished with her.'

'I don't know what to say. Good luck?'

'I don't know either. Matt, I have never felt this bad before in my entire life.'

'I know.'

'I might be able to stand up straight and walk and talk, but inside, inside everything is crumbling.'

'I know.'

'What if I never recover? At the moment, everything is

rushing around and I don't know how to process it, but what if I realise that I've lost everything and I can't cope?'

'I'll help you cope.' Matt gingerly pats Johnny's shoulder again. 'Come on, I'll drive you and wait outside.'

'I might be a while.'

'I know, it's fine. I'll sit there and wait.' It is the only useful thing he can think of to do. And also, Johnny and a car might not be the best idea under the circumstances.

'How could they do this to me?' They are in a traffic jam and Matt feels that it is not just the traffic that isn't going anywhere.

'Johnny, you have to speak to them. That's the only thing you can do. Now, where exactly am I going?'

'Come in.' Grace steps aside as Johnny walks into her flat.

'How are you?' He sounds normal but she can see he is not.

'Fine. You?'

'Horny.' Not what she was expecting. He is a stranger.

'Sorry?'

'I'm horny for you.' He moves towards her and kisses her, hard on the lips.

'Johnny, this isn't like you.' She pulls away, confused.

'I'm sorry but I can't stop thinking about you. I need you, don't you understand?' Finally as he says the words she has wished for, she leans in and kisses him. He tears at her clothes, and manages to get her down to her underwear.

'Shall we go to the bedroom?' she asks breathlessly. Finally passion has taken over; she is helpless.

'OK.'

He follows her, holding on to her hand tightly. She pushes him on the bed, where she unhooks her bra, and he pushes his head into her cleavage. She feels all the sexual tension that she has felt almost since their first meeting dissipate. She pulls off her knickers and starts to undo his trousers.

'Stop,' he shouts.

'Why?' she asks breathlessly. He pushes her off him and grabs her wrist harshly.

'You'd go that far for the bet? You would sleep with me for the bet?'

'Oh shit,' she replies.

She sits down on the bed, still naked, but unaware.

'Did she tell you?'

'No. She doesn't even know I know.'

'Johnny, I have to explain.'

'What? That you're a honey trapper and you tried to trap me. And congratulations, darling, you did a good job, because I fell for it. I was considering leaving my wife for you. Which would have made me look really silly, wouldn't it?'

'No.'

'What the fuck do you mean, "no"? I would have looked like a fucking idiot.'

'No you wouldn't because that's what I wanted. I love you, I really do love you. Yes, there was a bet but I forgot it ages ago.'

'Yeah, and I know what a great actress you are. Divorcee? Probably not. PA to a lawyer? Definitely not. Quit your job? I don't think so. Tell me, Grace, please fucking tell me where in all that is the truth.'

'I didn't intend for it to be like this.'

'Really? Well, it is. And thanks a fucking bunch for ruining my life.' He does up his trousers, which are still unbuttoned. 'Tell me, do you love golf? Do you love *Carry On* films?' He is fully clothed.

'Johnny, wait. Please let me explain. I really did fall in love with you. This has nothing to do with the bet, you have to believe me.' Tears are falling down her cheeks. Her insides are burning. She feels that she will collapse.

'Give the girl an Oscar. It has every fucking thing to do with the bet.' He storms out.

*

He climbs into the car, next to Matt and cries again. Matt gives him his customary pat on the shoulder.

'She tried to tell me she loved me.'

'Did it occur to you that she might do?'

'It doesn't matter now, because it was all lies. With both of them. And love doesn't have much to do with lies.'

'No. Where to now?'

'Home. I need to speak to Betty.'

She has never cried so hard in her life. Her sobs are rocking her body; they are so violent. She gets off the bed, where he left her, and she goes to get her robe. She is cold. Freezing cold. She cannot contemplate her life, and how empty it is now. She cannot contemplate what has just happened. She wants to die. She has never felt that. Even at her most unhappy she has never wanted to die, but now she does. She is not being dramatic, because she feels calm. But she will not die; that is not an option. It is a sin to take a life, even your own. Her mother taught her all about sins. And while she has committed most of them, that one she won't. Not now.

She is calm when she reaches the phone, and calm when she dials, but then when the voice answers she falls apart.

'Nicole.'

'What's wrong?'

'It's all gone wrong, all of it.'

'I'll be right over.' She hangs up before Grace can answer.

Grace has no idea what amount of time has passed before her buzzer goes and she lets Nicole in.

'I shouldn't be doing this. You'll sack me.' She manages a dull smile.

'I feel responsible. You go sit down and I'll make some coffee.' Grace hugs her legs to herself as she sits on the small sofa. Again, she has no idea how much time has lapsed before Nicole reappears and hands her a cup of coffee.

'It was so awful, so humiliating.'

'He found out?'

'Yeah. I'm still not sure how, but he said that it wasn't Betty.'

'Oh.'

'He came over and he said he wanted me. I was naked, on top of him, and he told me that he knew. He said, "How far were you prepared to go for the bet?" I felt so cheap. He thinks I'm a whore.' She collapses with a fresh batch of tears; Nicole takes her cup off her and puts it down.

'Did you tell him how you felt? How there is no way you were doing it for the bet?'

'I told him I loved him, but he didn't believe me. Now he's probably going to confront her. I messed up.'

'I feel responsible,' Nicole repeats. She puts her arms around Grace and holds her as if she is a child. That is the way she has always felt about her: weirdly maternal.

'You didn't give me the idea.'

'No, for that we have Fiona to thank, I know. But I pushed you into the article. I know you only did it because you were doing it for me.'

'I love him.'

'I know.'

'What am I going to do?'

'I have no idea.'

'What if he never wants to see either of us again? What if I've wrecked all our lives?'

'It wasn't just you. She agreed.'

'She agreed to the bet; she didn't agree to me falling in love.'

'You don't control who you love.'

'You really don't, do you? But I can't bear it if he hates me. I need to stop him from hating me.'

'Well, let him calm down and then call him and tell him you

need to explain. If he refuses to see you then you can write him a letter, write it all down.'

'I could, couldn't I? Do you think he'd read it?'

'Give it a day or two before contacting him. Listen, I've rearranged all your work this week, and I think you should stay with me.'

'I can't do that.'

'Why?'

'Because he won't know where I am.'

'Oh, honey, I wish we'd never gone near that feature.'

'But don't you see, if we hadn't I'd never have met him.'

'And you wouldn't be crying your heart out now.'

'No, but I wouldn't have had the wonderful feeling he gave me either, would I?'

'This is it,' Betty tells herself as she scoops up her bag and switches off the computer. 'This is when he tells me he doesn't want me any more.' She shakes as she puts her coat on.

'Where are you going?' Hannah asks.

'To find out if I still have a marriage,' Betty replies, as she walks out the door.

She hails a cab, unable to cope with public transport, but the traffic feels sluggish and she is so eager to get there that she begins to feel angry, impatient and out of control. As they stop at the hundredth red traffic light, she curses aloud and the driver shoots her a look. But her marriage is on the line, so she is allowed to swear.

'Are you sure you'll be all right?' Matt feels the inadequacy of the question as he asks it. He has been feeling inadequate all day.

'Do you mind if I stay at yours tonight? Will it be awkward because of Alison?'

'No, you stay. I am sure Alison will be with Betty, anyway.'

'I hate to think about that.'

'I know.'

'It's like our lives are all messed up.'

'I know.'

'If I'd gone with Grace, that's what I was thinking: how angry Alison would be, how our friendship would suffer as a result. I was trying to work out the right thing to do, but all along . . .'

'I know, mate. Listen, you call me when you're done and I'll pick you up.'

'No need. I'll walk.'

'OK.' Matt has an overwhelming urge not to leave Johnny alone, but he doesn't push it.

He is angry and hurt. He tries not to think of Grace, or hear her telling him she did love him, or picture her tears. Not now. The anger is his only weapon, his only guard. That is all he has.

He tours his home – the 'marital home' – thinking about how empty it feels. But then everything reminds him, not of who he is but of his marriage. Wedding photos on the mantelpiece; Cyril, his pet and her pet; the bathrobes on the back of the bathroom door; the books next to the bed. His, non-fiction, hers fiction. The two toothbrushes in the holder. His shaving stuff, her face stuff. The bed.

Anger is overwhelming now. He had all this, and even if he was tempted, it was she who nearly made him throw it all away.

The door opens and he walks downstairs. He sees her and remembers the first time he saw her. Her hair tumbling out of its clips, the stripy tights and the short, short skirt. The smile on her lips, the notebook, and her oversized bag. Everything is there in his head, and will be for ever. Along with Grace, and her magnificent legs, her huge eyes, her neatly coiffured hair, and her immaculate clothes. Anger is all he is.

*

'Hi,' Betty says. She can see that something is wrong, but he looks angry, not remorseful. She feels wrong-footed.

'I know,' he replies. No elaborate plan, like with Grace; he has no desire for her. Not even with his anger.

'You know what?' Betty feels fear rip through her like a knife. *He knows.*

'About the bet. About Grace, about the honey trapping.'

Betty collapses on to the nearest chair. She is deflated.

'Did she tell you?' she asks through the tears.

'No. But you should have done.'

'I'm sorry.' The words that are a red rag to a bull.

'Oh, fuck me, that's all right then. You make a bet with a stranger that she can't seduce me? You think that that is in any way acceptable? Remember how much you hated her because of what she did and you do the same.'

'It wasn't the same. I trusted you.'

'Then you should have told her to fuck her bet and told Fiona to get stuffed. How could you jeopardise everything?'

'I didn't think I was jeopardising anything. I thought you'd tell her to get lost.'

'Now don't you dare turn this round and blame me. I didn't kiss her, I didn't fuck her, although now I wish I had. I wish I fucked you both the way you've both fucked me.'

'Johnny—'

'Shut up. Just shut up. You lied to me, you deceived me, and I will never, ever forgive you. You hear me? I will never forgive you.' He slams the sitting-room door shut and goes upstairs to pack.

She sits there, but is not sure how long for. She hears the opening and closing of the wardrobe. She hears his footsteps. She hears the front door open and slam. He is gone. He is gone for ever. All because of the bet. The fight is over and neither of them won, and neither did Johnny. They are all big fat losers.

Chapter Thirty-Four

'I'd better go and see Betty,' Alison says as she stands in the kitchen with Matt. Johnny is in the sitting room.

'Do you think you should stay the night?'

'Probably. Do you mind?'

'No. I think Johnny's going to keep me occupied.'

'Oh God, I hate to think of what's happened to them.'

'I know. But, you know, I'm not sure we can fix this.'

'I doubt we can. But we have to be there for them.' Alison hugs Matt and goes to pack an overnight bag.

'Bye then.' She walks into the sitting room, feeling awkward.

'Are you going to my house?' Johnny asks, looking forlorn.

Alison nods.

'Make sure Cyril is all right,' he says.

She nods again.

Betty opens the door, looking awful. Instead of making a lame comment, Alison walks in and engulfs her in a hug. She sobs and sobs.

'Is there anything I can do to get him back?' she asks.

Alison just shrugs. Feisty Betty is feeling more than a bit hopeless.

Grace is sitting at home, trying to get her head together. It is refusing to be pulled into line. She doesn't have any work on.

Nicole has made sure of that, and she calls her every hour to make sure she is all right. They are meeting the following day for lunch, and Nicole has promised to help her sort things out. Grace is desperately trying to think of a way to put everything right; she wants him back. She doesn't know how she is going to get him.

'I am still so angry. It's going round and round in my head and I feel so hopeless. I need to do something, you know, physical. I wanted to hit someone earlier; I was almost looking for a fight. But you know that that's not me. Look what they've done to me.' Johnny is seesawing between crying and anger. His fists remain clenched, his eyes red. He cannot cope with his feelings because he has no control over them.

'I know. Look, how about going to the gym?' Matt is feeling completely out of his depth, and he doesn't know how to make the situation better.

'The gym?' Johnny looks at him with surprise.

'They have a punchbag, and I can hold focus pads for you. It's lame but I couldn't think of anything.'

'No, no, that's good. I can't sit here. I think I'm going mad. Maybe punching a bag will help.'

Matt breathes a huge sigh of relief. At least something will work.

'I fucking well need to get him back, but he's not coming.' Betty has stopped crying because she doesn't find tears useful.

'Not necessarily. Look, it's early days and he's angry and hurt. You have to give him time.'

'Ali, I screwed up. You warned me, but I screwed up. I remember when Fiona first told me about Grace – I knew that it was bad, I knew I didn't want to interview her. I wish I hadn't.'

'Does Fiona know?'

'No, but she will soon, because I hold her responsible as well. Her and Grace and me, and Johnny.'

'Johnny?'

'You don't understand. He's angry because we lied to him, but he fell for her. He admitted it. He was falling for her, and although he wasn't unfaithful he wanted to be.'

'I don't think—'

'Ali, I don't need protecting, not any more. There is no protection from this mess. I know that he fell for her; I could tell. And I bet he told Matt.'

Alison goes red and nods. 'But he didn't do anything,' she adds quickly.

'I know, but he wanted to. What kind of a marriage did we have?'

'A near-perfect one.' Now Alison is angry.

'Right. Fucking perfect, of course.'

'Betty, shut up. You're feeling sorry for yourself and I know that you're justified, but you put a beautiful woman in front of him, you made her interested in things he was interested in. You did it. And maybe he did fall for her, but she flattered him. It wasn't real, because Grace wasn't real. She was a fantasy figure and any man would have felt at least confused by her.'

'You're right. This isn't Johnny's fault, it's mine.'

Grace jumps when her buzzer goes and for a fleeting moment she imagines it will be Johnny. The voice on the other end surprises her. It is Oliver.

'You didn't call,' she says as she opens the door for him. She doesn't want to think about how she looks, with her face devoid of make-up, eyes red from crying and lack of sleep.

'I didn't think you'd let me come round if I did. You look awful.'

'Thanks.'

He notices that her spirit has deserted her. 'Let's have a drink and a chat, shall we?'

She realises as he walks into the kitchen to take charge that she is incredibly relieved no longer to be alone.

'So, don't you wonder at my timing?' Oliver asks as they sit down.

'You mean, this isn't a coincidence?' This has only just occurred to her.

'I called Nicole.'

'I didn't even know you knew Nicole.' The mundane nature of the conversation is oddly soothing.

'I know the company name – you've told me. I was worried about you so I called her.'

'You were prying.'

'Grace, we didn't part on the best of terms and I'm a busy man, used to getting what I want. I have no time to play games. It's hardly prying.'

'Sorry.'

'Anyway, it's a good job I called because she told me what a mess things were.'

'That's one way of putting it.'

'So, what are you going to do?'

'What am I going to do? Nothing. Why should I do anything?' She feels any strength of resolve disappear.

'About the mess. You're partly responsible.'

'Oh, you mean that I should sort things out. Yes, that has occurred to me, but somehow I don't think Johnny wants me any more.'

'I didn't mean that.'

'What then?'

'Don't you think you need to get everyone talking and everyone resolving things?'

'No. I love him. I don't care about her. I can't. You have to understand, Ollie, that I didn't think I could fall in love, but I did, with him. And I do love him.'

'Like you couldn't love me.'

'Don't be like that. I can't cope if you're like that.' She shudders because she is already ensconced in one other person's heart and she doesn't want to know about his.

'Sorry, that was wrong of me. I came here as a friend and I am your friend. You look like you could use one.'

'I could, Ollie, I really could.' She begins to cry and he holds her. 'I have to write him a letter, explaining everything.'

'Later, Grace. First we should talk.'

'I have to write him a letter, Ali.'

'What, explaining things?'

'Yeah. That way he'll read it. Well, he might read it but if I try to call—'

'And you are a writer.'

'Yes, yes, I am. Let's get started.'

Alison watches as Betty goes to get a pad and a pen and starts writing. She hopes that it might help her even if it won't help her marriage.

Betty writes from her heart. She won't give him up without a fight, that much she is sure of, because she loves him too much and she still believes deep down that he loves her.

'He might have thought he was falling for Grace but he wasn't, was he?' she asks, as if the conversation they had earlier hasn't taken place.

'No, Betts. He didn't know her; he loves only you. I'm pretty sure of that.'

'Will it work out?' Her voice is childlike, begging for reassurance.

'I'm sure it will. Come on, finish the letter,' is Alison's mother-like answer.

*

'I feel so much better.'

'Good, because I feel worse. Christ, you can really pack a punch.' They are in the changing rooms, about to go into the shower.

'Sorry, but it's good for you too.'

'Whatever.' Matt smiles though, because despite the fact he feels as if his shoulder might be dislocated, Johnny is slowly returning to humanity.

After they shower, Johnny suggests going to the pub.

'Are you sure?' Matt doesn't want to sound so wimpish but he doesn't think he could cope with Johnny breaking down in public.

'Yeah, if I'm in public I have to hold things together. It's better.'

Matt orders the drinks while Johnny finds a table.

'I'm going to see them,' he announces as Matt puts the drinks down.

'Isn't it a bit soon?'

'No, you don't understand. I'm going to see them together.'

'What?' Matt feels cold.

'I'm angry, right? And I need to expunge my anger. If I went to see a counsellor that is probably what they'd tell me. So I'm going to arrange to meet them together and then I'll ask questions.'

'It sounds a bit dodgy. Are you sure?'

'Yes.' Johnny smiles, and Matt's heart sinks.

'Do you think—'

'Yes, I do. I think it's the best thing. Only, don't tell Alison.'

'Oh, don't worry. Alison and I are getting quite good at keeping secrets from each other.' He doesn't mean it the way it sounds.

'Sorry,' Johnny says. 'I hate to think that you're being dragged into this.'

'Hey,' Matt replies, determined to make amends, 'it's not as if we're going through what you're going through. Listen, we both want you to sort things out. And I am on your side. Remember that.'

'The thing is that he loved me. I know that much. He felt torn apart with guilt for his wife, but he loved me and he was going to make a decision. I knew in my heart that I would be his decision.' Grace gets a dreamy look in her eyes. She is imagining her life with Johnny and how perfect it would be. They would be affectionate, laugh a lot, play golf, have dinner, huddle on the sofa, stay in bed for days.

'Right,' Oliver says, interrupting her thoughts. 'Have you thought about what you're saying?'

'Of course I have. I haven't thought about anything else.'

'So this love you speak of, have you really thought it through? He didn't know you, Grace, so how on earth could he love you?' She looks shocked, as if he has slapped her, but Oliver is not going to tell her what she wants to hear.

'He did know me.'

'He knew you as a divorcee, he knew you as a PA, he believes you love golf. You told me you hated it. You presented him with his perfect woman, not the real you.'

'I didn't hate golf as much with him.'

'But you didn't love it?'

'No,' she admits.

'So, now he knows the truth. He knows you're a detective, he knows you tempt men for their wives, he knows that you've never been married. He doesn't know you.'

'I hadn't thought of it like that.'

'Hadn't you?' His tone is sharp.

'Of course I had, but I love him. I love him so much and I can't give him up. I tried, but I couldn't.'

'You tried to walk away before it all blew up?'

'I did. Betty sounded awful and I thought that I couldn't do this, not to them. Even though I didn't like her, I didn't want her to wallow in misery.'

'But you couldn't walk away?'

'No, I couldn't.'

'Could you now?'

'I don't know.'

Betty finishes the letter with tears in her eyes – she can't stop them. She gives it to Alison to read and soon she is crying too.

'Oh God, this has to work out,' Alison says.

'I'd do anything to get him back.'

'I know. Do you want me to deliver this tomorrow?'

'I guess he'll be at yours still?'

'Betty, at least we know where he is, that's something.'

'I wonder what she's doing?'

'Grace? Repenting, I hope.'

'Maybe she's really missing him too.' Betty has a dreamy look in her eyes. 'I can't blame her for falling for him. After all, that's exactly what I did.'

'Sleep on it, and then decide,' Matt says, finally coming up with a solution that Johnny might agree to.

'OK. But if tomorrow I decide to confront them together, then I will, OK?'

'Sure. Another beer?'

'You know what, I think I need sleep.'

'Well, that's a good thing.'

'I know, I feel as if someone has put me through a mangle.'

'No offence, mate, but you look like it too.'

'I might make you spar with me again for that.' He almost laughs.

'Shit, anything but that.' Matt puts his arm around his friend as they leave the pub. He can give him affection. After all, he needs some, and Matt is proud of his friend because, all of a sudden, he thinks that he will be all right.

'You're suggesting I try to save their marriage?' There is a dull incredulity to Grace's tone.

'Yes. Look, Grace, when you go out to work you tempt the men by being a fantasy figure, and they fall for it because they're weak men who are probably happy to cheat. But Johnny wasn't. It hurt him to see you and his wife, and he refused to get physical. You have wrecked a perfectly good marriage.'

Grace falls silent. She sees the picture so clearly now. Betty with that twinkle in her eye every time she mentioned Johnny. Her slight blush when she talked about him. How Grace had seen how much she loved him from the start but ignored it because she disliked her.

When the bet started, she was cruel to her when Betty called her, panicking. Instead of understanding how much she loved him, Grace almost mocked Betty's feelings. She was jealous of her. All the time she wanted to have what Betty had and she almost got it. But at what price?

'Oh my God, I have, haven't I?'

'Yes, and the only thing to do, the right thing to do, is to try to put it together again.'

Grace knows Oliver is right, but when she thinks about it, and the letter she is desperate to write, she knows that she needs to try, one last time. She will tell him exactly how she feels about him. That is her right thing to do.

Chapter Thirty-Five

Betty is at home, having called Fiona that morning.

'Hi, Betts. What's up?'

'Johnny found out about the bet.'

'Oh, shit.'

'Yeah, and Grace fell for him properly and he fell for her, but just before he was going to leave me for her, he found out and left us both.'

'Holy shit.'

'So I thought I might not come in today, if you don't mind, my marriage being in tatters as it is.'

'Take as long as you want. Bye.' Fiona put the phone down rapidly and Betty almost laughed.

Alison went to work, but she left early to deliver the letter. As Betty sits down with a cup of coffee, she imagines Johnny reading it. His hair will flop a little over his forehead as he bends his neck to read. If she were there she would remind him that it needs a cut. His hands might shake a little, because, she knows, he will be angry and hurt. She hopes he cries at her words because they were sent straight from her heart to his. She hopes he won't stop halfway through but read it to the end. She knows that she will have to wait until he contacts her.

Johnny wakes, feeling alien, but he soon remembers why. He gets up and goes to the office, having decided that any normality he can get into his life is a good thing. He has the letter that Alison gave him that morning in his pocket, and he reads it when he gets to his office. His hands shake as he takes it out of the envelope. His hair falls on to his face as he begins to read and he pushes it back. He sees the words and they strike him in his heart, and he finds tears in his eyes. He stops halfway, angry that she is making him feel sad, and he folds the letter and puts it in his desk drawer. He has slept on his dilemma as Matt requested, and he still wants to confront both women together. But not yet. He knows that it is too soon.

Grace wakes, feeling slightly lighter, but still heavy-hearted. She feeds her fish, drinks her coffee and goes to her office as if on autopilot, but as she hasn't worked she has no reports to write and no jobs to prepare for. She has a long bath before she gets dressed. She still has two hours to kill before she needs to leave for lunch, but she has no idea how to fill them. She curls herself up on the sofa and watches her fish. She is interrupted by the phone. Still in the dating mindset she jumps to answer it.

'Grace, it's Oliver.'

'Hi.' She cannot help but feel slightly disappointed.

'I'm going to Paris this morning, but my mobile will be on and I want you to call if you need anything.' Her heart lifts.

'You are truly a good friend.' She sounds surprised; she is surprised.

'I know what it's like to be in love and lose someone,' he laughs, 'and that is not a dig at you, Gracie. But anytime you need me I'm here.'

'Thanks, Oliver, and I do love you – in my own way I do.'

'I know.'

She puts the phone down and picks up the sealed envelope that she put on her desk last night. Her heart is in that envelope. She doesn't know where Johnny will be, but she has a strong feeling that he will go to work. Without hesitation she calls for a courier and arranges to have the letter delivered there.

*

Fiona has been pacing her office since she put the phone down on Betty. She is experiencing a new emotion: guilt. She can't quite believe that that is what it is, but she is ashamed. Did she think it through? Of course she didn't. She wanted Betty to be like her, a bitter woman with a failed marriage. Or, a successful career woman with no time for men. It was time she stopped kidding herself, and it was time to come clean.

She grabs her coat and tells Michelle that there is an emergency she needs to attend to. Then she walks out of the office.

Betty is still in bed, only moving to answer her mobile when Alison calls her every five minutes. Alison doesn't want her to worry any more than she already does. Betty wonders if he has read the letter yet, but she cannot do anything. She has to wait.

When she hears the doorbell she thinks for a minute that it might be him. But then she remembers that he has a key and, even when angry, he would use it. She drags herself out of bed, walks sluggishly down the stairs and opens the door. She finds herself face to face with Fiona.

'Are you going to let me in?' Fiona finds it hard to be humble, even when she is about to deliver a grovelling apology. Betty doesn't say anything, she just stands aside. She leads her into the living room, where Fiona sits down on the sofa, while Betty remains standing.

'I think we should talk.'

'About?' Betty doesn't want her there; she wants to go back to wallowing in her bed.

'About the bet. About the fact that I am the one responsible for the bet.'

'Shit, Fiona, can't you just leave it? Yes, you pushed me into it and threatened to demote me and all sorts of horrible things, but I could have stood my ground. Now, if you're here to clear your conscience, then you can leave because I don't have the energy for this.'

'It's not that. Betty, the bet was my idea.'

'Grace, not you.'

'No, that's the thing, you see. I came up with the idea, and I talked Grace into it. I thought it all up and I went to see her. She was reluctant at first but I talked her into it by making you out to be, well, not very nice about her and she finally agreed. I told her that you were too judgemental in your ivory tower and needed to be taught a lesson and then I suggested the lesson.'

'Oh, shit.' Betty sits down in an armchair. She puts her head in her hands, takes it out, looks at Fiona and shakes her head.

'I'm a horrible, horrible person.' Fiona is sure that it will take more than that but apologies aren't her thing.

'You did this? You did this to me?' Betty cannot believe her ears. She's looking at the woman who has been responsible for her career. Her mentor. She knew that Fiona was a hard woman, a bitch at times, but she also trusted her. Which is why she had agreed to the bet – because she believed her boss knew what was best for her career. And now she is learning the truth.

'You must really hate me.'

'No, no, Betty. I don't hate you. You know I care about you.'

'How can you care about me? You tried to ruin my life.'

'No, I tried to make it better.'

'Hold on a minute. You seriously believe that?' Betty feels like laughing, but she thinks that is more a sign of her losing her mind than anything.

'No, of course I don't. I tried to tell myself that that was what I was doing but it wasn't. I don't have a defence, I don't. I'm such a bitch.'

'Carry on. This should be good.' Betty folds her arms and looks at her boss, as if seeing her for the first time.

'When we first met, I saw myself in you. You were so determined and I knew that you'd be a great journalist. I took you under my wing and I never regretted it, but I wanted to turn you into me.'

'That's why you pushed this feature on me?'

'Before the bet I needed you to see what men were like. I couldn't believe that you'd got a good one when I'd got the worst one ever. That didn't make sense. You were so like me in every other way, and I couldn't believe that your marriage should be more important to you than your career.'

'So you tried to wreck it.'

'I guess I did.'

'Because you wanted to turn me into you.'

'Yes.' Fiona cowers, as if Betty might hit her.

'You wanted Johnny to cheat on me so we could have that in common?'

Fiona nods.

Betty stands up and goes to the window. Life has taken a bizarre turn. She is unsure what to do or say next. But she knows one thing, and that is that she is not angry with Fiona. God knows why she isn't but she cannot be angry with her. 'You wanted Grace to wreck my marriage, you talked her into this bet.'

'I know, and I'm so ashamed and angry with myself.'

'You are?' Betty looks at her and sees a bitter, lonely woman. She doesn't fear her any more, she just feels sorry for her. Finally she finds a reaction. She laughs. Fiona couldn't look more shocked if she'd struck her.

'Why are you laughing?'

'Because, Fiona, this is a joke. You wanted to turn me into you, and you succeeded. What now? We can be man haters together?'

'Well, that's not exactly—'

'Fiona, I'm not you. I never will be. Shit, I don't believe this. Why didn't you talk to me?'

'I don't think I knew any of this until just now. I didn't realise what I was doing, or why. I just did it.'

'Well, it's done now.'

'But I wanted her to win. Don't you see, I kept you busy so she could have a clear go at him? I wanted him to be a cheater because then I would have known that we were the same and I was right. I'm sick and twisted and horrible and I don't know how you can bear to look at me.'

'Oh, Fiona, you are all those things, but I still listened to you.'

'Is that all you're going to say?'

'To be honest, it's all I can say. You might have come up with the bet but that doesn't matter much now. All that matters is me saving my marriage. Why did I ever listen to you?'

'I don't know but I don't think you should ever listen to me again.'

'Fiona, you're my boss.'

'Right, but if I say anything, ever, that you don't like, you must tell me.' Fiona is still taken aback, not only by her confession but by Betty's reaction.

'I will tell you. And now I'm going to try to win Johnny back. I don't suppose you have any ideas on how to do that?'

'I'm keeping quiet.'

'Fiona, that's the first sensible thing you've said.'

When Betty lets Fiona out, she hugs her goodbye. The look of confusion on Fiona's face is priceless. Betty feels better; almost calm about everything. Fiona wanted to turn Betty into a carbon copy of herself. It might have screwed up her life but at least it made sense of things. Because now one thing is clear to her: this whole business is her fault. She let Fiona manipulate her, she always did, and now she is paying the price. Johnny wasn't at fault, nor was Grace. Even Fiona could be exonerated. The only person Betty can blame is herself and the lesson she is learning is perhaps the most painful and the most valuable of her life.

She thinks back to the times when she let Johnny come second to her career. It has happened. Fiona was always behind it. Seeing the truth, finally, admitting that she isn't the perfect wife, gives her hope. Maybe she will get him back. And if she does, then she will never let Fiona influence her again.

Despite the way her life is crumbling she begins to see some good. She was immature, worried that single people and the word 'divorce' could contaminate her marriage. She was convinced her marriage was perfect but no marriage ever is. She sees it, finally, for what it is: two people in love, totally in love, but having to live together through the realities of modern life. Now she sees it she feels stronger, but she also hopes that it isn't too late.

Grace has lunch with Nicole, wearing enough make-up to mask her misery. She can barely string a sentence together or eat as she wonders if Johnny has her letter. But all she can do is wait.

Johnny's secretary brings him a courier delivery. He looks at the envelope and wonders if it is from her. Another bolt of unfamiliarity hits him as he realises that he doesn't know her handwriting. He opens it, and pulls out four pages of A4. He doesn't read it but looks at the bottom where she has signed her name. He feels sick. He takes out Betty's letter, and he holds one in each hand. Then he quickly stuffs both into his jacket pocket before they destroy him completely. He has their letters but he is not going to read them.

He gives up on work early. The worst thing is his inability to know what to do. His thoughts and feelings are killing him, but how does he stop that? Anger, fear, hurt, all ripping through him, and he doesn't know how to get rid of them. He needs to get out. Before he leaves, he does the 'sensible Johnny' thing and calls Matt. He tells him that he is going to visit a friend, to get some space, and will call him the following day. Instead, he gets rid of 'sensible Johnny', grabs his jacket and goes to get drunk.

The bar he chooses is unfamiliar, as is the drink he chooses, Jack Daniel's on the rocks. He drinks quickly, hoping that each burning mouthful will help him forget. Because that is the only thing he wants now: to forget. He switches his mobile off. He buys a packet of cigarettes. He hasn't smoked since university and that was only for a couple of months. But smoking and drinking are offering him a distraction. They are stopping him from going mad.

His head is too fuzzy. It is all too much to bear. One minute he wants revenge, the next he desperately wants to turn the clock back to before Grace. He was happy then. He didn't particularly want to change anything about his life. But now it has changed, and he has no idea what he is going to do about it.

He buries himself in the drink but thoughts keep flowing into his head. Where is he going to live? Will he get a divorce? What will he say to them, to the two women who thought it was a good idea to turn his life upside down?

What about his own near infidelity? He failed the test, if it was a test. He nearly buckled; he was about to succumb. He might have walked away, but now he will never know. He will never know which woman he would have chosen and that just adds to his confusion.

He misses the simplicity of life. Everything is so complicated and there is no way he can start simplifying it now. It is all too much.

He reaches into his pocket and pulls out the letters. One half read, the other unread. He cannot bring himself to read them; he doesn't yet want to hear their excuses or declarations of love. He doesn't want to exonerate either of them. At the moment hate is burning its brand on to his mind. Hate is safe waters; hate he can deal with. He does not enjoy it, but along with anger it is here, and it makes him feel for a while that he knows where he is.

Without his realising it, the pub is calling last orders. Johnny panics. What is he going to do now? He lied to Matt. He doesn't have a friend to stay with; his drink was his friend. He decides to go somewhere that 'sensible Johnny' wouldn't go. He goes to a club in Soho.

When he stands up the drink seems to hit him, and he wobbles his way out of the bar. He stands straight enough to hail a cab and get it to take him to his destination. When he gets there he pays the driver and wobbles in. It's a club that one of the guys at work talks about, it's 'full of scantily clad women who are all looking for a shag'. He remembers this. He walks into the club, pays an extortionate entrance fee and realises why they were all looking for shags. It is depressing. The girls are all wearing next to nothing, either standing at the bar watching the door or on the dance floor watching the door. Drunken men are wobbling around, just like Johnny, and girls are letting them breathe on them. It is not a strip club, it's not full of hookers. It's a club for London's lonely young people. It is depressing.

Johnny would never visit a club like this. He hasn't been to a club for years and his party was the nearest he's got. But Johnny isn't Johnny any more. He doesn't know who he is, but he is here. He walks to the bar and orders a drink. He pulls out his cigarettes (which he cannot even taste any more), and lights one. A girl smiles at him. He offers her a drink. She agrees. As he waits for the barman to give him change he looks at her. Through his 'drunk vision' she is all right. Not a patch on Grace, of course, and not a patch on Betty. But she is blonde and, as neither of them is, that is a positive attribute. She also has an enormous chest, which neither have. She is actually quite enormous all round (well, she is fleshy), nothing like the other two. He immediately smiles. Now he knows what to do.

'I'm Johnny.' His chat-up lines are a bit rusty.

'Sally.'

'Cheers, Sally.' He realises that he doesn't really know how to talk to her.

'So, what's a handsome man like you doing here?' He thinks that he might not need to do much talking.

'I just wanted a drink and a friendly chat.' He cannot believe how cheesy he sounds.

'Well, you came to the right place. Do you want to dance?'

They hit the dance floor, Johnny, still a little unsteady on his feet, but that doesn't matter because Sally is practically holding him up. She has pushed her ample chest right into him and, despite everything, he is getting turned on. She is nothing like the women he loves, but that is proving even more of a turn-on.

'What do you do?' he asks her, when they go back to the bar for another drink.

'I'm a waitress.' She doesn't ask him, but takes her drink, swallows it down in one and grabs him and kisses him. Johnny is not taken aback by the teenage nature of the snog – he doesn't care. This is all helping him.

'Can I take you home?' he says, realising that the music is giving him a headache and he is really too drunk. She nods and leads him out.

The first blast of the night air injects a tiny bit of sobriety into him. He looks at her again as they wait for a cab. She is overweight, her legs squeezed into a tiny skirt. Her hair is dyed blonde, and it is not a sophisticated style. Her make-up is clumsy and too brash to compliment her. Her shoes are too high and her fat feet are pouring out of them. She is not attractive to him; therefore she is.

A cab stops and Sally gives him her address. Johnny gets in after her and puts his hand on her thigh. They go back to their kiss.

There are a number of reasons that he finds himself with her.

One is that he is drunk. The second is that she kissed him. The third is that he has nowhere else to go.

Her flat is shared and reminds him of days when he first moved to London. There are no signs of any flatmates, but the place is depressing. It is messy, but she does not apologise for this. As soon as they are in the sitting room, she is sexily dancing towards him, but she is not sexy. He knows what he needs. He walks up to her and grabs her, like he means it.

'Your bedroom.' It is a command. She looks delighted as she leads him there.

The bedroom has a double bed, a wooden wardrobe and a mirror in it. It is tidy, unlike the rest of the flat, but also small. He feels as if he is regressing; this is a university type of bedroom, not one for grownups. Not like Grace's, or like his and Betty's. The thoughts make him even more angry. He kisses her hard, and then undoes her top. It is not easy pulling it off her, and they wrestle before it is free. He unclips her bra, which is too small, and watches, with a teenage glee, when her huge boobs spring free. As he kisses and teases the nipples she squeals in delight. It is not long before they are both naked.

He tells himself that she is sexy, but he no longer finds her sexy. She isn't attractive, but he tells himself she is. There is something sordid about the way he pushes her head to his crotch, but she loves it and when he reciprocates, burying his head in a tangle of pubic hair and thigh flesh, she orgasms for him. It is her gratitude that makes him decide to continue. He is nauseous from both her and the drink, but she thanks him over and over again for pleasing her, which makes him feel like a man. The bitches took away his balls, but Sally will give them back.

Sex is rough, both clawing at each other, in desperation rather than passion. Finally, they are finished and he kisses her and turns over.

He was so detached from the act, even when he came.

Afterwards he lies close to the edge of her small double bed, wishing he were anywhere but there. But he has nowhere else to go.

As soon as the sun makes an appearance he wakes up and sees that she is snoring next to him. His head pounds and all the memories come flooding back. She is not as unattractive as he told himself she was last night, but she is no beauty. He looks at her one last time, feeling rotten, feeling awful, feeling like a cad, before he grabs his clothes, puts them on and leaves.

It is only six in the morning, and he cannot remember where he is. He walks the streets, which are eerily quiet, before he sees a postcode sign and realises that he is really close to Grace's flat. This depresses him further. He does the only thing he can think of. He finds a taxi, and goes to Matt's.

He uses the key Matt gave him to get in, and he goes to the bathroom, to shower. By the time Matt and Alison get up he is sitting in the kitchen drinking juice.

'Are you all right?' Alison asks.

'I've got a hangover the size of London.'

'Where were you?' she continues.

'With a friend.' She doesn't believe him, but there is nothing she can do. All three of them leave for work, with depression sitting in their pockets.

Chapter Thirty-Six

Johnny feels awful until he gets to the office, where a new kind of awful overtakes him. He cannot feel guilty about Sally, or revulsion at the way he used her, because it is their fault. It is time for them to pay. He calls Matt.

'I'm doing it. I'm confronting them.'

'OK.' Matt has no arguments to give.

'There's no time like the present. I'm going to call them.'

'Now I know you feel nervous about this. You never use wanky phrases like "there's no time like the present".'

'That obvious?'

'Transparent.'

'Well, I am nervous, but I don't know why.'

'Call me after.'

'I will.'

Betty is watching daytime TV when the phone rings. She immediately snatches it up, hoping it is Johnny. It's been two days.

'Hi,' she says.

'It's me.' He sounds cold, but at least it is his voice.

'Oh, Johnny. Thank God.' She falters. 'Did you read the letter?'

'I want to meet you. Tonight.' He gives her the name and address of a bar.

'OK. Great, what time?' She cannot hide her excitement. She

believes it must be the letter that has brought this about, even though he still sounds a little cold.

'Eight.' He hangs up.

Betty jumps up and even though it is not yet lunchtime she goes to choose what she will wear.

Johnny is sweating. Despite the fact that he is the wronged man, he feels guilty because Betty obviously thought he wanted to talk to her following the letter that he's only half read. Be a man, he tells himself as he wipes his forehead and picks up the phone again.

Grace answers the phone after the first ring. 'Hello.'

'It's me.'

Despite everything Oliver said, she feels so many emotions hearing his voice. 'Oh, Johnny.' She has no idea what to say.

'I need to see you.'

'You do? Is it the letter?' She is elated and surprised. Maybe Oliver was wrong and, despite the lies, Johnny still loves her.

'Tonight, eight o'clock at a bar called Barnie's.'

'Fine, but where is it?' Johnny gives her the address and hangs up.

Grace leaves the flat to meet Nicole with new hope. She is going to see him and she just knows that he is going to tell her he loves her.

Johnny feels the sweat intensify. He calls Matt.

'Matt speaking.'

'It's me. I did it. They're meeting me tonight.'

'How did they sound?'

'Happy.'

'Oh.'

'I know. But I have to do this. I need it.'

'I understand, mate.' But Matt is terrified all the same.

*

'Alison, guess what. He called me.'

'He did? What did he say?'

'He wants to meet me tonight. Barnie's. It has to be a good sign, doesn't it?'

'Don't get your hopes up. He's probably still angry.' She doesn't add that she has no idea where he was last night, and that he was acting suspicious when he got in.

'I know but at least we're meeting, that's got to be a good thing, hasn't it?'

'I hope so.' Alison really does hope so.

'So I'm seeing him tonight.' Grace is on the phone to Nicole.

'You are?'

'Yeah, at eight. He called up and said he needed to speak to me.'

'Hopefully not another showdown.' Nicole is anxious.

'No, I've got a good feeling about this.'

'I hope you're right.'

'Nicole, don't worry.'

'I was hoping that Oliver would have helped you.'

'He did. He told me I should fix their marriage, but if Johnny really loves me then I can't fix it, can I?'

'I guess not,' Nicole replies, feeling inside that this meeting is not what Grace thinks it is.

Johnny is there early. He is drinking lager, and waiting. So far he feels composed, although he is still unsure what he is going to say. He wants to hurt them, he thinks, to get rid of some of his anger, because it is the anger that he can't cope with. The hurt he can, but not the anger, which is knotting him up inside and ensuring he cannot concentrate on anything.

Betty walks in first. He sees her and feels a pang. He remembers everything he loves about her, before the anger pushes it away. She walks up to him, and smiles. He does not smile back.

'Drink?' he asks.

'White wine, please?' She looks at him hopefully but he is giving nothing away.

Betty is sipping her drink and doesn't notice him turn to face the door. When Johnny sees Grace walk in, he remembers why he feels so much for her. She sees him, smiles and walks over. It is not long before the smile freezes on her lips as she sees Betty, at the exact same time that Betty sees her. They look at each other and then turn to Johnny.

'I thought that maybe we three could have a chat,' he says, asking the barman for another glass and handing it to a very shocked Grace.

Johnny walks over to a newly vacated table, but Grace and Betty stay rooted to the spot.

'I don't believe it,' Betty says.

'I had no idea,' Grace says. Johnny looks at them, and they slowly make their way over.

Betty doesn't even know if her legs are working. All the hope she had has gone. Grace's hand is shaking as she carries her drink. She is unsure what it is about, but a declaration of love is obviously not on the cards. This meeting has nothing to do with the letter.

'So, I guess I don't need to introduce you,' Johnny says. He knows that he doesn't sound like himself, as he hears the coldness in his voice, but he doesn't feel like himself. And they have done this to him. Suddenly the anger leaves him as he looks at the two women and feels empty. Betty, who he knew so well until this happened, and Grace, who he thought he knew but never really did.

'Johnny?' Betty asks.

'I wanted us all to meet, together. Maybe you could both tell me why you thought you would play with me. You,' he points at Grace, 'well, you hurt me, but you,' he points at Betty, 'you married me. So why would you do this?' He finds his words inadequate and realises that he has made a mistake. He doesn't want to be in the bar with them, he doesn't want to see either of them. Everything that they have done to him flows through his mind, and his body. He wants to cry. To crumple up into a ball.

'I am sorry. I didn't think you'd fall for her,' Betty says, her only defence.

'I didn't think I'd fall in love with you,' Grace adds, her only defence.

Johnny feels the walls closing in on him. He has to get out, he can't cope. He looks at Betty, the woman he married, the woman he loves, and he looks at Grace, the woman he thought he loved but the one he doesn't know.

'I hate you both for what you've done to me. And I will never ever forgive you,' he says before getting up and leaving. It is not what he planned, not what he wants, but it is all he can do.

He walks as fast as he can until he gets to Matt's house. He rings the doorbell, unable to get his hand in his pocket to get the key. Matt answers.

'What happened?' he asks, fearing the worst.

'You were right. I couldn't, couldn't do anything.' They both walk in. He tells Matt what happened, shaking quite violently. Matt pours him a drink and sits him down.

'You left them there?'

'I had to get out. I couldn't cope.'

'I understand.'

'Even my anger wasn't enough. Nothing is enough. Matt, what am I going to do?'

Matt doesn't have any answers. Alison walks in, having been at work late. She looks at Johnny and at Matt, and gestures for Matt to join her in the kitchen.

'What happened?'

Matt explains.

'Oh shit, why did he think it was a good idea for him to meet them both?'

'He's angry, Ali. He's not exactly thinking straight.'

'I know. Listen, I'll try to get hold of Betty. You take him home.'

'What if she's there?'

'Then you can come back here and I'll go over, but she might come here and he will be there. I'll try to call her and track her down.' Alison walks to the phone and calls Betty's mobile. She leaves a message. Then she calls their house and again leaves a message. She walks back into the living room and shakes her head.

'OK, mate, let's go home.' Johnny looks at Matt, but doesn't argue. He obediently gets up and follows Matt out. Even if it's not his home any longer, it is his territory, it was his home and it is familiar. He needs to check on Cyril; he had forgotten about Cyril. If Betty is there then he will leave, and maybe, if anger returns, he will throw her out.

Alison sinks down on the sofa, tired from the emotions that are flying around, and she tries to call Betty again.

'Should I go after him?'

'He's your husband, it's your decision.' Grace feels cold. It hits her, again, that Oliver was right. How could he love her when she was a total lie to him? She should have done the right thing.

'Some fucking decision. You heard what he said. To both of us.' Betty puts her head in her hands.

'Oh God.' Grace feels tears rolling down her cheeks, but she doesn't feel she has the right to them. She fell in love with someone else's husband, it all ended up as a mess, the tears are rightfully Betty's. The story of her sorry life.

'I just want to die. Or, actually, I want to kill you.' People are staring. For the first time, Grace notices what is going on around them.

'Betty,' she says gently, despite the death threat, 'Betty, let's get out of here.'

Betty looks at her in total bewilderment, as if she has never seen her before, but she allows Grace to help her out of the bar. Shock is setting in for Betty, as Grace hails a cab and puts Betty inside. Then she asks the driver to take them to Grace's flat. Betty just lets her do all this.

When they get to the flat, Grace helps her to the door. Although she is falling apart, she is familiar with the feeling, and she feels responsible for Betty. Instead of contenting herself with ruining her own life (something she is extremely good at), she had to go and ruin Betty and Johnny's as well. Guilt doesn't even begin to describe it.

They sit at the dining table (the chairs are upright and Grace feels that Betty needs propping up), with a bottle of brandy and two glasses.

'I hate brandy,' Betty finally speaks, but she drinks it anyway.

'I can get you something else. I just thought it might do us good.'

'Shock. They always give you brandy for shock. Well, they do in films anyway.' She laughs bitterly.

'It hurts so much.' Grace is thinking aloud.

'It does, more than I ever thought anything could hurt.' Betty pulls out the tissue that Grace foisted upon her in the taxi. It is near to total disintegration.

'Hold on, I'll get you another one.'

When Grace returns with a box of tissues, Betty says, 'Why are you being so nice to me?'

'I ruined your life. I guess that's as good a reason as any.'

'Fiona told me – how it was her idea, not yours, although you did ultimately agree. But you don't look too pleased with yourself.'

'No. No, I'm not. At the moment I feel wretched, totally, with myself but also for what I lost.'

'What you lost?'

'Johnny. Betty, I really fell for him.'

'I thought so.'

'Yeah, not for the bet, not to prove a point or to wipe the smug smile off your face. For me, for my emotions. I fell for him.'

'Blimey.' She takes another drink.

'But I shouldn't have done. He's your husband.'

'Not for much longer, by the look of things.'

'I'm sorry how it turned out.'

'Well, it looks like neither of us won the bet.'

'The bet stopped mattering a long time ago. Betty, I am sorry. I really didn't want all this.'

'But nothing happened.'

'No, nothing like that.'

'Right.'

'Honestly, you were right: you always had the perfect man. How could I not fall in love with him? He's handsome, and kind and funny and intelligent. Betty, I stopped trying to trap him a long time ago, and instead, well, I think I tried to get him to fall in love with me.'

'Which he did.'

'No, that's the sad thing. He didn't.'

'What do you mean?'

'I'm not real, Betty, don't you see? You were right all along. In the beginning when we met, and you interviewed me about my job you condemned me for what I was doing, saying that my looks made it unfair on the men, but that wasn't all. I protested, remember, saying that it was about more than looks, and I was right. I was never real. I was a fantasy figure. I would walk into a bar, dressed glamorously, and when I spoke to the man I was working to trap I would be interested in him. I would never dominate the conversation, I would ask endless questions about him and talk about only what he was interested in. I was a male fantasy; I was never real. So you were right, it was unfair to get me to trap them, because even though they were wrong to cheat, if their wives were at home covered in baby sick, or too tired to brush their hair, or have sex, or cook them dinner, then I was the opposite, the anti-wife. And you're right, it would take a strong man to resist something like that. A very strong man. Like Johnny.'

'But he just said, he fell for you.'

'He didn't fall for me, he didn't know me. Betty, I might not have tried such obvious tactics with him, but I didn't let him get to know me. I told him that my husband divorced me. I told him I loved golf. Christ, I even played golf with him. I hate golf.'

'Do you?' Betty feels confused, but she cannot cope with processing the information.

'I was a big fat fake.'

'So you're saying that Johnny didn't fall in love with you?'

'No, he fell in love with this illusion, that happened to like everything he liked. You know how much you hate *Carry On* films?' Betty nods. 'I even said that I loved them, because I planned to take him to a film at some point. I don't get *Carry On* films.'

'My God. You know what, I was doing the same.'

'What, saying you liked the same films?'

'No, I was being the perfect wife, but not me. God, I really humiliated myself doing it.'

'We're a couple of losers.'

'One thing I don't understand is how you fell in love with him if you didn't like the things he did.'

'Easy. I might not have liked them but I liked the way he liked things. You know what I mean. How when he talked about those films he had a smile on his face and in his eyes at all times.

When he played golf he would concentrate and become really competitive, although normally he's so gentle. Have I said too much?'

'Yes and no. You know him too well and that kills me. It really does.'

'It's you he loves. I was just a diversion.'

'You really think that?'

'I would rather it wasn't true, but yes, I believe that.'

'Well, it looks as if we've both lost him, anyway.'

'Betty, I will back off if you fight for him.' She can barely believe she is saying it. She knows she should have walked away – she knew it ages ago – but maybe it can be a case of better late than never.

'I know Johnny. He'll never forgive me for this.'

'You can't just give up.' It's suddenly important to Grace that Betty stay with him. She has to fix it and that's the only way. It will be one person alone, not three. That she can live with. She is good at alone.

'I don't see I have a choice.'

'I've ruined everything.'

'With a little help from me.'

'Yeah, what a team. Remind me never to see you again.'

'Sure thing. Grace?'

'Yeah.'

'I'm feeling a little drunk now, and totally destroyed, and my life is over and everything. What am I going to do?'

'I wish I knew. I wish I could turn back time and leave him alone.'

'But then you wouldn't have fallen in love.' Betty knows it is surreal, sitting here with Grace after everything they've been through.

'I know. It felt so good. Even though nothing happened between us, it made me feel good. Just to hear his voice.'

'I know. I wish you weren't talking about my husband, but I do know why.'

'He's amazing.'

Betty puts her head in her hands. 'What am I going to do?'

'Look, I know it's late, but if you give me the number of your friend – you know, the one who's married to his best friend – then I can call her and at least she can tell us if he's all right. Anyway, she is probably worried about you.'

'Yeah, Alison will know what to do.' Betty writes the number down and hands it to Grace.

'I can't believe we're here in this situation.' Grace is again voicing her thoughts.

'Me neither. Why on earth would I be sitting drinking brandy with my archenemy?'

'You got me.' They both smile weakly.

The phone was snatched up immediately.

'Hello.' She sounds panicked.

'Is that Alison?'

'Yes, who are you?'

'I'm Grace, but before you shout, I've got Betty.'

'She's with you? I've been worried sick. I've left her a million messages on her mobile. Shit, is she all right?'

'Not really. I just took her home because she fell apart in the bar. We both did. Look, I know this sounds weird, but it's so late and we've both been drinking, and I don't think we'll sleep any tonight, so I wondered if you could pick her up in the morning.'

'Of course. Give me your address.'

Grace dictates her address. 'Alison?'

'Yes.'

'One more thing. Is he all right?'

'No, he's far from all right, but Matt's with him. I don't

understand you, and I certainly didn't approve of what you both were doing, but even I didn't think it would end like this.'

'I know.'

'Tell Betty I love her and tell her I'll pick her up in the morning.' Alison hangs up and Grace feels even more full of questions. It's like he's dead now, dead to her, and perhaps that is how it has to be. Betty needs him, and although Grace feels she does too, she realises she has no right. She never, ever did.

Johnny is storming around his kitchen. Cyril is cowering under the kitchen table and Matt is tempted to do the same.

'I almost wish I hadn't told you.' Matt is thinking aloud.

'What, and let me go on being deceived by the two women I thought I loved?'

'No, you know I couldn't do that, which is why I didn't. But now . . . well, I hate to see you this hurt.'

'I am so angry. Not only angry, but confused, and what do I do next? Christ, how could she have done this to me?'

'Which she?'

'Betty. Grace – well, she was a stranger, so it doesn't matter so much. No, actually it fucking well does matter because she made me have feelings for her too, but Betty is worse because she was my wife, and I trusted her. Shit, Matt, please tell me this is just some fucking nightmare and it'll all go away.'

'I wish I could, but you know it's not.'

'No. What am I going to do?'

'Get through tonight, then tomorrow we'll think. It's too soon to know.'

'I never want to see either of them again.'

'Do you mean that?'

'No, I want to see both of them right now. You know, that's the worst thing. The setup is bad enough, but if I hadn't had any feelings for Grace then it wouldn't have been so bad. I mean, I blame myself. Because if I hadn't found out, or if it hadn't been a setup, I can't say, hand on heart, which woman I would have chosen to be with.'

'I think you'd have stayed with Betty.'

'Yeah, I like to think so too, but, Matt, I really fell for Grace.'

'But you know that she was there to be whoever you wanted her to be – of course you fell for her.'

'Yeah, I guess. I fell in love with perfection, but it wasn't real.'

'Shit, if perfection was real, then we'd be in big trouble.'

'In case you hadn't noticed, I already am.'

'Alison is coming over tomorrow morning.'

'What about Johnny?'

'He's with Matt. That's all she would say.'

'How could I let this happen?'

'I cajoled you into it, and your boss didn't exactly help.'

'Why, though? Why did you do it?' Betty is angry with Grace, although she knows that she cannot blame her for everything.

'Because you looked down on me.'

'But I didn't really. I was threatened by you. You represented everything I feared.'

'I guess I should have known. I was scared by you because I didn't believe in the total happiness you had with Johnny and you were threatened by me because I stood for everything that you didn't.'

'We were both blinded by our stubborn nature, I guess.'

'Our stupidity.'

'I'll drink to that.' They clink their glasses.

'I bet you were always popular at school.' Finally Grace says what she has wanted to say ever since she first met Betty.

'Nope actually. I was ugly, geeky and totally unpopular. I got bullied terribly.'

'You're kidding. But I thought—'

'That I had an idyllic life? But I didn't. I was so desperately unhappy growing up, which is why I assumed that you were always the popular bully.'

'I can't believe it. I was bullied too. I grew up in a council house with five siblings. The school I went to was really rough. Drugs, knives, the lot. Even the teachers were scared every day.'

'I guess we both got it wrong.'

'Oh, Betty, we got it so wrong.'

'I have to stop now. I feel sick,' Betty announces.

'Do you need the bathroom?'

'No, I need to lie down.'

Grace leads Betty to the sofa and goes to get a blanket and a pillow. She sits on the floor and watches her fish and Betty in turn. She is still there when Betty wakes and Grace looks out of the window and realises that a new day is welcoming them.

Chapter Thirty-Seven

Although she is not Betty's biggest fan, Grace feels very empty once Betty has been collected by Alison. That's it, that's her life. She is on her own again and she has to rebuild the ruins that she created. She calls Oliver and tells him she is taking his advice but she doesn't tell him about the previous night. She feels oddly calm. She needs to rebuild her life and she knows that she cannot rely on Oliver for that. She tells him that she is all right, because he has been better to her than she deserves. She also promises to keep in touch.

Finally she realises that what she needs first is sleep. Clarity is near, she believes that, but she cannot think straight. She is still a bit drunk, and if she isn't, she is hungover. She goes to bed and sleeps until the following day.

She wakes up feeling stronger. She needs to move on, because she will never have Johnny. She knows now what she has to do, but she has no idea how to do it. She calls Nicole for advice.

'I am so proud of you,' Nicole says when Grace explains.

'But I don't know what to do.'

'Actually, you know exactly what to do.'

'I do?'

'Yes. Listen, in your job you help women whose marriages are in jeopardy. Think along those lines.'

'That's what I did, and look what happened.'

'No, you tried to tempt Johnny, and I know that's your job but think about the times when you save the women from being hurt.'

'I still don't follow.'

'If you tested a marriage and the man doesn't cheat, or imply he will cheat how do you feel?'

'That there's hope?'

'And Johnny didn't cheat with you, he fell for you but he didn't cheat.'

'You mean I just have to get them both to see that.'

'Him, anyway. You can't convince her to save the marriage because she already wants to, although you can explain to him why she did it, from your point of view. What you need to do is point out to him that he fell for a fantasy, and that you're not real, but despite that he didn't cheat on his wife. Make him see that that means he has to stay with her.'

'Do you think it'll work?'

'It's worth a try.'

She feels better because she has a plan. The plan starts where the bet starts. She dresses plainly and goes to his office.

The receptionist recognises her and calls Johnny's assistant. She comes out to see Grace.

'You don't have an appointment,' she says.

'I know, but I have to see him. It's my mortgage. I've got some problems and they're really urgent.'

'I'll ask him if he's free.'

Grace is taking a gamble. She knows that Johnny won't want to make a scene at work, and he'll probably agree to see her in his office just so he can send her away. He does, although he makes her wait for half an hour. She is nervous because she has only one chance to get it right.

'Come in.' He sounds cold as he leads her to the office, although she is grateful that at least he is seeing her.

'Johnny, I know you're going to tell me to get lost as soon as the door is shut but give me a few minutes, please.'

'I was going to tell you to get lost actually. I still am.' He is shocked. He didn't expect to see her and he is totally unprepared for handling her.

'I'm not here to apologise to you.'

'Oh, good.'

'There's no point. You're not going to forgive me and quite frankly you're right not to.'

'So we're agreed.'

'Not quite. I want to sit down here and tell you a story.'

'You're good at that.'

'Just listen to me, and then I'll leave.'

'Why should I?'

'Because you're a wreck and maybe this might just help.' She wants to turn and run away, but she won't. She looks into the eyes that she loves and then she looks away. It is time for her to compose herself.

'I doubt it.'

'It's worth a try.'

'Perhaps.'

'Well, I'll begin.' She smiles, displaying bravery that she doesn't feel. One chance is all she has.

'My boss, Nicole, the detective agency boss, called me up and told me that we had a chance to be profiled in a glossy magazine, which would be like free advertising.'

'I'm not sure I want to listen to this.'

'Please. Be patient. Try.'

'Fine.' He folds his arms. It is so unlike him that Grace wants to laugh, but she cannot because there is nothing left for her in him now.

'I agreed because Nicole has been the best boss to me. She has made me into a success, advising me every step of the way. I've profited from honey trapping, as Betty used to call it. There are more unfaithful men than you can imagine and I have met a huge number of them. It's not cheap, maybe it's not ethical, but we only ever did what the wives or girlfriends wanted. Anyway, I'm not here to talk about me. I just want you to know the whole story.' She pauses and is relieved to see he seems to be listening.

'Well, then along comes Betty, and she's so together. Trendy, confident, funny, and she walks into my life. But she doesn't like me. She thinks I'm a slut, a marriage wrecker, and I had a few problems with that. We argued and it got bad, which is what you know. Then I pulled out.

'My boss said it was fine, but her boss didn't. She wanted that profile and threatened Betty with demotion.'

'I know this.'

'Yes, you do, but what you don't know is that Fiona came up with the idea of the bet, convinced me to do it and then I told Betty that it was the only way that I would let her finish and run the story. She thought it was my idea, although Fiona has come clean now. So I proposed it, and Fiona told her that it was a good idea to agree, based on the fact that you and she have such a rock-solid marriage that there would be no problem.'

'We did.'

'Yeah, but you see, Betty didn't ever want to do this. She was press-ganged into it and she tried to put a stop to it a number of times. I refused.'

'She did?'

'Yeah, and then I told her to work harder to keep you.'

'The sex toys.'

'I guess. I didn't ask for details. Anyway, the problem was that once I'd met you I fell for you too.'

'How nice.'

'Not really, because then I forgot all about the bet and tried to get you to fall in love with me.'

'By being someone you're not.'

'Johnny, you're right, but anyway, that isn't important now.' She wants to tell him that he knew most of her, but that isn't her purpose, and if he has read the letter he will know that.

'It's not.'

'Johnny, listen to me. I'm going to get up in a minute and you will never see me again. What I am here for is to make you think before you make a final decision. You never cheated on Betty. In my experience, and I can only talk from that, most men agree to cheat within an hour or two of meeting me. Now you weren't being tested because she thought you were a cheater, you were being tested because she loves her job.'

'She should love me more.'

'Oh, she does, and you know that.' Grace is angry, but then she realises she is on thin ice so she smiles. 'She wasn't in fear of losing you, she was in fear of losing her job. So she agreed. But I cheated, if you like, because my feelings came into it and I tried to make out I was this perfect woman, or the perfect woman for you.'

'You were.'

'But you know, I don't like golf and I hate *Carry On* films.'

'You do?'

'Yeah. I'm not the person you thought I was and I know that you know that. The divorce story was made up. But when I told you about my childhood, that was all true, I need you to believe that because I've never told anyone else.'

'OK.' He is softening because the anger is slowly leaving. It doesn't sound so bad when Grace explains it, as if it wasn't as serious as he makes out. But he knows that this is the last time he will see her.

'Now, Johnny, I think you can forgive Betty for agreeing to the bet and lying to you.'

'I can?' Johnny takes a minute to think about this, but he is unsure; unconvinced.

'Yes, what you can't forgive is that you actually considered leaving her. This isn't about what she did to you, it's about what you might have done to her.' Grace thanks God for Nicole's genius.

'It is?'

'Yes.' Grace is triumphant. She knows now that this is the truth. 'You feel guilty, but because we deceived you, you've got an outlet for your anger. I don't think you should feel guilty.'

'I shouldn't?'

'No, because you never cheated and the only reason you even considered it was because I was exactly your perfect woman.'

'You were. But then isn't that your job?'

'Yes, I suppose, but that's another question for me to ponder when I'm alone. Do I still want to do it? Is it right? I have no idea, but the point is that you didn't cheat.'

'I didn't.'

'Betty lied to you about the bet. You forgive her and she'll forgive you for lying to her when you were with me.'

'So, I'm in the wrong?' He is not sure how this has happened.

'You were wronged, that much is true, but you also were in the wrong a bit, but not much because you were completely manipulated. Which means that the only villain in this whole thing was me.' She smiles triumphantly.

'You?'

'Yes, and Fiona. So if you are angry with anyone, let it be me, or even her, but you cannot doubt how much Betty loves you, and I can't doubt how much you love her, so, to be honest, you'd be a bloody fool to throw all that away.'

'But you said you loved me – was that a lie?'

'No, I did, I do love you, but we haven't got a future, we never had. It was a fairy tale and I enjoyed it. I'll miss you.' She cannot convey how awful she feels knowing that she will never see him again. She wants to curl into a ball and stay in the corner of his office, but she won't.

'I'll miss you.' He has tears in his eyes.

'No, you'll miss perfect Grace, but not the Grace who has smelly feet and wears spot cream all the time.'

'I find that hard to believe.'

'Whatever, but you won't miss me. And I promise that I'll stop being such a bad person if you promise me something.' She is still smiling. Although her heart is breaking, she is happy because she knows she is doing the right thing. He is smiling for the first time in days, although he has no idea why.

'What?'

'Talk to her and try to work it out. The guilt is gone now; you have nothing to feel guilty about. Do you accept that?'

'Yes, I do.' He actually, surprisingly, did.

'And Betty loves you, and despite what she did, there was never any question about that. Do you accept that?'

'Actually I do.'

'Fine, then my work is done.' Grace giggles as she stands up and leaves. She does not look back, as finally she knows that, no matter how much it hurts, she has done the right thing.

Johnny shakes his head and smiles. Despite the fact that he didn't really get to know her, there is no denying that she is amazing. His amazing Grace. He will always remember her, he will never see her again, and he will stop missing her. He has nothing to feel guilty about because everything is clear. He loves Betty, and he always will. He reaches into his suit pocket and pulls out the two letters. For some reason, he reads Grace's first. He knows now, he knows that she did care about him and she wasn't playing a game. This makes him feel better. When he has finished, he has tears in his eyes but he moves straight on to Betty's letter.

When he finishes, he picks up the phone. For the first time in his marriage he has no idea where his wife is.

'Hello.'

'Betts, it's me.'

'Johnny?'

'Yes, Johnny, your husband.'

'My husband.'

'Don't tell me you've forgotten me already.' He laughs. He feels light-hearted.

'Johnny?' Confusion melts into her words.

'Look, I've been thinking. You were wrong to do what you did, but I was wrong too. And the only thing I know for sure now is that I love you. I read your letter and I know you love me, so how about we start again?' It really is that easy, he thinks, as all the anger and hurt leaves him. He won't forget, though. Never will he forget the lies, and he knows at times he will be angry still, but he can live with that because the alternative is to lose Betty and he knows, he is one hundred per cent sure, that he doesn't want to do that. He is in love with his wife.

'You mean it?' She can barely believe this is happening. Just yesterday she wanted to die, and now he is offering to save their marriage.

'Yes. Two conditions.'

'Name them, anything.'

'One, that you promise never to do anything like that again.'

'Absolutely.' She is nodding her head vigorously to the amusement of her secretary.

'Second, you take me on that holiday you promised.'

'Yes, yes, yes. I love you so much.'

'You know what? I love you too.' All his anger walked out of the door with Grace, as did the confusion of the past couple of months. He doesn't want to lose her, that much is clear, and Grace made him see that. He has her to thank for nearly destroying his life, but also for saving it.

Chapter Thirty-Eight

They are at Gatwick Airport, and Betty is on her mobile.

'Fiona, leave me alone. I'm about to get on a plane.'

'Yes, but I need to know where the celebrity diet feature is.' Despite everything, Betty has remained loyal to Fiona. At first Johnny tried to talk her into getting a new job, but when Betty explained how lonely Fiona was, and when she'd explained how in a way their marriage was better than ever now, he relented. He knew that Fiona wouldn't be risking ruining their marriage again.

'Hannah has everything. Now I'm going to go and I will see you when I get back.'

'Any chance of a postcard?'

Betty looks at Johnny. 'No, we'll be too busy to write postcards.'

She is at Heathrow Airport, on her mobile.

'Nicole, are you sure that the fish will be OK?'

'Grace, Helen is very responsible and you told her, what, oh, a thousand times, how to care for them, and yes, she will speak to them, and yes I'll speak to her daily to check that she's talking to them.'

'Thanks. How's the baby?'

'About the size of a pea at the moment and I'm not, touch wood, being sick. Look, enjoy yourself, you deserve this.'

'I'm only going as his friend.'

'Yikes, Grace, you only told me that one thousand times as well. Oliver is a good friend and if you shag him, then well, that wouldn't be so bad. You have done it before.'

'But, I didn't love him before so I doubt I will now.'

'Of course, but have fun.'

'I'm nervous. I'm used to my own terms.' Grace has spent a week packing for her holiday, and making lists and planning. It was like waiting for Christmas.

'You enjoy your holiday, and come back feeling great because I have so much work for you.'

'I think I'll miss the fidelity testing.'

'Nah, once you start running the agency you'll love it.'

'But are you sure you want to hand over the reins?'

'I want this baby. I'll be there for you, you know, part time in a very non-interfering kind of way.'

'I love you, Nicole.' Grace surprises herself with this. She has never said it before.

'I love you too, honey.'

FAITH BLEASDALE

Deranged Marriage

WOULD YOU EVER CONSIDER A MARRIAGE PACT?

Holly did. In a heartbroken and drunken haze, it all seemed to make perfect sense. George was her best friend, would always be her best friend and, if they both found themselves single at the age of thirty, well why not?

But when, a decade later, a man Holly hasn't seen for years says she's signed a contract and has to marry him, she realises exactly why not. Forget the fact that her career is going places, forget that she's head-over-heels in love with a gorgeous boyfriend, George wants the pact fulfilled and will stop at nothing to get his way.

'A sharp, funny read that will make you fight for the cause of love' *Cosmopolitan*

'The perfect tonic . . . hilarious' *OK!*

flame

FLAME
Hodder & Stoughton